Shamar

By

Lydia Staggs

W & B Publishers
USA

W & B Publishers

For information:
W & B Publishers
9001 Ridge Hill Street
Kernersville, NC 27284

www.a-argusbooks.com

ISBN: 9781942981503

Book Cover designed by Melissa Carrigee
Book Cover Art by Ashley Gaia
Printed in the United States of America

Dedication

For the people who are the most important in my life:
family and friends.

Acknowledgements

A special thanks to Jen Wilson-Cohen, who helped me along in this entire process, and made me hate the saying, "show not tell".

Chapter 1

A hike through Cumberland Gap National Park was exactly what Juliet needed today. Shades of greens and browns swirled around her in every direction as the strong smell of pine infused her nose. Even though this was a hike for work instead of leisure, it was still good to be out in the rejuvenating fresh air. Juliet rolled her head back and through translucent blue eyes gazed up at the thousands of trees stretching up into the sky, reminding her of a cathedral: soaring columns ending in elaborate, fanning buttresses of branches and leaves. Rays of light broke through the canopy from above to illuminate patches of the underbrush.

She envied Secret's ability to identify all the foliage in the National Park. Then again, her friend had worked for the ranger service for five years. It was Secret's job to know every species of fauna, and rock formation found within the park. Juliet could barely identify an oak tree. A large carpenter bee buzzed in front of Juliet's face, forcing her to direct her attention to the task ahead. *Today,* Juliet thought, as she stepped over a fallen tree, *today will be different.*

Secret marched ahead, unaware of the growing distance between them. After a time, she began to sense the gap, cocked her head and called to Juliet, "Hey, Princess, will you hurry up? You would think someone with your legs would be bounding over all these down trees with no problem."

"Easy for you to say when I'm carrying all the equipment, and you only have a backpack of food and water," Juliet shot back at her friend. "And don't call me Princess or else I'll call you – oh, I don't know what I'll call you, but it will be something you don't like."

A sly smile formed on her friend's face. "After nine years, I hoped you'd have a better comeback." Shaking her head. "I've taught you nothing."

In one motion Juliet bent down, picked up a marble-sized rock and hurled it, striking Secret in the arm. "You taught me how to throw!" she said quickly to stop the barrage of curses she knew were coming based on Secret's reddening face. The comment was enough to pacify her friend before the verbal explosion, and the two women smiled for a few seconds before Secret turned to continue through the thick forest.

Though an avid runner, Juliet was struggling to keep up. Her height was a definite disadvantage when trekking through the low-lying branches that hung in this section of the forest. Juliet had always enjoyed being a bean pole, but was currently envious of Secret's compact height as a branch caught her blond hair, snagging the long pony tail and jerking her head backwards. Juliet stopped to untangle herself, gazing ahead at Secret who resembled a forest sprite, easily maneuvering over the fallen trees and scrub brush snagging Juliet's pants.

Initially, people were quick to comment on how lucky she was to have "the perfect job". The majority of the population, she found, often romanticized her profession. Juliet silently pondered this while feeling perspiration all over her body. There was a recurring itch between her shoulder blades where the backpack of veterinary supplies she carried was preventing her from scratching it satisfactorily. The barrel of the large tranquilizer gun strapped to the pack kept catching on branches she didn't quite duck low enough to clear. Even though it was the end of June, it had been unseasonably warm. As she wiped the sweat from her brow again, the corner of her mouth turned up while reflecting about her current under-taking. It was not for the faint of heart and was most as-suredly not as easy as most people perceived, but there was no job she would rather have.

Secret swatted a deer fly trying to bite her. "You know, Jules, it is a good thing we're best friends, because only you could convince me to walk through this park looking for illegal traps when it's hotter than hell."

"I know, but you know you love me, and at least this gets you out of talking to tourists all day long." Juliet smiled back at her friend.

Secret only glared at her. "Gee, when you put it like that, how could I not resist?"

Juliet – Dr. Greene, as most people called her now – had recently completed her veterinary internship in small animal and exotic medicine. She was fortunate to land an internship soon after graduating from vet school at Au-burn University. For the past year, Juliet had honed her skills in internal medicine and surgery at a large clinic in Atlanta. Her favorite rotations always focused on surgery, since she liked to live by the motto, "A chance to cut is a chance to cure".

Her real passion, though, was wildlife medicine. Dogs and cats were wonderful, but a person could only handle so many cases of vomiting and diarrhea before getting bored. Wild animals always presented new chal-lenges with no two cases being the same. It was fortunate Secret was working at the ranger station near Middlesbo-ro, Kentucky, since she found out about the wildlife-related position before it was even advertised to the gen-eral community. In March, Juliet opened her email to find a job listing forwarded from Secret. One of the leading wildlife veterinarians in the country, Dr. Anthony Silver, was helping the National Park Service investigate a recent increase in poaching. Although Dr. Silver was a board certified small animal surgeon with a small animal clinic in town, he was known for his expertise in North American wildlife with a focus on wolf population health studies. Unable to efficiently balance the case load of the clinic with the demands of the Park Service, Dr. Silver had proposed a more proactive approach to combating the poaching by having a veterinarian ride along with the rangers during their weekly surveys of the forest. This way, any animal found trapped or injured in the park could be assessed immediately and some of the unfortunate deaths could, hopefully, be prevented. Since poaching was becoming a reoccurring problem, the Park Service had accepted the program.

When Juliet had read Secret's e-mail with the job description, her heart leapt -- living in the city had taught her how much she had missed the rolling hills and changing seasons of her childhood home. So excited at the prospect of getting away from the concrete jungle of Atlanta, it hadn't registered Secret would be there too until she read the e-mail again. This realization resulted in the type of phone conversation only best friends can have, with Juliet and Secret both talking at the same time and yet not missing a word. Despite being opposites in almost all categories, Juliet and Secret had always managed to find the perfect Yin and Yang relationship, using their strengths to balance the other's weaknesses.

Juliet had screamed so loudly when Dr. Silver had offered her the job it might have caused some hearing loss, since she had to repeat herself several times to him throughout the rest of the conversation. Everything had fallen into place after the phone call, from easily finding the perfect house to rent to everyone at the clinic being some of the best people she had worked with so far in her short career.

Even though Juliet was excited about their assignment, it hadn't exactly been the start she had imagined in her head. After six weeks of working at the clinic, this had been her first rotation out in the field, and they had only found empty traps or remains of animals who had not survived. Meaning a long week of necropsies and evidence collection instead of treating injured animals. She knew necropsies were extremely important. During the dissection of each body more evidence which might lead to who was poaching would be found, but being an animal CSI wasn't very exciting to her. Juliet was convinced she had hit the lowest point when they had to carry the maggot-covered body of a dead fox back to the truck so she could collect samples. Secret had certainly made her opinion on that particular task very clear.

"Jules, seriously?" Secret had said when Juliet told her they had to pick up the rotting carcass. "I know I majored in forestry and have made a career out of getting close to nature, but some things should just be left where they lie. That fox is one of them." Even though the body was too far along in its decomposition to have much scent left, Secret made a point of positioning herself upwind.

"I know you'd rather hang out in the forest taking soil samples and measuring water indexes, but we have to do this," Juliet had responded, as she plucked a piece of the larva-eaten liver out of the body and placed it in a evidence bag. "Look, nobody likes maggots – except sadistic entomologists. There was a guy in my vet school class who would throw up every time an animal came in like this. He couldn't be within fifty feet of the smell without hurling."

Today, they had not found any rotting carcasses. Juliet was secretly thankful for this, since she too, hated dealing with maggots, but would never admit to her friend. In case she did come across anything that smelled horrible, she always kept a small container of VapoRub in her vet bag. Just a small strip of the ointment under her nose and the smell of rotting flesh became somewhat manageable.

"I cannot believe you are spending your day off doing this. I know you went out every day this week with some of the other rangers, so don't try to pretend you're required to be out here today. Don't get me wrong, I love spending time with you and all, but I don't want you to burn out your first week. Why don't you do something normal like have fun?" Secret asked.

Juliet just rolled her eyes. "Not this again. I told you, I'm here to work, not to have fun. Well, actually, my work is fun when I'm not dissecting four-day-old dead animals rotting in ninety-degree heat."

"When was the last time you went out?" Secret asked. "Why don't you come to our Fourth of July party next weekend?"

It was time to change the subject. As far as Juliet was concerned, talking with drunk strangers sounded about as appealing as nails on a chalkboard. She'd be much happier curled up on the couch with her cat in her lap and a good book to read. Juliet went with her go to plan for steering the conversation away from her, "So, how was Kevin's shift last night with the full moon and everything?"

Secret moved a low tree branch out of her way as she continued into the woods. "Oh, you know, the usual, crazy people doing stupid stuff. Same as every other night."

Secret was all but legally married to Kevin O'Hara, an officer with the Middlesboro Police Department. He and Secret had started dating shortly after he arrived in Kentucky from Virginia two years earlier. They'd moved in with each other after about three months of dating and were the kind of couple that gave Juliet a toothache, seemingly connected at the hip. Juliet was lost in her thoughts when a loud, blood-chilling scream erupted from the forest.

"What the hell was that?" gasped Secret, stopping mid-stride and staring into the thicket ahead.

"How should I know?" retorted Juliet. "You're the ranger!"

Whatever had emitted the wail was still making a horrendous sound. Like doomed characters in a horror movie, they ran towards the sound rather than away from it. As they took off, Juliet was struck with the thought that this was not what most sane people would do. They ran about fifty feet through some knee-high shrubs and year-old saplings before coming to a small clearing. In front of a fallen oak tree was a writhing animal caught in what appeared to be a double jaw foot trap. The trap had closed on the front left leg of a remarkably large beast, and the poor creature was desperately pulling at it in an attempt to free itself. When it noticed the two women, it stopped suddenly, flattened its ears, bared its teeth, and let out a low growl. Both women froze like statues for several seconds.

Secret broke the silence between the women first. "That's a grey wolf!"

Juliet had already started moving closer to the animal. "I can see that."

Secret's face reddened as she crossed her arms in front of her chest. "Yes, I know that Jules. What I meant was why is there a *Canis lupus lupus* in Kentucky? They haven't lived in this area since the 1900s."

Juliet was too busy taking of her pack off and looking for the supplies she needed to think of a snide remark to Secret's defensive display of scientific knowledge. She pulled out the bottle she wanted and started filling a syringe with clear liquid.

"I don't know why, Secret, and, frankly, I don't care. What I do know is this is the first live animal I've seen all week. Go get the truck and bring it as close as you can," she said.

Secret just stared at her. "Why? What do you think you're doing?"

"My job," Juliet countered.

Secret's eyes widened. "You don't honestly think you are going to bring a *wolf* back to the clinic, do you?"

"That's exactly what I'm going to do," Juliet replied. She pulled the needle tip of the full syringe out of the bottle and looked straight at her friend. "Secret, this is why I'm here. What I'm supposed to do. Go get the truck, and let me handle this. I've sedated bigger and more dangerous animals than this before. By the time you get back, this big guy will be out, and we'll need to get him back to the clinic as quickly as possible."

Secret stood there for a few moments rocking back and forth on her legs. Juliet could see the internal debate going on in her friend. She gave a reassuring smile and locked eyes with her. Secret opened her mouth as if to say something but didn't. Instead she turned and went back through the woods from which they had come.

Juliet focused her attention on the still-growling animal. The truth was while she had sedated larger and more dangerous animals, it was during her many rotations in veterinary school and internship. This would be the first time she would be attempting to dart an animal without another veterinarian there to back her up if something went wrong. Her stomach clenched slightly with the thought. *So much for wading into the water*, she thought. She always did dive right into things.

She finished pulling up all the sedatives needed, and quickly loaded the dart. It wasn't until she placed her hands on the gun the wolf's reaction changed. The snarling intensified, and, for a split second, Juliet thought she heard a noise off to her right. The hair on the back of her neck stood up suddenly as she rose to her feet. A thought that she might be the one being hunted flashed through her mind. She turned to make sure nothing was behind her but could not see anything in the woods.

Juliet moved slowly towards the wolf with the dart gun in hand. It felt heavier than she remembered, and her voice trembled as she spoke, matching the unsteadiness of her nervous hands. "I know you don't understand me, big fella, but I'm here to help, not hurt you. You're scared and hurting, but I promise I'm going to make you feel better."

Maybe it was her imagination, but it seemed to Juliet the wolf stopped growling as loudly and his ears relaxed ever-so-slightly from their pinned down position against the back of its head. Juliet wondered for a moment if this change in behavior meant the wolf could sense a pack mate approaching, and felt her pulse quicken as she tightened the grip on the dart gun. *Steady*, she thought to herself. *You need to get this animal sedated*. Juliet took a deep breath and aimed the dart gun towards the back of the wolf, targeting the gluteal muscle, thus avoiding any major organs. Slowly exhaling, she squeezed the trigger and fired. It took a few seconds for Juliet to see if the dart had hit its target, as the wolf had spun away from her to look at the implanted projectile. She sighed with relief when the wolf turned, revealing the dart behind his right hip.

Juliet slowly lowered herself to the ground to wait for the wolf to feel the effects of the sedatives, trying not to make any loud noises or sudden movements, which would only prolong the time it took for the animal to fall asleep. More relaxed, she was able to admire how beautiful the creature was. Its light brown fur looked soft and clean causing her to wonder if it was as delicate as it appeared. The fur on the legs gradually changed from the light brown to white, giving the illusion the animal was wearing socks. As the medications began to take effect, the wolf stumbled drunkenly until finally collapsing onto the ground. The sedatives were working swiftly, and Juliet hoped they wouldn't wear off too soon. Quickly but quietly, she assembled her portable stretcher so they would be able to carry the animal back to the truck. For the first time in the past few minutes, Juliet took stock of her surroundings, and couldn't get over the feeling she was being watched. Once again, she scanned the woods, holding as still as possible, focusing all her energy on listening for any sounds of movement in the forest beyond. Snapping branches from behind made her jump. She turned around, not knowing what to expect, and saw Secret burst back into the small clearing.

"Why do you look like a deer in the head lights?" questioned Secret.

Juliet relaxed her shoulders. "Oh, I don't know. Maybe it's because you almost made me pee myself bursting out of nowhere."

Secret walked over and sat down by Juliet's backpack. "Well, thank God you're all right."

Juliet scowled at her friend. "Why would I not be?"

"Honestly?" Secret smiled. "You were never very graceful. I was worried you might have shot yourself or gotten eaten."

"Thanks for the vote of confidence," Juliet said as she turned back to the sleeping mound in front of her. "Help me un-anchor this trap so we can move him." She gestured at the wolf as she started to dig through her pack for a towel to place over its head.

Secret followed the chain to where it was grounded. "I got the truck as close as I could, but it's still about fifty yards away."

Juliet found the towel, slinging it over her shoulder as she pulled her stethoscope out of the backpack and wrapped it familiarly around her neck. She walked up to the wolf, looking for the gentle rise and fall of its chest. Draping the towel over the animal's eyes to shield them from the sun, she bent down next to it. Removing the stethoscope from around her neck, she fitted the ear tips into her ears and placed the bell on the smooth coat while watching for any signs of a reaction. It would be disastrous if she had given too little sedative or too much. Much to her relief, the wolf didn't react to her touch, and the heart rate and breathing seemed to be normal. Her eyebrows furrowed as she began to examine the injured leg. She winced when palpating the injury, it appeared the trap had fractured both long bones in the left front leg. As she pulled her hands away, she noticed the tissue was slowly being seared around the areas where the metal had pierced the skin. Suddenly, an overwhelming smell of burnt flesh invaded her nose. She closed her eyes and focused on keeping the food in her stomach from coming up and out of her mouth while she turned back to the pack to find her trusty VapoRub.

"Secret, careful with that chain! I think this trap is coated with some kind of acid because it's burning the tissue," she said, smearing the menthol paste under her nose. "Make sure you're wearing your gloves." Juliet looked over at her friend and saw the odd expression on her face. "What? Do I have VapoRub on my chin?"

Secret lifted the chain in her hand. "Jules, I don't think there's anything on the chain, but there is something not quite right about this trap."

Juliet leaned down to get a closer look at the metal. It looked like a regular stainless steel trap to her, but she really did not have time to examine it closely. Right now, she needed to focus on getting the wolf back to the clinic before the sedatives wore off.

She looked for the release mechanism. "I'm going to take this trap off here. We need to stop the damage it's causing. Bring me my bag so I can put a pressure wrap on the leg."

Secret nodded in agreement and moved the backpack next to Juliet, kneeling down beside her. In short time, the trap was off and the leg was bandaged. They slid the wolf onto the stretcher and strapped him to it for the trip back to the truck. Juliet regretted not working out more, since she struggled to lift the heavy animal through the woods. She had to stop and rest the stretcher on her leg for just a minute to give her trembling arms a break. By the time the women got to the truck they were both drenched in sweat. Juliet had never been so grateful to see a truck. They slid the stretcher into the bed and Juliet climbed in beside it carefully avoiding hitting her head on the topper. Unable to stand, she crouched down with the wolf, settling herself against the wheel well. After downing an entire bottle of water, she started making phone calls to some of the technicians at the clinic to prepare for an emergency surgery. She also left a message on Dr. Silver's phone about what was going on, and hoped the urgency in her voice would be enough to convince him to meet her there. Secret returned from the clearing with the backpack and trap, hopped into the cab and started the engine. As they pulled away, Juliet stared into the forest as it fell away behind them. She felt the same eerie tingling along the back of her neck like she was still being watched, but forced herself to look away from the receding trees and focus all her attention on her patient. "You're going to be okay," she whispered, placing a hand on the smooth fur.

Chapter 2

Twenty-five minutes later, three veterinary technicians greeted them as they were pulling up to Dr. Silver's clinic. From her limited view in the truck bed, Juliet could see them pacing back and forth in the parking lot. One of the techs was chewing her nails while another pulled at the bottom of her scrub top. Gina, Nicole, and Emily looked extremely nervous when Secret opened up the back of the truck. She noticed all three techs' faces blanched at the site of the injured wolf.

Juliet hopped out of the truck and grabbed the end of the stretcher. "Let's get him inside and intubated before we have an awake, painful animal on our hands."

The techs leapt into action, first transferring the wolf to a wheel stretcher and then rolling him into the clinic and straight into the treatment room. The women had already set up a portable anesthesia machines along with a variety of endotracheal tubes. Juliet picked a size she suspected would fit easily down the wolf's trachea. With Gina holding the mouth open, she inserted the tube into its windpipe. Quickly, she secured the tube by tying gauze around the portion sitting in the animal's mouth and then wrapping it around the back of the head and knotting it behind the ears. Gina connected the open end to the anesthesia machine and checked the connection for any leaks.

Once the wolf was safely intubated and under gas anesthesia, Juliet let out a deep breath she didn't realize she'd been holding. The last hour had been a whirlwind, and the realization of the entire situation was beginning to sink in. The techs were buzzing around the clinic preparing everything needed to stabilize the animal, Gina placed an IV catheter, Nicole measured the injured leg for radiographs, and Emily prepared the surgery room. As the women moved around her, Juliet decided to perform a complete physical exam of the patient to make sure no other obvious problems existed. As she checked the depth of anesthesia by looking at the rotation of the eyes, Juliet drew in a sharp breath when she noticed the color of the irises. *That's weird*, she thought to herself, since green eyes, though not impossible, were not a common eye color for wolves. Examining the teeth around the trachea tube, she noted his small, immature canines and molars indicating this was a young animal, much younger than his size would suggest. His upper right baby canine was missing. Based on his teeth alone, she would guess he was no more than five to six months of age, but he was easily the size of an average adult male wolf. She completed the rest of her exam consciously looking for other oddities but found nothing else that stood out.

Gina and Nicole rolled the wolf into the radiology room to take X-rays. Juliet made her way over to one of the computers in the treatment room to start typing her findings from the physical exam into the records. Images of the front leg soon appeared on the computer monitor in front of her. Just as she had suspected, both the left radius and ulna were fractured in the center of the bone. There was also a metal fragment from the trap broken off in the leg. Juliet started to visualize how she was going to stabilize the fracture while managing a dirty open wound. Closing her eyes, she created a mental picture of the fracture. Her fingers began to move in the air as she mimicked her surgical approach. Her thoughts were interrupted by a hand on her shoulder.

"First, what are you doing, and, second, is this something you can fix, or do you think you're going to have to euthanize this animal?" Secret asked, rotating the swivel chair so Juliet was facing her. Tucked underneath her arm was a cardboard box.

A crash made both women spin around. The metal tray containing the gauzes and the surgical scrub was at Gina's feet. Blue fluid from the scrub container covered the top of Gina's shoe and was spreading across the treatment room floor. She was staring at Juliet with wide eyes and almost looked like she was about to burst into tears.

Juliet got up from the computer station and walked over to the technician gently placing her had on her right shoulder. "Gina, are you okay?"

Gina blinked and then quickly snapped out of her trance. "I'm fine. Sorry." Juliet noticed a reluctant anger in Gina's voice. "It's just, Dr. Silver has never euthanized anything over a broken leg before. Maybe we need to wait until he gets here."

"I'm not going to euthanize this wolf," replied Juliet, a little taken aback by Gina's instant distrust in her abilities. "I can fix this."

Gina picked up the dropped equipment with a curt nod and headed to where Emily and Nicole were waiting with the wolf. Juliet turned to her friend, "To answer your earlier question, I was visualizing my surgery. It's something that helps me prepare before I have to do any type of procedure. Very relaxing; you should try it sometime," she said flatly, Gina's sudden change in attitude having put her on edge. When she saw the hurt expression flash across Secret's face, she quickly added, "Sorry, I'm just nervous and none of this –" she gestured at the spot where Gina had stood seconds before, "Is helping me to relax." Secret squeezed her friend's shoulder in silent understanding. Juliet looked down and pointed at the package under Secret's arm. "What's in the box?"

Secret carried the box over to the closest table, set it down, and unfolded the four pieces of cardboard at the top, opening it for Juliet to peer inside. "I didn't know what you wanted me to do with the trap."

Juliet looked from the trap to Secret, "Do you know where we could send this to run some tests to see what it was coated in?"

Secret pursed her lips, which was a habit Juliet had noticed she did when thinking. "I'll ask my boss at the ranger station to see what he says."

"I have to change into my scrubs for surgery. You don't need to hang around if you need to go." Juliet turned away from the tablet and headed towards a cabinet in the treatment room.

"Hey, Jules, before you go, come look at this chain." Secret lifted the chain in her gloved hand. "Something's not right with this metal. Most of the traps we find out here are made of stainless steel, which is a lighter metal. This trap is much heavier than it should be for its size."

Juliet leaned down to get a closer look at the metal. Not being of much help, she took her friend for her word. Right now, she needed to focus on getting the wolf healed. "I'm going to leave this in your capable hands. I'm sorry, Secret, but I have to go." She turned to walk out of the treatment room to go change.

"You're going to do fine you know," Secret spoke behind her. "You just need to start believing in yourself as much as I do."

Juliet turned back to her friend and smiled. "Thanks. I needed that."

By the time Juliet dressed into her scrubs, scrubbed her hands, and put on her sterile surgical gown and gloves, the three techs had the animal on the surgical table, removed the bandage from the leg, shaved the hair around the injury, performed a surgical scrub to decontaminate the skin, and had the animal completely draped for surgery. The computer monitor in the surgery room displayed images of the broken leg. As Emily hooked up the patient to the temperature probe, ECG lines, pulse oximeter, and capnograph – all used to monitor the animal under anesthesia – Juliet took another look at the radiographs. The broken piece of the trap was near the radius, and she hoped it had not damaged any major blood vessels or nerves. She had been so focused on the wound before she had failed to look at the entire radiograph. Her radiology professor's voice rang in her head, "You must read the entire radiograph from top to bottom. The image you see tells a story; don't just focus on the end, read the whole book."

When she redirected her vision to take in the complete image, she noticed the growth plates of each bone were still open. Puzzled, Juliet wondered just how big this animal would grow. The average adult male gray wolf weighed between 70-140 pounds, and this wolf was at least 100 pounds. Gina's buzzing phone brought her back from her thoughts.

"Hi, Dad," Gina said, stepping away from the surgical table to take the call. Juliet turned from the computer screen to face Gina, who was nodding to whatever was being said to her. When Gina made eye contact with Juliet, she held up a finger in a "hold on a second" motion. "Okay, I'll tell her," Gina said before ending the call. She looked at Juliet. "Dad – I mean, Dr. Silver – says he will be here shortly and to not do anything extreme."

Juliet was thankful her surgical mask covered the frown she was making. Even though she had only been working for Dr. Silver for little over a month, he had never once doubted her skills. Likewise, the techs all seem to like her and trust her, despite Gina's earlier outburst. Then again, Gina and Nicole were sisters who happened to work at their father's veterinary practice. Emily had worked for Dr. Silver since high school. Juliet told herself the extra precaution was due to this being her first time working on an injured wolf. She hoped soon she'd be trusted to handle things without Dr. Silver's direct input even though he was the "wolf expert".

Juliet straightened. "Well, we need to get this leg debrided sooner rather than later, and I want to get the piece of metal out as soon as possible. We can at least do that before he gets here, and then we'll work on getting the fractures stabilized."

Three sets of eyes looked at her in agreement, and then everyone fell into their unspoken roles to get the job at hand done. Juliet located the metal fragment embedded in one of the extensor muscles of the leg. Carefully peeling away the muscle fibers around the metal she grasped the piece with her thumb forceps and removed it without hitting any nerves or blood vessels. Juliet smiled for a moment as she thought about how this was just like playing the game "Operation" as a child, which had always been one of her favorites. Only, in this case, instead of an annoying sound and a big red nose that would light up when you touched the metal sides, you could royally screw something up and lose a leg.

The tissue surrounding the fragment appeared to be burnt. She asked Gina to lavage the wound with saline to try and get rid of any remaining chemicals. As Juliet started to debride the area, Dr. Silver's voice came on over the intercom, "Dr. Greene, please stop what you are doing and wait for me to finish scrubbing in before you proceed."

Juliet looked up at the window separating the surgery room from the surgical prep to see Dr. Silver staring at her. He already had his cap and mask on, but she could tell he was not very happy by the intense stare directed towards her. Her stomach began to ache, and she felt like a child who had just been reprimanded by her teacher. Before Dr. Silver finished his hand scrub, another man appeared next to him, seeming very agitated. She could hear his raised voice through the glass, but the words were muffled by the walls. Juliet wished she could hear the conversation taking place, or that both men were not wearing surgical masks so she could at least try to read their lips. She could watch each man's eyes, and as much as Dr. Silver seemed upset the unknown man was ten times as furious. Her stomach tightened even more.

Dr. Silver stepped away from the angry man and entered the surgery room. "Dr. Greene, what do we have here and what have you done so far?"

Juliet explained what had taken place both in the field and at the clinic. Dr. Sliver listened intently as she added her findings in regards to the size of the animal versus the open growth plates and incomplete set of adult teeth. When she mentioned this information, Dr. Silver's eyebrows furrowed.

"Interesting observation Dr. Greene, I'm sure I will take that into consideration when I finish fixing this fracture," Dr. Silver replied hastily.

Juliet stared at him for a moment before hesitantly saying, "But, Dr. Silver, I thought –"

"I think you have had a long enough day, especially since this is your day off," Dr. Silver cut her off authoritatively. "I can handle things from here. Thank you for your time; you may go home now." And with that, Dr. Silver turned his back to her and started working on the wolf's leg.

"But I thought I could stay and assist you in stabilizing the fracture."

"You've done a great job in what you have done so far, but now is not the time for me to teach you. I need you to go home and be ready for work on Monday," Dr. Silver dictated without even looking away from the surgery table.

Juliet looked around the room for some kind of support from the technicians and noticed none of them would look her in the eyes. Embarrassed she was being dismissed, she turned and walked out of the room. Once Juliet made it through the door, she started ripping off the top layer of gloves and tossing them towards the trash without looking to see if they made it in the garbage.

Before she could rip off her other pair of gloves, mask or gown, she was stopped abruptly by the unknown man Dr. Silver had been talking to through the glass. She tried to pass by him, but he moved to block her way of escape. He glared down at Juliet with the most piercing eyes she had ever seen. They were a dark blue like the ocean, but the waters she saw in them were dark and storming. Juliet was momentarily stunned by the unusual color, but forced her gaze away and made for the door. The man moved so she couldn't reach it.

"I hope for your sake you didn't screw anything up too badly," he hissed from behind the surgical mask he wore.

With that, he pushed past Juliet and joined the others in the surgery room. Juliet had had enough. She ripped off the rest of her surgical attire and threw it on the ground. Grabbing her car keys, she stomped out of the clinic without changing out of her scrubs, hopped into her truck, and peeled out of the parking lot.

Chapter 3

In the sanctuary of her truck, the tears of frustration she had refused to shed at the clinic came spilling out. She felt so stupid for crying, but she couldn't help it. When the mucus started flowing from her nose, Juliet knew she had to get her outburst under control. With some major will power, she was able to get the steady waterfall of tears down to the occasional trickle.

Juliet had gotten about halfway home when a set of police lights turned on behind her truck. Her already bad mood instantly worsened as she pulled over to the side of the road. Quickly, she wiped the remaining tears from her face, retrieved her purse, and started fishing through it to get her wallet for her license. She rolled down the window and turned to face the police officer who had approached. The smile on the officer's face immediately morphed into concern when he saw Juliet.

"Oh, hi, Kevin," Juliet managed to muster some sort of pleasant greeting. "What did I do wrong?"

Kevin removed his sunglasses revealing his brown eyes. Already the summer had given him the perfect bronze tan complimenting his eyes and sandy blond hair. It also helped to define the muscles in his forearms, which were exposed in his short-sleeved uniform. With his height, he was able to look straight at Juliet's face through her truck window and continued to give her a concerned look.

"Well, I had stopped you because I can't get ahold of Secret, and I was hoping you knew where she was. Now, though, I can see you look pretty upset, and, as a civil servant concerned for the well-being of the citizens of this town and the fact we're friends, I need to make sure you're not in distress," Kevin added.

Juliet knew this was some attempt to make her feel better, so she managed a half-hearted smile. "Why are you pulling me over to ask where your fiancée is when you could have called me? I mean don't get me wrong I'm glad to see you, but there are these things people have invented called cell phones. Perhaps you've heard of them?"

Kevin's smile broadened, but he still looked concerned. "There's the feistiness I know. I did call your phone, but you didn't answer. The odds of both of you not answering your phones are beyond calculation. I saw you drive by, so I just decided to pull you over to ask about Secret. I know," he added quickly, putting up his hands to block the rebuttal Juliet was about to throw at him, "I abused my position, but you cannot fault a guy for being worried about his fiancée. Besides, it looks like you needed to talk to someone."

Juliet pulled out her cell phone and indeed saw the missed call from Kevin. She checked the settings and realized the ringer had not been turned back on from when she set it on silent for her trip out into the forest. She turned back to Kevin. "Secret and I went out again this morning. She went back after she left me to log some evidence and take samples. My guess is she's still at the ranger station, and you know how horrible cell phone service is out there."

Kevin looked puzzled. "I didn't know you guys were going out this morning. Did you find something?"

This question brought Juliet back to why she was in a bad mood and why she wanted so badly to get home to pout alone. "Oh, we found something," Juliet's voice started to quiver as the anger and embarrassment of the situation came welling up again full force. "Kevin, no offense, but I do not want to talk about it right now."

To her relief, Kevin didn't push her further. "Okay, I can tell you're pretty beat up. Once you feel better, let me know who I have to arrest. I'll let Secret know you probably need to talk when she gets home. Oh, and Juliet," his look of concern morphed into a familiar lopsided smile, "make sure you take a shower, cause you stink pretty bad."

"Thanks, Kevin," Juliet rolled her eyes. "Next time, let a girl just have a bad day, okay?"

Kevin chuckled and slapped the side of Juliet's truck in response, giving her a nod. Juliet watched his relaxed figure get smaller in her rearview mirror as she pulled away.

Juliet was thankful to get back to the two-bedroom stone cottage she was renting for the year. It was the perfect place for her, both in size and rent. Her roommate, Shadow, met her at the front door purring louder than a train and rubbing his head at her ankles. She picked up the grey cat and gave him a big squeeze. She guessed she really did smell bad, because even he gave her a little huff of disgust and turned his head away.

Shadow had been adopted during her junior year of veterinary school. He had been one of her patients from the shelter that had come in for surgery class. There had been a large wound on his side requiring a skin graft and, of course, he needed to be neutered. Juliet had been the lead student surgeon for his case. Proud of the work she had done and becoming attached to her patient during the post-op care, she had adopted him. He'd been her "little shadow" from then on out, following from room to room in every place she lived. That was how many of the veterinary students in her class had come by most of their pets. As far as veterinarians and their pets were concerned, Juliet was an oddity with only having one. Since she knew she was going to be moving around a lot her first few years out of veterinary school, she didn't think it would be fair to have a menagerie like most of her colleagues had acquired. She looked down at the gray fur ball in her arms. "I only need you, anyway," she said, lifting his face up to hers and touching their noses together. Shadow jumped down in protest and proceeded to curl up on the couch.

Once Juliet had showered, she felt like a new person, at least scent-wise. After putting on her most comfortable pajama pants and an old, worn tee shirt, she headed into the kitchen to look for some kind of comfort food. She was still pissed this stranger – what was his connection to the clinic anyway? – had the audacity to insinuate she had harmful intentions regarding the wolf. Even though she was initially just confused by Dr. Silver's insistence she leave, after having some time to think about it, she was starting to become angry with him too. What was going on with the wolf she couldn't see? None of it made sense – Dr. Silver had created this job to increase animal survival rates, and, as far as she could reason while she replayed the day's events over and over, that was exactly what she had done. He was also supposed to be teaching her, and how was she going to learn anything if she was asked to leave every surgery? She scanned the cupboards and then opened the fridge. She needed junk food, stat. Two options met the criteria, a bowl of mac and cheese and a roll of cookie dough. She decided her mood warranted the ultimate guilty pleasure. As she grabbed the container out of the refrigerator, her cell phone started ringing. "Hello?"

"Jules, what happened after I left? Kevin said he saw you and you had been crying. Are you okay? Did the wolf die?" Secret's concerned voice resonated through the phone.

"I'm fine now," Juliet replied with the first bite of food in her mouth. "I'll be okay."

"What are you eating?" Secret asked.

"Nothing," Juliet responded mischievously.

"Juliet Greene, are you eating a bowl of macaroni and cheese?" accused Secret.

"No," Juliet gulped out as she spooned another piece of food in her mouth.

"Are you eating a tube of raw cookie dough?" Secret tried again.

Juliet stopped mid-bite and was thankful her friend could not see her guilty face. "Maybe."

"Shit, that bad. I am coming over." Secret hung up before Juliet could tell her she had the situation under control.

The cookie dough was halfway gone twenty minutes later when there was a knock on the door. Juliet opened it to see her friend standing there with two bottles of wine in her hands and a backpack over her shoulder. She immediately embraced Juliet, but, before making her way past the threshold, looked past Juliet into the living room. "Where is it?"

Juliet placed another spoonful of cookie dough in her mouth and rolled her eyes. "I'll never understand your unhealthy fear of cats."

"It's the eyes, they're just creepy." Secret shuddered as she eyed the tube of cookie dough. "It looks like I got here just in time for the self-pity and over-indulgence portion of the evening. I guess I have some catching up to do."

Juliet tightened her grip on what remained of the package and held it against her chest, removing the spoon from her mouth where she had been holding it so she had a free hand to close the door. "I'm fine," Juliet said, unable to keep a straight face in response to Secret's incredulous look. Raw cookie dough had become her coping mechanism in college when she was extremely stressed or upset about anything. The week she had waited for her acceptance letters from veterinary schools she had eaten so much of the stuff that Secret was worried she may have to take Juliet to the hospital for food poisoning.

Secret shook her head and gave Juliet a friendly nudge as she pushed past her to set down her supplies on the coffee table. Juliet closed the door and shuffled behind her, dropping onto the couch where she had been sitting before. Secret went to rummage through the kitchen, opening cabinets and then closing them again. "Where are your wine glasses?" Secret asked as she threw open another cupboard.

"Um, nowhere?" Juliet responded with a confused tone. "You know I don't drink anymore, so I don't have wine glasses."

Secret shot Juliet a look of mock exasperation. "Yes, but your friend drinks wine." She moved back to one of the cabinets she had already been through and pulled out a large Auburn sports cup. "Guess this will have to do." She brought the cup over to the couch and produced a bottle opener from her backpack. "So, cookie dough bad but not Juliet-touches-the-devil's-drink bad, huh?" Juliet nodded in response, because her mouth was occupied with another spoonful of cookie dough.

Secret poured herself a large cup of wine and sat there sipping.

"I guess you're not going to leave me alone until I tell you what happened?" Juliet asked while the next delicious bite was making its way down her esophagus.

Secret just looked at Juliet expectantly, peering over the top of her cup. Juliet recounted everything, in detail, about what had transpired after Secret's departure from the veterinary clinic. When finished, she actually felt much better, but could tell her friend was now irate. She waited for the tirade to begin. Her friend had always been the one to fight the battles for her.

"So." Secret took a drink of wine. "You're telling me Dr. Silver just waltzed in and dismissed you just like that? What an asshole. Who does he think he is? Who is this other ass who came in and yelled at you too?"

"I don't know," Juliet looked down. "I'm sure Dr. Silver had a good reason for why he did what he did."

Secret glared at her. "I wish you would stop letting people walk all over you."

"I'm not like you," sighed Juliet. "You've always been quick and witty and never let anybody push you around. I wish I had you're gumption." Juliet leaned her head into her hand. "As for the other guy, I was hoping you might know who he is."

"Let me think of all the tall, asshole guys I know with blue eyes," Secret paused as she poured more wine. "Oh, wait, I don't think we have enough paper for that list. Are you sure there was nothing else you noticed?"

"No, I told you, he was gowned up for surgery. The only thing you can see is a person's eyes when they're in all that stuff." Juliet shoved another spoonful of cookie dough in her mouth, conscious of how little remained in the package. "Ah, I think I should stop eating this before I make myself sick. And, on that note, you might really want to drink some water. I'm not holding your hair back while you vomit in my toilet."

Secret's eyes narrowed on her friend. "I'm fine. I don't have to work tomorrow since Sunday and Monday are my days off. So, we need to find out who mysterious, blue-eyed asshole is, why he was there, and why Dr. Silver was a jerk, because I always thought he was a nice guy but my opinion is quickly changing."

"Until today he's been the best boss," Juliet sighed. "I just wish I knew what I did wrong. Or what he thinks I did wrong. He seemed completely different from his usual self. I really hope the rest of the year isn't like this."

Secret took another sip of wine. "What are you going to do?"

Juliet put down the spoon and now empty cookie dough wrapper and buried her face in a couch pillow. "Like I said, I'll talk to him on Monday. He's always had a the-door's-always-open policy, and I've never had a problem asking him anything before." She lifted her face out of the pillow as a wave of anxiety washed over her. What if she had done something really wrong? Her face began to turn red. What if the rest of her employment here was miserable and awkward, with Dr. Silver and the techs second-guessing her every move. "I hope this wasn't a huge mistake: taking this job and coming here."

Secret reached out and patted her hand. "Jules, don't be so extreme." Juliet had to smirk– Secret was notorious for taking things too far. "You're going to be okay. Everything will work out for the best."

"Well, look who turned into miss fuzzy bunnies. When did you get so optimistic?" Juliet gave her friend a skeptical look.

Secret lifted up her glass. "Since it became wine-thirty. Always makes life a little better."

Juliet yawned and stretched her arms above her head. The emotional roller coaster of a day had taken its toll. Since she had hashed out everything with Secret, she felt better prepared for her next step. She would talk to Dr. Silver and get everything straightened out. Maybe she'd even find out who this mystery man was and get some answers to explain his behavior. In her exhausted state, she envisioned herself marching up to him to give him a piece of her mind. Oh the look that would wash over his smug face – a face she had to invent based around those piercing and spiteful eyes. Juliet smiled as she imagined the man being at first taken aback, then trying to rebuke her accusations, and finally lowering his head in shame and apologizing for his behavior, begging for Juliet's forgiveness, slinking away with his tail tucked between his legs. *Wait, what?* Juliet said to herself, shaking her head to wake up from the dreamlike place she had gone. She must have started to doze off.

She stood up from the couch, forcing Shadow, who had been curled up on her lap this entire time, to jump on the floor. He gave her a repugnant look and spread his claws, digging them into the carpet. "I think I'm going to go to bed. Are you going to stay here? Wait, don't answer. You're going to stay here, there's no way I'm letting you drive home. The guest bedroom is already made up, so help yourself. Oh, and shut the door if you don't want Shadow sleeping on your head, since I know how much you love it when he touches you."

"Very funny." Secret stood up from the couch and embraced Juliet. "Everything's going to be okay, Jules."

Juliet nodded. "Thanks." She turned and walked towards her bedroom, not sure if she was looking forward to or dreading the dreams of confronting the blue-eyed man she knew would come.

Chapter 4

In the morning, the events of the previous day were still with Juliet when she woke up. The anger from the night before had abated. Her dreams had been filled with wolves chasing her and confrontations with the masked man. The only satisfaction she had was, in her dreams, she had punched the man in the nose while the injured wolf from the forest bit his leg. That memory had her still smiling as she walked out of her bedroom.

Juliet almost burst into laughter at the scene laid out before her in the living room. Sprawled over the couch was Secret; her brown hair sticking out in all directions. She hadn't made it out of her clothes from the night before. The second wine bottle sat half empty next to Secret's cup on the coffee table. Shadow was sitting on top of her head licking his anus. When he completed this task, he turned his attention to Secret's brown hair. At this sight, Juliet lost all control and started laughing until she was hit by a flying couch pillow.

"Go away," Secret grumbled. "And get off my head."

Another giggle erupted from Juliet. "I'm not on your head, but my cat is, and he's giving you a shower."

Secret sprang up from the couch, launching Shadow in the air. She ran her hands through her hair. "Yuck, my hair is wet with cat drool. Why do you torture me with that animal? You know he freaks me out. Can't you do something with him?"

Juliet picked up Shadow and started scratching his head. "My house, my cat, my rules. Suck it up."

Secret scowled and then stuck out her tongue at her friend. "Why are you up so early anyway?"

"It's Sunday; I'm going to church," Juliet replied as she started getting things out to make breakfast. "You wanna come?"

Secret was picking up the wine bottle. "Ugh, I'll pass, thanks."

After breakfast, Juliet got ready for church while Secret finished cleaning up from the night before. They made plans to meet later after Secret had recovered from the previous night's activities. The two of them had been working on a scrapbook of photos from college, and it was almost finished.

Juliet had been brought up in the church. Her faith was deeply entwined with her day-to-day life. Since arriving in town, she'd gone to a different church each week trying to find one she liked. So far none of the churches had been the right fit. Today, she was headed to the First Christian Church of Middlesboro for the 10:45 service. The parking lot was packed as she pulled up to the building. Which made her wonder if there was a special celebration going on or if this was just typical.

As she walked into the vestibule of the church, she gazed at the large stained glass windows lining the sanctuary. Each window depicted different scenes from the Bible. One of her favorite stories as a child had been Noah's ark, which was of course, because of all the animals. She picked a not-so-crowded pew near a window displaying the animals lining up to go in to the ark as Noah counted each pair. In the scene, Noah was bent down with his hands on a pair of large wolves. One had green eyes and the other blue. *How odd*, she thought, *but it must be artistic interpretation.*

A group of familiar people passed by her vision, disrupting her thoughts. Dr. Silver, his wife, Brenda, Gina, and Nicole moved along the aisle and sat down in a pew closer to the front. They sat behind a large family, and she watched as everyone greeted Dr. Silver, his wife, and children. A young boy with black hair spun around to say hello to Nicole, but suddenly froze, gawking at Juliet.

Juliet looked around to see if she was incorrect to assume she was the focus of his attention. She had never seen him before in her life, but, as she scanned the area around her couldn't find anything else in his line of sight. Juliet immediately became self-conscious: biting her lip and twisting her fingers in her hands. Releasing her fingers, she brought her right hand to her face and wiped her hand across the top of her nose to remove anything that might be on it. Hopefully, there was nothing embarrassing on her face the child was starting at. She looked back at the boy, who was saying something to Dr. Silver. He turned and gazed back in her direction. Juliet wanted to melt into the pew. She grabbed her purse and shifted her weight to stand when the organ music started and more people filed into the pew, cutting off any chance of an easy escape.

The service began, and Juliet tried to focus. A few minutes in, the children were called up to the front for the beginning of children's message. Juliet watched as the boy who had stared at her went up front. When the kids were dismissed to go to children's church, the same child glared at Juliet with his brilliant green eyes as he walked past making Juliet squirm in her seat.

The choir began singing as the minister stood up and went to the pulpit. The pastor of the church was Reverend Sterling Archon. He was an older man with silver hair and a gentle but commanding voice. Juliet pictured him as someone that would be excellent as a narrator of children's stories. Even though she had been distracted by the earlier events, she found his words quite captivating.

When the service was over, people started to file out the door. Rev. Archon was there, greeting everyone and shaking each person's hand. She saw Dr. Silver say something to him and nod in her direction. Juliet felt her cheeks flair with warmth. She was getting tired of the whispering and the side glances. It was making her feel like she had done something terribly wrong. As soon as she made it past the minister, she resolved, she was going to catch Dr. Silver and say something.

The line moved quickly to the vestibule, and soon she was standing in front of the pastor. Reverend Archon grabbed Juliet's hand and began shaking it. "Welcome to our church, young lady. I'm so pleased you could be with us today."

"Thank you," Juliet could not help but smile back at the man. Up close, she was able to get a better look at him. His broad warm smile complemented his square jaw and rosy cheeks. She was surprised, not only by how tall he was – probably about 6' 3" – but also how strong he appeared to be for a man of his age. Her breath hitched as she noticed his eyes. Gazing down at her and bordered by friendly creases were aged versions of the eyes of the mysterious man from the veterinary clinic. In fact, she suspected if Rev. Archon had been about 30 years younger, his eyes would have been the exact same as the man from the day before.

"What is your name, young lady?" Rev. Archon inquired.

"Juliet Greene, sir."

"What a beautiful name for a beautiful person," Rev. Archon stated. "I hope you come again next week. We'd love to have you as part of our church family."

Juliet could not help but deepen her smile. "Thank you for the compliment, and, yes, I think I'll be back soon."

Rev. Archon released her hand. Juliet walked out of the church and, for a brief moment, forgot her plan of confronting Dr. Silver. As she walked down the outside steps, she noticed Dr. Silver and his family speaking to a police officer. She assumed by his uniform he was the Sheriff of Middlesboro. Juliet wondered what was going on; she could tell her boss was getting more distressed by whatever the Sheriff was telling him, since he kept running his fingers through his pepper-colored hair. Gina and Nicole stood by their father, watching the two men with wide eyes and pale faces. Juliet's earlier annoyance with Dr. Silver dissolved as she could see the increased agitation of her boss and his family.

Juliet hurried over to the group. "Dr. Silver, is everything okay?"

"No, it isn't," Dr. Silver frowned. "The Sheriff has just informed me that someone broke into the clinic last night."

Chapter 5

Juliet had mixed feelings driving to Dr. Sliver's clinic Monday morning. The last forty-eight hours had left her with more questions than answers. Her type-A personality disliked the feeling of not knowing what was going on. She tapped her fingers on the steering wheel and let her mind wander to the events that had unfolded after church the day before. The sheriff had said someone had cut the alarm to the clinic before smashing in a side window. The thief or thieves were suspected of looking for drugs since the damage was focused on the pharmacy area. The police had dusted for prints and were running whatever they had found through criminal databases. The only reason why the police had been alerted at all was because someone driving by the clinic had noticed shattered glass by the side entrance. That was all she was able to overhear before Dr. Silver told her the matter was none of her concern. As she walked away, she had pulled Nicole away from the group to find out how the wolf was doing. Much to her frustration, Nicole shrugged her shoulders and told her she could not tell her anything, though if it was because she didn't know or didn't want to tell, Juliet was unclear. Determined to get more details about the break in, she had cornered Kevin later on that evening when she went over for dinner, but even he was elusive, stating that it was "under police investigation and not subject for conversation."

Turning into the clinic, Juliet brought her mind back to the plan she and Secret had discussed the night before.

Secret said Juliet was allowing herself to be a human doormat, and she couldn't help but agree. With a pep talk from her friend, she was now prepared to confront her boss and get the answers to her questions, even if it meant getting fired. At least, that's what she had told herself the night before. Walking up to the front door now, her resolve to follow through was waning. Still, she walked with her head held high and ducked under the police investigation tape. All her gumption evaporated the minute she saw the pharmacy. It looked like a tornado had gone through the entire room. Bottles and pills were scattered everywhere. Shards of glass scattered the floor from the bottles of injectable medications that had been dropped. One of the shelves had been completely ripped off the wall. Juliet turned to look down at the safe that held the controlled drugs, expecting the door to be wide open. To her surprise, the safe was untouched.

She walked around the rest of the clinic looking for other staff members as well as other damage the robber or robbers had done. With every area she saw she became more overwhelmed by the senseless destruction. By the time she found Emily and Gina in the back dog kennel area, Juliet was nauseated. The metal cages which normally housed a variety of small-sized dogs had all the doors flung open, and the clean bedding for each cage was strewn on the floor. Even the large dog runs had their doors open and all the bedding had been removed. Both ladies acknowledged Juliet with a "Good morning, Dr. Greene."

"Good morning. Is there anything I can do to help you guys?"

Emily folded a large quilt in front of her. "We're good here. Have you seen your office yet?"

Her spirits plummeted. "No, and from the face you are both making, I take it I'm not going to like what I find."

The two techs frowned. Juliet turned and walked the hallway to the office she shared with the two other practice associates. The large rectangular room housed three desks, one on each wall, with a large bookshelf on the fourth wall. Each desk had been decorated per each doctor's personality. Dr. Robbins' workstation was closest to the door and had been a disorganized mess filled with journal papers, open textbooks, and who knows what else. Juliet often wondered how the woman had found anything on it. Dr. Fuller's space was on the wall next to Dr. Robbins and to the left of it one of the two windows in the office. She had decorated her desk with pictures of her kids and always had snacks in the drawers in case one of them or the staff needed something to eat. On the back wall was another window and Juliet's desk, which fit in the corner between the window and the edge of the bookshelf. Since she'd only been working at the clinic for a few weeks, her desk was relatively sparse with only two pictures sitting on top. One of her and Secret dressed in their caps and gowns on the day of their graduation from college, and one of her with her mom, dad, and brother at her graduation from veterinary school. Those pictures were now lying smashed on the ground in the room. Juliet's work laptop had been taken, too. For the first time since she'd arrived, she could see the polished wood on top of Dr. Robbins's desk, since all the crap piled on it was now scattered on the floor. Dr. Fuller's desk appeared to have sustained the least damage since only her photos had been knocked over and not smashed like Juliet's.

By now the rest of the staff had gotten to work. They were wandering in and out of the rooms assessing the damage and starting to clean up everything. Everyone had been asked to come in an hour early to help so at least the exam rooms would be ready to receive patients when the clinic opened that morning. Dr. Silver had a four-doctor practice with an office manager, a kennel tech, two dog and cat groomers, four receptionists, and ten technicians. All four doctors were splitting the daily workload of the clinic and the wildlife rotations in the park. Dr. Silver had been scheduled out this week to ride with the rangers, but appeared at the doorway of the office five minutes later. Juliet assumed it was because of the break in.

"Dr. Greene," he motioned with his right hand towards the office across the way. "Will you please come into my office?"

Juliet stood up and placed the pile of papers she'd been picking up on the first available flat surface. She took a slow deep breath, rolled her shoulders back, and forced herself to straighten to her full height. She walked behind Dr. Silver into his office. Before she got through the threshold of the door, she slowed her stride so as not to slip on the strewn papers covering the green carpet of the office. Dr. Silver's office had an oak roll top along the wall to the left of the entrance. Under normal circumstances, the desk would have an array of papers, books, and pins in each of the individual pigeonholes. The office phone would have sat on the left side, and in the center his laptop would have been ready for data entry on the latest case. Instead, like Dr. Robbins' desk, the entire surface was bare, and the contents had been tossed onto the floor. She stepped over what she suspected were the smashed pieces of the office phone and felt the crunching of plastic under her foot. All the pictures of different wildlife, ranging from an Alaskan Moose to a Florida Beach Mouse, had been ripped off the wall, and, like the papers, were scattered along the floor. Juliet attempted to not to press her full weight on her heels as she crept farther into the office, tried to avoid shards of glass. She slowly turned around as she heard the door close behind her.

Dr. Silver stepped forward and leaned down. He picked up one of the discarded office chairs and gestured with his right hand for Juliet to sit. Juliet tiptoed back over the broken glass and sat gingerly in the wooden chair. Dr. Silver walked away from where she was sitting and grabbed another overturned chair, brought it back, and placed it two feet in front of her. He sat slowly in his chair, keeping his gray eyes locked onto Juliet's the entire time. The scleras of his eyes were bloodshot and there were dark circles under his lower eyelids. His pepper colored hair which was always perfectly groomed was disheveled. Juliet wondered how long it had been since he'd slept. She was bothered by his slow, deliberate actions. Suddenly, the overwhelming sense she was about to get fired came over her.

Placing his hands together in his lap, Dr. Silver took a deep breath in through his nose. "Juliet, I want to talk to you about this weekend and thank you for everything you did."

Juliet sat stunned looking at Dr. Silver. After she felt her eyes starting to get dry, she consciously made herself blink. It wasn't until she was going to respond she realized her mouth was hanging open. "Thank you. I think."

Dr. Silver seemed unaware of her reaction and continued, "I don't think you realize the full extent of your actions, but your quick thinking and dedication saved the life of that young wolf. I'm in your debt and truly grateful you work for me. With that being said, though, I need to remind you everything we do here, even our work for the National Park Service, is completely confidential and should not be discussed with anyone."

He continued to look at her intently. "There is a small population of wolves living in this area. Most people, don't know about them, since they're protected. With the poaching problem we've had over the past few months, the last thing that needs to happen is to bring attention to such a rare species in this area. Do you understand?"

Leaning forward in the chair Juliet propped her elbows on her knees. A dozen emotions wrestled in her head, but she didn't want to blow her opportunity to get answers. She let out a long, slow breath. "I don't understand. I mean, I understand patient-doctor confidentiality, but I don't understand your reaction the past two days, I don't understand why you kicked me out of my own surgery, I don't understand what happened to the wolf, or who that man in the clinic was and why he was able to go into surgery with you." She had to steady her voice towards the end because it began to quiver. She took in another slow, deep breath and was thankful she would have a few seconds to concentrate on her breathing while listening to Dr. Silver's reply.

The edges of Dr. Silver's mouth turned down. "I cannot give you the answers you need, but I can tell you the wolf is safe."

Juliet would not be deterred. She leaned closer to Dr. Silver, locking her eyes onto his. "Who was that man? How is the wolf safe? Where is he?"

Dr. Silver shook his head and deepened his frown. He rubbed his eyes with his right thumb and pointer finger, bringing his fingers together at the sides of his nose. "All I'm allowed to say is the wolf is safe, and recovering in a place where he will be well taken care of by the man you met. I need you to just trust me on this."

Juliet opened her mouth, but, before she could speak the words in her mind, there was a knock on the office door. It opened slightly, and Nicole's head appeared through the gap. She looked between Juliet and Dr. Silver before speaking, "Hey, Dad. Rev. Archon is here to see you."

Dr. Silver stood up and, in response, so did Juliet. She turned to face the door opened by Nicole. Behind her stood the Reverend, dressed in khaki pants and a blue polo shirt that accentuated his eyes. Juliet saw his eyes narrow for a spilt second when he first saw the office, but they immediately relaxed when he saw her standing in the center of the room beside Dr. Silver. Rev. Archon took a step forward and extended his hand to her boss. "Anthony, I came to check and see how you folks were doing. It looks like the damage done will be able to be fixed pretty easily, I hope."

"Nothing a little hard work won't fix." Dr. Silver turned to Juliet and extended his arm towards her. "Where are my manners? Juliet Greene, this is Reverend Sterling Archon."

Rev. Archon flashed Juliet the same warm smile he had given her the day before. "Oh, yes, we met yesterday at church. How could I possibly forget such a beautiful young lady?"

Juliet looked down at the floor and felt a sudden surge of blood flood her checks. She twisted her fingers in her right hand. Though she never thought of herself as ugly, she was not used to compliments about her physical appearance. Any kind of attention in regards to her looks always made her feel embarrassed and awkward. "Thank you. I'll let you two speak alone."

"Actually," Rev. Archon lifted his right hand to signal her to stop. "I'm glad I ran into you. I know you are new to this area and wanted to invite you to our Fourth of July picnic on Friday afternoon. Now, before you say no, just know my wife will be making her famous apple pie."

Juliet looked up from the floor with every intention of gracefully declining the invitation. She was overwhelmed by the fatherly gaze that met her eyes. If she said no she knew she would completely disappoint him. If everyone felt this way around the Reverend, then no wonder he had gone into the ministry. "I guess I could swing by," her voice was barely above a whisper.

Rev. Archon clapped his hands together. "Excellent! Anthony, I trust you will give her the directions to our house."

"Of course, Sterling," Dr. Silver nodded in agreement. "Juliet, would you excuse us while I speak with the Reverend?"

"Yes, sir. I'll just head to my office to continue cleaning up. Good-bye, Reverend Archon. Thank you, again, for the invitation." Juliet made her way past the two men, closing the door behind her. She leaned her back against the wall next to Dr. Silver's door and closed her eyes. It looked like she was going to a Fourth of July party after all.

Chapter 6

On Thursday, her landlord called and said the exterminators would be coming by to spray and set traps on Friday. Two days after she had moved in, Juliet kept finding cockroaches coming out of her plumbing. Juliet loved animals, but she wouldn't bat an eye if cockroaches went extinct. Her evening showers had become quiet traumatic ever since two of the nasty bugs crawled across her foot one night while washing her hair. She had run from the bathroom with her head covered in shampoo and immediately called the landlord. Shadow, her defender from all things bug, had caught several and eaten them, but had, on occasion, left one or two half-eaten bodies on her pillow. The exterminators were evidently free to come on a holiday, and Juliet would have to drop Shadow off at the clinic before attending any Fourth of July events, since the pest control company had requested no animals be in the house while they worked.

The morning of the Fourth, Secret came over to Juliet's house to watch the town parade. Secret wasn't very happy with Juliet for ditching her Fourth of July party to go to Rev. Archon's. Using her chocolate-colored eyes, she had stared Juliet down. Now, instead of avoiding all parties, Juliet would be attending two.

Secret arrived at Juliet's house an hour before the parade began since the road would be closed once the festivities started. As they sat in the kitchen, eating the coffee cake Secret had brought, they discussed their weeks at work. Juliet filled Secret in about the cleanup at the vet clinic. Secret mentioned her boss had her send the metal trap to the state lab in Lexington. It would be after the holiday before they received any results.

When it was time, the two sat out on the cottage's covered porch – Secret drinking coffee, Juliet drinking water – and watched as the parade went by. They waved at all the people in different floats, clapped for the local high school band playing patriotic songs, and, of course, cheered the loudest when Kevin went by in his patrol car as part of the Sheriff's department. After the last red, white, and blue paper mâché float went by the house, Secret left to prepare for her party, but not before confirming with Juliet for the hundredth time she would be over at the house by five.

Juliet went inside to get ready for the day. There was a little less than two hours before she had to be at the first party. Her grand plan was to take Shadow to the clinic, get him settled, get to Rev. Archon's place around one p.m., and from there go to Secret's house. She'd originally planned on only spending about an hour at Rev. Archon's, but when she mentioned it at work earlier in the week, Nicole informed her otherwise.

Nicole had been assisting her while Juliet was lancing open an abscess on the back leg of an outdoor cat when they started talking about their plans for the Fourth. Nicole and her family were also attending Rev. Archon's party. Juliet had just sliced open the skin in the center of the soft swelling while telling Nicole she would only be able to attend for about an hour. Nicole had informed her she would probably have to stay at least three or four hours since Rev. Archon liked to introduce new people to everyone and there would be a lot of guests attending. This news had resulted in Juliet squeezing a little too hard on the pocket of puss, forcing the purulent discharge to spray from the wound and accidently hit Nicole in the face. She'd felt really bad and apologized several times to Nicole throughout the week.

Now, standing in her closet, Juliet stared at the clothes hanging in orderly sections. Each clothing category was grouped together, tee shirt, long sleeved tee shirts, sweat shirts, short sleeved dress tops, long sleeved blouses, dress pants, and then dresses. All the clothes were even hung in color groups within each category. The rest of the clothes were folded and stacked neatly in the square shelving units which were part of the walk-in closet. Her years at Auburn had greatly expanded her wardrobe from tee shirts and jeans to slacks, blouses, and dresses. The veterinary school had earned a reputation of having the strictest dress code in the country, by requiring men and women to wear professional dress from the first day of school to last. This dress code had carried over into the work place since Juliet had only ever worked for veterinarians who had attended Auburn, including Dr. Silver.

Tapping her fingers on her lips, she looked around at the selection of clothes. She needed one outfit for all day, something nice but comfortable and patriotic. Juliet finally decided on a pair of navy blue Capri pants, a white wrap-around sleeveless shirt that tied in the front, and flip flops embellished with sliver beads and clear rhinestones. She fixed her blond hair in her standard ponytail but added a red ribbon. After applying SPF 50 sunscreen on her exposed skin, she looked in the mirror in the bathroom to make sure she had completely rubbed in all the white lotion. On more than one occasion, she had gone out looking like a Japanese geisha, and she wanted to avoid any embarrassment today.

After fishing Shadow out from under the bed and shoving him backwards into the cat carrier, she was ready to go. With care, she placed Shadow's carrier on the passenger seat and threaded the seat belt through the handle.

She drove the wailing cat to the clinic and got him settled in one of the spacious cages in the cat ward.

Before starting her truck again, Juliet got out the hand written instructions Dr. Silver had given her. She had offered to just use the GPS on her smartphone, but Dr. Silver insisted it would lead her the wrong way and she'd end up lost in the National Park. She read over them again to figure out what direction she would be heading. Juliet started the truck and pulled out, heading east. She turned on the main road through town and followed it out of the city center and past the town line. Rev. Archon, she gathered, lived near the northwest border of the National Park. After missing the correct road twice, she turned on-to a gravel road lined with tall red maple trees. It was one of the few trees she recognized since it was one of the toxic plants she had to learn in school. She imagined the drive through this road would be breath taking in the fall when the leaves turned crimson. Careful not to let her mind wander too much and miss the next turn to the house, she kept her eyes glued to the road. She counted the small gravel road offshoots until she came to the seventh one and turned left. She continued another winding half mile, scanning back and forth for a house but only seeing forest. The canopy above was so thick she had to remove her sunglass to see. Like water bursting through a dam, the sun burst out above as the tree coverage suddenly stopped. She brought the truck to a grinding halt and stared out through the windshield.

Juliet didn't know exactly what she had expected but it certainly was not the scene before her. She wasn't sure what the difference between a house and a mansion was, but the structure she saw was enormous. Juliet couldn't fathom how the pastor and his wife could afford, let alone maintain, the residence she was seeing. In the center of the lush green glade was a massive two-story, log cabin-style house with a wraparound porch. Lining the porch were thousands of roses of all shapes, sizes, and colors, ranging from white to red to yellow. The roses wrapped around the base of the house like a protective barrier. Catching the sun, the stained glass door reflected the colored beams of light. Each gable was covered in what she assumed were green shingles.

She inched her truck forward and parked in the grass to the right of the house next to the other vehicles. Closing her eyes, she mentally prepared for the upcoming awkwardness she knew was to come when a new person walks into a group of people who are all friends and family. Juliet was fine with one-on-one conversations and enjoyed meeting new people on an individual basis, but group settings with complete strangers were overwhelming to her. It was like being an insect that was being stared and picked at by children. She'd never liked going to any of the parties on campus Secret had drug her to back in college. Clubs, bars, and any other similar situation were absolute avoid-at-all-costs scenarios. There were only a few cars, so hopefully it would be a small group, and she could get in and out fast.

As she approached the house, she heard music coming from around back. She was halfway up the white stone path to the front entrance when she hesitated. Juliet wondered if she should knock on the front door or just head towards the music. Her question was answered as several young children came racing around the corner of the house chasing each other and screaming with delight. The young boy who had stared at her in church stopped in his tracks, causing the teenage boy behind him to almost crash into him. Juliet could feel multiple sets of eyes settle on her. *And it begins*, she thought, drawing in a deep breath for courage.

The teenage boy straightened and approached her with the younger boy closely following at his heels, breaking away from the rest of the children who had resumed their game. He extended his hand. "You must be Miss Juliet. Welcome to our family's house. I'm Aiden."

Juliet took the young man's hand and shook it, noticing his strong grip. "Nice to meet you, Aiden."

"And this," releasing her hand, Aiden turned and gestured to the boy lingering a foot behind him, "is my brother, Mathew."

Juliet took a step towards the child and extended her hand. "Nice to meet you, Mathew."

Mathew took her hand and shook it but said nothing. Releasing her hand, he looked at his brother, and Juliet could tell by the movement between their eyes the two were having a silent conversation. She and Secret, having spent so many years as friends, could do the same thing. The resemblance between the two boys was unmistakable, except where Aiden had light brown hair and blue eyes his younger brother had raven hair and green eyes. Aiden turned back to her. "Do ya want to follow me? Everyone's there. Uncle Sterling's been waiting for you."

Juliet smiled and nodded in agreement. The Kentucky blue grass tickled the sides of her feet as she followed the boys. When she rounded the corner of the house, all hope of avoiding a large crowd went crashing to the ground along with her spirit. Dozens of tables lined with red- and white-checkered table clothes scattered the back yard of the house. The seats surrounding each table were filled with people of all ages. Rev. Archon was in the center of the controlled chaos talking with a middle-aged woman. The Reverend said something to the woman when he saw Juliet with the two boys and both turned to approach her. As he took his first step forward, Rev. Archon had immediately taken the woman's hand. Juliet noticed they entwined their fingers together, and knew this must be his wife.

Once the reverend and his wife were about two feet away, they released hands, and he stepped forward and embraced Juliet, giving her what she would describe as a bear hug. "So glad you could join us, young lady." Thankfully, he released her before he cracked any of her ribs. "Let me introduce you to my lovely bride, Cara."

Following suit, Cara stepped forward and embraced Juliet. "Welcome, my dear."

Juliet was grateful Cara didn't hug as tightly as her husband but could feel the strength in the woman's arms around her. "Thank you for having me, Rev. and Mrs. Archon," she said once she was set free from Cara's grip.

"Oh, please, call us Cara and Sterling. You're part of the family now, so there's no need to be formal around here," Cara gently scolded and then locked her arm around Juliet's. "Now, you're coming with me so we can get you fed, and, Sterling, please check on everyone and see if they need anything."

Before she could protest, Cara was dragging Juliet off towards a gigantic table filled with food. Juliet was overwhelmed by the selection before her. There were hamburgers, hotdogs, barbeque chicken, pork, brisket, every casserole common in the South, corn on the cob, watermelon and other assorted fruits, and the largest bowls of potato and pasta salad Juliet had ever seen. Cara shoved a paper plate in her hands and waited for Juliet to fill it up. At the end of the table, Juliet grabbed a plastic cup already filled with ice and poured herself some lemonade from a pitcher.

"Come, dear, let me show you where you can sit." Cara took the cup of lemonade from Juliet and led her past several tables full of people to a round table that was under a gigantic oak tree. The table only had one occupant: a child, who was eating a hamburger. There were several half-empty cups sitting on the table, and Juliet assumed the owners of the drinks had already finished eating and were socializing. The boy turned his green eyes up from his meal, which first went to Cara then to Juliet then back to Cara. "Jacob, this is Miss Juliet. Juliet, this is my grandson, Jacob. Please make yourself comfortable, my dear. Jacob, you keep Miss Juliet company while I go and find your mamma. I'll be back soon."

Juliet and the boy, who she guessed was around 8 or 9, just stared at each other for a moment. Juliet blinked first and sat down next to the child. As much as she hated meeting new people, Juliet felt completely at ease with children. She found their untamed honesty refreshing and their indestructible mentality inspiring. She gave the child a toothy grin. "Hi, Jacob. How are you doing today?"

Jacob was mid-chew on a piece of his hamburger. "Fine."

"Is it always this crowded? I didn't know there were so many people at your grandfather's church," Juliet asked while placing a fork full of potato salad in her mouth. *Oh my, this is good*, she thought after the food hit her taste buds.

Jacob was about to take another bite of his food, then stopped with his mouth halfway open. The gap from his missing right upper tooth now became noticeable. He looked around the sea of people and chairs and then turned his attention back to Juliet. "Miss Juliet, this is my family."

Juliet choked on the bite of potato salad she had just shoveled into her mouth. *All these people are his family. Are they rabbits?* Maybe she had misunderstood. She pointed to the crowd. "You're related to all these people? Is this a family reunion?"

Jacob shook his head. "No, ma'am. These are just the family members that live in Middlesboro."

Juliet was about to ask where everyone was staying when she noticed a long wide scar that wrapped around Jacob's entire left arm. The band of tissue was less pigmented then the rest of the arm and was shiny. The scientist in her wanted to ask how he got the scar, but, luckily, her mouth filter was in full working force today. Juliet bit down on another forkful of potato salad. Without warning, she felt something on her right leg, which almost sent her flying out of her chair and knocking over the table. Before she reacted and made a complete fool of herself, she noticed the "thing" touching her leg was a small girl.

The little girl had red ringlet hair, bright green eyes, and soft freckled checks. She reminded Juliet of a Strawberry Short Cake doll. Behind her were several other girls who were all glancing sheepishly at Juliet. Looking at all their faces she doubted any of the girls in the group were older than seven. The little redheaded girl put both arms towards Juliet. "Up, please."

Juliet indulged the child and picked her up, setting her on her lap. "And what's your name?"

She straightened her back and faced Juliet. "Nora Barman."

"What a pretty name," Juliet commented. "And how old are you, Nora Barman?"

Nora held up three fingers. "Three."

Juliet cocked her head down towards Nora's face. "That's a very mature age; you're practically a grown up."

Nora giggled along with the rest of the girls who had encircled Juliet. Juliet looked over at Jacob, who seemed to be ignoring the entire conversation and was continuing to eat his food. She turned her attention back to Nora, who was now touching Juliet's ponytail hanging over her left shoulder. "I like you hair. It's soooooo pretty."

It was Juliet's turn to let out a small giggle, "Why, thank you. You have pretty hair too. I like your curls."

The smiling child abruptly flattened her mouth and narrowed her eyes. She flung her arms around Juliet's neck, hugging her tightly. "Thank you for saving my brother."

A flurry of activity quickly took place as Jacob spilt his drink all over the table, Juliet, and Nora. Nora started screaming in Juliet's ear about being wet while still clinging onto her neck, and Juliet stood up, trying to avoid any more of the brown liquid from getting on her clothes. The group of girls scattered from the area, leaving Juliet, Nora, and a white-as-a-sheet Jacob at the table.

"Nora, there you are. Mommy's been looking everywhere for you. You can't wander off even if we are at Daddaw and LaLa's house," gently scolded a woman with matching red hair who took Nora from Juliet's arms. "I'm sorry she if she was bothering you. I'm Lorna, Nora and Jacob's mom, and you are?"

Juliet extended her hand towards Lorna. "Juliet Greene, and your children weren't bothering me at all. In fact, they're a delight."

Juliet noticed Lorna's quick inhale. She shifted Nora onto her left hip and, instead of shaking Juliet's hand, she hugged her so forcefully Juliet thought she might pass out. *What's with all the hugging?* she wondered. Before Juliet began to see dark spots, Lorna released her. Juliet thought she noticed Lorna's eyes were a bit glassy as she blinked rapidly. "We are so glad you could come today. If there is anything you need, anything at all, please let me know." Turning her attention to Nora she said, "Nora, baby, why is your back wet?"

Nora pointed an accusatory finger at her brother. "Jacob got his drink on me."

"It was an accident," whined Jacob as he tried to contain the liquid continuing to drip off the table.

With Nora still on her left hip, Lorna grabbed some napkins off the table with her right hand and started helping her son. "It's fine, Jacob. No whining."

Juliet picked up her now soaked plate of food. "Here, let me help you."

"Oh dear, what's going on over here?" Juliet heard Cara from behind her.

She glanced over her shoulder to see the kind-faced woman standing there with three other people. Juliet assumed these were more family members Cara had brought to introduce her to.

"Just a small spill, Mom. No big deal," Lorna replied as she soaked up the last bit of brown liquid with a napkin. "I'm going to go change Nora. Can you keep an eye on the other three? Jacob, go put these wet things in the trash."

Jacob took the plateful of large napkins and left in one direction while Lorna carried Nora off in another after telling Juliet she would see her later. Juliet stood under the sprawling tree looking between the three unfamiliar faces and then finally to Cara. She picked up her cup of lemonade to keep her from fidgeting with her hands. So began the onslaught of introductions. For the next several hours, Cara escorted her around, introducing her to everyone at the picnic. Juliet felt a headache coming on trying to keep track of how everyone was related to each other. She would suggest next time all introductions should come with a family tree. It was amazing the ethnic diversity she found in one family. An array of skin tones painted the crowd, but after several introductions she began to notice the predominance of green and blue eye colors. Expecting to hear the familiar southern accent, she was pleasantly surprised by the unique dialects that tickled her ears.

And then there was the hugging; *dear Lord, these people love to hug.* No one seemed to understand personal body space. Juliet did feel a twinge of guilt with this thought since everyone was so warm, welcoming and truly seemed to be excited she was there. When she saw Dr. Silver, Nicole, and Gina, Juliet excused herself from Cara, telling her that she wanted to say hi to them. She was fifty feet from her escape when she heard a familiar voice behind her, "Juliet, my dear, how are you liking everything?"

Juliet whirled around to face Sterling. "It's so wonderful, thank you. Everyone's so kind."

Sterling winked at her and the right side of his mouth angled upward. "You're overwhelmed aren't you?"

Juliet opened her mouth to speak and then closed it again. She didn't want to be rude, but she was a worse liar. She opened her mouth again and shut it again. Words just weren't going to come. Sterling gave a deep-throated laugh and patted her on the shoulder. "It's okay. We know we're a little intense sometimes. We don't get too many new people, so we tend to overdo it a little."

Juliet felt her shoulders relax for the first time that day. She took a deep breath in through her nose; a technique she learned to do to stall a few more seconds to help compose her thoughts before she spoke. It was in that breath she caught a sudden scent which caused her thoughts to go from somewhat coherent to pure pandemonium. In all her life, Juliet had never smelled something so wonderful. She really could not describe it, but the closest words she could use would be vanilla mixed with patchouli. Her eyes flew open and she tried to subtly look around to see where the smell was coming from. Sterling was saying something to her, but she couldn't pay attention to the words coming from his mouth. She prayed she wasn't being obvious. It wasn't until he placed his left hand on her right arm and was gently forcing her to turn around that she focused on what he was saying, "Juliet, this is my son, Gabriel."

When Juliet turned, her eyes immediately met a chest. Her gaze quickly traveled up from there to a face, where it came to a screeching halt at the man's eyes. This was the man who had been so rude to her for no apparent reason. She took another deep breath to tell him exactly what she thought of him. To relay all the conversations she had rehearsed in her head for when she finally came face to face with him. It was in that breath the alluring scent from earlier intensified. Juliet blinked and took a small step back as she realized he was the source of this aroma. She refocused her attention back to his face, noticing his nostrils were flared and jaw set with the left side of it twitching. His blue eyes were so focused she felt like they were going to pierce through her head. She knew he recognized her as much as she did him from their encounter at the clinic. The urge to continue stepping back was countered by her stubbornness to stand her ground. Lifting her head up so her eyes met his, a quick thought raced through her mind, *Yep, I'm in trouble.*

Chapter 7

Like a clap of thunder, Sterling's voice broke the silence, "Gabriel, this is Juliet Greene. She's our special guest today. Be the polite gentleman I raised and say hello."

Gabriel blinked and finally relaxed. "Pardon me." He extended his hand. "Sometimes I forget my manners when I've been working all day and my father drags me off just before I get a chance to eat something." He shot a sarcastic but sweet smile at Sterling before turning his attention back to Juliet. "Forgive me."

Juliet almost got whiplash from the 180-degree turn in attitude in less than two seconds. How could he be pissed at her one minute and then docile after his father spoke to him? She took his hand and gave a firm handshake, making a mental note he hadn't inherited his family's obsession with hugging. The mention of food reminded her of the two bites of potato salad she'd had hours earlier. Her stomach emitted a loud grumble. Juliet placed her hands on her abdomen as her face flooded with blood. Worse, her tongue and mouth had chosen to stop working, so she could not even attempt say something witty. Years of professional accomplishments and then one normal bodily function had reduced her to a mute, self-conscious idiot.

Gabriel cocked his head to the right while his eyebrows lifted. "Didn't you eat?" He turned to his father. "You and Mom haven't fed her?"

Juliet pulled her hand free from his and waved it in front of her. "Oh no, they tried, but there was a spilling incident we don't need to go into right now. It's fine."

"Well, you can eat with me now," Gabriel said as he lightly took her arm and wrapped it around his.

Juliet immediately pulled away from him and backed up. Father and son gave her the same quizzical look. She knew she was about to make a scene, and it was rude to do so, but this was the man who had yelled at her less than a week ago. "I can find the food myself, thank you."

Gabriel looked at her cautiously. "I'm sorry, did I offend you? I know I was rude for about thirty seconds, but I just apologized."

"Yes, but you forgot to apologize for threatening me on Saturday when you and Dr. Silver kicked me out of my own surgery." Juliet's words came out a little bit louder then she had meant them too. Several family members turned to look at her.

"Son, I think this is yours to resolve. Remember, you reap what you sow." Sterling patted his son on the back. Juliet noted he had a smirk on his face as he walked past her, as if he was part of an inside joke of which she was definitely on the outside.

Gabriel shook his head. "I'm sorry, what are you talking about?"

You coy son of a bitch she thought to herself and the thing lit Juliet up like a Roman candle. She'd have strangled the man had it not been for his mass or the dozens of relations close by. It took two beats of her heart to collect herself and produce as civil a tone as she could muster. "At Dr. Silver's clinic last Sunday, I was operating on a wolf and you yelled at me for no reason. I get no explanation as to what condition my patient is in, or where he is except that he's recuperating, and you're taking care of him. We meet for real and you're ready to take off my head until your dad reels you in. Now, you're playing nice and offering to get me food."

His eyes grew round. "What are you talking about? How did you know it was me? You never saw my face."

Juliet threw her hands up in the air. "That's not an apology or an explanation, and, to answer your question, it's your eyes. I recognize them from the other day." She whipped around and headed straight for the table of food, leaving him standing dumbfounded.

Juliet grabbed a plate and silently filled it with food, making sure she got more of the potato salad. The hair on her neck stood up as she became aware of Gabriel behind her. He reached past her, taking care not to touch her, and grabbed a piece of fried chicken. Juliet finished filling her plate and walked to the table she had started to eat at earlier, which was now completely empty. Much to her dismay, Gabriel walked to the same table and sat down next to her. The same alluring smell drifted into her nose. Ignoring him, she started eating.

She heard him clear his throat, and looked up. Any easiness in Gabriel's face had vanished, and in its place was a thin set mouth making him look solemn. "You're right, I shouldn't have snapped at you. I know that now, but I didn't know what was going on at the time."

Juliet nearly choked on her food. "Was that an apology? Because normally you are supposed to say the words 'I'm sorry'."

"Listen, I'm trying to be nice. If you want to hold a grudge, that's your problem; I don't have to explain myself to you," he snapped.

This was escalating, and Juliet knew it. She didn't want to back down, but she didn't want to make a scene either. Sterling and Cara had offered her every hospitality and to further disrespect their home was not her intention. She'd made it known to Gabriel how she felt and he'd half assed apologized. Her anger abated some and she elected to follow childhood advice, if she couldn't say anything nice, she wouldn't say anything at all. If she ignored him, maybe he would go away and leave her to eat in peace. Juliet turned her attention back to her food. It was after inhaling the last of the chicken she even bothered to look up. The man sitting next to her had his eyes fixed on her and was cracking a smile. Juliet felt a flush spread to her face as she realized how ridiculous she must look but was equally upset he had the audacity to laugh at her.

"It's refreshing to see a girl your size with such a healthy appetite," Gabriel chuckled.

Juliet almost choked on the baked beans she was currently chewing, but managed to swallow without aspirating any of it down her trachea. "What the hell is that supposed to mean?" she said, balling up the napkin in her hand.

Gabriel put up his hands in front of him. "Easy there, killer, don't take it the wrong way. I was actually trying to give you a compliment. Other than the women in my family, I've never seen a female enjoy eating as much."

She calmly placed the napkin back into her lap and looked Gabriel in the eye. "Let me guess, you hang out with anorexic models," she sneered. "I know you're probably not use to strong, intelligent women outside of your family who actually think for a living, but this one does. Any attempt at winning my good graces should include 'Juliet, your magnanimous veterinary skill saved the life of one of my favorite wild animals, I am forever in your debt. Please forgive my transgression last week, the fault is singularly mine.'"

Once again, Juliet turned her attention to her food. In her mind, she was hurtling insult after insult at him. She really wished he would leave, but the man persisted. When finished, she'd go, but until then, she wouldn't allow him to run her off while she ate.

"I'm sorry."

Juliet looked up. "What was that?"

Gabriel took a deep breath in. "I said, 'I'm sorry.' You're right, I was a total jerk, and I took my anger out on you. I didn't know what you were doing at the time, but I realize now you were just trying to help."

Holy crap, he just apologized. Juliet was too stunned to say anything for several seconds. Finally, she stammered out, "Thank you."

They sat there for what felt like several minutes, just staring at each other and their plates. With those few, simple words, Gabriel had deflated some of the anger, but the volcano still loomed inside ready to erupt with the slightest bit of provocation. She wondered who would make the next move.

Gabriel was the first to break the silence, "Can I risk giving you a compliment again?"

"If it's an actual compliment, most certainly."

"Your skills of observation are impressive."

"They must be; lives depend on my perception." Juliet knew she was being arrogant, but she didn't care.

The two sat there once again in an awkward silence. Laughter of everyone around them resonated in her ears as the family mingled amongst themselves. It didn't go unnoticed several people had been staring at the two of them, but no one dared approach the table. There was an invisible fence of social awkwardness surrounding them. Taking matters into her own hands, she started asking the questions that had plagued her for a week. She would either get her answers or drive him off trying. "Is stomping into people's operating rooms and taking them over something you do all the time?"

"Actually, that's exactly what I do all the time, and I get paid for it, I'm a trauma surgeon at Middlesboro Appalachian Regional Hospital," he replied.

"Human surgeon; explains the arrogance," she took a sip of her drink, pondering his previous response. Juliet knew many times veterinarians would call in physicians to help with cases. However, why did Dr. Silver feel the need to kick her out when she could have assisted both of them? Dr. Silver had told her the man sitting across from her had taken the wolf, but unless he rehabbed wolves too, why would a surgeon have the animal? She felt he knew more than he was letting on.

Gabriel squinted his eyes. "I don't know if you're being serious or teasing me. I'm trying to be nice, you know."

Juliet had never been good at looking down on people, but she gave her best indifferent look to him. "Oh, I know."

Gabriel shifted in his seat. "You're not making this very easy."

"Why should I?" she baulked. "Is it because you're a doctor and most women fall all over you? Are you used to getting whatever you want by flashing a smile and winking those blue eyes to make ladies swoon?"

She was becoming more animated as she spoke. Her hands waving in the air. "News flash, a handsome face doesn't work on me. The only thing I know about you is your propensity to berate people at their place of business."

Gabriel stood up, grabbed his plate, and walked away. She sighed in relief when he was gone. Only then did she realize the one person who might be able to answer her questions had just left. Silently, she scolded herself for letting her anger get the best of her. She rubbed her face with her hands. It was time to leave.

A plate appeared before her filled with four different pieces of pie with a glob of vanilla ice cream in the center. Gabriel slid back into the seat next to her. *What is he up to now?*

Gabriel handed her a fork. "Just listen, please."

Juliet had to give him credit for his persistence. But why would this man be so stubborn? Any other person would have blown her off by now as being too much of a pain to put up with. What was his game? No one in her life had ever made this much of an effort to get on her good side.

When she didn't storm off or scream at him, Gabriel's face relaxed slightly. "You're right. You don't know me, but I'd like to start this over again." Juliet stuck a spoonful of ice cream in her mouth. "Hello, my name is Gabriel Archon. I'm a trauma surgeon at the local hospital. Now it's your turn."

Juliet took another bite of the vanilla ice cream. She let the coldness run down her throat to sooth her temper. Once again, she reminded herself she needed answers. No one who seemed to be on her side so far was talking, so he was her last hope. That thought stung a little as she took her second bite. His eyes never left her face, giving her the impression he was waiting for her to reveal something about herself.

Juliet sighed and rested her spoon against the plate. She decided to play along. "Nice to meet you. I'm Juliet Greene, local veterinarian." Gabriel smiled, and Juliet tried to steer the conversation back to where she wanted it to be. "Jacob said everyone here was family. Does that make you and Dr. Silver cousins?"

"Are you always this persistent?" he asked.

"Yes."

He pushed his plate away from him. "You're not going to let this go, are you?"

"Nope." She took another bite of her dessert.

"Yes, Dr. Silver and I are related." Gabriel leaned closer to her. "What else can I tell you?"

Another wave of desirable aroma hit her and almost made her miss the window Juliet had been hoping for.

"I'd like to know what happened to my patient. You know: a certain wolf you stomped in on while I was trying to fix his leg. And don't tell me you don't know, because Dr. Silver told me he left the wolf in your hands, although I can't for the life of me figure out why he would do that."

Without missing a beat, Gabriel answered, "I delivered the wolf to where he needed to be."

"So, you're telling me you rehab wolves in your free time?"

"No, I'm saying he's where he needs to be."

"And where is that exactly?"

"In a safe place."

Juliet blew air out through her nose. The abated anger was beginning to well up again. "Listen, I'm just trying to follow up on things and make sure my patient is receiving proper treatment. Not to mention the paper work involved in all of this and the fact that there's a 100-pound animal that isn't supposed to be living in Kentucky – that you and Dr. Silver are so calm about now – but you were so upset about less than a week ago. Am I really supposed to believe all this?"

Gabriel swallowed his food and stared into Juliet's eyes. "Yes."

Not to be defeated, Juliet stared back. "You're lying to me."

Gabriel just shrugged his shoulders but didn't remove his gaze. Juliet refused to back down and kept her eyes locked on the man across from her. She would stare him down if she had to. Unfortunately, at that moment, the ringtone she had set for Secret started playing. Reluctantly, Juliet forfeited her staring contest to answer the phone. She barely had it to her ear when Secret's voice came screeching out the other end, "Where are you?"

Juliet checked the time to see it was 5:30. "Sorry, I got caught up here. I'm coming straight there. I'll see you in a few minutes." She hung up the phone and looked at Gabriel. "I'm leaving, but don't think this conversation is over."

She stood up, gathering her garbage. Gabriel stood from his seat and reached to take the plate from her hands. Juliet pulled away, backed-up from the table, and proceeded to collide into Jacob who was walking by with a plate full of cherry pie. A muffled *damn* came out of her mouth as the pie landed on Juliet's white shirt and created a red streak down the front. Jacob's eyes widened, and he shrank back away from Juliet and Gabriel.

"I-I-I'm so sorry, Miss Juliet," Jacob stuttered. "It was an accident, Gabriel. I promise."

"It's just a shirt. I can wash it," Juliet reassured him. She set her phone down on the table and picked up some napkins to brush the pie remnants off the shirt onto the ground.

"Jacob, you need to pay better attention to things. Now go on now before you get yourself into more trouble," scolded Gabriel.

Juliet gave Gabriel a weary look then continued to clean her shirt. "It was an accident. The only victim is this shirt, which I'll need to change."

Gabriel's gaze followed Jacob as he scurried away from the two adults. "That boy needs to learn to pay attention to his surroundings before he gets into more trouble than he can get out of."

Juliet thought about defending the boy, but decided against it. Gabriel opened his mouth like he was going to say something else, but instead closed it and walked away. Juliet muttered something unkind under her breath. She found Sterling and Cara to say goodbye. Climbing in her truck, she couldn't wait to get home and change.

Chapter 8

When Juliet pulled into the driveway of her house, a white van was parked in her usual spot. It took a second, but she remembered the exterminators were there to fumigate. For a split second, she wondered why they were working so late, but the thought was replaced by the need to let Secret know what was going on. She reached for her phone to call her friend about having to change before coming to the party. Much to her surprise, she couldn't find her phone anywhere. Juliet huffed in frustration, realizing she must have left it on the table at the Archon's while cleaning the pie off her shirt. There wasn't time to go back now. She would just call her phone when she got to Secret's and hope someone would answer. Maybe she could pick it up tomorrow.

These and other thoughts consumed Juliet as she walked through the front door. She didn't see the duffle bag laying in the entry way which she tripped over and caught herself before falling. Confusion morphed into fear as an arm seized her from behind and a hand was placed over her mouth. A man walked out of the bedroom, "Hey, Ryan, stop making –" he stopped and stared at Juliet like a deer in the headlights. "Shit."

Juliet's hands flew up to the arm wrapped around her chest. She kicked wildly as the man behind her tightened his grip and lifted her off the floor. Her feet couldn't gain traction. Midair, she gazed at the other man. He was white with dark hair and eyes. There was an odd tattoo on his right forearm. In those few moments, the self-defense classes Secret made her go to after her freshman year of vet school came exploding to her forebrain. She stopped struggling and let her body go limp. This worked to her advantage as the man slightly loosened his grip and lowered her so she could plant her feet on the floor. She took advantage of this mistake by forcing her head back and smashing it into the face of her attacker. Juliet followed this with a forceful stomp to the foot. Her attacker must have sensed her next step since he shifted his hip to the side to protect his groin. She countered by shifting her hips in the opposite direction, exposing his groin. She grabbed it and twisted. The man screamed in agony and let go of Juliet. She twisted around towards the door and felt a sharp pain across the back of her head. The darkness came swiftly as she felt herself crumbling to the floor.

She could smell smoke, but her eyes refused to open. Juliet could feel arms wrapping around her. Her body was being lifted, but her eyes wouldn't cooperate. Her lungs filled with smoke, and she began coughing. The arms around her tightened, and she felt like she was moving faster. Her mind drifted back into the abyss.

A constant, high-pitched beeping broke through Juliet's subconscious, slowly coaxing her awake. Her eyes felt weighted down with cement. There was a dull ache in the back of her head, and she was lying down on something soft. The smell of rubbing alcohol mixed with the wonderful smell from the picnic penetrated her nostrils. Finally, her eyes blinked opened, but the small amount of light hurt them, and she shut them quickly.

A male voice cut through the fogginess of her brain, "I'll dim the lights more if they hurt."

The sound of the voice made Juliet force her eyes open as she attempted to sit up. That movement caused her head to swim, and she immediately lay back down and closed her eyes. There was something attached to her left hand and chest. A small panic arose with the realization she was not in her clothes. Cautiously, she opened her eyes again to look at her surroundings. An IV catheter had been placed in her left hand and was being held there with several layers of tape. There was a plastic cover with a red light over her pointer finger. Juliet immediately recognized the pulse oxygen unit used to measure her blood oxygen level. Wires were shooting out of the top of her hospital gown, which she followed with her eyes to where they connected to a monitor. Recognizing the waves on the screen as the electrical conduction of her heart, she watched the pulsing heart icon next to the waves beat with the number 70 over it.

Juliet searched the room for the origin of the voice, and found Gabriel sitting on a chair in the corner with his hands grasped together in front of his mouth leaning forward. Out of all the people she was expecting to see, he was the last. Why was he here? Why was she here? Her thoughts were hazy. Slowly the events of the evening started to come back to her.

She focused more on the man sitting in the corner. Even from her bed, she could see his eyes blazing with anger. Juliet prayed his fury was not directed at her, because she couldn't go another round with him right now with her head pounding and body aching.

Gabriel was in scrubs with a stethoscope draped around his neck. Dropping his hands to his lap, he stood up and walked over to the right side of the bed. "Juliet, you're safe. You're in the hospital."

Now that he was closer, Juliet could see there were black smudge marks on his face. Her mind filled with questions. "What happened?" was all she managed to get out through the gravel in her voice. She reflexively placed a hand on her throat as the pain from trying to speak surprised her.

Gabriel's muscles tensed as his hands balled into fists at his side. Juliet looked to his face and noticed the twitch in his set chin and thinned lips of a scowl. She wanted to ask why he was so angry, but any thoughts were interrupted by the shrill timbre of Secret's voice outside her room, "You let me see her right now, or I swear I'll destroy every room until I get to her!"

The door burst open, and Secret dashed into the room followed by a haggard nurse trying to grab her. Kevin followed both women into the room with his standard, nonchalant walk. He seemed to garnish a morbid amusement from the scene. Secret rushed to the left side of the bed and grabbed Juliet's hand. The nurse reached out to take Secret's arm, but, before she touched her, Gabriel's commanding voice interrupted the chaos, "Betsy, I'll handle this."

The nurse paused and pulled her arm back. Somehow Secret had missed the domineering man on the other side of Juliet when she first entered and now stood with her eyes wide staring at Gabriel. The nurse turned and left the room as Kevin made his way to stand behind Secret. He wrapped his right arm around her waist and pulled her closer to him. If Juliet's head weren't pounding, she would have laughed at the mounting standoff between Secret and Gabriel. Without blinking, Gabriel spoke in a low, deliberate tone, "Who are you, and what makes you think you can come into this hospital and disturb the patients here?"

Secret lifted her chin in the air. "I'm her best friend, and who the hell do you think you are?"

Gabriel broke eye contact with Secret, looked down at Juliet, and then returned to the staring contest with her best friend. "I'm Dr. Archon, Ms. Greene's physician."

Secret crossed her arms against her chest and leaned back into Kevin. "Then you can tell me why my best friend is in the hospital and what happened."

Juliet could see Gabriel's jaw twitch on the left side ever so slightly. Her pain medication-filled head made her open her mouth to ask him about this tic, but her common sense and hoarse throat stopped her. He gripped the bed rails with both hands so tightly his knuckles went white. "I'm not at liberty to discuss anything with you. There are several things I need to talk over with Ms. Greene, so I'll kindly ask you to step outside until she is medically ready for visitors."

"That's horseshit!" screamed Secret as her face glowed crimson.

Kevin tightened his grip around his fiancée. Juliet suspected he was trying to keep the pint-size pixie from catapulting over the bed and punching Gabriel. The drugs in her system had her mind pondering all sorts of odd scenarios to come from the events unfolding in the hospital room. She wondered in that moment, if Secret did throw a punch, would Gabriel hit a woman? She was never to find out since there was a knock. The door opened and the Sheriff came through. Kevin straightened himself as soon as he saw the man. "Sheriff Archon. Hello, sir."

"Hello, Kevin." The Sheriff nodded. "Secret, nice to see you." He turned his attention to Gabriel. "Is Ms. Greene okay to speak with me for a few minutes?"

Secret threw her arms up in the air and pulled away from Kevin. "Wait a damn minute. Why are you here?" She pointed towards the Sheriff. "And what do you want with Juliet?"

Kevin stepped between Secret and the Sheriff. "Secret, honey, I need you to calm down. I'm sure there is a good explanation for what's going on, but if the Sheriff is here, then he needs to do his job." He turned and looked at his boss. "Sorry, Sheriff, she's been drinking, and she's worried about her best friend."

Juliet appreciated her friend's defense of her, but the screaming was not helping her massive headache. "Secret, I'm fine," Juliet managed to croak.

Secret whirled around to face her friend. A look of disappointment and worry splashed across her face. She spoke with her eyes in a way only a best friend could read: *Are you sure? I don't want to leave you.* Juliet could only muster up a nod and a faint smile. Secret stood still for another moment, leaned over to hug her friend. She stood up, pushed past Kevin and the Sheriff, and stomped out of the room. Kevin looked between the two men left in the room and silently followed his fiancée, closing the door behind him.

The Sheriff approached Juliet's bed and pulled out a small, spiral-bound notebook and a pen. He turned to Gabriel. "After I'm done questioning her, I will need to ask you a few questions. I'll come get you when I'm done."

Gabriel straightened but remained positioned on the other side of Juliet's bed. He focused his gaze on the other man. "I'm not going anywhere. I'm her doctor, and I'll tell you when she's had enough. I won't let you compromise her health for answers."

"Gabriel, this is police business," the Sheriff replied.

"Marcus, I'm staying, and you don't outrank me in this situation," countered Gabriel.

"You know each other?" Juliet spoke softly.

Both men turned to look at her. The left corner of the Sheriff's mouth turned upward, and he nodded his head in Gabriel's direction. "He's my nephew, and as stubborn as a mule."

That would explain the same last name. The IV drip of morphine was certainly making it harder to make sense of things. She turned to Gabriel. "Are you related to everyone?"

Gabriel ignored her question and turned back to Marcus. The smile vanished. "You have five minutes."

"Juliet, can you tell me what you remember?" the Sheriff asked.

Juliet tried to recall the events before she woke up in the hospital. "I saw a white van in my driveway. My landlord had called me this week and told me the exterminators would be at my house today, so I walked into my house thinking it was them."

Her throat felt like it was on fire. Gabriel handed her some water which she slowly sipped. The cool liquid eased the pain. "Someone grabbed me from behind. There was another man coming out from my room. I saw his face. He was white with black hair and brown eyes." She paused letting her throat rest until the Sheriff stopped scribbling and nodded for her to continue. "He had a tattoo on the inside of his right arm. It was a weird symbol. Something I've never seen before." She squeezed her eyes closed trying to bring the image of the tattoo to her forethoughts so she could describe it, but her brain screamed in pain the more she concentrated.

"I think we need to stop for now," she heard Gabriel say.

Juliet opened her eyes. "No, I'm alright." She turned to the Sheriff. "I'm sorry, I can't describe it right now, but I'll think of it. The man who was holding me, I'm pretty sure I broke his nose. I never saw him, but I slammed my head into his nose to get away, and he may have trouble walking for a few days after what I did to his groin region."

Juliet noticed both men reflexively shift uncomfortably at the last part of her statement. *Why do men always get so sensitive when anybody talks about hurting their man parts?* "I was trying to get away when I felt a sharp pain, and then I was out. How did I get here, anyhow?"

Marcus looked at his nephew, who was now gazing down at Juliet's hand. He seemed fixated, like her fingers were the most fascinating things he had ever seen, and yet, Gabriel looked like he was scowling. Juliet was not sure if it was the pain medicine messing with her head, but she really couldn't understand why he'd be angry. Through gritted teeth he mumbled something Juliet almost missed. "It was me."

Juliet was confused. "What?"

He focused his attention to her face, his nostrils flared slightly. "I said, 'it was me.' I found your phone on the table and drove to your place, because you said you were going to go home and change. Dr. Silver told me where you lived," he added when he glanced up to see the confused expression on her face. "When I got to your house, it was on fire. I broke down the door and found you on the floor. I brought you here and called Marcus."

Juliet sat stunned by the words that had come from his mouth. He had saved her life. The black smudges on his face must have been from the fire. "Are you alright? Did you get hurt?"

Those questions made Gabriel take a step back away from the bed. He looked exasperated and rolled his eyes at her. "You've just been attacked, and your house was set on fire, and you're worried about me?"

Maybe he was the one with the head injury. "Sorry I asked," she snapped.

"I'm fine," Gabriel grumbled as he looked back at Marcus. "I think we are done for now. I trust you'll do everything in your power to find these men."

Marcus looked from Gabriel to Juliet. He reached out and patted her on the hand. "Ms. Greene, I'm going to find these men, don't worry. I'm impressed by the way you handled yourself. It'll be hard to hide a broken nose around here for a few days. That's the good thing about small towns." He glanced over at Gabriel, turned, and walked out of the room.

Juliet suddenly felt like she had run a marathon. Before she let sleep over take her, she reached out and touched Gabriel's hand still holding the bed railing. "Thank you for saving my life." She never saw his reaction, because her eyes closed bringing much needed sleep.

Chapter 9

When Juliet emerged from her slumber, the fogginess in her mind had somewhat lifted and she was able to think more clearly. Looking to her left she saw the pump controlling her morphine drip had been set at a very low rate. Gabriel was gone, and Secret was sleeping in a chair next to her. Her friend was in the same clothes as when she had first burst into the room. By the contorted way she was curled, Juliet knew Secret would be sore when she woke up. The door to her room opened and Kevin walked in, holding two coffee cups in his hands. He looked showered and refreshed in his uniform. Obviously, he had decided not to accompany Secret on her bedside vigil. He walked over and waved the coffee cup in front of Secret's nose. The smell brought her back to life.

"Oh my God, I feel like shit. They need to get better chairs," Secret grumbled.

"I don't think you're supposed to sleep in them." Juliet was thankful: the pain in her throat was not as severe.

"You're awake!" Secret leapt out of the chair and hugged her friend. "You smell horrible. We need to work on your hygiene, but I'm glad you're okay."

Juliet embraced her friend. "That's the pot calling the kettle black. At least I have an excuse for looking like crap."

Secret released her friend and grinned ear to ear. "You wish you could look half as sexy as me after sleeping in a hospital chair all night." She turned to Kevin, grabbed the coffee cup in his hands, and kissed him on the cheek. "I knew there was a reason I kept you around."

Secret took a long, slow sip of coffee then looked down at her friend. "Alright, Jules. Spill."

Juliet really did not want to recount the entire scenario to Secret and Kevin, but she felt like she owed it to her to explain what had happened. The woman had slept here after all. She told them about coming home and being attacked, pausing only when Secret gloated to Kevin she was the one to make Juliet take those self-defense classes. She left out the part about Gabriel being the one to come to her rescue and instead said the neighbors must've called 9-1-1 when they saw the fire. Juliet didn't know why, but she got the feeling he did not want anyone to know what he had done. Besides, it was his story to tell, not hers.

Kevin walked up to the other side of the bed. "So, you have no idea what those guys were doing?"

"No, I assumed they were the exterminators. Instead, they were robbing my house." Juliet shrugged her shoulders and looked over to Secret to see if she might have a better idea.

Secret had a blank look on her face and shrugged. Kevin continued with his questions. "Do you think you could identify the one man if you saw him? If I brought you a book of tattoos do you think you could recognize it?"

Juliet scratched one of the electrodes attached to her chest under her hospital gown. The glue holding them to her was very itchy. "Yes, I'm pretty sure I could."

Kevin took a sip of his coffee. "I'll get some tattoo books from the station and bring them by for you to look at." He looked at Secret. "Honey, I need to get you home before I go to work, so we need to leave."

Secret bent down and kissed her friend on top of the head. "I'll come by later to see you and bring you some proper clothes. Oh, and definitely a toothbrush."

Kevin and Secret began to walk out of the room as the door opened and Gabriel walked in. He was wearing a white doctor's coat over a shirt and tie. His coal black hair was neatly combed on top of his head. As Secret walked by, she paused next to him. "Thank you for letting me stay here last night." Gabriel acknowledged her statement with a nod and a smile.

When Secret and Kevin left, Gabriel walked over to Juliet. "Good morning. I just need to check your chart before I look you over." He had an electronic tablet in his hand. His eyes moved back and forth reading something on the screen. Removing the stethoscope from around his neck and placing it on her chest, he began to listen to her heart. "I'm going to help you sit up now so I can listen to your lungs," he said, gingerly moving her forward. He placed the bell of the stethoscope to her back. "Take a deep breath." Juliet did as he requested. "Again," he said moving the instrument to another section of her back. Once finished, he placed the stethoscope over his neck. He took out a penlight and began shinning it in her eyes. Juliet closed her eyes, trying to shield them from the light. Finally, he looked at the back of her head, examining something.

Gabriel started typing on his tablet. "How are you feeling this morning?"

Juliet rubbed the back of her head. Her fingers felt something foreign sticking out from her scalp. "Better, but my head still is a little sore. Do I have stitches?"

"Yes, whoever hit you left a pretty nasty gash on the back of your head. It took sixteen stiches to close the wound." Gabriel looked up from his tablet. "You've been stable all night, and I'm going to discharge you, but you must rest today and tomorrow. You have a concussion, so if you overdo it you'll land yourself right back in the hospital."

"Do I even have a home to go to after the fire?" Juliet's eyes began to fill with tears, but she refused to spill them out.

Another deep voice filled the room. "You're coming home with us."

Juliet looked past Gabriel and saw Rev. Archon and Cara standing at the entrance to her room. The couple made their way into the room and stood next to their son. Gabriel's intense eyes fixated on his father. "Dad, I don't think that's a good idea. Why would Juliet want to stay with complete strangers?"

Juliet didn't that like he answered before she could and wanted to say something to save face, even if she shared Gabriel's sentiment. "That's very kind of you, but I don't want to impose on your family. I'll just see if I can stay with my friend Secret and her fiancé."

Cara clasped Juliet's hand. "Now, don't be ridiculous. Someone needs to take care of you. If one of our children were away from home, we would hope someone would do the same after such an ordeal." Cara turned and stared down Gabriel. "She's coming home with us and that's final."

Juliet got the feeling any protest would just be futile. "Thank you, you're too kind." Her response was met with warm smiles from Rev. Archon and his wife, but Gabriel continued to scowl. The look on his face reminded Juliet of an important detail. "Um, Mrs. Archon, I mean, Cara, I think you guys need to know I have a cat. Is that going to be a problem?"

Cara smiled down at her. "That's no problem since we are going to have you stay in the guest house. You and your feline friend will have plenty of room."

It looked like Juliet had a new place to stay.

Chapter 10

Juliet was released a few hours later. Sterling, Cara, and another daughter, Sabra, picked Juliet up and took her to what remained of her house. Most of it was destroyed along with the majority of her possessions, but the back bedrooms were still standing. Even though this had only been her home for a few weeks, she was saddened by the loss. Grateful Shadow was safe at the clinic and not amongst the damage, she made her way to her bedroom. Her clothes in the closet were waterlogged and wreaked of smoke. Most of her casual clothes were salvageable, but the nicer dress clothes which couldn't be easily cleaned were a loss. It looked like the only pair of shoes she would be able to wear were the ones on her feet. Sabra helped Juliet throw all her clothes into garbage bags while Sterling and Cara looked for anything else salvable. It took less than 30 minutes to pack up her few remaining possessions. Her keys had somehow survived the fire, and she handed them to Sabra to drive her truck. The two vehicles went to the clinic, where she picked up Shadow and some supplies for him.

When they pulled into the driveway of the Archon's house, she was curious as to where she would be staying. Instead of parking by the house, the cars detoured to the right down a gravel driveway and pulled up to another structure hidden by several large trees. Cara turned around from the front seat of the car. "This is where you'll be staying. I hope it's okay."

Okay was a minor understatement. Standing before Juliet was her dream house. The two-story Victorian looked like something she'd imagined out of a storybook, with its purple-painted hardy board and decorative white trim. Purple and blue flowers cascaded out of hanging baskets along the long covered porch. Above each window were half-moon stained glass window accents.

"This –" Juliet stuttered. "This is where I'm staying?"

The corner of Cara's eyes wrinkled. "Why, of course. You are a professional woman, and our house is very noisy at times with all the children coming and going, so we wanted to make sure you had a quiet place to yourself. Come, dear, let's get you inside and settled."

Juliet got out of the SUV and carried the cat carrier up the stairs. She stopped in front of the door to admire the stained glass inset. It was a scene of four wolves hunting in the snow. Each wolf was a different color and the swirls of the glass gave the illusion the fur was real. Sterling opened the door to the house.

She stepped into the foyer and took in everything. The first floor was a modern, open-concept floor plan, but the furniture and décor was a mixture of classic and southern style. To her right was a large living room decorated in warm, rich tones of reds, browns, and gold. There was a large stone fireplace in the center of the room. The dining area had a long, sleek mahogany table with six matching seats. Juliet walked farther into the house to see what was past the wooden staircase. Next to the dining area was the kitchen containing stainless steel appliances, with a large island in the center. The butcher-block countertops gave the contrasting metal a warm tone. Cara pointed out a half bathroom and an office with a small library also on the first floor.

The three women went upstairs, leaving Sterling to bring in the rest of Juliet's few belongings. On the second floor, Cara showed Juliet the laundry area where they deposited some of the bags of dirty clothes. She pointed out the three other bedrooms all with attached full bathrooms. Each one was decorated in a blue, yellow, or green motif. Cara led Juliet to the master suite, which was just as grand as the rest of the house. The king-sized sleigh bed was in the center of the room with a gas fireplace across from it on the inside wall. There was a sitting area with two plush chairs next to floor-to-ceiling windows. The en suite bathroom had a shower and a large claw-foot soaker tub.

Sabra grabbed her hand and drug Juliet out of the bathroom into the closet. The room was bigger than her bedroom at her rental. She noticed most of the racks were filled with women's clothing. Confused, she turned to a beaming Sabra and pointed. "Whose clothes are these?"

"They're yours. Mom and Dad told me what happened. I'm a fashion major and have tons of extra clothes, so I thought I'd let you borrow them. I even have shoes because it looks like you and I are the same size," Sabra squealed. "What do you think?"

"Cara, Sabra, this is way too much. I can't accept this." Juliet felt overwhelmed and leaned against the doorframe of the closet. She wasn't accustomed to needing or accepting this much generosity.

Cara waved off her comment. "Oh, you can and you will. Now, let's get some of those clothes washed."

While Cara put some clothes in the washing machine for her, Juliet let Shadow out of his carrier. He sniffed the air in the strange new house and immediately ran under the bed. Cara walked back into the room. "Now, Juliet, I want you to climb in bed and rest. Gabriel said you needed to take it easy. Lord knows, we don't want to disobey the doctor's orders. We'll be eating dinner at five p.m., so come over to the main house. Please don't even think about objecting. It will just be the four of us tonight, so you should have a nice, quiet dinner."

Juliet said the only thing she could, "Yes, ma'am."

After the three left, Juliet filled the large soaker tub to take a bubble bath. Stripping off her clothes, she eased herself into the water. As much as she wanted to wash her hair, her sutures couldn't get wet until tomorrow. The warm water on her skin felt amazing and it allowed her sore muscles to relax. She lost track of time and her fingers had long ago started to prune. Juliet finally forced herself to get out. She wrapped herself in a white terry cloth robe she found in the closet, letting the soft material hug her body.

Juliet crawled into the huge bed to rest, but her cell phone had a different idea as its shrill ring tone broke her serenity. "Hey, Secret, what's up?"

The voice from the receiver was eerily calm and quiet. "Can you tell me why I am standing in your hospital room with a bag full of clothes and supplies and you're not in it?"

Juliet slapped her hand to her forehead. "Oh crap, I'm so sorry I didn't call you. I'm the worst friend ever. I got released from the hospital, and I'm staying with Reverend and Mrs. Archon. They brought me home."

"And you didn't think it might be important to tell your friend who spent the entire night sleeping next to your bed?"

The chill in her voice was dropping every second. Juliet knew if she did not fix this fast Secret might go postal on her butt. "I'm sorry, please don't hate me. I'll make it up to you, I promise."

"Mmm-hmmm."

"Okay, how about you come over and see where I'm staying tomorrow. We can make popcorn and watch movies all afternoon. Besides, I do have a head injury, so my forgetting to tell you might be because I have brain damage. You can't stay mad at someone with that condition, can you?" Juliet was hoping the stupid jokes and bribe would break through to her friend.

"Fine, but you're making the kettle corn kind not the plain crap you always make me eat, and I get to pick the movies." The tension in Secret's voice was gone.

"Deal! I'll text you the address and see you tomorrow. Talk to you later, and, Secret, I really am sorry."

"I know," she heard Secret sigh into the phone. "You're a spaz; always have been. That's why I love you. See you tomorrow."

The rest of the afternoon, Juliet rested in bed until it was time to go over to the main house. Juliet tried on some of the borrowed clothes from the closet to dress for dinner. Hoping this was a casual dinner, she settled for some linen pants with a cotton tank top. Sabra had been right about the shoe size, since the sandals were a perfect fit. Following the white marble path to the house, she noticed there were several other paths with the same white stones leading away from the house into the woods. She wondered if these were nature trails around the property.

The stained glass door to the exquisite log home was a coat of arms. The gold shield had two wolves at the base of a tree. The animals had what appeared to be snakes in their mouths. Above the tree was a red cross. Juliet pondered the meaning behind the crest. She knocked on the door, and Sabra answered it, swinging the large wooden door back so Juliet could step inside.

The guest house was squalor compared to the grandeur of the main house. Sabra took her on a tour of the first floor. They stopped in the kitchen to say hello to Cara before moving on to the other rooms. Juliet noticed the hallways were decorated with family portraits. There were so many pictures of family members, many of whom she'd met at the Fourth of July party, Juliet lost count. The family room had a huge, vaulted ceiling with dark wooden beams spaced every few feet. A large stone fireplace took up most of the far wall and climbed all the way up to the ceiling. Above the hearth there was a thick, polished mantel home to several more family pictures. Juliet's eyes zeroed in on one in particular. In the portrait was a beautiful woman a little younger than Juliet's age and flanked on either side were two men, one of which Juliet recognized as a younger Gabriel. She pointed to the frame. "Sabra, who is in the picture with Gabriel?"

Sabra's expression became solemn. "My brother, Michael and Gabriel's fiancée, Natalia. They were killed in a car accident about three years ago."

Juliet shifted uncomfortably. "I'm so sorry."

This small bit of information tugged at her sympathy. She could not imagine losing a brother and someone you wanted to spend the rest of your life with all in one tragic incident. Juliet suddenly felt sorry for the man she'd been yelling at the day before.

Sabra and Juliet looked at each other as the awkward silence between them grew, but Sterling entered the room to announce dinner was ready. Both were grateful for the interruption as they followed him back to the dinner table. Cara had prepared another feast for the family. Sterling said the blessing before they placed the food on their plates. Juliet did not realize how hungry she was until she smelled the food.

"How do you like the house, Juliet?" Sterling asked as he ate.

Juliet looked around and made eye contact with all three of them as she spoke. "It is the most beautiful house I've ever stayed in. Thank you all so much for your generosity. Please let me know how much I owe you for all of this. I promise I'll start looking for a new place to live on Monday."

Cara patted her on the hand. "Don't rush to find a new place. I'm sure we will work something out when you're feeling better. As you can see, we have plenty of room."

"Thank you." Juliet turned to Sabra. "And thank you for the clothes, they fit perfectly."

Sabra beamed. "I knew you'd like it. I studied in Paris last semester and brought back more than I should have. I'm glad somebody can wear the clothes."

"I always wished I could've spent a semester abroad, but it never panned out. I bet it was amazing. Did you just stay in France or did you travel all over Europe?" Juliet asked.

"All over. Greece was my favorite. The people are so generous and the landscape is breath taking."

"We were lucky she came back home after her adventures," chortled Cara. "Juliet, dear, why don't you tell us about yourself?"

"Well, there's not much to tell." Three pair of eyes sat fixed on her. "I was born and raised in Northern Kentucky. Mom and Dad still live there. Dad's an actuary, and Mom's a librarian at the county library. My brother is an engineer and works in Cincinnati. I went to vet school at Auburn, did an internship in Atlanta, and then came here to work for Dr. Silver before I apply for a residency this fall," Juliet paused. "Cara, if you don't mind me asking, where are you from? I've noticed your accent, but I can't place it."

"I'm originally from Greenland," answered Cara. "And I bet your next question is going to be how did I end up here?" Juliet nodded yes. Cara reached over and placed her hand on Sterling. "Our parents knew each other, they're the reason why we're together. I moved here thirty-six years ago to marry my husband."

The couple looked at each other, absolutely forgetting the two other people at the table for a moment. Sabra cleared her throat breaking them from their trance. Cara turned her attention back to Juliet. "As you know, Sterling is a pastor, and I'm a teacher at the elementary school. We come from a very large family, in case you couldn't tell from the party. Gabriel is our oldest son. Lorna is our oldest daughter. She and her husband are both lawyers. Sabra is the only one who still lives at the house with us when she is not in school."

Juliet thought it was sad they had such a big house with only one child living part-time at home. At that moment, a random thought popped into her mind, "Cara, as I was walking over here, I noticed a bunch of trails like the one from the guest house all seem to lead to this house. Are those all hiking trails?"

The three individuals all started laughing. Evidently, Juliet had said something they found funny, but the joke was lost to her. Sterling responded first, "They are trails but not hiking trails. Our family has lived on this piece of property since before Kentucky became a state. The land borders one side of the National Park. Over the years, the family did not want to divide the land, so we kept it intact. If someone in our family chooses to live here, we have plenty of room. Those trails you saw are paths to the other houses on the land."

This statement startled Juliet. "I'm sorry, I don't think I understand. Did you say your entire family lives here?"

Sterling cleared his throat. "Well, not everyone lives here, but, for instance, Lorna and her family live two houses down. Everyone has their own separate entrances to their houses and each house is built for each family's needs and wants. The paths just link all the houses together so no one has to drive. The children love being able to run back and forth."

Even though Juliet was caught off guard by this information, it was actually pretty impressive at the same time. "Does Dr. Silver live here? Well, not *here* here, but, you know, on this land?"

"No, he and his family live in the city." Sterling pushed away from the table. "I'll go get the dessert."

Sterling returned with four bowls containing a brownie topped with vanilla ice cream. As she looked at the dessert, Juliet seriously pondered the idea of asking them to adopt her so she could eat like this the rest of her life. She reconsidered this since she figured it might be a little creepy. Wanting to get to know these people who had been so kind to her better she said, "I'd love to hear some stories about your family growing up."

Sterling turned to Cara. "That we can do very easily. Would you like to begin, my love?"

Cara reached over and took Sterling's hand in hers. "Let's see." She tapped the side of her face with her other hand. "When the children were younger, they were constantly getting into trouble. Gabriel, especially, went through a major teething phase. He chewed up everything. I remember when Lorna had just been born, and Gabriel had just turned two. He had wandered out of my sight for just a few minutes, and I found him in the baby room. He had chewed the baby oil and baby powder and it covered the entire room. It took forever to get out of the carpet, not to mention he was pooping pieces of plastic for days."

"His teeth were so strong he chewed a hole through plastic?" Juliet was sure she had misheard Cara. There was no way a human child could chew up a plastic bottle.

"Oh, no. Whoops!" Cara cleared her throat. "We had a dog at the time who chewed open the bottle, and he and Gabriel just went to town making a mess of things before I found them." Cara looked at her husband. "Sterling, I'm sure you have a tale you'd like to tell."

The rest of the stories over dessert were full of the escapades of Sterling and Cara's four children. Most of them seemed to center around their eldest son, who, although he was a bit of a rascal as a child, seemed to be a happy, vibrant kid. Juliet wondered if the accident Sabra had spoken of had changed that in Gabriel. She felt the question would be inappropriate to ask at this time. Juliet enjoyed the conversation, and it was nice to be around a family that cared about each other. Before saying goodnight, Sterling asked her if she would be attending church with them in the morning. Juliet said she would, and Sabra volunteered to drive her.

When Juliet got back to her house, she felt full and sleepy. The mattress was soft and inviting and she burrowed under the covers. Shadow decided to come out from his hiding place and join her. He curled up next to her head and the loud purring, which normally would have kept her awake, was a calming reassurance of familiarity to her. She closed her eyes and the feline motor lulled her to sleep.

Chapter 11

The ride to church had been a harrowing endeavor. Never before was Juliet so thankful to be alive. She was dreading getting back into the car with Sabra when the service was over. To say the college student was an awful driver would be a major understatement. Juliet never knew curves could be taken at such a high velocity. Most of her trip was spent with her eyes closed and her hands gripping the doorframe. The blood was just now returning to her knuckles. She had literally jumped from the SUV when they had pulled into the parking lot.

When they entered the church, Sabra had ushered her down towards the front with the rest of the family. The news of the last 48 hours had spread like wildfire through the clan. Once again, she received hugs from everyone, with questions about her health and how she was doing.

Her saving grace was the organ music starting, signaling everyone to take their seats. Juliet sat between Lorna and Sabra. The two fiery red heads looked so much alike down to their emerald green eyes. She wondered what it would be like to have a sister. She and her brother were close, but there were just some things you could only do with a sister. As Juliet was daydreaming, she noticed Sabra turn and look behind her. Juliet followed her gaze to discover Gabriel walking down the side aisle towards the group and slid in next to Sabra. As he settled into the pew, she recalled Sabra's story the night before and sympathy welled up inside of her. Did his anger manifest itself from that event? Her thoughts were broken up by his amazing scent. She took in a sharp breath, and her heartbeat quickened. *Why does he smell so incredible?* Juliet looked at Lorna and then Sabra to see if they gave any indication of noticing the powerful cologne their brother was wearing. Sabra saw Juliet's face and giggled. Gabriel nudged his sister and then glanced at Juliet, who quickly turned her head to focus on the church choir.

Throughout the service, Juliet found her eyes wandering over to the man sitting to her right. She didn't realize how often she was looking over until Sabra cleared her throat and looked directly at her. After that, she concentrated on keeping her wandering eyes forward. Juliet scolded herself for being so silly. Why did she feel the need to look at him? Yes, he'd saved her life, his family adored him, he'd experienced a terrible tragedy, but he was still a liar, had a bad temper, and was arrogant. These weren't qualities she found desirable, yet there was something about him nagging her soul. She had dealt with men like him in her past and never thought twice about them. Why was he so different?

Juliet was so lost in thought she didn't realize people had started getting up to leave. She blinked as her mind focused on the present world before her. Lorna was smiling at her. "I know you're not deep in thought over my father's sermon."

Juliet gave her a sheepish grin. "It's nothing. Just thinking about work."

"Sure you are." Lorna stood up and turned to her husband, Ben, who had just finished speaking with Cara. "Honey, let's go get the kids from children's church."

Sabra leaned over. "Are you ready for me to drive you back to the house?"

"*You* drove Juliet to church?" Gabriel interrupted. He was already standing and had taken several steps towards the end of the pew, but now backtracked towards his sister.

Sabra rose to her feet, scowling at her older brother. "Of course I drove her to church. Don't you remember you were the one who didn't want her driving all weekend long? Dad and Mom get here super early, so that left me."

"You're a horrible driver. Don't deny it," Gabriel quipped back. "You also forgot the part about how she is supposed to be resting and not having a lot of stress which your driving will cause."

Juliet was annoyed the siblings were discussing her like she was not there.

Gabriel turned his focus from his sister to her. "I'm driving you home."

Silently thankful for not having to endure the demolition derby-style driving of Sabra, Juliet's inner-feminist refused to let a man dictate her actions. She also didn't like how distracted she had been around him in church. The thought of being in a closed, confined space with him made her nervous, but she could not put her finger on why. "No, you're not. You don't get to make decisions for me outside of the hospital, and I'm perfectly happy riding with Sabra."

Gabriel seemed taken aback for a moment. Juliet could see his face tense and then relax. "If you want to ride with my sister, that's fine."

Juliet became immediately suspicious of how she won the argument so easily. Though she did not know him very well, the one thing she had learned in the last two days was he did not back down from something when he was determined. She also was annoyed with herself she had just elected to get back in a car with Sabra behind the wheel. But, she'd committed to this, and she was not going to change her mind now. "Come on, Sabra. Let's go."

Sabra and Juliet walked out of church with Gabriel following them. When they got to Sabra's SUV, Gabriel stepped in front of the driver's-side door and held his hand out to his sister. "Hand over the keys."

Sabra baulked at the offense. "No! This is my car."

Gabriel crossed his arms and laughed. "Let's see you get past me."

Juliet was accustomed to having sibling spats, but these two were acting like teenagers. She hoped they normally acted their age when she wasn't around. Juliet stepped into the middle of the two and tilted her chin up towards Gabriel. "You agreed I was going to go with Sabra."

A sly smile crossed Gabriel's lips. "No, I agreed you would ride with my sister. I never said I would let her drive."

Juliet placed her hands on her hips. "Are you serious? Where do you get off ordering people around? Don't you think you're a little old to be a bully?"

"I'm not a bully; I'm just looking out for you," he said matter-of-factly.

Juliet really wished she could hit him. He had somehow put her between the proverbial rock and a hard place. Either decision she made was a losing one, if she agreed to go with him, then he won the battle which would be humiliating, but she didn't want Sabra to be degraded by her brother, especially since she had already been more than kind to Juliet. She looked back at Sabra, who was silently pleading with her to back down. "Fine," she sighed. "Where's your car?"

Triumphant in his mission, Gabriel moved and opened the car door for his sister. When she had gotten in, he closed the door and turned to Juliet. "Follow me, please."

Begrudgingly, Juliet walked next to Gabriel. She refused to look at him, seething every step of the way. The relief she felt over not having to get into the car with Sabra was countered by the fury of Gabriel's demanding and protective attitude. Juliet was not a damsel in distress who needed rescuing every five minutes. She realized some of this anger was misdirected from enduring years of "southern male good ole boy" attitudes while in school. This was a sore spot with her. He just managed to evoke that walled-off sensitivity every time he was around.

Gabriel approached a black sports car in the parking lot and opened the passenger side door for her. Juliet walked past him and sat down in the car's leather seat. *Great, even his car smells like him.* She willed herself not to take deep breaths, even though her body wanted to. Why was his scent like a drug to her? She couldn't get enough of it, and, to make matters worse, it always distracted her from her anger with him. He closed the passenger door and made his way around to the driver's side. By the time Gabriel sat in his seat, Juliet had her seatbelt on, her arms crossed, and was staring as hard as she could outside her window trying to focus on all his personality flaws. It was completely immature, and she knew it. They had barely pulled out of the church parking lot when he called her out about her behavior, "You know, the silent treatment is something I thought most people stopped doing after elementary school."

The goading had just gone a little too far, and Juliet had to let it out. "Who the hell do you think you are? First, you're a jerk. Then, you try and be nice to me at your parents' house only to then lie to me later on. You scold a child for an accident; you save my life, and then you're angry about it; you don't want me to stay at your parents place, and now you order me out of your sister's car because you are, quote, 'looking out for me.' I can't keep up with the mood swings. Do you like torturing people or just me?"

Through her blazing eyes she could see a flash of hurt go across his face. His mouth thinned to a flat line. "Believe it or not, I'm trying to do what is in your best interest." His voice softened. "I'm normally not like this, I promise. It's just, things are very complicated right now."

"Well, if you're sincere, why don't you start telling me the truth? And, while we're at it, asking me politely for things instead of ordering me around?" The words were flowing now as she became more and more flustered with the situation. Her hands were waving wildly in the air. "I'm not a child, in case you haven't noticed. Stop ordering me around and start looking at me as a woman. I mean, treating me like a woman."

"Good God, Juliet, you drive me nuts!" Gabriel barked back. "I've been trying to treat you like a lady, but you won't let me. Maybe if you weren't so head strong and accepted my apology, then we could actually get along."

Juliet felt like she'd been slapped across the face. As much as she really didn't want to admit he was right, she realized she hadn't forgiven him for their first encounter after he apologized. For a person who was so used to seeing the good in people, why was she only looking at the bad? Her conscience suddenly handed out a heavy dose of guilt. Her mouth felt dry, and it began to feel uncomfortably hot. Juliet looked down at her lap.

"I want to forgive you." Her voice was just above a whisper.

"Then why don't you?" Gabriel's voice was flat. He made the turn leading them out of town.

Juliet chewed the bottom of her lip. There was a battle going on within her conscience. She felt like she had the devil and angel cartoon characters arguing inside her head, both screaming as loudly as possible their opinions on the entire situation. One side telling her to not to give in and to hold a grudge while the other preaching the only person she was hurting was herself if she did not let her anger go. She inhaled and then blew the air out of her mouth. "Look, I'll work on the forgiveness thing, but I need you to stop being so dominant."

"I'll take into consideration your feelings and be better about asking your opinion." Gabriel's eyes diverted to her face for a second before he returned them to the road. "Dominant? That's an interesting term."

Juliet shrugged her shoulders. "I deal with animals all the time. It was the first word that came to mind."

Not wanting him to see the small smile trying to form, she turned to look out the car window. The wildflowers along the road created a sea of colors. Sometimes she forgot about the simple joys in life. Reminding herself that getting tangled up in petty grudges distracted her from fully appreciating the beauty of the things around her, she turned back to the man sitting to her left. Juliet became cognizant of his physical attributes beyond the alluring smell. She could appreciate the masculine quality of the lines of his face. His chiseled jaw was relaxed. Now that he wasn't flushed with anger, his face had a light bronze color. When Gabriel next spoke, Juliet was jolted out of her reverie. She hoped he didn't see her jump.

"So does this mean we're going to try and have a conversation without being at each other's throats?" Gabriel kept his eyes straight ahead.

"I'll try if you'll try." Juliet realized how intensely she had been staring at him and dropped her gaze to her lap. She reflexively played with the hem of her dress with her fingers. "Will you start answering some of my questions?"

Gabriel turned onto the main road to his parent's house. "Only the ones I can answer."

Juliet opened her mouth to protest but reconsidered. Arguing would lead her back to square one. For now, she would be happy with their peace treaty. Gabriel's grip on the steering wheel relaxed, and for a moment he took his right hand off the wheel and moved it in Juliet's direction. She saw the movement out of the corner of her eye and was suddenly filled with so many conflicting emotions her face combined them into a frantic grimace. Gabriel turned to look at her, and, when he saw her face, his hand immediately retreated back to the steering wheel. Juliet let out a small sigh -- of relief or disappointment she couldn't quite tell. *I really need to get out of this car so I can think straight*, she reassured herself.

Gabriel pulled slowly into the gravel driveway and parked the car. Even though she was in a hurry to get out of the vehicle and into fresh, unscented air, Juliet knew Gabriel would open the door for her, as this gesture hadn't been lost on her the first time he'd done it. She sat for what seemed far longer than the ten seconds it took him to walk from his side of the car to hers, making sure to only inhale through her mouth. Some people would scoff at the idea of not opening her own door, but she had to admit she appreciated the gentlemanly gesture. When he finally swung open the passenger-side door, Juliet hopped out. "Thank you," she said with a smile.

He shut the car door once she had gotten out. "You're welcome. Would you like me to walk you to the door?"

Juliet's stomach fluttered. It was essential she get some distance from this man. "No, thank you, but thanks for asking." She walked up the porch stairs and unlocked the door. Giving him a quick glance, she sighed and headed into the house.

Chapter 12

By the time Juliet had walked over to have lunch with the Archon family, she felt more in control of her emotions. Gabriel was the key to a huge amount of questions she had. Since she hadn't gotten anywhere in the past week questioning Dr. Silver and the three staff members involved in the wolf situation, Gabriel was her only hope. Juliet would take the advice her mother had always given her, she could attract more flies with honey than vinegar. Gabriel Archon was the fly, and she'd be the honey. She would not allow herself to get distracted by him, but would be her normal, kind self while maintaining her distance. She told herself he was like every other man she'd interacted with in her adult life. There was nothing special about him.

When Juliet walked up the main steps, Aiden was on the front porch with his two sisters, Hanna and Ava. The teenagers were busy looking at something on a smart phone. Aiden looked up and smiled at Juliet. "Hey, Juliet. Just go inside; there's no need to knock. I have to warn you, they're going to put you to work in the kitchen. That's why we're hiding out here."

Juliet smiled then and opened the door. "Thanks for the warning."

When Juliet entered the house, she was greeted with children's laughter echoing down the hall. Making her way towards the kitchen, she paused at the study. Through the closed, glass French doors she could see Sterling and Gabriel talking. Sterling's hand was on Gabriel's shoulder. The conversation wasn't heated, but she could tell whatever they were discussing was something serious. Not wanting to be caught prying, Juliet continued her way down the hall. The smell of food filled her nostrils as she approached the kitchen.

Cara and Lorna were in the kitchen along with Sterling's sister, Leah, and her daughter, Kayla. The four women had created another feast in a little over an hour since church had let out. *I really do need to learn how to cook.* Juliet turned to Kayla. "Your son said I would be put to work if I came in here. So, where do you need me?"

Kayla handed her a bowl full of tomatoes. "You can slice these for the salad. By the way, where are my children?"

Taking the bowl and sitting it on the center island Juliet searched for a cutting board, which she found in one of the island drawers. She took a knife from the butcher block on the counter and began slicing. "Aiden, Hanna, and Ava are all out on the porch looking at something on their phone. I didn't see Mathew."

Lorna brought over a bowl of freshly washed spinach leaves and roman lettuce and set it next to Juliet to put the tomatoes in. "Mathew is probably with Jacob. Those two have been thick as thieves since they were born."

Juliet dumped several sliced tomatoes into the bowl. "Where are your little ones, Lorna?"

"Last time I checked, Ben was taking Caleb to help fix something in the tree house by the lake. Sabra was entertaining Eve and Nora." Lorna was adding cheese into the salad bowl.

"I don't know how y'all do it. Have as many children as you do and work at the same time. I'm impressed and intimidated." Juliet finished slicing the last of the tomatoes.

"It's called help." Leah pulled out rolls from the oven. "Cara, Kayla, and I all teach, so in the summer we are able to watch the children while everyone else works. When you have this big of a family there is always someone to help out. You'll see someday."

Juliet laughed, "Right now I'm just working on my career and taking care of my cat. A family is a long way off."

"Oh, that reminds me: Juliet, I have a huge favor to ask of you." Lorna was grinning ear to ear. "So, every year we have a fall gala for the hospital to raise money for our St. Francis fund. We auction off single men or women to be dates for someone for the evening. This year is the women's turn, so I have to find as many eligible ladies as possible. Sabra is going to do it, and I was wondering if I could talk you into possibly being one of those people this year?"

Juliet grimaced and then immediately tried to cover it up with a fake smile on her face. "Um, I don't know. I mean, nobody would want to bid on me, and then I would look like an idiot. Besides, big social events are not really my thing."

Lorna reached out and clasped both of Juliet's hands. "Juliet, I know it sounds kind of scary, but it's a lot of fun! You'd be helping me out, and it's for a good cause. Sabra can even design a dress for you. You'll look gorgeous. I promise you, the single men in this town would love a chance to be your date for the evening."

Juliet really had to learn to say no, but today would not be that day. "Alright, but if no one bids on me, I don't want you getting mad if I don't make you any money."

Lorna threw her arms around her. "Thank you! I promise you won't regret it."

"What won't she regret?" asked Sterling as he and Gabriel walked into the kitchen.

"I just talked Juliet into being one of the people auctioned off at the hospital gala. She's going to be great," Lorna beamed.

"She'll be wonderful." Sterling clapped his hands together. "Now, let us help you carry this stuff to the table."

Juliet had looked to Gabriel to see his reaction, but he hadn't even glanced in her direction. She didn't know why she cared what he thought about her volunteering for his sister's charity event. Gabriel took a tray of food from his mother and walked out the door. Juliet helped the other women in the kitchen carry the remaining food into the other room.

After the blessing, adults ate in the dining room while the kids ate at the kitchen table. Gabriel sat across from Juliet where he joined in the conversation, but never spoke directly to her. She mentally reminded herself to be patient. She couldn't start questioning him in front of his family. When Juliet saw the other members of the dinner party had finished eating and were leaving the table, she stood up. "Can I take anyone's plate for them?" she asked as she looked at the faces remaining. Her eyes fell last on Gabriel.

Gabriel blinked at her a few times before the words she had just spoken seemed to register in his mind. "Yes, thank you."

"You're welcome. Is there anything else you might need?" Maybe she was laying it on a bit too thick.

Gabriel eyed her suspiciously. "No, I'm fine, thank you."

Juliet pivoted to head towards the kitchen. Her eyes caught Cara's knowing ones for a split second. In that moment, she could see Cara was very aware of what Juliet was up to. The matriarch gave her an insightful smile. Juliet turned away from the table so no one could see the heat rising to her face.

Back in the kitchen, Juliet put the dirty plates in the dishwasher. When she turned around, Nora was standing in front of her. "Hello, Nora. How are you today?"

"Good." Nora lifted her arms. "Up, please."

Juliet picked her up and the little girl giggled. "Will you spin me?" Nora asked.

Juliet looked around at the kitchen full of sharp objects. This was not the ideal location to be spinning a child in the air. "Let's go into the other room, and I'll spin you there. How's that sound?"

"Okay," Nora agreed.

Juliet carried the girl into the family room, which was open and not full of potential crashing hazards. Most of the children were already lounging on the couches in the room. Juliet spun around in a circle a few times, holding the little redheaded girl so her feet sailed out from Juliet. Nora laughed out loud.

When Juliet stopped Nora immediately shouted, "Again! Again!"

Juliet was a little dizzy but picked the child up again. She waited a moment till she felt better and began spinning. Juliet quickly realized she'd made a mistake. She suddenly felt like she was going to fall. Before losing her balance, she was able to stop and put Nora on the ground. The dizziness was overwhelming, and Juliet felt her body pitch sideways. A hand shot out and caught her arm. She saw Aiden was by her side, keeping her from falling. "Uncle Gabriel!" he shouted.

Within seconds, a pair of arms wrapped around her, and Gabriel picked her up. "I'm fine," she protested. "I just got a little dizzy."

He placed her gently on the couch. Juliet's world was still spinning, so she closed her eyes. "Oh dear, is she going to be okay?" she heard Cara ask.

"I need to examine her, but I think she will be fine if she would just listen to me and rest." Gabriel's tone was a mix of tension and concern.

"I just over did it," Juliet said but kept her eyes closed. "I'll be fine."

"Are you always this stubborn?" he asked.

"Only when I'm around you," Juliet murmured. Why did he have to ask her questions when she couldn't think straight?

Juliet opened her eyes and saw multiple faces staring down at her. The dizziness had subsided, but she still felt a little light-headed. Not ready to attempt getting up, she laid still feeling very self-conscious. Cara began shooing everyone out of the room to give her more space. Some of the children whined about being kicked out, but most of the adults herded them away with a promise they could play some game outside. With the room now much less crowded, she gingerly sat up on the couch. This was her first severe injury, and being hit over the head had really done a number on her. She wondered when she would be back to herself again. Juliet managed a weak smile at the set of blue eyes staring at her.

Gabriel offered his hand to her. "Let's get you back to the guesthouse. Do you think you can walk, or do I need to carry you?"

"I can walk." Accepting his hand, she slowly stood and made her way out of the room. Juliet didn't protest when she felt Gabriel's firm hand pressed around her waist, thankful for the support. The heat from his hand radiated through her clothes to the small of her back. Deep down Juliet knew she should have accepted his offer of being carried, but her pride refused to let him know just how weak she felt.

Taking her time, Juliet made it the guesthouse without passing out or needing to be carried. She appreciated how patient he'd been on the slow trek from the main house to the guesthouse. Along the way, he told her she was 'doing great' and to 'take her time'. She recognized the tone as the same one she used when speaking to a wounded animal.

"I know part of our deal is I don't order you around, but I'm guessing you can't make it up the stairs. If you'll allow me, I'm going to carry you." Gabriel waited for Juliet to nod her head yes before he scooped her up in his arms.

Enveloped as she was in his arms and against his chest, there was now no escaping the narcotic effect Gabriel's smell had on her nervous system. Even if she'd held her breath it permeated her pores, and she could taste it on her tongue. It gave her the sensation she was floating on air in a dreamlike state she didn't want to end. In the seconds it took for them to ascend the porch steps, she allowed her mind to articulate the dichotomous nature of feelings he evoked within her. She was intoxicated by his very existence, yet she harbored a healthy discontent toward him because of his deception concerning many things. On one hand he is an educated, logical man from a good family; however, he was purposely lying to protect something. One question, more important now than any other ricocheted inside her head. The question to answer all others. What was he protecting, himself, or something else?

By now they'd reached the front door and the time traveling trip her mind sometimes took came to an end. She allowed herself one last deep breath. Instead of setting her down on the porch, he opened the door and brought her to the couch. A moment later, Aiden entered the house holding a medical bag. He handed it to Gabriel, looked at Juliet, gave her a reassuring smile, and then left.

Gabriel collected several things from the bag. He took the penlight and flashed it in her eyes. She knew he was checking to make sure if her eyes were reacting correctly to the bright light, but it blinded her for a split second. He clicked off the light and placed his right pointer finger in front of her. "Follow my finger, please, without moving your head," he stated. She did as she was instructed. He checked her reflexes and then finally reached for his stethoscope. He placed the bell of the stethoscope to her chest, and she could feel her heart beat quicken. *What is wrong with me?* She hoped by some small miracle he hadn't noticed, but knew that would be impossible. He moved from her heart to her lungs. She took deep breaths and let them out slowly.

"I need you to stay in bed or on the couch today. Now, I'm going to trust you will listen to me, but, if I have to, I will make someone stay with you. I've got to run to the hospital for a little bit, but when I get back, I'm going to check on you again."

"Secret's coming over. She should be here any minute. We were planning on watching movies all afternoon and hanging out." As if on cue, there was a knock on the door.

Gabriel rose and answered the door. Secret peeked past the doorframe and looked around. When her eyes met Juliet, she entered the house and walked over to her friend. Secret dropped the bag she had over her shoulder onto the floor, and looked from Juliet to Gabriel. "What has she done now?"

Gabriel closed the door and walked to stand over the couch. "She didn't listen to me and got dizzy. If you're staying with her for a while, I'm putting you in charge of making sure she stays put and doesn't get up."

"I can take care of myself," pouted Juliet.

They both responded in unison, "No, you can't."

Secret and Gabriel looked at each other and then back at her. In that instant, Juliet could tell the two had come to an agreement. She would have to remind Secret, as her best friend, she was always supposed to be on her side.

"Good, I'll leave you ladies to your afternoon of movies," Gabriel said as he grabbed his medical bag and walked out the door.

Secret watched Gabriel as he left and plopped down on the couch at Juliet's feet. "I think I'm beginning to like him."

Juliet threw a pillow at her friend. "Traitor!"

"What? You have your own personal physician. His family is putting you up in this house, which, by the way, holy cow awesome! He seems to be very concerned about you. Not to mention, he is gorgeous." Secret gave her friend a toothy grin. "Why don't you like him again?"

"Do you want the entire list or the abridged version?" Juliet huffed. She looked down at the pillow in her lap so as not to look directly into her friend's eyes. "He's not that attractive anyway."

Secret rolled her eyes and stuck her finger in Juliet's ribs. "Whatever. Juliet, I love you, but you're hopeless. If you're not careful, you're going to become a nun."

Juliet wrinkled her nose. "Ha-ha. Very funny. There are no Protestant nuns."

Secret dismissed this comment and was looking around the room. "Hey, do you mind if I check out the rest of the house before we start watching movies?"

"Sure, go ahead. Will you bring me my PJ's from the master bedroom when you go upstairs?"

After Secret explored the house, she came back downstairs with the pajamas. Juliet went to the bathroom to change while Secret made popcorn. Once they were all settled in front of the TV with the first movie playing, Secret asked, "Hey, you want to go out to dinner with me and Kevin on Friday? You've had a lot going on, and I thought it might be fun."

"Sure. Just let me know what time." Juliet crunched down on the popcorn.

Secret smacked her hand to her forehead. "That reminds me, Kevin told me to tell you he's going to bring a tattoo book by tomorrow at your work so you can take a look at it."

After the first movie, Juliet was feeling back to her old self. During the second movie, they painted their toenails. Secret went with a bright orange while Juliet had chosen purple. Cara brought dinner to Juliet around five o'clock. Juliet introduced her to Secret and the two chatted for a few minutes before Cara left to go back to the house. Right before the end of the third movie, there was a knock at the door. Secret answered it, and Gabriel entered.

"Did she stay on the couch this afternoon?" Gabriel asked Secret after he observed Juliet was sitting where he had left her hours earlier.

"Yes, doctor." Secret nodded her head. Juliet rolled her eyes. She could tell Secret was loving every minute of this.

Gabriel seemed unaware of her friend's mockery. "Any problems? I know you'll tell me before she will."

"No, she seems fine." Secret gave Juliet a sly smile before speaking again. "I don't think she's absolutely a hundred percent though, so she may need you to stay for a while. I would, but I need to get home since I have a lot of stuff to do."

Secret collected her things. "Jules, I'm going to take off now since I know you are in capable hands. Oh, and remember, Friday night dinner."

Juliet didn't even have time to protest before Secret was out the door, and she found herself in an awkward silence with Gabriel. He sat in the chair across from her and looked around. "So, did you have fun with Secret?"

"Yes, I did."

"What movies did you watch?"

"The Princess Bride, Pirates of the Caribbean, and The Crow." Juliet studied his face for any reaction to the movie selection.

Gabriel cocked his head sideway. "That's an odd combination."

Juliet shrugged her shoulders. "What can I say? Secret and I have an eclectic taste in movies."

"So, you're going out to dinner with Secret on Friday?"

"Well, Secret and Kevin, her fiancé. She thought it would be fun for me."

Gabriel did not respond to this comment. Instead a silence fell over the two of them. She avoided eye contact with him and looked around the room for something – anything – to talk about. When she found nothing of interest, Juliet decided to ask the most obvious question, "How was work?"

Gabriel sat back in his chair. He looked at ease sitting in the big leather recliner. "Interesting but I can't really discuss much. Patient-doctor confidentiality you know."

Juliet smiled. "Oh, I know, but my patients tend not to talk."

"I envy you that," replied Gabriel. His eyes locked on hers, and for what seemed like several minutes the two of them just looked at each other. He blinked and then shifted forward in his seat. "It's getting late. I know you will just fight with me about going to work tomorrow, so as long as you don't strain yourself, I'm going to let you go. But, I'm calling Anthony and telling him if you don't feel well you need to come home. Deal?"

"Deal."

Gabriel stood from the chair. "Now, let me help you up the stairs."

"What happened to asking and not telling?" Juliet gave him a wry smile.

"Dear God, woman, do you ever let up?" he lightly chastised her. "Juliet, would you please allow me to help you up the stairs?" Gabriel extended his hand towards her.

Juliet accepted his open palm as she stood up from the couch. He followed her up the stairs, and she was grateful she didn't need to be carried. She paused at the doorway to her bedroom and looked up at him. Much to her surprise he had an amused smile on his face. "What?" she asked.

"I think our little truce is working. Isn't this better than squabbling?" reflected Gabriel.

Juliet had to admit she could get used to this. "Yes, this is nice. Maybe we should try it again."

"Maybe." He looked down at her. "Goodnight. Juliet."

"Goodnight, Gabriel." She closed the bedroom door and leaned her body against it. *Crap!* Her heart was beating faster again.

Chapter 13

As instructed, Juliet took it easy on Monday. Dr. Silver and the rest of the staff made sure she didn't overdo it. Gina had even stopped her from picking up a two-pound kitten at one point during the day. She hated to admit it was nice to have a day full of puppy and kitten vaccines instead of vomiting and diarrhea cases or the uncontrollable, diabetic cat. Gabriel and his family had called to check on her throughout the day. Cara had even stopped by during lunch to see if Juliet needed anything.

The only downside of the day was when Kevin stopped by towards the end with the tattoo book. It was an ugly reminder of her assault. The pages contained known gang tattoos for her to look at. She spent the last thirty minutes of her workday sitting in her office going over the pages with Kevin. Nothing looked even vaguely familiar. Juliet knew if she saw the tattoo again she would remember it. She didn't know why her mind choose not to remember that important detail. When it came to her, she would draw the tattoo on a piece of paper and give it to Kevin.

By Wednesday, she felt back to normal. After the past week and a half, it looked like her life would return to some semblance of its boring self. Those reassuring thoughts were dashed on Thursday, when Kevin showed up at the vet clinic in the middle of the busy workday. The receptionist escorted him to the back area where Juliet was ultrasounding a dog, a sullen look on his face. Juliet immediately got butterflies in her stomach. She quickly finished her evaluation of the dog's spleen and excused herself. Kevin followed her to the office where she closed the door behind them.

"What's wrong?" Juliet asked.

Kevin scratched the back of his head. "Juliet, I need you to come down to the station with me for a little bit."

Juliet was taken aback for a minute. "Am I in some kind of trouble or something?"

"No, it's just…" Kevin fumbled with something in his hands. "It's just we found two bodies, Juliet, and I need you to see if you recognize them."

A million thoughts were racing through her mind. She ran a checklist in her head and had talked to or seen Secret and almost the entire Archon family in the last twenty-four hours. "Oh my God, Kevin, who is it?"

Kevin reached out and touched her arm. "Nooo, I'm sorry, everyone's safe. I should've led with that. I can't tell you much right now, but we think it might be part of what happened to you the other night."

"Oh, thank God. Don't scare me like that!" She pulled away from Kevin and gave him a friendly punch on the arm. "Let me finish up here and then I'll take my lunch. I can go with you then. Dr. Silver should be in a room or his office. Can you find him and let him know what is going on?"

Though relieved no one close to her was hurt, she was sick to her stomach. Human death bothered her deeply. Her hands were shaking when she reached for the doorknob. When she walked out of the office, the staff scattered from the door like cockroaches. She headed to the receptionist's area to see how busy her schedule was for the afternoon. Nothing was booked in the slots immediately after lunch. She went to the waiting room where the owners of the dog she had been ultrasounding were. After going over her findings with them, she finished the medical notes. She found Kevin in the hallway with Dr.

Silver, who looked grim. He told her not to worry about her patients and to take as much time as she needed.

Kevin drove her to the police station where she was met by Sheriff Archon. The two men escorted her into an office area, and she took a seat on one of the hard wooden chairs. Looking up at Marcus, she wondered if she should call him by his first name or by his title. Juliet decided to go with the formal title since this was an official setting. "Sheriff, what's happened? Kevin, I mean, Officer O'Hara, said this involved some bodies that were found. What does it have to do with me?"

The Sheriff cleared his throat. "We found two bodies outside of the city along the side of the road. The medical examiner stated both men had broken necks. One had a broken nose and several bruises and the other matched the facial description you gave me of your attacker. I want to show you some pictures and see if you recognize either man."

The Sheriff pulled pictures from a manila envelope. "I should warn you these photos are quite graphic," he said before placing them on his desk in front of Juliet. She took a deep breath in before looking. Her stomach lurched as she gazed at the lifeless forms. The man with the obvious broken nose was not familiar to her, but the second man was definitely the one from the attack. She pointed to him. "That's the man from the other night. Do you know who he is?"

The Sheriff nodded. "Both men had records for burglary and assault. We're working on how they knew each other, but they were definitely not from this area."

"So you think they were just stealing from me and I walked in at the wrong time?" Juliet asked. "Did you guys look into the exterminators? Did you call my landlord? Was anything connected?"

Kevin jumped into the conversation. "Juliet, I know you are trying to figure out what happened the other night and want a more in-depth explanation, but sometimes it is just coincidence. These guys are known for breaking and entering."

The Sheriff reached over and touched her shoulder. "I personally called your landlord and everything checked out with him. As for the exterminators, the company is legitimate, and they did have a call in to come to your house, but it was on a different day. We're still investigating that angle."

Like with the break in at the clinic, Juliet's gut told her something else was going on. "What about the tattoo?"

Kevin ran his fingers through his hair. "What about it? Did you remember something since Monday?"

Juliet shook her head. "No, I just was wondering if you took a picture of it on the man's body. I would like to see it."

"There was serious scavenging to both bodies. Most of this man's arm was completely eaten and the area where you said the tattoo was located wasn't able to be recovered," Sheriff Archon stated.

As much as Juliet dealt with gross things all day, the thought of animals eating a body made her stomach turn. "What about the clinic? Could there be link between the robbery at the vet clinic and my house? Were there any finger prints?"

The Sheriff put the case file down on the desk. "No finger prints were found at the clinic, so we really have no leads."

"And you know clinics are a major target for drug addicts, so that is most likely the case," added Kevin.

"Kevin, that makes no sense. Why would people looking to break into the clinic for drugs not bust open the drug safe with the controlled drugs? I saw it after the break in and it was untouched." Juliet sat back in her chair and looked back and forth between the two men.

Kevin crossed his arms. "I'm sorry, Juliet, but we just don't have a better explanation right now."

Juliet opened her mouth to reply but closed it again. Every reason she had thought of since the break in seemed unreasonable to her. "Is there anything else you need to know from me, or can I go back to work?"

The Sheriff gave her a reassuring smile. "I think that is all for now. We'll let you know if anything else comes up. Kevin can take you back to work now."

Juliet got out of her seat and shook the Sheriff's hand. She and Kevin barely spoke in the car back to the office. When they pulled into the clinic, Kevin turned to her. "Hey, I'm sorry you had to see those pictures, but at least we know the guys who did this to you won't be a problem. You can rest easier now."

Juliet gave him a half-hearted smile. "I don't know, Kevin, something feels off. They just happened to be found on the side of the road, and the significant evidence which might lead somewhere was eaten by wild animals? It just seems too convenient."

Kevin patted her on the shoulder. "I know, it doesn't make much sense. But you let me and the Sheriff worry about that. It has nothing to do with you. You need to just put this behind you."

Juliet appreciated his sentiment, but she knew it would be a long time before she could get the images of the dead men out of her head. "I guess you're right," she said, not wanting to talk about it anymore. She climbed out of the car.

Kevin rolled down the window. "I'll see you tomorrow night!"

She had forgotten about dinner with him and Secret. "Yeah, see you tomorrow."

She turned and headed into the clinic. Juliet's world was growing stranger by the moment. So much so she began to question her perception of reality or maybe this regular small town drama. She wanted to lose herself in work and not think about anything having to do with break-ins, dead bodies, or mysterious disappearing animals.

That night, she had a nightmare the two dead men from the photos were chasing her. They grabbed her and held her down, choking her. The injured wolf she'd saved pounced on the men and started to eat them. Gabriel suddenly appeared and told her everything would be all right. He reached out to her as the wolf crept towards him. Juliet screamed to warn him, but instead her screams woke her up. She sat up in the bed drenched in sweat. Juliet laid there for an hour trying to figure out what the dream could have meant.

By the end of the next workday, she was dragging. It had taken her over an hour after the dream to finally fall asleep. When she had, Juliet tossed and turned until morning. Now, instead of being able to go back to the house and vegetate, she was getting ready to meet Secret and Kevin. She had brought clothes to change into so she could leave straight from the clinic.

Juliet drove to the recently opened Italian restaurant, parked, and called Secret to let her know she was there. Secret told her they were already inside. She found the couple sitting at a table holding hands and deep in conversation.

"Hey, Juliet." Kevin got up and pulled out her chair. "Have a seat."

"Thank you." Juliet sat in the chair, and he pushed it in for her. He went back around the table and took his seat next to Secret. Their eyes darted from each other to Juliet.

"What?" She crossed her arms in front of her chest, leaning back in her chair.

"Kevin's got a question for you." Secret's eyes slid over to her fiancé. "I just want you to hear him out."

"Okay," responded Juliet, but she didn't like when her friends were being mysterious.

Kevin cleared his throat. "Secret said you wouldn't go for it, but I was wondering if you would let me set you up."

The waitress arrived to take their drink orders before she could answer. When she left, Juliet just continued to stare at Kevin as she pursed her lips together. She was not happy at all about the question. In college, Secret had tried setting Juliet up on numerous first dates, all of which were horrible. Much to the dismay of her friend, Juliet had spent most of her weekends in the library studying. She did have one serious boyfriend during vet school and it ended in disaster. Juliet had to remind herself she had attended Auburn to get her DVM, not a MRS degree. Since moving to town, Juliet had been pleasantly surprised Secret hadn't gone back to her old habits of setting her up, especially since Secret knew about everything that had happened in vet school.

"I think this is an excellent time to look at the menu," interjected Secret.

When the waitress came back with the drinks, they placed their orders. After the waitress left, Kevin broke the awkward silence. "You see, Juliet, my new partner – his name's Joe – is a really great guy. I just thought we could go out on a double date or something."

"Stop right there." Juliet held up her hand. "Kevin, I know you mean well, but I don't do blind dates. I'm sure Secret has probably told you about some of my dating disasters in college."

"Oh, I did!" confirmed Secret.

"Don't get me wrong; I really appreciate the gesture, but when it comes to my dating life, I can handle that on my own." Juliet smiled at Kevin, but hoped her eyes expressed the seriousness about this point.

Kevin would not be deterred. "Come on, you're my friend, and I want to see you happy. I know lots of single guys."

The smile of Juliet's face flattened. "Drop it, Kevin."

Luckily, the food arrived, giving her a reprieve to the current conversation. After everyone had taken several bites of food, Juliet was thankful the dialog turned into inconsequential small talk. When it came time to order dessert, Juliet was much more relaxed.

"So how's finding a place going?" Secret said as she finished chewing a piece of cheesecake.

"Not so good." Juliet picked at her brownie. "It's weird, but it's like all the rentals suddenly disappeared or they're way out of my price range."

Secret shrugged her shoulders. "Something will turn up, and in the mean time you can enjoy the view you have right now."

Juliet scrunched her face together. "What's that supposed to mean?"

"A certain doctor who has been taking care of you. Even you have to admit he's gorgeous." Secret nudged her leg under the table.

"Yeah, what's up with Archon?" Kevin leaned over the table. "You just met him and now you're staying at his house. You're fine with that but won't go on a date with my partner?"

"I'm not staying at his house. His *parents* are letting me stay in *their* guesthouse. Gabriel and I are barely friends." Kevin raised his eyebrows at Juliet. "Nothing's going on."

"He just happens to be there every time you're in trouble, right?" Secret placed the back of her hand on her head and dramatically pretended to swoon. "Oh tall, dark, and handsome doctor, please help! I might faint from your sexiness."

Juliet smacked her friend's arm. "You can't be serious. He just happened to be my doctor when I was brought in from the fire. Will you two stop looking at me!" Secret and Kevin's faces were perfectly matched: a mix of not believing a word Juliet was saying and enjoying every minute of her trying to explain herself. "I was going to stay with you guys, but somebody has an unreasonable fear of cats." She stared at Secret, who shrugged nonchalantly.

"As the male friend in your life, I think I should come by and check Archon out. Make sure he's not trying to take advantage of your injured state." Kevin smiled before he lifted his beer to his mouth.

"Thanks for your concern, but no." Juliet resisted the urge to stick her tongue out at him. The mere mention of Gabriel's name sent a jolt through Juliet's body. She was being silly, and she knew it. The two of them were just now beginning to get along, why couldn't she just be normal about it?

Kevin's cell phone rang and he excused himself from the table. Secret leaned over to her friend. "Jules, I'm really worried about you. It's been a long time since…you know. You can't keep living in the past; it's not healthy. I'd feel a lot better if you at least admitted some members of the opposite sex are attractive."

"Thank you for your concern, but I'm here to work." She reached out and squeezed Secret's hand.

Chapter 14

Even though Juliet had been exhausted when she went to bed Friday night, she awoke the next morning at 5 a.m. Unable to go back to sleep, she decided to go for a run. She hadn't been running since the break-in and was eager to stretch her muscles. After putting on her running clothes and brushing her teeth, she headed for the front door. Pulling the door open, she stopped dead in her tracks and had to stifle the scream wanting to come up out of her body. Sprawled out on her front porch was a large, sleeping wolf. This animal was twice the size of the one she had rescued from the forest. As quietly and quickly as she could she backed into the house and shut the door.

She grabbed her phone and debated whom to call. After a few seconds, she made up her mind and called the person physically closest to her. Cara answered the phone. "Hello?"

Juliet was grateful she'd answered the phone at such an early hour. The words rushed out of her mouth as her voice went up by an octave, "Cara, I'm so sorry to call this early, but I opened the door to go for a run, and there is a large wolf sleeping on my porch!"

"Now dear, just calm down." Cara's voice on the other end of the phone was even and matter of fact. "Are you sure there's wolf on your porch?"

"Cara, I'm looking at it through the window. It's massive!" Juliet added, as though this would somehow make the fact a live wolf was on her porch more believable. Juliet peered through the window while tapping her right foot on the floor. "I don't know what to do!"

"Don't worry, hon', Sterling will handle it. Just sit tight." And, with that, Cara hung up.

Juliet looked at her phone and was befuddled. How could Cara be so nonchalant about a huge, wild animal sitting on her front porch? Juliet was supposed to be the professional and even this had rattled her. Bunnies and squirrels on the outside of the door were one thing, but a predator – and a massive one – was another.

If the wolf wasn't disturbing enough, what Juliet witnessed next made her think she must be trapped in a dream. Sterling came walking around the corner of the porch, walked up the stairs towards the wolf, and looked at Juliet through the window. His forehead creased before turning his attention to the still-sleeping animal. Sterling casually walked up to the creature and touched it on the shoulder. Juliet thought she might vomit from the impossible knot in her stomach. *What is he doing?!* she screamed in her head. To her utter amazement, the animal blinked his eyes open and looked up at the man. Juliet braced herself for the inevitable attack. She wanted to look away, but couldn't. Several tense seconds passed, but the wolf made no show of aggression. Juliet didn't know what to think. Watching with disbelief as Sterling appeared to say something to the wolf and then pointed towards the woods. As if it understood, the wolf stood up, stretching languidly, and turned in the direction of Sterling's outstretched arm. If she had not known better, Juliet would have sworn the animal looked back at her before dropping its head as it went down the stairs. The wolf sauntered along the driveway a few paces and then took off into the forest beyond.

"Holy shit." The words escaped her before she realized it. Her hands flew up to her mouth as she gawked out the window.

Sterling straightened, walked over to the door, and knocked. As if on autopilot, Juliet walked to the door and opened it just a few inches, peering between the door and its frame at the gentleman in front of her. "May I come in?" Sterling asked.

Juliet just nodded silently, opening the door wider to allow him in. She shut the door hurriedly, fearing another wolf could appear at any moment. As she turned around to look at Sterling, her emotions came tumbling out. "How did you do that? What did you do? What just happened?" she said in one breath, stepping forward and raising her arms in the air in confused exasperation.

Sterling held his hand up to signal her to stop. "All in good time. Why don't we make some tea while we wait?"

"Tea?" Juliet coughed out in surprise. She had just seen one of the most bizarre and, she was just beginning to realize, awesome things of her life, and he wanted to make tea. Either she had lost her mind or he had. Thoughts of how he could rationally explain the situation raced through her mind as she followed him into the kitchen. She watched him get the teakettle out and fill it with water before placing it on the burner. Juliet gave herself a quick pinch to make sure this wasn't a dream, and she had been very much awake to witness this *Twilight Zone* situation.

Sterling moved around the kitchen casually, opening the cupboard containing mugs and pulled two out. Juliet could barely contain her desire to grab and shake him until he said something. She was about to open her mouth to speak when Gabriel burst through the door followed a few moments later by his mother. In Juliet's mildly irrational state, her first thought was how stupid she had been to not lock the door. There were wild animals outside! Big – *really, really big!* she thought – potentially very dangerous wild animals who somehow understood human speech and followed directions. Juliet looked frantically at the two new comers, hoping they would share her sentiment. Cara looked to be as calm as she had sounded on the phone, but Gabriel's blue eyes were wild and his face was flushed. Finally, someone was reacting the way she expected. Juliet could not figure out if he was mad, scared, or both. They all seemed like acceptable reactions to her. She was ignorant of how word had gotten to Gabriel, but she was relieved he was acting like a normal human being. Gabriel looked from his father to Juliet and then back to Sterling. "What happened?" he demanded angrily.

"Son, calm down. Everything is fine. Juliet just found one of our family members on the front porch. I was just making some tea so we can all sit down and discuss it rationally." Sterling walked over to the cabinet and pulled out two more mugs.

"Family member?" Juliet blurted out at the exact same time Gabriel stated, "Shit."

"Gabriel Hamon Archon, you watch your mouth!" Cara smacked her son on the shoulder. "I raised you better than that."

"Sorry, Mom," Gabriel looked down at the floor for a moment before he looked once again at his father.

"Excuse me." Juliet cleared her throat. "Can we go back to the part where you said I found one of your *family members* sleeping on the front porch? Actually, no, I don't even want to think about what it could possibly mean right now. How about someone explaining to me what I just saw and how it is in any way possible?" The volume of Juliet's voice had risen to just below yelling, but the two faces stared back at her didn't seem to register her tone. Juliet could see Gabriel pacing to her right. None of the Archons moved to speak. Juliet tried to compose herself. "Does anyone have something to say?"

As if in response, the teakettle whistled, and Sterling lifted it off the stove while Cara placed tea bags in the mugs. Juliet waited with her arms crossed and toe tapping for either one of them to begin to explain, but Sterling just poured the water and Cara set the steaming mugs on the kitchen table along with a plate of sugar cubes and some spoons. They both sat, gesturing at Juliet to do the same. She stared at them in disbelief, barely containing her anger. She wanted to make them talk, but she didn't know what else to do. Reluctantly, she pulled out a chair and sat, pulling a mug close to her and wrapping her hands around its warm surface. Juliet took several deep breaths, inhaling the flower-scented steam before looking back up, tapping the side of her cup with her fingernails. To her surprise, Sterling and Cara were both looking at Gabriel, who had continued to pace between the kitchen and living room. Juliet wondered what he could possibly have to do with any part of the morning's events. She suddenly remembered Gabriel's evasive comments about the whereabouts of the wolf with the broken leg, and it occurred to her maybe he did know what was going on. Gabriel seemed to sense the shift in attention towards him, and he stopped his movements, turning toward the gathering at the table. Juliet could now see his face had turned to a deep shade of crimson.

Sterling dropped two sugar cubes into his tea and stirred his drink, tapping the spoon with a light clinking sound on the side when he was done. "I think Juliet deserves to know the truth." Sterling's gaze was still directed towards his son.

"We agreed this was my decision," Gabriel countered.

"Yes, we did. But, as you can see, Juliet has seen us, and I believe you owe it to her to answer her questions." Gabriel's expression turned dark, and Sterling lifted a hand to stop Gabriel's protest. "I'm only voicing my opinion." Sterling shook his head side to side as he leaned back against the kitchen chair.

Gabriel let out a long slow breath before he turned to Juliet. "The wolf you saw this morning is special."

"A 200 pound wolf that understands English is special," Juliet responded haughtily. "Now tell me why?"

She finally had someone to direct her pent up frustration at, and the comment came out more biting than she had intended. Gabriel looked back at her, crossing his arms as if he wasn't going to have this conversation until she calmed down. Juliet closed her eyes for a moment and inhaled deeply. When she opened them, she met Gabriel's eyes again.

"I'm sorry, but you must realize how strange and...impossible this all seems!" she said, trying to level her voice in spite of her emotions. "Your father just talked the largest wolf I've ever seen down from my porch, which is crazy, but now, I think I'm more concerned that I seem to be the only one freaking out about it! So, please, explain how any of this is happening and I will shut up and listen." She turned her whole body to face him, placing her hands in her lap like an attentive student to prove her point.

Gabriel seemed reluctant to continue, but finally approached the table and sat down in the seat next to Juliet. He placed his hands on the table and stared at his fists before appearing to make up his mind. "Anthony told you there is a rare wolf pack which runs on the National Park land. Well, that's true, but they don't live in the National Park. They live here."

The words were barely out of his mouth before Juliet interrupted with a barrage of questions. "You mean live here like on your land? Like pets? You keep wolves as pets?" She paused to take a breath, and Gabriel looked like he was about to say something in reply when a new thought suddenly occurred to her. "Wait. The wolf from last week, do you own him too?"

Gabriel's eyes drew together. "I'm not sure I'd put it that way, but, yes, he lives here too."

A sense of satisfaction washed over her. "All this time wondering what happened, and he's been here the whole time," she murmured. "Is he okay? Can I see him? I can't believe you have wolves running around your un-fenced property. That's so… so… so…" she was going to say "dangerous" or "insane", but meeting Gabriel's eye she could see voicing her opinion on the subject might not get her the answers she had been so desperately seeking. "I shouldn't jump to conclusions. Let me clarify my earlier statement: I assume you've hand raised them to acclimate them to people, right?"

Gabriel's face relaxed and the red pigment started to lighten. "Yeah, that's right. We've raised these wolves here for years. We've kept their existence here a secret. That's why I didn't want you to know about the wolf you saved. They're part of our family and have been for centuries."

Things were remarkably beginning to make sense to Juliet. "Okay, so the whole family has been breeding wolves and letting them run free?" She turned to Sterling. "From what I saw this morning, they're pretty well trained. Amazingly well trained. But how do you know they won't run off and hurt someone?"

Sterling looked directly at Gabriel as he spoke. "I guess you could say they understand the property line."

Juliet could barely contain her confusion and excitement, and she started fidgeting in her seat. She was getting answers, but each one just created more questions. "Okay, I'll accept that, I guess. It's just…I see people all the time who have injuries from cat bites or trying to break up a dog fight. And those are domestic animals. I don't understand how a pastor, a surgeon, and the rest of your family can possibly have the time and skills to train wolves."

Gabriel sighed. "Juliet, they've been here for centuries. We all grew up together. No one trains them; the only way I can think to explain it is they train each other. They've never hurt an innocent human."

Juliet stared at him, dumbfounded. She didn't know if this was an acceptable answer or if it scared her even more. Gabriel turned to face her. "The most important thing for you to understand is their existence must remain a secret. There are people out there who would harm them. I cannot stress that enough."

Juliet nodded, the gravity of the situation suddenly hitting her full-force. "I promise you: I won't say a thing. Your family has been so kind to me, and I would do anything to protect you and your animals. I know this must have been hard for you: deciding to let a stranger know. Thank you for trusting me enough to tell me the truth about them."

Cara started coughing. Sterling placed his hand on her back. "Are you okay, dear?"

"I'm fine," Cara croaked. "Some tea went down the wrong pipe." She continued to cough for a few more seconds. "Really, I'm okay."

The brief distraction had given Juliet time to consider some of the more fascinating pieces of what she had been brought into. An isolated wolf pack, bred for centuries, kept as pets – though that seemed like the wrong term to use now – and it was just a routine part of life for this family. "And they're so big," she murmured in awe.

"Yes, they were meant to be protectors, so they've always been selected for size. That's part of what makes them...unique," Gabriel answered slowly.

Juliet looked between all three family members. "I've got so many questions, I don't know where to start."

Gabriel leaned across the table. "Since it looks like you're dressed to run, can I assume that was what you were going to do this morning?" Juliet nodded, and Gabriel continued, "If you go running with me every day, I'll answer your questions as we go. Provided you can keep up with me." He smiled teasingly, and Juliet felt her heart flutter and her anxiety melt away. *It must be okay*, she told herself. There was no way the town, the police – the federal government, for that matter – would allow such a thing to happen if anyone had ever been seriously injured. In a flash, she remembered the photos of the men who attacked her and then Marcus and Kevin's evasive answers when she pressed them about what had happened. Did Kevin know about the wolves? There was no way to ask him without breaking her promise to the Archons. She pushed the thoughts out of her head and focused on the man in front of her.

"It's a deal as long as you answer one last question first." Juliet could not help herself from grinning. After almost two weeks of trying to figure out what had happened, she was going to get her answers.

"Agreed," Gabriel replied.

"Can I see the wolf I saved?"

Chapter 15

Gabriel's eyes grew wide. "Um… that might be a little difficult right now."

"Why?" Juliet crossed her arms over her chest.

"Yes, son, why is it so difficult?" Sterling took a slow sip of his tea while his eyes fixed on Gabriel.

Gabriel scratched the back of his head. "You see, Lorna and Ben have raised that particular wolf. Since he was injured, they've kept him pretty close to home. As you know, they went to go visit Ben's parents, and they elected to take him with them, so, until they get back, I can't show him to you."

Juliet frowned and raised one eyebrow. "You're telling me Lorna, Ben, and their four children took an injured wolf on a road trip with them, and I'm supposed to believe that? Seriously, I just learned your entire family keeps a secret wolf pack. You don't need to lie to me anymore. If you don't want to show him to me, just say so. Don't make up a stupid story like that. Give me a little credit."

Gabriel's voice softened. "Juliet, I'm serious: that wolf is not on this property right now, but I promise you I will show him to you. Do you believe me when I tell you he is doing well thanks to you?"

Juliet looked straight into Gabriel's eyes. She was trying to read them to see if he was lying to her. He looked sincere enough. She broke eye contact and looked at Cara and Sterling who seemed to express the same gratitude on their faces. Juliet sighed and turned back to Gabriel. "At least tell me his name?"

Gabriel's eyebrows drew together. "Whose name?"

Juliet looked up to the ceiling while moving her head back and forth. "The wolf. Who else would I be asking about? What's his name?"

"Oh, right," Gabriel paused and looked at his mother, who smiled back at her son but said nothing. "The wolf's name is Iacobus."

"Really? What language is it even from?" Juliet questioned.

Gabriel got up from his chair and took his untouched mug to the sink where he dumped it out. He put the empty container in the dishwasher. "It's Latin."

Juliet turned in her chair so she could watch Gabriel as he walked around the kitchen. "Okay. What about the wolf on the porch this morning: what's his – or her – name?"

Gabriel held up his finger and shook his head. "No, more questions until we run; that was the deal."

Juliet leaned back in her chair as she stuck her bottom lip out. Sterling rose to his feet and held out his hand to Cara, who accepted it and got up from her chair. Juliet admired how sweet the older couple was. The two of them glanced in her direction. "Juliet, this family is in your debt for what you did to save our wolf. I hope you know now." Sterling looked at Juliet and then to his son. "Well, we'll let you two get on with your day." He flashed a smile at Juliet as he and Cara walked to the front door. "Give him a run for his money."

The right corner of her mouth turned upward. "Oh, I will," Juliet replied.

As Sterling walked past Gabriel, he said, "Walk me out, son."

Juliet had a feeling Sterling wanted to say something private to Gabriel. She watched all three of them walk out of the house and close the door. Curiosity got the best of her, and she made her way towards the entrance. The only disadvantage to the house was all the windows. Someone could not eavesdrop from the inside very well without being caught. Juliet crept around the side of the family room and pressed her body into the wall next to one of the widows. She could hear the two men talking but did not dare peak out. She heard Sterling say, "You're playing with fire." To which Gabriel responded with, "I know what I'm doing."

The next thing she knew, she heard footsteps going in opposite directions: two sets down the front porch stairs and the other coming inside. With cat-like reflexes, she ran as fast as she could and jumped onto the couch just as Gabriel opened the front door. He walked over to her slowly, his eyes fixed on her. His eyes were slanted, and his mouth was a straight line. She gave him a wide, innocent smile and blinked a few times for effect.

He pointed towards the front door again. "I've got to go change. Do you mind waiting here for me? I'll be back in a few minutes."

"Sure."

Gabriel left the house, and Juliet gave a sigh of relief he hadn't figured out what she had been doing. Part of Juliet wanted to go with him so she could see his house. She wondered where on the property he lived and what his house looked like. She shifted uncomfortably on the couch. Juliet was becoming more interested in this man than she wanted to admit. *He's just a source of answers,* she reminded herself.

Getting up off the couch, Juliet headed outside to begin to stretch her muscles. It was getting warm, and she could feel the humidity on her skin. Their run wouldn't be long in this heat. She stripped off her long-sleeved shirt and dropped it on the porch. Juliet dressed in layers since she could go from cold to hot and back so easily. She had a purple Nike running tank top on underneath her long-sleeved shirt. The sun's rays felt nice on her bare arms.

Staying in the yard, she walked around swinging her arms back and forth. Long ago, she had learned static stretching wasn't good before running. Her body soon felt warm and relaxed. The muscles loose and blood flowing. Closing her eyes, she faced the sky, taking in the peaceful moment, committing it to memory. Breathing deeply through her nose she was inundated with Gabriel's alluring aroma. Her eyes flew open, and she scanned the area to find him leaning against a tree by the trail. Curious as to why he would load up on cologne before running, she decided to bring that question up during their run. He was dressed in shorts and an Emory tee shirt. There was a strange look on his face she couldn't interpret. "Everything okay?"

Gabriel blinked. His faced looked flushed. "Yes, of course. Are you ready?"

There was a strain in his voice when he answered. For a second, she was puzzled as to why she had gotten such a gruff response from him. She wondered if she would ever figure out this man's ever-changing behavior. Juliet decided to brush off the remark and nodded her head yes. Without saying a word, Gabriel turned on his heels and headed back down the path, not bothering to wait for her. He didn't set an agonizing pace, but by his gait looked as though he could hold it for hours. Seven minute miles she guessed.

Juliet followed in his footsteps and quickly caught up to him. Gabriel veered down one of the white stone paths she had yet to explore. The path snaked its way through thousands of trees until it opened onto a beach near a lake. Distracted by this beautiful scene, Juliet stopped to admire the landscape. The water mirrored the trees surrounding it. As she gazed around the lake, she imagined how beautiful this would be when the leaves changed colors in the fall.

Noticing his running partner was not following anymore, Gabriel stopped and turned around. "You tired already?"

"Seriously?" Juliet rolled her eyes as the word dripped with sarcasm. She figured they were half a mile out and her breathing had increased quicker than normal in the heat and humidity. His wasn't above normal yet. Juliet wondered just how good of shape he was in. "No, I was just admiring this." She opened her arms wide to gesture to everything around her.

"You haven't seen this yet?" he asked.

"No, I haven't really done a lot of exploring since I got here. I'm jealous you grew up here, looking at things like this all the time." Juliet continued to look in every direction.

"We'll run around the lake and I'll point out everything of interest. That'll be about three miles and then back to the house. Can you make it?"

Juliet didn't even say yes. She leaned back and looked up at the man who had indirectly insulted her running abilities. She lifted her eyebrows and cocked her head to the side. Taking the hint, Gabriel turned and started running again. As they ran around, Gabriel would slow down to point out all the separate paths that led to different family members' homes. According to her guide, there was even a gym on the far side of the lake the family had built years ago. She made a metal note to go and investigate it on one of their runs.

As they approached the beach area where they would turn to go back to the guesthouse, Gabriel pointed out a rather ornate tree house. It rested in a huge water oak tree. This must be the tree Lorna's children were constantly playing in. She remembered Gabriel had pointed out the trail leading to their house a few moments before. Her inner child wanted to stop and explore the treehouse, but the adult side wanted to continue the run. The adult side won the battle this time.

Soon both of them were climbing the stairs to the guesthouse. Juliet was drenched in sweat, whereas Gabriel was barely perspiring. As they had been running, she had fallen behind in several places where the path was too narrow to run side-by-side, and had found herself admiring his well-developed calves and biceps. She had not really paid attention before to how defined they were. His clothing had inhibited her from studying the rest of his frame, but she was pretty sure the man had the body of an Olympic athlete. Standing at the top of the stairs, Juliet realized she was staring at his arms and blushed.

She turned to face the door. Without looking back at him she asked, "Would you like some water?"

"Maybe next time. I've got to go. See you later." Gabriel was down the stairs before Juliet could turn back around.

As she walked in the house, a realization smacked her in the face: the entire time they had run, she had been so preoccupied by the scenery she didn't ask a single question. She shook her head in disgust. After he had been so willing to give her answers, she had allowed herself to get caught up by the beauty and charm of everything he had pointed out. Tomorrow would be different.

Chapter 16

The violent pelting of rain against the bedroom windows woke Juliet the next morning. Shadow snuggled against her under the covers, protesting her movement by lightly digging his claws into her side. The sky illuminated with lightning followed by the angry answer of thunder. Still shaking off the effects of sleep, Juliet rolled over to check the time on her phone. As she picked it up, the phone vibrated, and a message flashed across the screen:

No running today. Be by in 10 minutes. Have to remove your sutures.

Juliet launched herself out of the bed. Shadow cried out and glared at her. Twitching his tail, he tunneled his way back under the covers. Juliet sprinted to the bathroom to wash her face and brush her teeth. She had all but forgotten about the stitches in her head. The only time she remembered was when she snagged them on the brush when fixing her hair in the mornings. Before being able to change out of her PJs, she heard a car pull into the driveway. Seconds later, there was a loud knock on the door.

She quickly made her way down the steps. As she opened the door, lighting flashed across the sky and instantly a large boom rattled the windows of the house. Reflexively, she jumped, startled by the sound. Gabriel walked into the house carrying his doctor bag. The rain had wet his long-sleeved shirt, tie, and slacks. Water droplets made his already shiny black hair glisten more.

There was a smirk across his face. "Scared of a little storm? Do you need someone to protect you?"

She looked up at him with one side of her mouth slanted downward. "Um, no. Besides, don't you think it is a bit ominous Mother Nature decided to put on that little display right when I opened the door to let you in? Maybe it's a sign. The good doctor could be a wolf in sheep's clothing."

"Hmm," he muttered in response. The smirk had vanished, and a stoic expression had appeared. "Let's get a look at that head."

Juliet picked up on the sudden change in temperament. *So sensitive. He can dish it out, but he certainly can't take it.*

She walked past Gabriel and sat down on the couch. He followed and sat down next to her. Juliet turned away from him so he could look at the back of her head. She felt his fingers touch her hair and begin to part it. There was a light tug, and then the feeling of the cold metal suture scissors against her scalp. Every few seconds, she heard the clipping of the scissors followed by a slight pulling sensation. She felt his fingers skim the back of her neck, sending a shiver down her spine. His movement stopped, and then he placed the strands of her hair back into their original positions.

Gabriel was up and off the couch before she could turn around. "Everything is healing well."

"Thank you for coming by and taking the sutures out." Juliet stood up. "Do you want something to drink or maybe breakfast?"

Gabriel started making his way towards the door. "No, thank you. I have to go in to the hospital this morning and wanted to stop by to take those out before I did."

He placed his hand on the doorknob. "I have to be in early tomorrow morning, so I figure we can run after work."

"Oh, okay. I guess I'll see you tomorrow evening then." Juliet gave him a smile but felt a twinge of disappointment inside of her.

After she closed the door, she got ready for church. This time, she drove Sabra, and the car ride was much more pleasant. Afterwards, she joined the family again for their Sunday lunch. Juliet was truly thankful they had taken her in. Sabra, Hanna, and Ava had drug her upstairs to Sabra's room after lunch to hang out. Sabra had been horrified to discover Juliet hadn't had a manicure in her life and was not overly impressed with the job she'd done painting her toenails with Secret. The two teenagers were Sabra's partners in the nail painting makeover. Juliet felt like she was at a ninth grade slumber party. Hanna seemed interested in veterinary medicine and bombarded Juliet with questions about getting into the field. Juliet was happy to answer them since she liked to encourage girls who took an interest in science. She even recommended Hanna come by and volunteer at the clinic.

The next day, Juliet sat at her desk looking at her French manicured fingernails. She smiled begrudgingly, realizing she had fun with the three girls the previous day. A knock at her door redirected her attention to one of the receptionists standing in the doorframe.

"Hey, doc, you might want to come up front." The receptionist had a huge smile on her face and almost seemed giddy.

Juliet eyed her suspiciously. "Why? What is it?"

"Oh, you'll see," was the only response the receptionist gave her before turning and walking away.

Curiosity got the best of her. Juliet followed her to the front of the clinic. There was a man she didn't recognize holding a vase full of the most beautiful red roses she had ever seen. "Are you Juliet Greene?" he asked.

"Yes."

He handed her the flowers. "These are for you."

Juliet took the flowers. "Who are they from?"

"I'll bring in the card with the next set of flowers," the deliveryman said.

"There's more?" But the man was already out the door. Juliet stared at the beautiful roses in her hands.

Gina had made her way up to the front and looked curiously between Juliet and the flowers. "Who are the flowers from?"

Juliet shrugged her shoulders. "No idea."

The man returned carrying two more vases. One was full of calla lilies and the other bright yellow daisies. He placed them on the receptionist's desk and handed Juliet a card. Without saying a word, he turned and walked out the door. Juliet handed the roses to Gina and opened the card.

I wanted to send you flowers, but I didn't know which kind you liked.
Your secret admirer.

Juliet could feel Gina peering over her shoulder reading the note. She could also feel her entire face turning bright red. Her thoughts raced and her stomach fluttered with nervousness and fear. The door swung open again and more flowers appeared in the office.

Juliet looked at the deliveryman. "How many flowers are you bringing in here?"

"A dozen vases," he replied as he handed over a bouquet filled with bird of paradise to Nicole, who had joined the growing group of people from the clinic curious as to what was going on.

Juliet pivoted, grabbed the roses from Gina, and headed back to her office. She placed the container on her desk and slumped into her chair. Putting her hands on her face she took several deep breathes. Some people would think this was romantic, but she found it very unsettling.

Who would send her all these flowers? She needed a moment to collect her thoughts. That didn't happen as Dr. Silver knocked on the office door and stepped in. Juliet only spread her fingers over her eyes, but didn't immediately remove them from her face. She wanted to stay hidden as long as possible.

"Why does my veterinary clinic look like a florist shop?" he asked, pointing out the office door.

Juliet removed her hands from her face. "I'm so sorry."

Dr. Silver gave her a sympathetic smile. "Dr. Greene – Juliet – it's fine. I'm not mad. I was just curious. We do, however, need to find a place for all these flowers till you can get them home."

"I'll get them out of the way." Juliet took another slow breath in.

Dr. Silver patted her on the shoulder. "I know it can be overwhelming, but you should be flattered. The Archon men overdo it at times when they care about someone."

Juliet looked up and turned her head. "What are you talking about?"

"Gabriel, of course. Didn't he send you all these flowers?" Dr. Silver studied her reaction.

Juliet's voice caught in her throat. She handed the note to her boss. Dr. Silver's eyes widened and his cheeks flushed. "I'm sorry; I must have been mistaken." He shifted and looked around the office, avoiding eye contact with her. "You know what, let me take care of the flowers. You just sit in here and take a few minutes."

Based upon his treatment of her thus far, she and Gabriel were just acquaintances, slowly becoming friends. He had given her no indication his intentions were anything but platonic. Could he have sent all these flowers? She thought about calling him, but decided to ask him when they went running tonight.

Juliet picked up the phone and dialed Secret.

"Hey Jules. What's up?"

"Somebody just sent a bunch of flowers to me at the clinic."

Secret's voice became a pitch higher. "Did it come with a card?"

"Yes, but it was only signed as a secret admirer."

"You don't think-"

"No, I don't think it was him," Juliet interrupted as she shuddered.

"Are you okay?"

Juliet blew out another breath. "Not really, but I will be."

Chapter 17

Dr. Silver had the receptionists place the flowers in the lobby, her office, and at the receptionist desk. Nicole and Gina had loaded several bouquets into the cab of her truck. The thought of having them throw every bouquet away did cross her mind, but would only lead to more questions about the situation.

Juliet passed Hanna and Sabra walking along the driveway to the guest house. They waved and she stopped and rolled down the window. "Hey, what are you two up to?"

"We just got off babysitting duty, so we're walking around in the peace and quiet," said Sabra.

"Could I sweet talk you two into helping me unload these flowers?" Juliet pointed to the garden sitting to her right.

Hanna and Sabra peered into the truck. They looked wide-eyed at the flowers and then to Juliet. Hanna beat Sabra in asking the question, "Who sent you all of those?"

"It's a long story, but I will be happy to share if you help me. Climb in the back and I'll give you a lift," replied Juliet.

She waited for the two girls to climb in and slowly finished driving to the house. Sabra and Hanna commented on the beauty of the flowers as they carried each vase into the house. Juliet even offered bouquets to both of them to take home. Hanna picked the yellow daisies while Sabra picked the pink tulips. Once each arrangement was positioned nicely in the house, Juliet turned to answer the question the girls had patiently been waiting to ask.

Sabra twirled one of the tulips in her hand. "Soooo, who sent you all these flowers?"

Juliet looked down at the floor as she felt the heat on her face. "I don't know. The card just said a secret admirer."

Hanna let out a small squeal and jumped up and down. "That's so romantic."

Sabra turned to Juliet and looked very serious. "Do you have any idea who it might be?"

She was not helping the already growing anxiety Juliet felt about receiving dozens of flowers from some unknown person. "Not really, but I was going to ask around."

Sabra crossed her arms in front of her. "I want you to be careful. There're a lot of creeps in this world, and you just never know."

"Well, I think it's romantic," sighed Hanna.

"You're sixteen; what do you know?" snapped Sabra.

Juliet felt the truth behind Sabra's reaction, and was relieved to hear she wasn't the only one thinking the flowers were far from romantic. A wave of anxiety clutched at her throat, and she suddenly felt like bursting into tears. Not wanting to make a scene, she thanked the girls for their help and excused herself to change for her run with Gabriel.

As she finished tying the sneakers there was a knock on the door. She went bounding down the stairs ready to get rid of some of the nervous energy pent up inside. Gabriel's smiling face greeted her as she opened the door. He sniffed the air and looked at her with a puzzled expression. "Are you wearing perfume?"

"No," Juliet said. She wanted to add, "But you always wear cologne when we run, so why is perfume so weird?", but she didn't want to embarrass him. Instead, she continued, "You must be smelling all the flowers. I didn't realize they were that potent. I guess I got use to the smell."

Gabriel leaned past her and peered into the house. She watched his eyes move from flower to flower. His expression was stoic. "Where did all the flowers come from?"

"Someone sent them to me." Juliet walked out onto the porch. She really didn't want to have this conversation right now. Especially with him.

Gabriel turned and shut the door behind him. "May I ask who sent them?"

"I don't know," she said a little too forcefully, realizing she'd secretly hoped he would take ownership of the stunt. Even though she wasn't sure if she wanted Gabriel as her 'secret admirer', knowing who had sent the flowers would be a lot better than wondering. Suddenly clouded with frustration, she snapped, "So can we just go running?" Without giving him time to answer, she darted down the steps.

"Hey, Juliet, wait!" he called after her. Within seconds he had caught up to her. "Why are you upset?"

There were no words; she just felt like an exposed nerve. Juliet just needed to run. Not talk. Her eyes pleaded with Gabriel. He seemed to pick up on her need for space and didn't push. They were halfway around the lake when Juliet felt like she could talk. She didn't want to bring up the flora currently sitting in the house. Instead, she picked their previously agreed upon topic. "So, how many wolves are there?"

Gabriel seemed completely caught off guard by the question, stumbling a few steps before regaining his stride. "Humph! Well, let me think." They continued to run. "There's around fifty living on this property."

Juliet almost stumbled herself but managed to keep her composure. There were fifty wolves running around, and she had only encountered two? "Fifty? I know you said they stay close, but that seems like way too many to keep track of."

"Well, it's one huge pack," Gabriel responded. "Like I said before, they've been here so long they understand this is their home. They don't want to leave."

Juliet still found this hard to believe, but no one around town seemed to be complaining of free-roaming predators. "Why have I only seen two of them?"

"They're not used to you. Our family has had a hand in raising every one of them. They know us. You're a stranger and they sense that. You only saw Iacobus because he ran into trouble. If he hadn't stepped in that trap, I doubt you would've known about any of this." Gabriel increased his speed just a little.

Juliet managed to keep up with him but was struggling. "Fair enough. You said they've lived here for centuries, and that Lorna and Ben took Iacobus with them on their road trip. Then there was that whole thing with your dad, the wolf whisperer. So do some of them live in the house like pets?"

Gabriel cleared his throat. "None of the wolves are pets, but, yes, they can live in our houses if they want."

Juliet's eyes widened. Once she had gotten past the initial shock of the wolves living here, she had convinced herself it was a rational situation. She didn't quite believe the set up was safe, but she assumed the Archon family had enough experience with the wolves to be taking the necessary precautions. With Gabriel's admission the wolves not only ran free but could also be invited into the families' homes, Juliet began to realize the hard reality of the situation. It was illegal to own wolves in the state, and, from what she had seen, these animals were no ordinary wolves. She had seen the results of people who kept wildlife as pets, and it made her extremely nervous. Gabriel must have sensed Juliet's uneasiness, because he stopped so abruptly she almost slammed into him. He turned so he was directly looking at her and placed one of his hands on her arm. "Look, I know you think we're crazy and this is dangerous. But none of these animals would hurt anybody in this family. They never have and they never will."

She wanted to believe him. "Gabriel, do you know how many times I've heard that from people, and the next thing I know I'm euthanizing the animal they swore would never hurt them, because it tore their face off? What about the kids? I barely trust a golden retriever around a small child. One good yank of a tail from a two year old and the kid is toast."

Gabriel took in a deep breath and his brow furrowed. Juliet watched his eyes move back and forth as she could see the internal debate going on in his head. "What if I showed you one of them and at least prove no harm would ever come to you? Would you believe me then?"

"Gabriel, I don't think that's possible—"

He put his hand up, cutting her off. "Would you believe me if I could prove it to you?"

Juliet stared at him for a moment, then nodded. "I'll try. That's all I can promise."

"Then I'll show you."

Chapter 18

Juliet paced the beach by the lake. Gabriel had told her to wait there so he could show her his proof the wolves weren't a threat. Waiting out in the open made her uncomfortable. The forest had an eerily intentional stillness offering no succor to her comfort level. She could hear the blood rushing through her ears with every increased heartbeat. A sound from behind made her nearly jump out of her skin. She whirled around to find Sterling and Cara hand in hand walking down one of the trails. They both waved as they approached her.

"Well, hello, my dear. How are you this fine evening?" greeted Sterling.

Juliet tugged on the bottom of her tee shirt. She really didn't want to insult the people who had taken her in, but she wanted to be honest. It was for their safety she needed to voice her concern. "Well, actually, I need to talk to you guys about something. You see…I mean…I really am concerned you have a bunch of wolves living among you." Okay, that was not subtle or delicate.

Sterling seemed unphased by the comment. "I see. And you were waiting here to tell us?"

"Well, no. Gabriel and I were running, and I brought up my concerns about all the wolves living here. He wanted me to wait here so he can prove everything's safe." Juliet's hands and arms were animated. It was a bad habit she'd had for years. The more excited she became, the more her arms flailed. Secret joked if she couldn't use her hands, she wouldn't be able to talk. "I would never want to offend you, since you've been so wonderful and kind to me, but no matter what Gabriel brings back here, I'm still going to think this is dangerous."

"Humph." Sterling placed his thumb and pointer finger over his jaw. "Exactly how is my son going to convince you to change your mind?"

Juliet shrugged. "Your guess is as good as mine."

Cara nodded her head past Juliet. "I think your proof has just arrived."

Juliet turned around and the hair on the back of her neck stood on end. She stepped back, pressing into Cara and Sterling, who hadn't moved. Before her was a solid black wolf. He was terrifyingly magnificent. His sleek, ebony hair reflected the setting sun's light perfectly. Though he stood not much higher than a Great Dane, he was at least eight feet in length from his nose to his tail. The wolf slowly approached and laid down about foot from her.

"What is it doing?" she whispered.

Sterling's voice was calm and even. "That's one of the alphas. I think this is the proof Gabriel wanted you to see."

"And what am I supposed to do?" her voice strained.

It was Cara who spoke this time. "I think he's waiting for you to say hello."

Juliet turned her head, wide-eyed, and looked at them. "Are you two nuts? I'm not going anywhere near it without some kind of protection. He could easily-" Her thought was cut off mid-sentence as she felt something soft and furry in the palm of her hand. She looked down to her left to see her hand resting on top of the wolf's muzzle.

Complete terror froze her in place. She willed her hand to move away from the animal, but it would not listen to her brain. The animal repositioned his head and licked the tip of her fingers. He then sat down and looked up at her. His blue eyes stared into hers.

Sterling's voice broke through the fear. "Juliet. Are you okay?"

"He licked me," were the only words she could utter.

Sterling chuckled. "Yes, he did. I think he's quite taken with you. He would no more harm you than he would one of us."

"But, this is impossible!" The wolf was leaning against her leg now. He had managed to push his head up under her left hand so her fingers were sitting between his ears. The softness of his fur tickled her skin.

"My dear Juliet, nothing is impossible." Sterling walked in front of her. He looked down at the wolf and then back at her. "As Gabriel told you, they've been part of our family for generations. I hope your mind can be at ease now."

Juliet nodded her head yes although not completely sure how to feel at the moment. She realized her hand was reflexively petting the top of the animal's head. Sterling and Cara turned and started to walk away.

"Hey, where are you guys going?" There was panic in her voice.

Sterling looked over his shoulder but kept walking. "We're going to finish our walk. You'll be fine."

Juliet wanted to yell at them to come back. The animal by her side moved away and positioned himself in front of her and looked up. There was nothing threatening in his posture – he was sitting with his right hip cocked out to the side – but Juliet got the sense he didn't want her to walk after Cara and Sterling. She looked once again at his face. There was so much expression to it. The brows above his eyes had been moving up and down while she had been talking with the Archons. His ears were constantly moving, and she suspected he was listening to every sound in the immediate area.

"Well, I don't know what you want me to do, but I'm not going to stand here all night just looking at you." She placed her right hand on her hip.

The wolf stood up and placed his head once again in her left hand. She began scratching the top of it, gently with one hand at first, then, as he leaned into her, she used both hands to ruffle his fur. She kneeled down next to him and scratched all the way down his back. A deep-throated rumbling sound came from his mouth. Juliet would characterize it as a sound of contentment. A giggle escaped her throat. Gabriel had been right, though she didn't know if she could admit it to him. The thought of Gabriel made her stop ruffling her four-legged companion's hair. Where was Gabriel? With the sudden stop of movement, her animal friend turned back to look at her and let out a whine.

"Oh, stop whining. I thought you were a big, bad alpha," she teased as she scratched behind his ears. The wolf's eyes caught her attention. He had blue eyes. Beautiful blue eyes, which was impossible. Adult wolves didn't have blue eyes unless they were hybrids of some kind. One more thing she would have to ask about. "You're absolutely gorgeous; you know that, right? It's a good thing you don't understand English or else you would be as arrogant as Gabriel." She patted his head. "Speaking of whom, it's nice he kind of abandoned me out here. I need to go find him."

Before she was able to stand up, the wolf came over and licked her on the cheek. He turned and ran back into the woods. This, by far, was the weirdest thing she had ever experienced. Totally awesome and unbelievable, but definitely weird.

Juliet made her way up the trail to the guest house where she'd call Gabriel and ask him where he'd gone. As she climbed the staircase to the front porch, he came around the corner of the house wearing a devilish grin.

She turned around on the step to face him. "You left me, quite literally, to the wolves, and you think your smile is all you need to disarm me? What happened and why do you have that stupid grin on your face?"

"I didn't leave you. I went to get you proof, and from the sound of it, you got it." He stopped on the step below where she stood, his face almost even with hers.

Juliet became very aware of just how close he was standing to her. Chill bumps went down her front arms. She placed her left foot behind her onto the next step but didn't step up. "Yes, one of your wolves came: a monstrous black one, in fact, and if it wasn't for your mom and dad I would have freaked out."

Gabriel leaned in a little closer and almost whispered. "You liked him, didn't you?"

He was too close, she couldn't think straight. She retreated up the step. "He was okay. What's his name?"

Gabriel cocked one of his eyebrows up. "Okay? He was just okay? He's an alpha. I'd think you'd appreciate him a bit more than just 'okay'. And his name is Adir."

Juliet felt a slight tinge of guilt for telling Gabriel the beautiful creature she had just interacted with was 'okay', but didn't want to show him just how wonderful she thought the experience was. She decided to ignore his question and redirect the conversation. "Adir? What does that mean?"

He came up onto the step she had just left, getting closer again to Juliet. "It's Hebrew. It means strong and mighty."

Again, she backed up a stair. "Who named him?"

He ascended the next step. "I named him. He lives in my house. He was born to be an alpha. To protect his own and hurt those who threaten anyone he cares about."

Juliet reached back with her foot to go up the next stair not realizing she had reached the top. She lost her balance and fell backwards. Gabriel's hand shot out, grabbing hers, while the other arm encircled Juliet, keeping her from falling. He pulled her up and pressed her against his body. Her face was dangerously too close to his. She put her hands on his chest to push away and discovered it was very solid. Gabriel's scent was overpowering at this distance now. His hand fell to the small of her back and as her toes touched ground again her face moved forward into the cavern between his neck and collar bone. Gabriel's jaw line ran down the right side of her head smelling her hair the entire way until their cheeks brushed. They stood silently there for a time. Juliet was the first to move.

"I need… must…go." She was trying not to breathe.

The arms around her loosened, and she retreated back to the door. Even with the distance, his smell was still too much. *I have got to figure out why he smells like this.*

"Thank you for everything. I'll see you tomorrow." She opened the door and flew in before he could respond and raced up the stairs to take a very cold shower.

Chapter 19

"I thank you for rescuing me from poker night at the house," Secret said while scouring through the pile of invitations strewn all over the coffee table. "I thought you said you were going to help me with this stuff maid of honor?"

"In a minute, I need to finish this article I found that might help me with one of my cases." Juliet peered over the veterinary journal at the pile of multicolored paper surrounding her friend.

"Let me guess, it is some disease nobody's ever heard of and cannot be pronounced by most of the population." Secret picked up a pink card with white hearts and grimaced before throwing it into the ever growing trash pile.

"I think most people have heard of diabetes, but you're right about people not being able to pronounce it correctly." She folded the journal down. "Am I snob, or does improper grammar drive you nuts?"

Secret flashed her a wicked smile. "I ain't knowin' what you is talkin' bout, but I seen somewheres on the TV that you can take classes to make you speak good."

"You're horrible," she laughed leaning closer to the table. "What's that?"

Secret lifted the invitation off the table. "Oh this is supposed to have a picture printed onto the velum and it goes over the writing on the card stock. See." She said, placing the thin material over the card stock.

"Oh, that's cool... I guess."

"Your enthusiasm is overwhelming."

"Whatever." A sudden thought occurred to her. "Hey, I never did ask you, did you ever get a report back on the trap?"

"Wow, that's random." Secret shifted in front of her. "Yeah, it came in yesterday. I meant to call you and forgot."

Juliet leaned in closer. "Well, what did it say?"

"There were no chemicals or residues anywhere on it." Secret hesitated. "Jules, it was made of one-hundred percent silver. Why would anybody make a trap like that?"

Juliet shrugged her shoulders. "Your guess is as good as mine, but, yeah, really weird."

A knock on the door suddenly interrupted the conversation. Through the window, Gabriel's silhouette was visible. Juliet opened the door, bracing herself for any scrumptious smells, only to be disappointed when there wasn't. "Hey you."

"Hey." Gabriel shifted his weight causing the wooden boards beneath him to creak.

"Hey Gabriel," shouted Secret from her perch in the living room. "Juliet, why don't you invite him in already?"

"Would you like to come in?" Warmth flooded Juliet's cheeks as she gave Secret a death look. It wasn't that she didn't want him in the house. It was the lasciviousness in Secret's voice she could do without.

Gabriel took a step backwards. "I don't want to interrupt your time with Secret."

"Oh, no, it's fine. Besides if you don't come in, she's just going to chase you down and harass you until you do." She opened the door wider.

Passing through the door frame, Gabriel quickly surveyed the scene before him. "What are you two lovely ladies up to this fine evening?"

"We're multitasking," replied Juliet. "I'm researching a case while, Martha Stewart here is in wedding planning bliss."

"And what have we done this evening for you to grace us with your *fine* presence." Secret batted her eyes at Gabriel causing Juliet to gawk at her friend in horrific amazement. Was this some bad version of *Gone with the Wind*? Secret was officially on tonight's shit list.

"I just came by to tell you I can't run with you tomorrow. I have an early meeting, and I'm scheduled until midnight," he said.

"Okay, thanks for coming by and telling me." Juliet couldn't keep herself from smiling at the man.

Gabriel looked around. "Well, I'll let you ladies get back to your evening."

"Hold on a minute." Secret extended a hand out. "I think I need a male perspective with these invitations."

"Don't you want to ask, Kevin about that," questioned Juliet.

"No, I don't. I think the good doctor here would do nicely. He seems like a man of fine culture and taste." Secret's eyes danced from Juliet to Gabriel, then focused on her friend relaying the message: *Will you shut up and let me talk.*

Oblivious to what her friend was up to Juliet settled back in her chair. Gabriel sat down on the couch next to Secret. "I'll see if I can help, but I really don't think I'm what you need."

"Oh, I think you're exactly what we need." Secret snapped her fingers. "Jules, get your nose out of that journal and pay attention. You might learn something. In fact, come over here and sit with us so you don't have to strain your neck"

Two pair of eyes watched as she moved to the couch on the opposite side of Secret. Now with the full attention of both parties the bride-to-be began displaying an assortment of textured paper of all shapes, sizes, and colors. Gabriel, gracefully nodded offering opinions when asked. This was about as interesting as watching paint dry for Juliet. She followed his lead, but to mix things up, would occasionally disagree with some of the selections.

"What about this one. I think I like this one the best." Secret held up an opal colored invitation with black embossing. It looked the same as the last 25 invitations.

"I think Officer O'Hara, is a lucky man to have a fiancée with such great taste." Gabriel looked over Secret's head and winked at Juliet who suppressed a giggle.

Secret turned to him. "You're really helpful with this stuff. It's like you've done this before."

Juliet's mouth went dry and she had the sudden urge to kick her friend. Secret's comment instantly destroyed the banter they'd built up for over the past half hour and left the room a frozen morgue. Juliet didn't want to, but looked at Gabriel. The shadow that crossed his face would have made saints cry. And then it was gone. So brief she wondered if it was ever even there. His face morphed into a statue, masking all emotion. "Thank you ladies, I think I'll leave you for tonight. My work here is finished." He rose from the couch. "I'll see myself out."

And then she knew it. His mercurial behavior toward her wasn't unwarranted. For every action, there is an equal and opposite reaction. The great carnage he'd experienced had affected him deeply. Yet he was obviously making an attempt to move past it. For this she could only admire him more.

Secret glared at Juliet and then in Gabriel's direction. Her friend's eyes reddened as she punched Juliet's leg, "Go after him."

Juliet stumbled her way to the door, but had no idea what to say. "Wait."

He paused halfway down the stair case pivoting to come back up. She suppressed the urge to wrap her arms around his neck in order to comfort him. Now what was she supposed to do? "I'm so sorry. I know it must have been difficult for you to sit there, so thanks for doing it."

"It's fine."

And like that the incident passed over into the ether. In her head, she marveled and wondered at the stuff this family was really made of. He gestured to the house with his head. "She loves looking through wedding invitations."

"Yeah, I just pray I don't have to sit through the linen selection for the reception. I think I'm missing the wedding gene that makes this stuff so much fun."

A light chuckle escaped him. "I don't think picking out linens is fun for anybody."

"I wanted to let you know Secret and I are going out into the park to search for traps next week. I wouldn't want to run into any of your *friends*." Juliet raised her eyebrows. "We also had the trap we found analyzed. It was pure silver. Weird huh?"

Gabriel's jaw clinched and his lips thinned. "Yes, very odd. Thanks for the heads up."

She twisted to leave, but stopped when he spoke again. "Isn't Hanna volunteering at the office with you?"

"Yes."

"How is she doing?"

"Hanna's great. She's really learning a lot, very attentive. Why do you ask?"

"Would you do me a favor? Take her next time you go into the park? I think she'd be very helpful if you guys accidently encountered one of the wolves."

"Sure, but I'll have to run it by Dr. Silver."

Gabriel shook his head. "It's okay. I can talk to Anthony about it."

"Oh, that's right; I forget you guys are related."

The two lingered on the steps between the lull in conversation. "Is there anything else," he asked finally breaking the awkward silence.

"I was wondering how Adir was doing?" She looked down, embarrassed about asking about a wolf.

"He's fine. Thanks for asking." His voice grew softer. "Do you want to see him again?"

"Yes. I mean…" Juliet's voice trailed off before finding her courage again. "Well…you see… it's just he's so cool. This relationship you have with them is amazing. I do this because I love animals and their variety, but nowhere in the literature is this breed mentioned. I don't know why, but the other day I felt at peace around him. Forget it. I'm being stupid."

She turned to go inside, but Gabriel reached out and touched her arm. "It's not stupid. I'm glad you feel comfortable around him."

"Really, you don't think it's dumb?"

Gabriel cocked an eyebrow upward in response. Juliet's face flushed with heat. "Oh, I forgot you live with some of them in the house."

"I'm sure you'll see him running around here soon enough." He descended down the steps. "Unfortunately, I really have to go. Tell Secret the only place in the house you can spy out of the downstairs without being seen is the place that you tried to hide when I was talking to my dad."

Juliet's mouth fell agape as Gabriel moved down the steps to the driveway. She marched back inside, mortified he'd known she was eavesdropping. Secret stood ghost white in the living room almost in tears.

"I'm so sorry, I had no idea. So what happened," she asked.

"He lost his brother and his fiancée in the same car wreck."

Secret shook her head. "I'm so stupid."

Juliet gave her a hug and told her what had transpired out on the porch leaving out the part about the wolves. Secret's world was again made whole and she returned to herself. She started shaking her head. "My friend you're so oblivious."

"To what?"

"To Mister I'm So Hot I Make Butter Melt, that's what. Why do you think he came over here tonight, and why does he spend so much time with you? He looks at you like a starved dog looks at a steak."

"We've just been running together. That's it. He's just a friend."

"Right, and I'm marrying the next President of the United States."

"NOTHING is going on between us!" Juliet shot back.

"You don't have to lie to me. I know what I just saw." Secret gathered up the stack of wedding stuff. She stopped in front of Juliet and gave her a hug. "You know I tease because I love you."

"I know."

"You need to start opening your eyes and thinking with this." Secret pointed to the left side of Juliet's chest.

"I'll try." Juliet reached over and hugged her friend. "Night, Secret. Tell Kevin, I said hi."

"Night, Jules."

Juliet walked her friend out and watched Secret pull away in her car. Instead of going back inside, she sat in the porch swing. The gentle rocking brought about a sense of solace. Tonight had been interesting. She needed time to digest it all. A goodnight's sleep would bring perspective.

A soft wrestling in the yard diverted her attention and dark figure sat down at the bottom of the steps. "Hey, Adir, what are you doing here?"

The animal just looked at her before ascending the stairs. When he got up to the landing, the great wolf pawed at her leg. She bent over and scratched him behind the ears. "I was just talking about you."

Those amazing blue eyes looked back at her. She whispered compliments and continued to scratch behind his ears, until the drowsiness began to take over. She stood up from the swing and took his face in both her hands. "You'd better go home. I bet Gabriel's wondering where you are. Thank you for coming to visit."

Adir just licked his lips and walked down the steps. He sat there for a minute and watched her move towards the door. When Juliet got inside the house, she turned and looked out the window to see if Adir was still there, but he was gone.

Chapter 20

A twig snapped under the weight of her foot as she walked between Secret and Hanna through the forest. So far, this excursion hadn't been as exciting as her last time out with Secret. The details of the last wolf had luckily continued to be kept under wraps. She had always wondered why the National Park Service hadn't investigated why the wolf she and Secret found had mysteriously disappeared. That riddle was solved when she had been talking with Sabra and Kayla this past weekend. In a conversation about the Archon family tree, she discovered Kayla's brother was Secret's boss. Though no one directly said it, she was sure Secret's report on the incident had conveniently been buried in mounds of paper work. The family seemed to have all their bases covered.

"What are you smiling about?" Secret had turned to look back at her.

Juliet dropped the curved corners of her mouth. "Nothing."

Hanna reached from behind Juliet and brushed something off her shoulder. "You had a horsefly on you."

"Thanks. Those guys hurt." She stepped over a shrub.

Juliet heard a few loud pops and the narrow tree next to her splintered. Before she knew what was happening, she had dropped to the ground with Hanna next to her. Confusion morphed into horror with the realization they were being shot at.

Looking forward, she saw that Secret was lying down on the ground also. Fear of drawing more attention prevented her from yelling to her friend. *Why are we being shot at? It's not like hunting is allowed and this could be accidental.* A sick pit grew in her stomach, with the thought that maybe these were the same poachers setting the traps.

As quickly as the firing had started, it stopped. There was complete silence. "Stay here," she whispered to Hanna.

Juliet refused to get up, so she army-crawled to her friend. Before even making it halfway, she noticed something was horribly wrong. Secret was twitching uncontrollably, her left arm tucked underneath her body and the right splayed out to the side. Juliet moved faster until she came up closer to her friend. Lying on her stomach, Secret's head was twisted to the left. Juliet could see Secret's left eye searching wildly as blood trickled out of the corner of her mouth.

Streams of tears moistened the sides of her face. "Secret," she sobbed.

Secret just looked up at Juliet but didn't say anything. Juliet wanted to touch her friend and help her but her muscles were frozen. Her mind began to shut down. Black spots covered her field of vision. Confusion and fear were battling inside of her.

"Help…me," Secret pleaded.

The words reached the back of Juliet's mind and comprehension of what Secret said refocused her thoughts. With the haze Juliet was in briefly broken, she braced herself with one arm and took out the pocketknife she had. Her hands shook uncontrollably as she managed to cut the straps to the backpack Secret wore and lifted it off. There were no signs of blood or bullet wounds. For a few small, glimmering seconds there was a sense of hope Juliet was wrong and her friend had not been shot. Her stomach lurched as she realized she must turn her friend over to check the front.

"Okay, I'm going to turn you over now. This might hurt a little." Juliet sat up and rolled Secret over as gently as she could.

The bile rose up from her stomach, and Juliet could not keep it inside. She turned and threw up. Wiping her mouth with the back of her hand she started breathing quickly trying to get oxygen into her lungs. She blinked desperately trying to keep her vision focused. After scanning Secret's injuries, she had to look away to prevent from vomiting again. Gathering every ounce of strength left, she twisted back to her friend. She focused on Secret's face mustering up the strength to look below her neck. Stopping at the first signs of blood soaking Secret's olive green uniform, she looked up in the air and took several breathes before returning to the bullet hole in the right side of the chest. Her eyes traveled down and discovered another gaping hole in the center of her abdomen with blood welling up from it. The brief moment of clarity Juliet had earlier came crashing down around her.

"It...hurts," the words gurgled out of Secret.

"Shhh, don't talk. We are going to get you some help." The tears were trickling down the side of her face.

By this time, Hanna had crawled over next to the two friends. "Oh, shit!" The teenager sat up next to Juliet and immediately put her hands over the two holes in Secret and applied pressure. She began speaking to Juliet, but the words were incoherent. To her the girl sounded like a babbling baby.

When Juliet didn't respond to something she'd said, Hanna looked at her. "Dr. Greene, I don't know what to do. Tell me, please."

The panic in Hanna's voice churned through Juliet's head. Her thoughts came slowly, like molasses in the winter. "Gauze. We need to place gauze over the wounds."

Mechanically, Juliet took off her backpack and dug through it until she found the gauze. She handed it to

Hanna who placed a healthy quantity of the squares over each wound and applied pressure. The squares saturated with blood almost immediately. Hanna changed them out, dropping the completely red ones next to Juliet in the ground. Juliet focused on the blood dripping from the sponges mixing with dirt to form a tar-colored mud.

"We need to get her to the hospital. Fast. Do you think you can help me carry her?" Juliet reached over to change out another of the blood-soaked gauzes. She began applying pressure to the chest wound while Hanna kept her hands on the abdominal wound.

Hanna nodded yes. Juliet looked at Secret. "Secret, we are going to pick you up, and it's probably going to hurt, but we've gotta do it, okay?"

Secret nodded and closed her eyes. Hanna helped put the medical bag back on Juliet's shoulders then the two of them scooped Secret up while Juliet wished there was a third person to continue to keep pressure on the wounds. Secret moaned, causing Juliet to wince. They moved as fast as they could back to the truck. Luckily, it was less than a quarter mile away. She decided Hanna would drive to the hospital and call 9-1-1 on the way. Hopefully, they could get a police escort to the hospital or meet an ambulance half way. Juliet would be in the back with Secret. They got Secret inside the bed and Juliet was at least thankful the topper was still on the back to shield them from the wind.

Juliet put the keys in Hanna's hand with the gravest look she could muster. "The pedal never leaves the floor unless you're turning."

Hanna gave her hand a squeeze to say she was on board. Before Hanna even got the truck started, Juliet wrapped cargo straps around both of Secrets forearms and hands and put the hooks into the bed's tie-downs. She pulled the slack out of the straps and locked them down. Hanna floored the truck almost throwing Juliet out the back. She used the last cargo strap to lash her own torso to the bed.

Juliet worked to quickly pressure wrap Secret's abdominal wound and then compression bandaged the thoracic wound. Secret screamed as she swaddled the holes and the sound was too much for her to take.

"The police are meeting us at the highway" Hanna yelled back through the opening from the front to the back.

Juliet peered back at Secret who was staring back at her but not speaking. Her breathing was labored, and Juliet knew she was in a great deal of pain. She dug out her phone, hit one of the numbers in her contact list, and put it on speaker.

"Please pick up. Please pick up. Please pick up," she recited as the phone rang.

"Hello?"

"Secret's been shot, and we're coming to the hospital!" She was screaming at the phone.

"Juliet? I don't know what you're saying. I need you to calm down and take a deep breath. Tell me again, but slowly." Gabriel's voice was steady.

"Secret's been shot, but I think I've controlled the bleeding. We're coming to the hospital," Juliet cried, and she looked down at her friend who was moaning.

"It's going to be okay. I'm going to talk you through this. What happened and where are you?"

"We were in the park looking for traps. Somebody shot at us! Secret was shot twice." Juliet was breathing between every other word, and she was feeling lightheaded. Her words were coming too quickly.

"I can hear you hyperventilating. You're going to pass out if you don't get yourself under control. Deep breaths, Juliet."

She realized Secrets eyes were level with hers in the back of the truck as Secret turned her head to look at her.

It was a soft and distant look that shattered her heart. It was too much. *Why would someone have done this to three women in the National Park? Who was capable of such random destruction?*

She took a deep breathe in and out. "Again," Gabriel directed.

Juliet inhaled again, trying to focus her thoughts. With each breath a stronger presence of mind came to her. The faintness subsided along with the uncontrollable tears.

"Where is she shot?"

"On the right side of her chest and in her abdomen." Secret started coughing and more blood came up out of her mouth. "She's coughing up blood."

"Are you applying pressure to the wounds?"

"I've got pressure bandages on the wounds. I don't know what else to do." Juliet heard the wail of a siren behind them and then saw a sheriff's vehicle go around them. "The police are here."

"Good, you have an escort, so you'll be here soon. I'm going to hang up now. I'll see you in a few minutes."

Juliet hung up the phone but held onto it like it was some kind of security blanket. Secret moved her hand to touch her friend on the arm. Juliet grabbed her hand and squeezed it. "You're going to be alright. We'll be there soon, and Gabriel will fix you, you'll see."

"You were...always a...bad liar," Secret gasped. More blood trickled down the side of her mouth.

"Please don't die on me," Juliet pleaded. The tears had started flowing again. "I need somebody to take care of me. I can't do this without you."

"Worry...too...much." Secret's eyes were starting to close.

"Hey. Hey. Hey." Juliet patted the side of Secret's face trying to wake her. Secret didn't open her eyes but continued to breath. Guilt flooded Juliet's veins, and it felt like her heart was being ripped out of her chest. She bent over her friend, pressing her forehead against Secret's. "I'm so sorry, Secret. I love you so much."

Juliet was so concentrated on Secret, she hadn't noticed the truck had stopped until the tailgate flew open. Gabriel and a huge medical team were standing there. They quickly and efficiently got Secret out of the truck onto a hospital gurney. Gabriel turned back at Juliet. She was on her knees in the bed of the truck. She could only mouth, "Please" and then slumped down in the truck like a bloody ragdoll.

Gabriel focused his attention and began giving orders as they wheeled Secret through the doors of the emergency room. A nurse came to the truck as Hanna walked around the vehicle. With her friend out of sight and safely in Gabriel's skilled hands, Juliet began to shake.

The nurse climbed in and put her arm around Juliet. "Come inside, let's get you looked at."

"I need to call my mom," said Hanna as she pulled out her phone and stepped away.

The police officer that had escorted them to the hospital came over to Juliet. "Is there anybody we need to contact?"

Juliet's voice was barely a whisper. "Kevin O'Hara, he's her fiancé."

"I'll let him know." The officer placed his hand on her shoulder and squeezed it.

The nurse wheeled Juliet inside and got her into one of the hospital beds in the emergency room. "Juliet, Dr. Archon told me to take good care of you. My name's Betsey. I was one of the nurses that cared for you when he brought you in after the fire." She brought over a thermometer. "Let's get your vitals."

Betsey checked her temperature, pulse, respiration, and blood pressure. She worked quickly, all the while making casual conversation. "You were very brave, dear. It takes a lot of strength to do what you did."

She looked down and saw that she was smeared in her friend's blood. Juliet just looked at Betsey and pointed at her clothes. "There's blood on me."

"Yes, child, there is. Let's get you cleaned up and get you something to drink." Betsey went out of the room and returned shortly with a pair of scrubs. "Let me help you get those clothes off."

Like a child that needed to be changed, Juliet allowed the nurse to take the blood-soaked clothes off. Betsey helped her into the scrubs before leading Juliet over to the sink to wash her hands and face. Her body felt like it had been injected with Novocain, as the numbness inside Juliet spread. She could barely feel anything touching her. There was a vague awareness of Betsey handing her something to drink before escorting her down to a lounge. The nurse had Juliet sit down on a couch and placed a thin hospital blanket over her lap.

"Your vital signs are normal, and I have no reason to keep you in the ER. I don't think Dr. Archon would want you waiting in the surgical lounge, so this is one of the doctor's lounges. I'll keep checking on you, and I'll even bring your friend down here when she's done with the officer. Is there anybody I can call?" Betsey asked.

Juliet shook her head no. She wanted very much to be alone so she could fall apart in peace. The older woman gave her a sympathetic smile and left. The room was quiet except of the hum for the fluorescent lights above. The tears that came so freely just minutes before were now reclusive. She closed her eyes, wishing the nightmare would end. How had they gotten here?

The lounge door opened, and in walked Kevin. He was not wearing his work clothes, but was dressed in jeans and a tee shirt. Kevin stared down at her. His eyes were rimed in red. Juliet could not find the words to speak to him.

"Have you called her mom yet?" Kevin asked.

"No," was all that Juliet managed to say.

"I'll do it," Kevin whispered. He swung open the lounge door, causing it to bang against the wall and stormed out.

The room suddenly felt too small. Juliet got up and roamed the hallways, searching for a place to escape and hide from the world. Juliet passed rooms with beeping machines, saw orderlies rolling people in beds and wheelchairs down the hall, and a few of the hospital staff rushed passed her without so much as a second glance. She came to a room with a small plaque on the outside that simply read: CHAPEL. Juliet opened the door and peered inside. It was empty. Taking a few more steps inside, she allowed her eyes to adjust to the dimly lit space. Several small pews took up most of the room in front of an altar. Towards the back, there was a table that contained small candles. Making her way down the aisle, she sat down on one of the front pews. The quiet was peaceful and started to ease her over-stimulated nerves.

Closing her eyes, she let her thoughts form words for a prayer. She prayed for her friend to live, for Gabriel to fix Secret's broken body, for strength, but mostly she prayed for help. Normally, she would feel peace after doing this, but that feeling was absent. The numbness inside still enveloped her spirit. Devoid of all thought and feeling, she stared at the wooden cross on the altar. Juliet felt someone sit down next to her but did not turn to see who it was.

"Juliet, honey, everybody's been looking for you." Lorna's voice broke through the fog.

"Okay," Juliet said as she continued to look forward.

Lorna touched the hair that had fallen out of Juliet's ponytail and tucked it behind her ear. "Are you alright?"

"No."

Lorna hesitated. "Do you want to talk about it?"

"No."

They continued to sit in silence. Lorna pulled out her phone and her fingers tapped rapidly on the screen. "I'm just going to let everybody know I found you and you're safe." A little whoosh sound emitted from the speaker, and then Lorna put the phone away.

Still continuing her gaze forward, Juliet asked, "Why are you here?"

"I'm a lawyer for the hospital, remember? I have an office on the second floor," Lorna replied.

"I know. I mean, why are you here with me?" Juliet's voice was monotone.

"The staff was alerted when you went missing from the doctor's lounge. Due to the circumstances of what happened today, there was fear something may have happened to you. We wanted to find you and make sure you were safe." Lorna spoke to her as if she was a child needing to be soothed. "I had a feeling you might come here. I don't know you that well, but from what I've gathered, we seem a lot alike." Lorna shifted. "As for why I'm sitting here with you, I will sit here in silence until you need something else. I know you need your space, but you don't need to be alone," she added.

There was a light knock on the chapel door, and Lorna rose up and went to open it. She went outside and shortly came back in. Sitting back down next to Juliet, Lorna asked, "Do you know who we can contact for Secret's family?"

Juliet turned to face Gabriel's sister. "Why? What's happened?"

"I don't know. Someone came to tell me Gabriel's out of surgery, and he needs to speak with Secret's family. Do you have their phone number?" Lorna's eyes darted around the room, avoiding direct eye contact with Juliet.

"There's just her mother and Kevin. I have her mom's number in my phone. I'll have to go back to the lounge to get it." Juliet got up and walked past her. The knot that had already formed in her stomach grew larger and more painful. She had no idea what time it was, but it seemed way too early for Gabriel to be finished with surgery. With every step down the hall, the pain got worse until she could barely stand it. When they entered the lounge, Hanna, Kayla, and Kevin were there sitting at the table in the center of the room. Kayla had her arm around her daughter. Kevin was staring at his phone. He got up and crossed over to Juliet, placing her phone in her hand. "I thought you might need this. I found it lying on the couch when we came back."

Juliet scrolled through her contact list until she came to the information for Secret's mother. She showed the number to Lorna who pulled out her phone and started texting. Juliet sat again on the couch. Kevin went to sit by her, but Juliet shifted away. Her body was on sensory overload, and she was desperate not to have a complete melt down. A hug would send her over the edge.

Kevin was saying something, but Juliet could not focus on his words. Lorna had taken a seat over in the corner of the lounge, and her eyes flickered between all four people and the door. Kevin's voice cut off, and Juliet became aware that all the people in the room had directed their attention to the doorway. Gabriel walked in, and everyone except Juliet stood up. Juliet saw his face and immediately knew the words he was about to speak. The expression he wore was the same one she had donned many times when talking with clients. A look of dread mixed with determination because the kind of news you were about to give would change the lives of others forever. That what you had to say must be told, but you hated to be the one to have to tell them there was more bad news than good. The pain Juliet felt inside was unbearable. She wanted to be wrong. Maybe Secret was alive but in critical condition. As Gabriel spoke to Kevin, he used words like "inoperable repair", "too severe", and "did everything we could". With every word he spoke, a piece inside Juliet felt like it was dying. Never once did Gabriel glance in Juliet's direction; his eyes locked on Kevin. "I'm sorry. Secret is dead."

Kevin stormed out of the room. Gabriel looked at his family, turned his back to Juliet and exited the room. Juliet sat still. She couldn't breathe. It felt like something was stabbing her in the heart. Her best friend was gone; she'd failed when Secret needed her the most. All she wanted to do was curl up in a fetal position on the couch, but was overcome with the need to get as far away from this place of death. Not caring about where she ended up, Juliet sprinted out of the room and down the hallway until she burst through a door to the outside. There was a parking lot ahead and she recognized the Park Service truck parked one row away. Juliet ran over to the truck, opened the cab door, and hoisted herself inside. There was Secret's ranger jacket lying across the seat, and Juliet grabbed the rumpled material, covered her mouth with it, and began to scream.

Chapter 21

Secret's death tore a hole through her soul she knew would never be filled. The day after, Juliet had driven to Lexington to be with Secret's mother. Juliet held her as the woman broke down in her arms, clinging to Juliet for support and comfort. Juliet took over as the role of caretaker and did everything possible to help out. Pushing down her own sorrow, she felt an overwhelming need to be strong for everyone else. She'd failed her best friend and owed her this.

For the next few days, Juliet helped Secret's mother make funeral arrangements, and ran errands around town so she didn't have to leave the house. Juliet stood by her side during the visitation, doting on her and receiving condolences from other mourners.

The anger Kevin had shown at the hospital turned into uncontrollable sorrow by the funeral. He arrived a weeping mess in Lexington the day after Juliet. There were several times Kevin clung to her as he fell apart. Plagued by guilt, his sobs magnified everything. Battling her own demons, she wasn't prepared to comfort him.

She allowed people to hug her whilst they cried. She silently consoled them, but something was taking place inside her. Something she consciously suppressed, but it was happening all the same. When she was asked to give the eulogy, Juliet did so without hesitation. She stood at the gravesite and watched Secret's casket being lowered into the ground. Juliet did all this without shedding a tear.

As the casket touched down, she filled her chest with air for the first time in days. The air tasted different. It wasn't as sweet, and carried a tinge of musk if she didn't know better. A series of misfortunate events strung over a significant period of time. When she opened her eyes and exhaled, whatever change that had been at work inside was finished. The veil was drawn. Life had lost a bit of its taste, the sun would never shine as bright.

A few days after the funeral, Kevin came by the clinic to check on her. Sitting in her office eating the Chinese he had brought the two of them for lunch, he asked how she was holding up. Juliet gave him a weak smile and continued to pick at the sweet and sour chicken. Kevin talked about the memories he had of Secret and all the struggles he was going through right now. Juliet had never been so thankful to have an emergency come in the door. She excused herself to go tend the dog that had been hit by a car.

Over the next week, Kevin came by the clinic or called her on her phone several times a day. Juliet listened as best she could, but he only exacerbated the remaining guilt inside her. She wanted to beg Kevin for forgiveness, but could not bring herself to do it. To make matters worse, he didn't blame her, but instead was grateful for everything she'd done to try and save Secret. If only he'd known how she'd faltered in the forest.

One Saturday, Kevin texted her asking if he could come over. She sent him the directions and got ready. When she opened the door to let him in, the sadness on his face was too much. "Hey, I'm sorry to drop by, but I just needed to talk with somebody."

"Come in." Juliet opened to the door wider for him to enter.

Kevin entered the house and immediately went to the couch, where he slunk down on the cushions. Juliet joined him, but not before she grabbed a box of tissues. "What's up?"

Kevin stared down at the floor. She could see the muscles in his face twitching. "The house is so lonely without her."

Juliet placed a hand on Kevin's back. "I know, and I'm sorry."

"I was thinking." Kevin looked up at her. "You need a place to live, and I hate being in that house alone. I thought maybe you would want to move into the spare bedroom."

That was not what Juliet had expected to hear. Her hand slid off his back. It took her a few seconds to think of a tactful way to respond. "I really appreciate the offer, but I can't, at least not right now."

"I get it." Kevin shrugged. "I just thought it might help both of us." Kevin stood up. "I won't keep you from your day. I'll see you around."

Juliet stood. Kevin leaned in and embraced her. She patted him on the back while returning the hug. Kevin started to pull away and then stopped. He looked at her with a sudden intensity, leaned in, and kissed her. A pit formed in her stomach while her inner voice screamed this was wrong. She pushed him away.

"I think you should leave," she said.

"I'm sorry. I shouldn't have done that," stammered Kevin.

Juliet walked to the door and opened it. With his head dropped, Kevin pushed past her and went down the stairs. Walking out onto the porch, she watched his truck slowly reverse down the gravel driveway. Juliet took a long deep breathe in and blew it out. A sudden movement caused her to notice two pairs of blue eyes looking out from the woods. Juliet walked down the steps and approached the tree line. The wolf she had first seen sleeping on her porch stepped out of the covering. On her runs with Gabriel before the shooting, she had learned the animal's name was Ardent.

When Ardent was a few feet from her, he turned around to look back at the other wolf still in the trees. By now Juliet's eyes had focused on the remaining animal and could see it was Adir. "Hey, big fella. I haven't seen you in a few weeks. Are you checking up on me?"

Adir backed up into the woods, letting the shade of the forest canopy consume him in the darkness. A howl emanated from the same region causing Ardent to turn around and go bounding into the woodland. Saddened they had left, Juliet turned and went back inside.

Later that morning, Sabra stopped by to check on her and to bring over some fresh fruit salad. She saw that Juliet was halfway through her movie and asked to join her. Juliet agreed after Sabra promised to watch in silence. When the movie was over, Sabra got up and left but not before inviting Juliet to join her for dinner with Sterling and Cara. Sabra wasn't insistent or demanding but made a simple, kind gesture. Juliet appreciated that. These were remarkable people she'd somehow found herself amongst.

She ended up joining them that evening, and other than asking her how she was doing, the family didn't pry about her emotional wellbeing. In fact, they filled the majority of the conversation with the simple things that had been occurring in their lives. Walking back to the guesthouse, it dawned on her how much she missed being around a loving family that could support her during this time.

Her parents and brother had come down for Secret's funeral where they'd met Rev. and Mrs. Archon, who, much to the surprise of Juliet, had attended. The two couples had seemed to hit it off with each other from what Juliet had gathered talking with her parents later on. Too preoccupied with her own thoughts at the time, she had left the two families to talk with each other. Mr. Greene had commented to his daughter he was worried about her but grateful she was staying with such a wonderful family. One night while eating dinner at the Rev. and Mrs. Archon's house, her parents called them. She discovered the two families had exchanged phone numbers, and Juliet suspected, were communicating to each other about her grieving process.

As the weeks went by, Juliet was thankful for the Archon family. In their own ways, they showed her the kindness and support she desperately needed but was too stubborn to ask. Each day they managed to get Juliet to join them in some activity, whether it was something as simple as helping Cara in her garden to Sunday family lunches or just stopping by to say hello. In the weeks following the funeral, she became increasingly close to several of the Archon women but especially Sabra and Lorna.

Sabra had a lightheartedness typical of most college students. At times Juliet felt like Sabra's personal doll, as she would come over and make her try on new clothes or fix her hair. Sometimes she was joined by Hanna, Ava, or both girls. Juliet would listen to them talk for hours about the upcoming school year, their plans for the future, boys they liked. These simple, optimistic views of life gave her a short escape from the darkness that had consumed her.

Being a working mom, Lorna brought a mature, calming demeanor to her interactions with Juliet. When she discovered Juliet was an avid reader, Lorna lent her some of her books. Lorna would invite Juliet over to sit on her porch while the children played in the yard to discuss the latest novel with its plot twists and characters. She would ask Juliet how work was going and about interesting cases she may have had. One morning, Lorna appeared on Juliet's doorstep. When Juliet walked out on the porch to greet her, Lorna turned and pointed to the front yard. Iacobus, who she had not seen for two months, was sitting in the grass. Lorna called the animal to her, and he came bounding up the stairs. Juliet bent down to get a closer look at him. Other than a band of missing fur around his front leg where the trap had been wrapped around, he looked perfectly fine. She was grateful to Lorna for finally letting her see Iacobus, but the memory of who Juliet was with during their encounter with the animal brought back the sadness that had momentarily been put aside.

In fact, the pain eased when she was around any member of the Archon family and worsened when alone with her thoughts. At night she would barely sleep, tossing and turning in bed. Shadow had gotten so annoyed with her thrashing he had permanently taken up residence in one of the other bedrooms. Unable to sleep, she would get up in the mornings and run until her legs gave out or her lungs felt like they were on fire. There were several mornings she had collapsed on the ground, dry heaving stomach acid. Despite all this, the tears she longed to spill out never came.

The morning after Kevin had stopped by, she heard something following her as she ran. Turning her head, she saw Adir running several feet behind her. Eventually, he increased his speed so as to run next to her. When she dropped to the ground in exhaustion the black wolf circled her and whined. He sat next to her until her breathing returned to normal. She ran her fingers through his soft fur, letting her blood pressure settle. This ritual was repeated every morning. His presence was a relief to her strained mental state but was a reminder of the one person she had not seen since that awful day in the hospital.

Even with her attending several Archon family activities, Gabriel's presence had been noticeably absent. Juliet was a mix of emotions about this. Initially, consumed with grief and anger, she wanted to blame anyone but herself. She was upset Gabriel hadn't saved Secret. He was the doctor. He was supposed to save her best friend.

However, animosity turned into guilt as she inwardly came to blame herself for everything that happened to her friend. She hadn't done enough. If she had been thinking clearly she could have gotten Secret to him in better shape. It was her fault, not his. Juliet realized Gabriel was probably avoiding her because he was ashamed of how she had handled the situation. She was the weak one. He was probably disgusted with her.

Everything and everyone had changed around her. She felt like a shell of her former self, going through the routines of day-to-day life. The guilt that was felt the day of her friend's death would not abate with time, but instead grew with each passing day.

These were the thoughts filling her mind as she ran next to Adir one morning in mid-August, exactly one month after the shooting. The physical pain pushed her body to hit a tipping point. Her legs gave out, and she stumbled to the ground. Lying on the dirt path, the emotions that had been held inside for a month began to manifest. The dam holding back the tears burst and spilled freely over her eyelids. The anguished sobs wretched out from the depths of her soul.

Through her cries she heard Adir whining. She lifted her face to see the giant animal pacing back and forth on the path. He came over and started licking the tears flowing down her cheeks. He continued to make high-pitched sounds and pawed at her back. Slowly, she pushed herself off the ground into an upright position and curled her knees into her chest. She wrapped her arms around her legs, hugging herself. Juliet did not know how long she sat there rocking and crying. Mucus was running out of her nose and down her face. She kept wiping it on her tee-shirt's sleeve but couldn't keep up.

Adir nuzzled his way under her arm so his head was between it and her knees. Juliet started to pat the top of his head then began to scratch behind his ears. He pushed forward so her arm now draped around his massive chest, and she was forced to shift so as to not fall backwards. With her knees now underneath her, Adir placed the front part of his body on her lap. She wrapped her arms around him and buried her face into his fur, continuing to cry. Adir's silky pelt tickled the inside of her nose, resulting in a series of sneezes. Snot flew out of her nostrils and onto the wolf who promptly turned and gave her an indignant look. Despite everything, Juliet giggled.

This momentary reprieve made her realize the sad state she was in. Through puffy eyes, she looked down to see her entire body was covered in dirt and leaves. Some of the cuts on her arms and legs were now bleeding. She saw her sleeve was soaked in snot and tears. Strands of hair had fallen out of the ponytail and were stuck to the sides of her face. Pushing against Adir, she attempted to get up. The great beast looked back and then moved away, allowing her to stand. Using her hands, she wiped the remaining tears away and started walking back towards the house. Adir trotted by her side and positioned himself so her hand was once again resting on his head. He followed her to the house and climbed up the steps where he turned around and sat on the porch as she went inside. When Juliet emerged an hour later to go to work, he was still sitting in the same position as if on guard. Only when she got into the truck did he leave and disappear into the woods.

That evening she was driving home from the clinic thinking about the events of that day. The temporary peace felt by expressing her emotions that morning had been side tracked at the clinic. Dr. Silver had called her into his office to inform her the veterinary wildlife program at the National Park, which had been temporarily suspended after the shooting, had officially been cancelled. This was devastating information. Something so important had again been taken away. Juliet's mind went back to the shooting, replaying each minute in slow motion, causing her to, once again, blame herself for everything. In her mind, she was now responsible for the cancellation of a program Dr. Silver had created.

A debate rose up inside her whether or not to quit the practice and start over somewhere else. Since living here, nothing but chaos and tragedy had befallen her. Between being attacked herself, having her house burn down, Secret being killed, and now the program had been cancelled, Juliet didn't know if she should stay here. The internal argument had her so distracted she didn't realize she'd missed the turn to her house until the vehicle came to a dead end. The house at the end of the road was a large, modern structure of metal, wood, and enormous sheets of glass, which she suspected were windows. Juliet pulled into the driveway to turn around and head back when she noticed Gabriel's black car parked near the front door. She flinched at the realization this was his house.

Shifting the car into reverse, Juliet wanted to escape before Gabriel noticed her. As her foot was about to press the accelerator, the front door opened, and Gabriel stepped out. He looked at Juliet's truck, and because of the distance, she couldn't tell what his expression was. He walked down the steps and came towards her vehicle. Too late to leave without making the situation more awkward, Juliet threw the truck into park.

Gabriel approached with a blank expression on his face. Juliet rolled down the window. "Hey," she said softly, refusing to look him in the eyes.

"Hey," he replied, lacking his normal commanding tone.

Juliet looked at the steering wheel. "I'm sorry. I was lost in thought and wasn't paying attention. I didn't know you lived up here. I didn't mean to bother you. I'm leaving." Her voice was quivering.

"Juliet," his voice was tender and filled with concern. "Are you okay?"

Not here and not now, she thought to herself. She was so drained and work was the last piece of string keeping her together. It too had now broke. Before she could stop it, a tear escaped and ran down her face. That tear was quickly chased by another and then another.

Before she knew it, the door was open, and Gabriel placed a hand on her shoulder. "Hey, why don't you turn off the truck?" His tone was soft.

Juliet reached for the ignition and turned the key causing the engine to stop. She placed her head on top of her arms that were crossed over the steering wheel and sobbed uncontrollably. Feeling the tightness of the seat belt across her chest, she undid it with one hand, not bothering to lift her head. The seat belt whipped across her chest sending the metal buckle into her left armpit.

Gabriel stood next to the open door with one of his hands placed on the center of her back. "Breathe. I know you need to let it out, but you've got to breathe."

Lifting up her head, she took a long, ragged breath in. The ache inside was unbearable. It felt like she was suffocating while at the same time being poked with a thousand needles. The pain needed to stop. At this moment she needed someone to tell her it was okay. Someone to say they would be there for her. Juliet thought of all the time she had spent comforting others during the funeral when she was the one that needed the support. The weeks after not allowing herself to mourn. The anger and the guilt over losing her friend, and Kevin's need to be close to her ending with the kiss. All these pent-up emotions came crashing down. She turned toward Gabriel, her knees pressed up against his chest, and bent over to put her head on his shoulder where she continued to cry. Leaning into him, her weight shifted, and she slid out of the truck, pressed her face into his chest, and continued to weep. His arms encircled her like a warm, soft blanket that could keep her safe from the outside world. Just as she had felt this morning with Adir, she felt secure and protected.

"Let's get you inside and find something to eat." Gabriel's words were heavy with worry.

Still crying, Juliet nodded her head yes and allowed him to guide her to his house. Inside, he led her over to an oversized leather couch where she sat. Disappearing for a moment, he returned with a box of Kleenex. Juliet accepted them and blew her nose before it started running out of control. Gabriel walked into the kitchen and returned with a glass of water, which he placed on the coffee table next to her.

"Can I get you something else?" he asked.

She shook her head no, still unable to talk without blubbering. Her insecurity from the belief he perceived her as weak for not saving Secret brought on a new wave of tears. She covered her face with her hands trying to conceal the shame. Juliet felt the weight of his body cause the couch cushion to sink. Once again, he held her in his protective embrace, patting her back with one of his hands.

"I'm sorry, I caused this." There was a strain in his voice.

The statement caught her attention, and she managed an audible "it's all my fault" before breaking down even more. Gabriel broke away from her and leaned back, still holding her shoulders. He turned so that he could look directly at her. "Don't blame yourself for what happened to Secret." His face was flushed.

"But she's…dead…because of…me," she wailed and tried to hide her face from him with her hands.

Gabriel took her hands in his. "Look at me." When she refused, he repeated his words. "Juliet, please look at me."

She gradually brought her face up to meet his, but diverted her eyes, not having the courage to look into his. "Secret is not dead because of you. Someone shot her. You're not taught to deal with something like that. I don't care how great a veterinarian you are; unless you've been trained to deal with that situation and, even then, to ask you to save your best friend is impossible."

Using the tissue, she dabbed the tears from her face. Taking a deep, staggered breath in, Juliet managed to compose herself enough to talk. "I should've tried harder. I froze out there. What kind of friend am I?"

"You're the kind of friend who got Secret to the hospital and was with her when she needed you the most."

"But it wasn't enough." A lump formed in Juliet's throat.

"I am going to keep saying this until you believe me: it is not your fault." Determination resounded in his words.

"So, you haven't been avoiding me because you think I was pathetic out there? You aren't disgusted by me?" Juliet spoke softly; fearful of the answer he might give.

"Is that what you think?" He moved his face so he could look into her eyes. "I've never thought that. I just told you without training it was impossible for you to do anything more. This is a horrible situation. Lorna and Sabra have both told me how strong you've been." Gabriel looked down at the floor. "I haven't been around, because I didn't think you wanted to see me. This is my fault."

A rush of air blew out of Juliet's mouth. "You couldn't have saved her with what happened. I remember what you told Kevin. The damage was too severe. Stop blaming yourself."

Gabriel let go of her hands and ran his fingers through his hair. He furrowed his brow and got up off the couch, pacing around the room. She watched him walk back and forth a few times before he sat back down on the couch facing her.

"I need to tell you something," he said with conviction.

"Okay." Juliet blew her nose.

He took her hands in his again. "You see, what I'm about to tell you is going to seem impossible. In fact, you're going to think I'm crazy," he paused, looking at her face for any signs of a reaction. Evidently satisfied by what he saw, Gabriel continued, "I just need to tell you the truth, and I'm afraid when you hear it you'll hate me forever."

Gabriel looked so torn with guilt Juliet was becoming concerned for him. She felt like he was the one who now needed to be comforted. Before she could react or he could say anything else, his cell phone started ringing.

He once again let go of her hands and got up to walk over to the device. Looking at the screen, he turned back to face her. "I'm sorry. I need to take this."

Gabriel answered the phone, walked over to a bookshelf, and appeared to disappear into it. Curious, Juliet walked over to the area where Gabriel had just vanished. Now that she wasn't crying, she could appreciate the inside of his house. The large main room was completely open with two-story ceilings. The space was made up of three different areas: the family room, the kitchen, and then what Juliet would best describe as a study. The front and back walls of the house were floor-to-ceiling glass with the two interior opaque sidewalls. The kitchen took up most of the left side of the room. It was the definition of sophistication with its stainless steel appliances, dark wood cabinets, and black granite countertops. To the right of the kitchen was the family room, which was decorated with leather and dark wooden tones. A gargantuan stone fireplace lined the center of the right wall and extended to the ceiling. The rest of the walls on both sides were occupied with bookshelves filled with thousands of books. Looking closer, the shelves had been arranged so that it gave the illusion of being one solid wall. When she reached out to where Gabriel had been she discovered there was actually a space leading to a hallway.

Not wanting to pry, Juliet decided to save the hallway inspection. She instead focused her attention on the remaining study area. This was at the very back of the room. In the center of this space was a black baby grand piano. Juliet walked over and tickled the piano keys while looking out through the giant panes of glass. The forest surrounded the house, and the glass was so translucent, it almost felt as if there was no separation between the inside and the elements.

"Do you play?"

His voice came from behind her, and Juliet jumped. Catching her breath, she turned around to face Gabriel. "I did, but I haven't touched a piano since I got into vet school. I miss it."

"You could come play here anytime you like." He stepped up to the keyboard and started playing a soft melody. Juliet recognized it as something from Brahms but couldn't place the title. "I started playing when I was a child. I don't know what I would do if I couldn't." After a few more chords, he stopped playing. "I think it's time you were fed."

"No, I really should go." Juliet went to step past him, but he blocked her way.

"Please, let me make you dinner. I'm worried about you, and it would make me feel better. I can tell you haven't been eating much. You and I both know it's unhealthy. Please…stay." There was no demand in his tone but a simple request.

He was right. Juliet had lost weight over the past month. Her voracious appetite was barely above nonexistent. What little food she was able to consume caused such pain she had to space out meals. Her clothes had become looser. Juliet had started drinking Ensure to get some kind of calories into her system.

"I'll stay and eat with you, but then I really should get home." She managed a small smile.

Gabriel turned and walked towards the kitchen and Juliet followed. He motioned for her to take a seat on one of the bar stools behind the countertop. She sat and watched him pull out some cookware and then make his way to the refrigerator where he pulled out a bunch of vegetables. After he washed them, he started slicing them on a cutting board. Juliet observed the precision of his hands with the kitchen knife. She wondered what it would be like to watch him in surgery. He threw everything into a skillet and started cooking.

"What were you going to tell me?" she asked.

He stopped what he was doing. "What was that?"

"Earlier, before the phone call, you said you needed to tell me something. What was it?"

Gabriel went back to cooking. "It was nothing. It doesn't matter right now. What does matter is that I make sure I don't burn the vegetables."

"Can I help?"

Gabriel glanced over to her. "Yes, you can sit there and tell me about your day."

Juliet sighed. Work had been part of the reason for her little melt down earlier. "They cancelled the program that was helping deter poaching in the park."

Gabriel reached into a cabinet and pulled out some plates. "I'm sorry to hear that."

"Yeah, I'm thinking about leaving," she mumbled.

Gabriel stopped cooking, put down the spatula, came over, and stood across from Juliet. "I know things are tough, and you are struggling right now. Please, don't quit, not just yet anyway."

Juliet appreciated his words but wondered why he cared so much what happened to her. Before the shooting, Secret had said she was oblivious to the way he acted around her. "My life here has fallen apart. Secret's dead. The National Park program has been cancelled. I'm living in your parent's guesthouse because my place burned down. I think I should just move on and start over."

"First, my family adores you, so stop thinking you are being a burden to anyone by living in the guesthouse. Second, give the Park Service thing some time. You never know what may happen." Gabriel paused and put his hands on the kitchen counter. "I know you loved your friend dearly. I didn't know her well, but what I knew, I really liked. She seemed like a go-getter. Am I right?"

"She was," Juliet reflected.

"Would she want you to quit?"

Juliet's eyes glistened. "It's not fair to ask me that."

Gabriel walked around the counter to stand next to Juliet. "I should've been there for you. Let me be there for you now."

For the first time in weeks, something stirred inside of her other than guilt and pain. "Okay."

Gabriel returned to the stove and began plating the food. He carried both dishes over to the table and placed them there. Pulling out a chair, he motioned for Juliet to come over and sit. She did this, and he scooted the chair in for her. Juliet sat as he placed utensils and a glass of water on the table. He sat down across the table and gestured for her to start eating. Tentatively, she took a bite of the food he had prepared, bracing for her stomach to protest. When nothing happened, she took another bite. Gabriel gave her a warm smile before eating.

"So, tell me about your house. I like the way you have the book shelves so it looks like a solid wall."

Gabriel beamed. "I'm glad you like it. Unlike my parents, I like a more modern approach to architecture. I wanted to feel like I was in the woods, hence all the glass. The bookshelves hide the stairs and the entrance to the other rooms. My bedroom and study are on the left side of the house and the right side has the guest bedrooms. Underneath is my workshop for my cars."

"Your cars?"

"Come on, I'm a guy. You think I wouldn't have a garage full of cars to work on?" he teased.

"Point taken." Juliet looked down to get another bite of food and realized she had already eaten the entire plate full without knowing it. An "oh" escaped her lips.

"What's wrong?"

Juliet looked up. "I can't believe I ate everything," she commented.

"Would you like some more?"

"No, I think I better not push my luck, but thank you." She smiled at Gabriel. "You're a pretty good cook."

"I'm not as good as the women in my family, but I do all right." He got up and took her plate. "Why don't you sit on the couch while I clean up?"

"Are you sure I can't help?"

Gabriel looked back at her. "Yes, I've got this. Now, go relax on the couch. I'll be there in a minute so we can finish talking."

Juliet sat down on the large, soft, leather couch. Now noticing how comfortable it was. Kicking off her shoes, she tucked her feet under her and leaned back against the cushions. Exhaustion set in, and she felt her eyes becoming heavy. There would be no harm in closing them for just a minute until Gabriel joined her.

Chapter 22

The amazing smell that had become synonymous with Gabriel drifted into her nose and brought her mind out of her slumber. Juliet could feel herself surrounded by softness as she stirred. Blinking her eyes open so as to adjust them to the bright light that flooded the room, she became aware she was in a bed and it wasn't hers. Juliet sat up and immediately looked down at herself. Breathing a sigh of relief that she was in her clothes from the night before, she scanned the room to take in her settings.

Juliet observed she was lying in a king-size bed positioned in one of the largest bedrooms she had ever seen. Based on the sheer size and the décor, she assumed this was the master bedroom in Gabriel's house. The majority of the room was wall-to-wall glass that overlooked the forest. To the left of the bed appeared to be what Juliet assumed was the entrance to the master bathroom. To the right of the bed was a sitting area occupied by two large, leather ottomans. Directly across from the bed was another stone fireplace, though it was much smaller than the one in Gabriel's living room. Lying in front on it was Adir. His head was up; ears at attention. He looked at Juliet and gave a soft low vocalization.

"Well, good morning to you. I didn't realize you slept in the house. How come I didn't see you last night?"

Adir stood and stretched. He padded over to the left side of the bed and pawed at a black duffle bag sitting next to the bedside table. Juliet swung her legs out over the edge of the mattress, reached out, and grabbed the bag. Before opening it she leaned over and gave Adir a scratch behind his ears. In the bag there was a note on top with a few of her clothes underneath.

I didn't want to wake you. I hope you don't mind but I had Sabra bring you some things from your house. Take your time getting ready, and I will see you downstairs. Gabriel

Juliet read the note again and then inadvertently put the tip of the paper to her mouth and smiled. She saw that Adir was just staring at her. "Oh, what are you looking at?" she scolded.

She put the bag aside and stood up to stretch. Checking her watch, she was comforted there was plenty of time to get to work. It was odd, but last night had been the first time in weeks she had slept soundly. Juliet would have to remember to ask Gabriel what kind of mattress he had because it was amazingly soft. She turned around to face the bed and started to take off her shirt. Juliet heard the clicking of nails on the wooden floor behind her. When she turned to see what Adir was up to, she saw his tail disappearing out of the bedroom. Juliet finished undressing, grabbed the bag, and headed for the bathroom.

When she walked into the space, she was impressed by the unique design of the room. Once again, there was a classic touch, with sharp, clean lines and dark tones. The shower was massive in size, and Juliet imagined that several people could easily fit inside. This elicited an unsettling feeling inside her.

Juliet reached inside to turn on the water, and a gentle cascade of liquid came out of the raindrop showerhead. When the temperature was just right, she stepped inside, taking with her the shampoo and soap Sabra had packed. The water was refreshing and she let it run over her body.

Juliet noticed there were several other showerheads that were positioned around the shower at different levels and angles. She fancied the idea of such an experience if she only knew how to turn them on. Once clean, she dried off and got dressed for work.

Juliet looked around to figure out where to put her used towel. The single hook was already occupied by a jet black towel. She opened a door only to discover a room that was completely empty. The floor was concrete with exposed pipes erupting from the center. Why would Gabriel have an incomplete bathroom?

Juliet shut the door and opted to fold the towel and lay it on the corner of the double vanity. Before leaving the bedroom, she made the bed and then picked up her bag to carry it downstairs. The smell of bacon floated up the stairway as she descended causing her mouth to water.

Gabriel was once again in the kitchen and looked to be almost finished making breakfast. His hair was ruffled, and he was wearing a tattered tee-shirt, gym shorts, and was barefoot. Ever since she had met him, Gabriel was always well groomed, almost like a piece of art with nothing out of place. Even when they went running together, there was never anything disheveled about him. This was the first time he ever seemed relaxed, and she liked it.

"Hey, I see you found my note. I hope it was okay I had Sabra go by your place and get some things for you." He handed her a cup of hot tea.

She took a sip and let the warmth soothe her insides. "Yes, thank you. You know you didn't need to do that. You could've just woke me up last night."

He grabbed the plates of food and headed to the kitchen table. Juliet followed and once again sat in the seat he pulled out for her. "You looked exhausted, and I wasn't about to awaken you and make you drive home. My parents would have skinned me alive if I did something like that." He sat down across from her.

"You aren't going to be late for work are you?" She started eating a piece of bacon.

"Oh, no, I don't have to go in until later. I have a meeting this morning." He passed her an orange slice, which she gladly accepted.

"So not fair," she commented.

He stopped eating and looked at her. "What's not fair?"

"You get to go to work later than I do. You make more than me. Sometimes I think I picked the wrong profession."

"Yeah, but you said you can't handle all the people stuff," Gabriel said off handedly, and then, when he saw Juliet's guilt-ridden face, realized his mistake. "I'm sorry. I didn't mean that."

She shook her head. "No, it's okay. I know what you meant."

The two of them sat and ate in awkward silence until Juliet could not stand it. "So, where is Adir? I didn't see him when I came downstairs."

Gabriel coughed and then took a drink. "Eating breakfast."

"Oh." Assuming Gabriel meant Adir was out hunting for something to eat, Juliet decided to change the subject. "I do feel bad I inadvertently kicked you out of your own room. You could have just left me on the couch."

He finished swallowing some eggs. "My male pride wouldn't allow me to sleep in my bed and leave you on the couch." Gabriel lifted up his mug and took a drink. "In all seriousness, it does worry me you don't know what chivalry is."

Juliet felt her entire body get warm. "I know it's a lost concept on most 21st-century men."

"Not the real ones." His gaze held her eyes until she averted them.

Thankful she was full, Juliet picked up her plate and headed towards the sink. Giving it a quick rinse she placed everything in the dishwasher. "I've got to get to work. Thank you, again, for everything."

He got up from the table and walked with her to the front door. "Kayla said you might join us for Aiden's football game tonight."

"Yeah, probably. Are you going to be there?"

"I wouldn't miss it. Aiden is one of the best receivers in the state." Gabriel beamed as he opened the door.

"I'll see you tonight then," she said and headed to her truck.

Juliet climbed into the truck and noticed Gabriel watched her from his doorway until she pulled out of the driveway. *He really is a good person*, she thought, appreciating that even though he could be a little over protective at times, deep down his heart was in the right place.

Chapter 23

Hurrying up the walkway towards the high school, Juliet checked her watch to see just how late she was. Shadow had vomited multiple hairballs all over the carpet, and it had taken a little longer than expected to clean them up. The cheer of the crowd increased as sounds of trumpets and drums filled the air with what sounded like a fight song. Approaching the entrance to buy a ticket, she noticed Kevin standing at the gate with his trainee Joe. She felt her shoulders tensing upwards the closer she got to the two men. Walking over to the ticket booth she paid and went to step past Kevin, who put out a hand to block her.

"Hey, Juliet." His voice had a hint of regret. He reached for Juliet and embraced her, squeezing just a little too hard.

"Hey, Kevin." Juliet took a step back after he released her from the hug. "How've you been?"

Kevin stepped to the side. "It's been a rough few weeks, but it's getting easier. I'm really sorry about...you know."

Juliet clenched and unclenched her hands. She had avoided him since he had kissed her, feeling extremely awkward about the entire situation. "It was a mistake. You were grieving and emotions were running high."

"Thanks. You're one of my closest friends, and I don't want to lose you. I guess I made a hard situation worse, and I really am sorry." Kevin rested his hand on top of his gun. "I wanted to see if you would mind coming over tomorrow and help me go through some of Secret's things. I think there's some stuff she would want you to have."

A sharp pain radiated from the left side of her chest. Her hands became cold and clammy. "I don't know if I'm ready to do that, Kevin."

He took a step closer to her. "I can't do this by myself, but I can't keep looking at her things. It just keeps reminding me of what happened."

Juliet was desperately blinking back the tears and so far was winning the battle. "I'll try and get over there tomorrow, but no promises," she stammered.

"Thank you." Kevin embraced her one more time before letting her enter into the gates.

Juliet walked in at a quick but steady pace, taking every bit of control to fight the internal urge to flee as fast as she could from Kevin. Using her hand, she wiped the few tears that had managed to escape away from her eyes. Not until she felt a little lightheaded did she realize she was hyperventilating. Juliet leaned on the wall of the concession stand in front of her, closed her eyes, and took in several deep breaths.

The roar of the crowd caused Juliet to open her eyes and look in the direction of the football field to see what had happened. Several young men wearing the hometown high school's colors were jumping up and down in the end zone. The scoreboard changed to 6-0.

Juliet scanned the stands trying to find the Archon family. In the middle, almost every member she had met at the Fourth of July picnic was sitting in the stands cheering loudly. Aiden was the only family member currently on the varsity team. One of his cousins was in the band and another was a cheerleader, though Juliet could not remember their names.

Climbing the stairs of the stands, Juliet looked for a place to sit. Some of the older children in the family were sitting at the very top of the stadium. She could see some of the kids huddled together actively ignoring their parents several rows below. Sabra waved and called out her name. She was next to Gabriel, Lorna, and Ben. Eve, Jacob, Caleb, and Mathew were sitting in between Ben and Travis, Kayla's husband. Nora was balanced on Gabriel's shoulders waving a shaker of white and gold.

Stepping out of the aisle, Juliet maneuvered her way to the family. Sabra moved over one seat so Juliet sat between her and Gabriel. Nora looked down from her perch and screamed, "Jew-wee-et!" The three-year-old opened her arms and leaned down over the top of Gabriel's head towards Juliet. With the assistance of Gabriel, Nora landed safely in her lap.

"Look at my shaker, Jew-wee-et." As Nora shook it wildly in her hands almost hitting all three adults surrounding her.

"I see it. It's very pretty," commented Juliet as she smiled down at the child.

"I glad you here. Uncle Gabree was worried you not be here." Nora turned to Gabriel. "Look, she here. You happy now."

Juliet tried very hard not to laugh as she looked at a red faced Gabriel. He reached over and plucked Nora off her lap. Gabriel lifted her up in the air over his head jiggling her back and forth. The little girl squealed in delight. He lowered her back down in his lap. "I think it's time for you to go sit with your daddy for a while."

"Okay." Nora gave her uncle a hug. "I go now cause Jew-wee-et is here. She makes you happy." With that, the little girl climbed off Gabriel's lab and headed over to Ben.

Gabriel rubbed the back of his neck with his hand. He gave Juliet a sheepish smile. "Gotta love kids."

"She adores you." Juliet nodded in Nora's direction.

"Yeah, she's great." He looked over towards the child and then back at Juliet. "We were getting a little worried since it was the end of the first quarter and you weren't here yet."

"I had to clean up a few hairballs Shadow decided to leave around the house." Juliet heard the crowd booing and turned to look at the field. She had no clue what was going on. "What happened?" she asked Gabriel.

He shrugged his shoulders. "I don't know; I was talking with you."

Sabra leaned over. "If you two paid attention, you'd know that the refs just called pass interference on our team."

Sabra sat back in her seat. Gabriel had his lips pressed together in an attempt not to smile and winked at her. The football game was pretty evenly matched the rest of the first half. In the second half, Aiden caught three long passes for touchdowns, allowing the home team to break away and win. Slowly, everyone filtered out of the stands. Sabra was chatting with Juliet about ideas for the dress she was making for the hospital charity ball that was fast approaching. Both agreed on a midnight blue color, and obviously, since this was a very formal event, the dress would be long. Other than those two things, the women had creative differences on how the dress should look. While debating the merits of strapless versus non-strapless, Kevin broke through the crowd to walk alongside Juliet. She felt the muscles around her shoulders and neck tense.

"I wanted to let you know I have something I need to do tomorrow afternoon, so do you think you could be at my house in the morning?" Kevin spoke directly to Juliet.

She really wasn't emotionally ready to do this, but knew it was something that needed to be done. "I'll be there around nine."

"I'll see you then." With that, Kevin drifted back into the crowd.

"What was that all about?" asked Sabra.

Juliet's stomach was beginning to hurt. "He wants me to help clean out Secret's things tomorrow."

"Oh." Sabra twirled her hair with her finger. "Do you want me to go with you?"

"I think I need to do this by myself." Juliet exhaled loudly.

"If you change your mind, let me know. Any one of us will go with you." She put her arm around Juliet and smiled. "Now, let's talk about how long we are going to make the slit for your dress."

Chapter 24

Juliet stared down at the boxes she had just carried into her house as if they contained the most venomous snakes on Earth. Secret's life had been reduced to seven boxes and three garbage bags full of clothes. It had taken every ounce of strength this morning to get up and drive to Kevin's house. When she had arrived, he was waiting outside next to a pile of boxes. Kevin blubbered apologies to her and said he just couldn't go through Secret's stuff while quickly loading the boxes in the back of the truck. Despite everything that had transpired between the two of them in the past few weeks, she silently promised herself she would be there more for Kevin. Secret would have wanted the two of them to take care of each other. She mustered a smile and gave him a hug, while assuring him everything would get easier.

Now all of those things were sitting in the middle of her living room. Shadow sniffed each one and then proceeded to file his nails on the side of the largest box. At this moment in time, Juliet really wished she drank, because this really called for some kind of adult beverage. Her hands shook as they passed over the top of one of the boxes. Using her fingernails, she started to pick at the tape closing the top and then stopped. Juliet got up off the floor and plopped down on the couch. Shifting positions, she couldn't get comfortable, so instead she got up and started pacing back and forth, all the while keeping her eyes on the objects in the middle of the room. Her cat perched on one, watching her movements. Occasionally, she would walk over, attempt to open one of the boxes, and then retreat back.

In the midst of attempting to open a box for the fifth time there was a knock on the door, startling her. Turning, she could see through the windows who was standing outside. With a sigh of relief, she walked over and opened the door fully. Once again, Gabriel looked very relaxed in his gym shorts and tee-shirt. He also had a bag of chocolate of some kind in his hand. "I thought I'd swing by and see how you were doing."

Juliet crossed her arms and eyed him suspiciously. "Sabra told you."

Opening his eyes wider, he feigned innocence. "Told me what?"

"She told you I was going over to Kevin's to help go through Secret's things." Juliet pointed to the bag in his hands. "I also bet she told you I love chocolate-covered almonds. I assume that's what you're holding."

"Oh, these?" Gabriel looked down at the bag. "I had these lying around and thought I might bring them by, but now that you mention it, I think Sabra might have told me that."

Juliet raised one eyebrow. "You couldn't be any more obvious if you tried." She was trying not to smile.

He leaned on the doorframe. "In all seriousness: how are you doing?"

Juliet swept her arm to the left. "Come in and see for yourself."

Gabriel walked through the door and made his way to the boxes. Shadow hopped down, sniffed him, and walked upstairs. Gabriel knelt down next to one of the larger ones and placed his hand on the top of it. Without looking, he handed Juliet the bag full of the chocolate-covered almonds. "How long have you been trying to open them?"

"I think at least an hour, maybe more." Juliet's voice began to quiver again. "I don't think I can do this."

Gabriel stood up and placed his hand on her shoulder. "You don't have to do this today. You don't have to do this tomorrow. You can do it whenever you feel ready."

"But I need to do this." She looked at the items on the floor. A single tear fell from her right eye. "I just don't want to do this alone."

"Remember what I told you the other night. I'm here for you."

Juliet turned away from him and wiped the wetness off her cheek. She placed the gift he brought on the kitchen counter, turned, and walked back to him. "Pick a box."

Gabriel's eyebrows furrowed. "I don't understand."

Juliet sat on the couch. "Pick a box and open it. I can't do it, so I want you to pick a box and open it for me. I think once it is open I might be able to look."

"Only if you're sure."

Juliet leaned her head to the left and glanced up at Gabriel. She slumped over and put her elbow on her knee, hand on her chin. "I'm not sure, but, unless I want a bunch of cardboard greeting me every time I walk in the door, I need to do this."

Gabriel hesitated then picked up a medium-size box and brought it to Juliet. He placed it on the couch next to her and then sat on the other side. With one last reassuring look, Gabriel pulled the tape off the top and opened the four sides. Juliet moved toward the opening at a snail's pace. Peering inside, a lump formed in her throat. She recognized the contents immediately and instantly regretted her decision. Inside were several scrapbooks and photo albums.

The tears began falling again. Without a word, Gabriel got up and disappeared around the corner, then returned with a roll of toilet paper. He also grabbed the chocolate off the countertop and handed both of the items to Juliet before reclaiming his seat. "I'm going to sit here with you until you're ready, and if you decide we need to do this another day, I'm going to take all of Secret's stuff and put it upstairs in one of the guest bedroom's closets so you can't see it."

"Okay," Juliet whispered.

The two of them sat there looking between the box and each other. It was so quiet she could hear the ticking of the second-hand on Gabriel's wristwatch. The silence was occasionally broken by her blowing her nose. The pile of used toilet paper next to her was growing steadily. Juliet closed her eyes, reached into the box, and lifted out the first thing she felt. The object sat on her lap, and Juliet held her eyes closed until she was ready to open them.

The name of her undergraduate college was pasted across the top of the book. Her tears made large, wet circles on the front cover, which she quickly wiped away with her hand. She opened it, and saw a picture of her and Secret on their first day of college when they had met as roommates: both young, smiling girls with nothing but the future in their eyes. She turned the album around and showed Gabriel. "First day," was all that she was able to squeak out.

Gabriel removed the carton between them and moved closer to her on the couch. She flipped to the next page and the next. Occasionally she would say something, but most of the time she just thought back to the memories each picture evoked. By the time she was done, the tears had stopped. The rest of the box contained other photos, which were of Secret's childhood, and there was a smaller album of more recent pictures. Most of those contained pictures of Kevin, which Juliet quickly flipped through.

"How do you feel?" asked Gabriel.

Juliet sat cross-legged on the couch, the books sitting on her lap. "A little better, but I don't think I can do any more today."

Gabriel got up off the couch. "Tell you what. How about I come over every night after work, and we open one box per day? Afterwards, we'll do something fun, if that's okay with you."

Juliet managed a weak smile. "I'd like that very much. Thank you."

Gabriel started piling the boxes on top of each other. "Now, I'm going to take these upstairs and put them in the blue bedroom. Why don't you go downstairs to the basement and pick out some kind of board game?"

That was the last thing Juliet expected him to say. "What?"

"You heard me: a board game. The basement should be full of them. It's about to rain outside, in case you haven't noticed, and we need to do something to get your mind off everything." He grabbed all three of the trash bags and started carrying them upstairs.

Juliet put the scrapbooks on the coffee table and opened the door to the basement. Since moving in, she'd never been down there. Truthfully, ever since she was a child, she had actually been scared of basements and made an effort to avoid them. Like everything else she had come to expect from the Archon family, the basement was decorated flawlessly. Along one of the walls were shelves full of every board game imaginable. After scanning the selection, she picked out two of her favorite childhood games and brought them upstairs.

Gabriel had finished carrying everything to the bedroom and was in the kitchen. He looked at the games in her hand and smirked. "Candyland and Chutes and Ladders? I would've never thought that."

Juliet frowned. "You said to pick out some games. These are fun. Besides, I'm not up for anything that requires a lot of thinking." She put the games on the island in the kitchen. "Are you scared I might beat you?"

"I was the family champion of Chutes and Ladders when I was a kid." He grabbed some bread and started buttering it.

Juliet rolled her eyes. "Of course you were."

Gabriel smiled back and opened the fridge door. "I'm making tomato soup and grilled cheese. Do you like yours toasted lightly or burnt?"

"Toasted lightly, please."

Juliet set up Candyland on the kitchen table and got drinks for both of them while Gabriel made lunch. The heavens opened up and rain pelted the windows. She flicked on several lights so they could see the board better. The grilled cheese melted in her mouth and filled her belly. Two games later, she had won both times in Candyland.

"Are you pouting?" she teased.

"No." He crossed his arms. "I've never liked this one. It's too girly for me."

"Sour grapes," she muttered.

"What was that?"

"Nothing." She smiled innocently.

Gabriel grabbed the other game. "How about we play this one?"

After a very lofty back and forth battle to see who could get to the top, Juliet had the unlucky turn of landing on the long chute that took her back down to the beginning. "Hey, if it's alright with you, I'd like to go lay down for a while."

He looked up from the game. "You okay?"

"Yes, but I haven't slept well for a month. It's catching up to me lately."

"You go on upstairs. I'll clean up and let myself out." He started putting away the game pieces.

"Are you sure?"

"Absolutely, I'll see you tomorrow. I have to work so I won't be at church, but I'll call you on my way home and we can tackle another box if you want."

"Thanks."

Chapter 25

True to his word, Gabriel came every night to help Juliet sort through a box of Secret's things. Every new box Juliet opened made her cry, but she felt better for having done so when the box was empty. In time, the chasm between the two emotions fell away and began a progression in the opposite direction. After sorting through the boxes she and Gabriel would watch a movie, or cook dinner, and one night he took her to play put-put golf. Only on Wednesday night when he got caught up in a surgery did Lorna and Sabra come over to help Juliet go through the bag of clothes. Since she was a completely different size than her friend, and only kept a few tee-shirts. The rest was packed up for Goodwill.

Late Saturday morning, she was standing in Sabra's bedroom draped in midnight blue material. The red head was measuring and pinning while mumbling to herself. Juliet had no idea what kind of material it was but it was soft and silky.

"Will you hold still?" Sabra lightly smacked her leg.

"Sorry, it's just that I'm going to meet Gabriel soon to open the last box of Secret's things, then we're meeting everybody down at the lake to go swimming, and afterwards we're watching the Auburn game. I have a very full day." Juliet shifted her weight again.

"I've got one week before I go back to school to get this finished and you're whining about swimming and football." Sabra was pinning the hem line.

"You're my friend and I will have to forgive your disparaging remark concerning college football…this time. But, we can't let it happen again. The Lord has seen fit to afford us only twelve games a year. If people are ignorant enough to schedule their functions on college game day then there can only be two reasons. They desire for nobody to attend, or they're half-wits." Sabra looked up into Juliet's face expecting a jovial one. None was there to be had.

Sabra huffed. "Not you too. The men and half the women in my family go nuts every Saturday."

"Your loss."

Sabra grunted. "Okay, you need to let me show off some kind of skin. This is a charity event, and if you look like Mother Teresa we're not going to raise a lot of money."

Juliet groaned. "Not this again. We are going with the one shoulder look, isn't that enough?"

Sabra crossed her arms. "No, pick a feature you like to show off, and it cannot be your face, arms, or feet."

"Fine." Juliet chewed on her bottom lip and exhaled loudly. "My back."

Sabra drew her eyebrows together. "Not what I was looking for, but I'll make it work."

There was light knock on the bedroom door. Both women turned and looked. Gabriel was standing in the doorway grinning at the scene before him. "Hey, I came to see if you were ready?"

Juliet glanced down at Sabra. "Can I go now?"

Sabra threw her arms up in the air. "Yes, you may go."

They walked over to her house and could hear the laughter and shouts of the family down at the lake. Juliet was ready to go through the last contents and be done with the process. Today she would open the smallest of all the boxes. As they had done the other days, the two sat down on the couch, and she opened the lid. Juliet already had a hunch what may be inside. She carefully lifted up a hand carved, cedar jewelry box. Secret's father had given it to her when she was a little girl before he had passed away from cancer. It was one of the most precious things to her. Inside, every necklace, ring, bracelet, and earrings Secret owned lay neatly in each slot or hook. Juliet picked up a thick, silver-cuffed bracelet she had always borrowed from her friend when they dressed up for formal events.

"This was always one of my favorite pieces." Juliet went to hand it to Gabriel who withdrew his hand.

"No, why don't you put it on so I can see it," he suggested.

She placed the bracelet on her slender wrist. Gabriel smiled. "It looks good on you."

"Thanks. I'd give it back in a heartbeat if I could just have my friend back."

His voice was soft. "I know you would."

Juliet looked down at the other pieces. None of the gold, silver, or precious stones would ever bring her friend back. She'd have to keep Secret's memory alive and help the police catch the person who did this.

"What would you like to do now?" asked Gabriel.

Juliet closed the lid on the wooden box and stood up. "I think I'm going to take this upstairs and change into my bathing suit."

Gabriel stood also. "That sounds like a good idea. I'll wait for you outside."

Taking the jewelry box with her, Juliet went upstairs and quickly changed into her, or really Sabra's, bathing suit, which was a purple bikini. She also took a minute to pin her hair up in a bun, since when it was wet it almost took on a life of its own and had a tendency to wrap around her neck and arms. Feeling a little body conscious, she threw a tee-shirt on and grabbed a beach towel. She walked out on the porch to discover that Gabriel had not changed out of his tee-shirt and jeans.

She pointed to him. "Aren't you going swimming?"

"Nope, I thought I'd sit and watch everybody else." He pointed to Juliet's wrist. "You might want to take that off. The water will tarnish it if you don't lose it."

Juliet looked down to see she was still wearing Secret's silver bracelet. "Oops."

She took it off, walked back inside, and placed it on the table. She joined Gabriel outside, and they proceeded to make their way down to the lake. Most of the family was scattered around the beach area. Some of the children were building sand castles. The older ones were swimming or swinging off a rope tied to a tree and landing in the water. Several of the adults were lounging in the Adirondack chairs that lined the lake. Cara and Sterling were sitting in two white chairs side by side drinking ice tea.

"Juliet, come on in," called Sabra who was in the water about twenty feet away next to Lorna.

Juliet dropped the towel down on the ground and slipped off her flip-flops. She headed towards the water. Before she could step in, Sabra yelled, "Take off your shirt. There's no point in wearing a bikini if you are going to stay covered."

She felt her face get hot and wanted to sink into the sand. Looking around to see if anybody else had heard Sabra, she was relieved nobody was looking in her direction. She walked back to where her towel was. Gabriel was still standing next to it.

"You know you don't have to let my sister bully you."

"I know." The words were spoken through gritted teeth.

Juliet turned her back to Gabriel and removed her shirt. She let it fall carelessly onto the sand. Taking a deep breath in, she caught the scent of Gabriel's fabulous cologne, which caused her to turn around. She wondered why he had gotten so close to her that she could smell it, but when she looked he had not moved from the original spot he had been standing in.

She squinted her eyes a little bit and cocked her head to the side. "What is it?"

"You look very nice," he replied.

Juliet smiled. "Thank you."

With that, she turned and walked down to the edge of the lake. The water felt refreshing as she swam out to Sabra. Where Sabra was, the water was about chest deep. Once she had her feet firmly planted, she splashed the red-haired vixen. "Hey, what was that for?"

"That is for calling me out about the tee-shirt."

Lorna laughed, "Serves you right."

Sabra splashed Lorna and then Juliet. "Shut up both of you." Her mouth curved upwards. "I think you look great. If you'd just trust me in all things clothing, I could make you a model.

Juliet shook her head. "Whatever." She glanced back to the beach. "Can I ask you guys a question?"

"Do either one of you know why Gabriel doesn't want to go swimming?" Juliet really wanted to ask why their brother would put on cologne to come outside.

Sabra sneered, "He's just being a fuddy dud."

"Leave him alone, Sabra," scolded Lorna.

Juliet felt like she was missing a part of an inside conversation. Lorna changed the subject to talk about the charity event in a few weeks. She wanted to get opinions about the final catering decisions on food. Lorna continued to chat with Juliet as Sabra headed towards shore. Juliet saw her whispering to Travis, Ben, and Kayla's brother, Luke. All three men looked at each other and then at Gabriel who was sitting next to Sterling talking with his parents.

She had an idea of what they were scheming and was curious how this would play out. The three men crept towards Gabriel who was deep in conversation. When they were a few feet away, Gabriel swiveled in his chair towards them, but it was too late. The three men grabbed Gabriel and lifted him off his feet. Sterling was laughing alongside Cara. The children were shouting encouragement. Gabriel managed to break free of the bear hug grip Travis had on him but was unable to shake Ben and Luke off before he was tossed into the water.

Gabriel emerged soaking wet and looking for revenge. The three culprits backed away, laughing and pointing to Sabra in the water calling out it was her idea. Gabriel turned to look at his sister with a wicked smile on his face.

Sabra quickly swam backwards. "You stay away."

Gabriel launched himself forward and dunked his sister under the water. She came up sputtering with her hair falling over her face like red seaweed. Sabra parted her red hair so her green eyes were now visible. "Guess what? Payback sucks, and I've got something special planned for you." She looked back at Juliet.

"Well, I think I need something to drink." Lorna swam to her sister. "Come on, Sabra, let's get you something." She nudged her sister forward.

Juliet unexplainably felt very awkward. She looked around trying to give herself time to figure out something to say. "Sooo, fancy seeing you here." It was not very clever, but it was the best she could come up with at the moment.

A chuckle escaped his mouth. "Imagine that. Do you come here often?"

"Oh you know. Only when it's blisteringly hot." Juliet shrugged.

"Do you mind if I leave you for a second?"

"Sure," she replied, hoping he could not detect the disappointment she was feeling.

Gabriel went to the shoreline and removed his shoes, cell phone, and, finally, his shirt and tossed it onto the sand. He turned around to swim back towards her. Juliet's eyes grew wide and she realized her mouth was hanging to the side. She'd imagined what he looked like shirtless watching him run, but this eclipsed that. The sun illuminated the bronze skin of his body, which accentuated each abdominal muscle forming the perfect 'six-pack' she did not realize could actually exist on a human being. The pectoral muscles composing his hairless, broad chest looked like they had been sculpted out of marble. He gave Michelangelo's *David* a run for his money.

He approached her. "That's better." He slicked his hands back through his hair. "Oh, sorry, I think I got water on your face."

Juliet snapped out of her trance. "What?"

"I think I splashed some water on your face. It's next to your mouth." He pointed to her right side.

Juliet took her hand and wiped her mouth. *Oh, dear God, I was drooling.* Hoping to regain some composure, she said the first thing that came to her mind. "How's your cell phone?"

"What about it?"

"Well, did it get ruined being thrown in the water?"

Gabriel swam past her a little ways and turned back around. "No, it's in a waterproof case, so it should be good. I'm pretty hard on things, so I got the most durable case I could find."

"Oh, that's good."

"Jew-wee-et come see my sand castle," called Nora.

"I've been summoned." She turned, heading towards the little girl.

"I'll come with you," she heard him say.

Juliet approached Nora, who was beaming with pride over her sand castle. "I did it all by myself."

"Very good. It is so pretty, just like you."

The little girl squealed with delight and hugged her. Juliet helped Nora build a mote around the castle. As they were finishing it, Juliet heard male hollering and then a splash. Ben had ended up in the water with Gabriel's deep-throated laughter filling the air. A shiver ran down her spine. She excused herself from the little girl and headed to get her towel. As she was patting her hair dry, Gabriel approached her. "I think I'm going to head to the house and get ready for the game."

He stepped a little closer. "Can I walk you there?"

"You don't have to if you don't want to."

"I'd like to, besides, if you don't mind, I would really like to grab a towel from the bathroom."

"Of course."

Juliet bent over and grabbed her shirt and put on her flip-flops. "Don't you want your shoes?"

"Na, it's fine. My feet are all calloused anyway."

They made their way to the house, walking in silence. Still dripping wet, Gabriel asked if she would mind grabbing a towel so he would not get the floor wet. Juliet reached for the doorknob to twist it open only to discover it was locked. "Are you kidding me?"

"What's wrong?" Gabriel asked from behind her.

"I guess when I came out I somehow managed to lock the door." Juliet turned around. "We'll need to go get the key from your parents."

"Hold on a minute." Gabriel walked to the door. "Maybe we can pick the lock."

Juliet crossed her arms in front of her chest and gave him a skeptical look. "How would you know how to pick locks? Were you a thief in a former life?"

His devious smile and twinkling eyes made her heart flutter ever so slightly. "It's something I learned to do as a kid; it came in handy sometimes. I'll show you. All I need is one of those bobby pins in your hair."

Slowly, Juliet unfolded her arms, reaching for one of the bobby pins in her hair. Handing it to him, she was doubtful this would work. Gabriel took the pin and broke it where it naturally bent in half, and then curved the straight piece of the pin to form a ninety-degree angle.

He bent down in front of the lock and waved his hand for her to come towards him. Moving aside to make room for her, Gabriel positioned her in front of him with his wet arms dripping on her shoulders. "I've made this straight part of the bobby pin into a tension wrench. Now, I want you to take it and place it securely into the bottom of the lock." He placed his hands on top of hers to help guide them.

"Take the handle of the pin and point it in the direction the lock would normally open. The door key opens to the right so have the handle pointing to your right." He moved her hand to the right.

"Put some pressure on the wrench by pushing down on it slightly with your thumb." Gabriel handed her the other portion of the bobby pin. "Now, insert this – the pick – into the top part of the lock and wiggle it around until the lock comes undone." His breath was warm on her neck.

She could feel the water dripping off him onto her skin making it very hard to focus on the task at hand. By pushing on the lock, she inadvertently started to lean back into his chest, the warmth radiating through her back. Gabriel shifted, resulting in his face being right next to hers. "As you wiggle the pick, continue putting more pressure on the tension wrench, pushing it in the direction the lock would normally open."

There was an audible click, and Juliet turned the doorknob. Giddy as a schoolgirl, she stood up and squealed. Juliet turned around and threw her arms around

Gabriel who was now standing. "Thank you! That was awesome!"

Realizing what she was doing, Juliet released her grip around his neck. Gabriel turned his face towards one of her descending hands, and Juliet could have sworn he inhaled deeply as her wrist passed near his nose. She could smell his amazing cologne again, but it was overwhelming. Gabriel reached up and took her hand in his, pulling it in close to his chest, causing her to step forward. His other hand wrapped around her waist and pulled her even closer. Caught off guard, Juliet looked up to ask him what he was doing, but his lips met her mouth before she could.

Her heart skipped a beat, and her stomach fluttered. For a second, everything went silent. Her skin felt like a low current was going through it, and her nose was being inundated with his amazing smell. His lips tasted like honey. She wanted more and eagerly returned the kiss. The hand not being held made its way to the base of his neck and encouraged his head to stay bent down towards her face.

A low growl of desire escaped his chest as a response. His mouth opened wider and his tongue encouraged hers to do the same. She reciprocated and felt his grip tighten. Warmth flowed through every part of her body like molten lava.

For a moment, everything was perfect. In that one instance, she felt happy and alive inside, and then, in the back recesses of her mind, a painful memory from her past came out of her subconscious. An awareness that they were both soaking wet and half naked magnified the intensity of the dark thought. What was she doing?

Juliet broke her lips away from his. His chest was heaving up and down. "I can't do this." Juliet pushed away from him and retreated into her house.

Chapter 26

Everything had gotten so complicated since Gabriel had kissed her yesterday. She needed to get her head on straight before seeing him again. Her insides were chaos and her hormones were raging up and down worse than when she had gone through puberty.

Looking for answers to questions and problems, Juliet had always turned to books. Her safety net was knowledge. They'd always revealed the answers, but this time, there were no books for her questions. Her mind, emotions, and fears were waging a three-way battle.

Right now, she couldn't face Gabriel; not until her mind was clear. Picking up her phone, she sent a quick text to Lorna and Sabra saying that she would be skipping church and would see them later. This gave her a few more hours to think.

Long after she knew everyone would be at church, she decided to get out of the house. The fresh air would be cathartic. She had every intention to go running. The blistering August sun was pelting down and the humidity made the air feel like she was trapped in a sauna. By the time she got to the lake, any desire to run had evaporated. The glassy surface of the water was inviting. She took off her tee-shirt and kicked off her shoes. Even though there was no one around, she wasn't brave enough to go skinny-dipping, so she left her sports bra and shorts on. Wading out into the lake, she let the coolness soothe her skin.

She swam farther from the shore, enjoying the peace and tranquility of everything. Floating around in the water, Juliet saw the massive tree house she always ran past but never once had climbed. Taking her time, she made her way to the side of the lake and walked ashore. The area at the base of the tree was lined in soft bluegrass.

She scaled the steps up into the branches and came to the landing. Every attention to detail she had come to expect had been placed into this structure as well. There was a safety railing that wrapped around the deck of the house to prevent anyone from falling through. Little chairs and benches were strategically placed everywhere for the children to be able to sit and play outside. The wooden door had another carving of a wolf on it which made Juliet smile now knowing the meaning behind the fascination with these animals. She opened the door and was mesmerized by what she saw.

The inside was something from one of her childhood fairy tales. Where most kids piece together their own playhouse with things they find, this looked to have come with its own interior designer. There were plush couches and an area for crafts, bookshelves that were lined with toys, books, and even binoculars. A child's tea set sat on a carved wooden table with four matching chairs. Dress up clothes were hanging from pegs on the wall. Everything was amazing. Juliet walked back outside so she wouldn't get anything wet. She sat down in one of the chairs, thankful her butt fit, and looked out over the water. The birds filled the air with vibrant songs while the slight breeze stirred the leaves in the treetops. She leaned her head back against the wall and a sense of tranquility washed over her.

Letting her mind wander, she replayed the episode from the day before. Never before had she responded so viscerally to someone. There was no denying she was attracted to him. Through his actions over the past few months, she'd come to trust him. Maybe he would be different.

Juliet had no idea how long she sat there. Gabriel's voice shouting her name broke the tranquility. The sun was high in the sky now. He called out her name again, and she detected a strain in his voice. Rising to her feet, she saw a distant figure walking the lakeshore. Instead of calling out, Juliet went back inside and grabbed a pair of binoculars she had seen earlier.

Looking through them, she saw Gabriel. He'd picked up her pile of clothes and looked at them then scanned the lake. He turned around suddenly, and Juliet panned the area to find out what he was looking at. She saw Lorna walk down, and start speaking with him. Gabriel was pacing back and forth like a caged animal. He looked frustrated or worried. He was talking to Lorna and held up Juliet's clothing to her.

Juliet saw Lorna reach out to him, but Gabriel turned his back to her. Lorna said something else and walked away. He lifted up her shirt to his nose. *What on Earth is he doing?* If his actions weren't confusing enough, he started taking off his clothes. He was obviously looking for her. She owed it to him to make herself known, but the dark side she so often ignored wanted to keep watching and enjoy the show.

He dropped his dress shirt next to her clothes and then started to take of his shoes and then his pants. Juliet dropped the binoculars and was thankful she had put the strap over her neck or else they would've fallen onto the ground. After a small moment of recovery, she peered once again through the eyepieces, disappointed a shrub was blocking her view of his bottom half. She noticed something very strange taking place. His skin began to ripple and black hair was growing out of his arms and chest. Juliet blinked several times, thinking she had to be hallucinating. Gabriel's mouth began to elongate, and she saw his teeth extend into sharp canines. Juliet closed her eyes again, and, when she opened them, Gabriel was gone and a big, black, familiar wolf had appeared: Adir.

A sound, barely audible escaped her throat. She leaned back against the chair and pressed her head against the wall. It was all she could do to remember to breath. Every fiber of her existence was fighting an ascending panic attack. Fear and confusion swept through her. What in the world was happening? This couldn't be real. She looked again and saw Adir was sniffing the ground. He lifted his head up and howled then headed off into the opposite direction from where she was.

One thought screamed louder than any other: RUN! She scampered down the steps of the tree house, scraping the side of her leg. Ignoring the pain, she went bounding through the grass. Barefoot, she wasn't able to walk on the stone path without stabbing the bottoms of her soft feet. Her only option was to hug the shore of the lake then grab her shoes. She prayed he wouldn't see her. After getting her shoes, she'd run back to the house, grab the keys, and get the hell out of there before anyone suspected anything.

With adrenaline coursing her veins, she made it to her shoes in short time. Grabbing them, she stuffed her feet inside. When she turned to head back up to the house, Juliet came face to face with a pair of blue eyes that belonged to Adir.

Juliet surprised herself when she felt not just fear but rage. "Get out of my way," she said in an icy tone. The wolf didn't move, but instead moved his ears forward. "I said move." The big black animal ducked his head and side stepped to the right. Trying to remain composed, Juliet stared straight ahead as she marched past the massive figure.

She started running, heading straight for her house. When her foot stepped onto the edge of the yard, she heard him calling her name. "Hey, Juliet, wait up I've been looking everywhere for you."

Juliet felt his hand on her shoulder. She wheeled around, breaking free. "Don't touch me!"

Shock coursed through his face. "Hey, what's wrong? If this is about yesterday—"

"I saw you, Gabriel," she spat, hoping the words would hit him like venom.

His eyes widened, the healthy tan color of his face turning ashen. "What are you talking about?"

"I saw you change by the lake! One minute you were human and the next you were a wolf." She reflexively took another step closer to the house.

"Juliet, please, let me explain," he pleaded as he reached for her hand.

Her anger bordered on hysteria. Wrenching her hand free and backing up against the porch stairs, her fight or flight instincts were screaming at her to get away. If she ran, he'd easily overtake her, and she wouldn't last long in a fight. "Stay away from me." Every muscle in her body tensed up, and she fought the bile trying to rise up into her throat.

Gabriel kept his distance and ran his hands through his hair. "I just…It's not what you think."

Juliet placed a hand on the railing and began slowly backing away from him up the steps. "I don't care!" Her voice caught in her throat. "Please, leave me alone," she said, trying to sound calm, but the statement rose in pitch like a question.

He stepped closer to her, covering the distance she had put between them in two strides. "I'm not going to hurt you. I'm still the same person."

"No, you're not. I don't know what you are and I don't want to." Juliet took another step up so she was standing just a few inches taller than Gabriel. "All I want is for you to go." Her ability to keep her voice steady was fading. Gabriel made no move to leave, and he stared up at Juliet without blinking. His eyes – Adir's eyes; how had she not seen it before? – seemed to look beyond hers, and she felt a new panic, the one she kept tucked away deep inside, starting to reach for the surface. "Please," she said, her voice softer. "You're scaring me."

Something seemed to shift within Gabriel, and he took a step backward, dropping his gaze to the ground. Juliet let out the breath she'd been holding, and quickly scaled the remaining steps to the porch. Turning back around, she could see Gabriel watching, but he made no move to stop her. She could see his fists clenching and unclenching at his sides and the now-familiar tightness in his jaw.

"I'm sorry," he said, his voice quiet. "I don't want you to be afraid. But I need you to listen to me."

"Leave me alone!" She didn't know what else to say.

"Please," he said. For a moment, Juliet thought she saw fear flash across his face. "I know this doesn't make sense, but you have to believe me: you're not safe on your own."

The knot in Juliet's stomach instantly tightened. "Why would you say that?" she half-whispered, reaching blindly behind her for the door handle, ready to duck inside at the slightest hint of danger.

"Because Secret—" he said, stopping mid-sentence when what little color remained drained from Juliet's face. She slowly turned the doorknob, keeping her eyes focused on Gabriel while her attention was on her actions. Gabriel seemed to sense his time was running out, because he inhaled deeply before speaking with new gravity, "She died because of what I am, and they will kill you too."

Chapter 27

Sterling's large wooden desk loomed in front of her. The flat surface was relatively clean with the exception of a lamp and a picture frame containing a family portrait. The patriarch of the Archon family was sitting behind his desk looking at her with the same kind eyes as always. Cara stood next to him holding a thick, leather-bound book with a matching expression to her husband's. Gabriel leaned against one of the bookshelves expressionless, his body tense like a guitar string. Juliet couldn't remember a time she felt more uncomfortable, especially in a place that had started to feel like a second home. The urge to bolt for the door was strong, but Gabriel's words kept her in her seat: Secret's death was not an accident. Weeks of not knowing why her friend had died still haunted her, and as much as she wanted to run, she needed to hear what they had to say. What Gabriel had to say, although Juliet couldn't imagine any explanation would lead her to forgive him. For what, she wasn't exactly sure; there were too many things to name right now. For being overbearing, for lying to her, for kissing her, for – tears stung her eyes at the thought – being more responsible for Secret's death than Juliet had ever thought possible. "She died because of what I am." She could hear his words clearly in her mind, and a chill went through her body. Juliet had changed out of her wet clothes before walking to the house, but her damp hair combined with her nerves left her feeling cold. She rubbed her hands over her arms in an attempt to remove the goose bumps. She wasn't sure how long she had been sitting in front of them, but if they didn't start talking soon, she was leaving. And this time, she would not be coming back, no matter what new twist they threw at her.

"Would you like a blanket or a jacket before we begin?" asked Cara.

"No, thank you," she stated as unemotionally as she could manage. She stared straight at Cara's husband.

Cara handed Sterling the book. He opened it and flipped through, stopping at a page to look up at her. Sterling took in a breath and then began to speak. "What would you say if I told you our family's roots are integral to the story of Adam and Eve?"

Juliet crossed her arms. "I would say I don't have time for another story, no matter how 'true' you claim it is," she said, using her fingers to mime the implied quotation around the word "true".

"Juliet, the truth can set people free, but it can also imprison them with knowledge. Truth is knowledge, but this comes with a burden and responsibility not all can handle." Sterling leaned back in his chair.

Juliet looked from him over to Gabriel, who had not so much as moved a muscle. His face was blank. "I didn't come here for a sermon, Reverend." The biting tone surprised her. "I want answers, and I need the truth." She paused to give Sterling time to respond, but he sat unmoving in his chair. Despite the bitterness in Juliet's voice, Sterling's face hadn't changed. In it all she saw was fatherly concern, and Juliet tried to swallow back her anger before speaking again. "I deserve the truth," she said with less force.

Sterling's eyes darted to his son before refocusing on Juliet. "You're absolutely right," he stated, leaning forward in his chair and pushing the book towards Juliet while keeping his palms over the open pages. "But before I begin, you have to understand what you want to know is not easy to explain. It requires some storytelling. Stories we believe to be true." He paused and then turned the book around so Juliet could see the beautiful hand-painted picture in it. It was of a blue-eyed wolf with a snake in its mouth. The snake had glowing, red eyes. "For centuries, our ancestors' stories were passed down by word of mouth until it was written down."

Juliet looked up from the book. Her mind flashed through all of the images of wolves she had seen since meeting the Archons: the family crest, the stained glass on doors and windows, the depiction of Noah's ark in the church. A burst of panic hit her: they were all wolves. She had been so focused on Gabriel's transformation and his mention of Secret she hadn't once stopped to think of the danger she had put herself in. Sitting in a closed room with three of these creatures… In a rush, Juliet stood up from her chair, moving to stand behind it and gripping the wooden seatback as tightly as she could. She had every intention of defending herself if necessary. Sterling, Cara, and Gabriel remained where they were, doing nothing but watching Juliet's spasmodic actions. She quickly glanced between the three of them, but they were still. Riding her newest wave of fear, she blurted out, "You're were-wolves!"

"We're not werewolves," snapped Gabriel. Reflexively, Juliet picked up the chair, pointing the legs in Gabriel's direction. Still leaning against the bookcase, Gabriel raised his eyebrows at her, as if daring her to make a move. "Put the chair down, Juliet," he commanded, his tone almost mocking. "No one is going to hurt you." His voice was gentler now.

She kept her stance with her wooden weapon poised for attack. "You said Secret died because of what you are, and I'm supposed to believe that I'm safe here?"

"Just stop freaking out and listen!" Gabriel said with unconcealed frustration. "You should be grateful: we don't have to tell you anything."

"Enough!" Sterling's voice was barely raised, but his words were firm. Gabriel scowled. Juliet turned back towards Sterling and gently placed the chair back on the ground but remained standing behind it. "Gabriel, if you can't control yourself, leave," his father said without looking at him. "Juliet, I hope our relationship up to this point has shown you that you can trust us." He gestured to the empty chair. "Please, sit down. I promise you are safe with us." Juliet hesitated for a moment, but reluctantly sat down. Her previous panic was receding and rational thought was beginning to once again take control. Sterling was right: he and Cara had been nothing but warm and kind towards Juliet. Not trusting herself to speak, Juliet merely nodded her head in Sterling's direction.

"Thank you," Sterling said, readjusting his position in his seat. "We are not werewolves. Those mythical monsters were created by our enemies to stir up fear and hatred. Yes, we're both wolf and human, but we are also much more." Sterling paused and looked down at the open book on the desk. He rested his pointer finger over the image on the page. "After the fall of man and their removal from Eden, God created a guardian to battle the enemy in all its forms. These creations were called the Ze'ev Shamar, which means 'wolf protector'. We refer to ourselves as just Shamar, or protector."

Juliet leaned forward and touched the page. The material felt different from normal paper; it was soft and smooth like a polished stone. She ran her fingers over the image of the wolf, feeling the detail of the fur. Even the snake had tiny scales. The craftsmanship reminded her of etchings from the medieval ages. Juliet wondered just how old the book was.

"So," Juliet began, removing her hand from the book and looking up at Sterling. "You're telling me that you transform into wolves to…hunt evil snakes?" The disbelief was impossible for her to hide.

Gabriel let out a low grunt. "If only it were that easy."

Sterling ignored his son. "You see, that snake – the snake that tempted Adam and Eve – was Lucifer's temptation of humans."

"Yes, I've read Genesis." Juliet's mind was trying to comprehend what she was hearing. "But I've never read the part about a wolf eating the snake afterwards."

"No, you wouldn't have. That part is only known to us." Sterling stopped and examined Juliet's quizzical expression. "Although we keep our roles in history a secret, what I'm telling you is true. We are protectors: our purpose is not to gain fame but to protect humans from the workings of Lucifer. That snake was the very first of its kind. Lucifer's first attempt to separate God from his creation. God alone has the ability to create. But, the world has fallen and Lucifer's power and influence in the weak minded creatures of the world, be they man or beast is real. He managed to twist God's creation of flesh and blood to his own will. Those in whom he has affected are known as the Amoveo." Sterling turned the page, and Juliet saw a new image: a man with red eyes whispering into a person's ears. There was writing in a language she did not understand on the opposite page. "The Amoveo are a race of people who can shift into any creature they want, except wolves. Throughout history, there are stories of animals wreaking havoc or destroying lives. Those stories are based on them."

Juliet's head was spinning. Yes, she had spent years reading fiction about fantastical creatures, but they were illusions, the products of imagination. If she hadn't seen it with her own eyes she would have laughed at Sterling's explanation. It was overwhelming. She started seeing black dots in her vision. Juliet folded over in the chair and placed her head in between her knees trying to keep herself from passing out. Her stomach clenched. A hand rested on her back. "Don't touch me!" she ordered. The hand she knew belonged to Gabriel withdrew.

After a few moments of silence, the feeling of faintness passed but the stomach pain remained. She lifted her head. "How do I know you're not the ones who are evil and manipulating me now?"

"We're not evil." Sterling's words were soft but firm. "The Amoveo have influenced history and culture to portray us as ruthless, man-killing beasts. This is far from the truth. Like the Amoveo, we can shift into humans or exist in our wolf form. But we are warriors born to hunt and destroy these creatures and only them. Not to hurt mankind."

Juliet felt vaguely reassured, but there was something else preventing her from being convinced. "But...Secret..." Juliet almost whispered. Gabriel had said he had caused Secret's death, and despite the Archons' repeated reassurances she was safe, Juliet had to know the truth about what had happened before she could ever start to believe them. None of the other people in the room said anything, so Juliet continued, "You tell me you are the protectors of humans, but where were you when Secret needed you?"

"We are fallible." Sterling's face was kind. "If we had known what was to happen, we would have been there."

Juliet looked down at the image in the book before her. The red eyes of the Amoveo had a sinister gleam. "What did happen?" Juliet asked, the pain in her stomach causing her to lean forward.

Sterling sighed. "Unfortunately, the Amoveo have gathered a following. Through their lies and deceptions, they have convinced humans we are the real enemy. They call themselves the Venator." Sterling stopped and looked down at the book on the desk. He pulled it back towards him and flipped through several pages, settling on one before pushing it back towards Juliet. When she looked down at the image before her, Juliet gasped. Staring back at her was the tattoo she had struggled to remember, the one on the arm of the man who attacked her. The symbol she previously could not remember now seemed so vivid drawn on the page. When she had first seen it, the tattoo had looked just like scribble, but now that she could sit and study it, there was a discernible pattern. The black lines were sharp and entwined like barbed wire crisscrossing to make narrow, jagged, tilted rectangles with a vaguely discernible 'V' in the center. "Venator" was written on the top of the page.

"The tattoo." The words escaped from her mouth.

Juliet saw the confirmation on Sterling's face with her recognition as he continued his explanation, "Next to the Amoveo, these are the most dangerous people you will ever meet. They are zealots. Anyone or anything they suspect as non-human they will destroy. They are secretive, and, when they strike, they leave destruction and carnage. These people don't care about innocent lives. We knew someone was hunting us after the incident with Jacob this summer, and suspected they may be the ones, but had no proof… until now."

Juliet's head was swimming. *They knew? They knew and they didn't warn us?* "But you knew we were going into the park. Why didn't you say anything? Make up some reason why we shouldn't go? You –" Juliet could feel her anger welling up again. "You sent Hanna with us!"

"We kept out of the National Park after Jacob was trapped. It was my decision not to tell you who and what we were." Gabriel said, stepping forward to the side of his father's desk. "I sent Hanna to look for signs of other traps. I never thought the Venator would be in the woods."

"But she's a kid!" Juliet yelled, standing up from her chair. She had forgotten her fear, and only focused on the thought that Gabriel had put everyone in danger. "Secret died because you didn't tell me these people were out there! We all could have died!"

"Would you have believed me if I had told you the truth?" Gabriel said, his previously calm voice now rising to match Juliet's. Juliet didn't know what to say, but stood in defiance although she knew he was right. Fists clenched, nails digging into her palms, the tears that had built up in her eyes were silently rolling down her face. She could feel her anger turning into grief, and fought to keep her fury. Even so, her shoulders slumped.

"I am so sorry, Juliet. If I had known..." His voice was much softer than before. "I never should have let any of you go out that day. I thought that Hanna—" Her eyes, tears no longer flowing, darted to his face. She cut Gabriel off with a snort, folding her arms across her chest. Gabriel rested a hand on his father's desk. "She may be young, but she's a trained fighter."

Juliet just continued to look at him with disbelief and disdain. Gabriel shifted, removing his hand from the desk and straightening to his full height. "It doesn't matter; none of it would have made a difference. I miscalculated the situation and people got hurt. I'm sorry." He looked directly at Juliet, his blue eyes boring in to hers. "Truly, truly sorry. You must know that."

Somewhere deep inside, she knew everything he had done these past 6 weeks was his way of proving to her how sorry he was, how guilty he felt. Still, she wasn't ready to forgive him. Not for this.

Juliet sat back down in the chair and slapped her hands on her knees. "Well, now that you said that, I feel so much better," she spouted off sarcastically, the only affect she felt confident would keep her balanced between yelling and sobbing.

Gabriel said nothing in return. He only stood there looking more pitiful than Juliet could remember ever seeing him, which made her furious until she couldn't bear to watch him anymore. Juliet scanned the room, avoiding Sterling and Cara's faces, trying to decide if she could just get up and leave now that she had heard all she needed to hear, when a piece of Sterling's words came back to her. She focused her attention on the seated figure before her. "Jacob is Iacobus, the wolf in the trap, he's…Shamar, right? "

"Correct," replied Sterling, the slightest hint of relief in his voice. "My son couldn't tell you the real names of the wolves when you asked, so he used our Latin names. He and Mathew were playing in the forest that day when Jacob got caught in the trap." Juliet thought back to the Fourth of July picnic, to Jacob's scar and Nora's odd comment. Now that it was laid out in front of her, it seemed so obvious.

"We were so fortunate you were the first one to find him," Sterling continued. "Of course, at first, when Mathew came back and said he had seen someone unfamiliar dart and take Jacob we assumed the worst." Sterling glanced at his son.

It took Juliet a moment to realize what he was implying. "You thought I was a Venator?" she asked incredulously. Then another thought hit her. "And that's why you came to the clinic that day?" she demanded, directing her question towards Gabriel.

All of a sudden his overreaction at their first meeting made sense, although knowing it was Gabriel's nephew on the operating table that day still didn't make Juliet excuse his behavior. "How did you know I wasn't?" she asked Sterling.

A small smile formed on Sterling's face. "Even a Venator trying to get close to us wouldn't pass up the chance to kill a Shamar. They consider it their greatest accomplishment. When Anthony, Dr. Silver, called after the surgery to report all of your efforts had been to save Jacob, not destroy him, we knew you were someone who could be trusted."

Cara moved from her husband's side and kneeled next to Juliet. "Which is why when you were attacked the first time, we took great measures to keep you close to us." There was a hint of sadness in Cara's voice as she spoke.

Juliet was about to make a sarcastic quip about just how far that trust had been abused when the door to the office opened, and Marcus walked in followed by Lorna, Ben, Kayla, Travis, and Sabra. She noticed Cara slipped out of the study after the others had entered. Juliet sat and listened to Sterling explain to the others why Juliet now knew the truth. While he spoke, Juliet desperately tried to process the information that had been thrown at her. The conversation had been was such a rollercoaster of emotions and information and she wasn't sure she'd be able to digest it all. Juliet was in the middle of a holy war, and Secret had been a casualty. She studied the face of each family member before her with a different view. These were warriors. She could now see the strength behind each of them. Juliet wanted to respect them, but they were also liars. She didn't care they had lied to safeguard their family. Her friend was dead because of it.

The center of her anger focused on Gabriel. She'd forgotten his previous apologies and focused on the one element of his story that could feed her fury: he claimed to be a protector, but he hadn't protected Secret. If he was born to defend humans, why hadn't he watched over her friend? He'd failed. Juliet's face grew hot with anger as her gaze found Gabriel among his family members in the office. He no longer looked defeated or ashamed. His assumed the countenance of a hardened veteran weathered by tragedy, who no longer saw the faces of the fallen in his fight for good versus evil. He hadn't even mourned Secret's death, despite his admonition of guilt. He'd continued with his life, and even used Juliet's sorrow to get closer to her. She suddenly had the desire to get up and slap him, but elected to stew in silence. She was so deep in her own mind she didn't realize everyone had stopped talking and was looking at her. "What?"

Marcus straightened. "I said I think the Venator are tracking you and think you may be able to lead them to us. We found listening devices in your rental after the fire. They were probably installing them the day they broke into your house. When you caught them, they panicked and tried to kill you."

His mentioning her attackers brought the memory of their dead bodies to her mind. Kevin had said the bodies had been scavenged by animals. "Did you kill them? The bodies had animal marks on them was it you? Did you see the tattoo and know then, what was out there?"

Marcus' face remained neutral. "No, we didn't. Whoever killed them did it to hide who they were from us."

Gabriel knelt down next to her. "I need you to think back and tell me if you told anybody about me rescuing you that night."

Juliet deliberately turned her head and let out, in as slow and smoldering tone as she could conjure, "Oh, wait, are you asking if I kept an important secret that might have gotten you or someone you care about killed?" Juliet did nothing to hide the rage.

Gabriel's face reddened. "Juliet, please. I thought—" He lowered his voice so only she could hear. "I don't know how else to apologize. I need your help now."

She could feel the muscles in her jaw quivering. "No, I didn't even tell Secret."

Gabriel blew out a deep breath and stood back up to address the whole room. "Then chances are they still don't know exactly who any of us are yet or they would've attacked by now."

Sterling rose from his chair. "No, son, I think we need to assume they do know who we are, but not all of us. They have one shot, and they know it. They're going to want to take down this entire family all at once."

Lorna stepped forward. "So what do we do now?"

"We stick together, but still act normal. No one is to run off this property, especially the children. The National Park is off limits. We'll divide up nightly patrols amongst the family. Sabra, darling, I need you to postpone going back to school this semester until we know what we are up against. We've lost one family member to them by being separated; I will not lose you."

Sabra looked down; her face had lost its normal glow. "Yes, Father. I understand."

Sterling turned to Juliet. "My dear, you are an amazing woman. Don't forget that. If you have any questions, please ask, but, for now, could you please excuse us? I have much to discuss with my family."

Chapter 28

Practically running down the hallway, she burst out through the front door onto the porch. She didn't care they had just told her everything; this was too much for one person to handle let alone stick around. Her feet clapped loudly along the stairs. When her shoes hit the gravel sidewalk, she heard her name being called. Juliet ignored the voice and started running. She needed to get away. Now. The person calling out her name increased her volume and urgency. Juliet stopped about twenty feet from the house and whirled around to see Cara sitting on a rocking chair on the porch. Like prey being hunted, Juliet froze.

"You're going to leave, aren't you?" Cara's voice was even.

"No." Lying seemed like the best option at this point in time.

Cara rose from the chair. "Before you pack up, I want to show you something."

The older woman opened the door and stood there waiting for Juliet. Reluctant, she put one foot in front of the other and made her way back up the steps. Once inside, she followed Cara to the family room where they stopped in front of a picture frame.

Cara pointed to it, and Juliet recognized it from the night she first had dinner with the Archon family. Gabriel, Michael, and Gabriel's fiancée, Natalia, stood together smiling. Cara sat in the closest chair and motioned for Juliet to sit across from her. Her voice had hardened. "We've all *lost* someone. Some more than others."

She opened her arms and looked all around to indicate infinity. "Our existence here is sometimes defined by depravity, loss and sacrifice. It is our burden here to bear." Cara looked to the picture and pointed again. "We are raised knowing life is fragile and can be taken away at any time, but nothing can ever prepare you to lose a son."

Juliet continued looking at the picture. She did not know how any of this related to her situation. Cara had lost her son in an accident; Juliet's best friend had been murdered. The comparison was not the same, which only churned the anger inside. "Sabra told me they died in a car accident."

"Michael and Natalia were never in a car accident. That is what we tell people outside of the family. They were murdered by the Venator."

Juliet's mouth opened but no words came out. "Everyone in this family knows what it feels like to lose someone you care about to these people. You're not alone." Cara continued, "Gabriel was finishing his residency in Atlanta. Michael and Natalia went down to visit him."

Cara walked over to the picture and took it down. "Michael had just graduated from college and missed Gabriel so much; he wanted him to come home." She touched the picture of Michael with her fingertip. "Gabriel doesn't speak much of what happened that day. It almost destroyed him."

The sadness was evident in Cara's face. "He had left his apartment and got a phone call from Natalia. She was screaming that men had broken into the apartment and killed Michael. She escaped, but they were chasing her. Natalia was in the car trying to get to the police station. Gabriel heard her screams through the phone and then nothing."

Juliet stood up wide-eyed listening to the woman's story. A cold shiver went down her spine while the hairs on the back of her neck stood up. Cara continued, "When Gabriel got back to the apartment, he found Michael's body. They had—" There was a crack in her voice.

Cara cleared her throat. "Gabriel searched for Natalia. He followed different paths to the nearest police station. On his way, he came across an accident at a bridge. A car had crashed through the railing and plunged into the water. Gabriel stood there for hours waiting. In the end, the police pulled Natalia's car out of the water. They never found her body, but there were bullet holes going through the driver's side. The investigators found several silver bullets embedded in the car frame, some had traces of her blood on them."

Cara took a box off the mantel and handed it to Juliet. "Gabriel found a silver ring searing the inside of Michael's hand. It had that horrible symbol you recognized engraved all around it. We think he managed to pull it off one of the men when they fought."

Opening the box, she discovered a ring with the Venator symbol emblazoned on the metal. Juliet held it in her fingers before returning it to the box. She closed it and handed it back.

Cara took the box from her. "We failed your friend. And for that, we are sorry. No attempt with words to assuage your grief will suffice. You must appreciate how thin the line my family walks and how few of us there are to complete the task at hand. If you leave now, your friend's sacrifice may go in vain. Stay and you will participate in seeing God's justice metered out in full. These are the things being discussed in that office."

Juliet stood speechless. The words washed over, and settled in her mind.

"You saved my grandson, and I've never truthfully thanked you for it. Thank you." Cara reached out and gently squeezed Juliet's hand.

"You're welcome," Juliet replied.

"Mom." Both women looked up at Gabriel who was standing at the edge of the room. "Dad wanted me to come check on you."

Cara walked out of the family room, but not before she stopped and patted her son of the arm. "I think I'll leave you two and go speak with your father."

"We need to talk." Gabriel said to Juliet, though his voice was distant.

"That's the last thing I want to do right now." She headed out of the room and towards the front door.

Gabriel followed her out the door and down the path. "Juliet. Juliet, please, just talk to me."

She kept walking.

"I'm sorry."

An inexplicable rage flared up at these words, and Juliet stopped and turned on him. "Sorry about which part, exactly? Where you lied? Where your family hid everything from me and played me for a fool? Where Secret died because you didn't have the guts to tell me about some vigilante group that is hunting you? Or are you sorry you got caught? Which is it, Gabriel, because it seems you've got a lot to be sorry about."

Gabriel focused on her face. "I'm sorry we – I – didn't keep you and Secret safe. I'm sorry you're afraid, angry, and probably confused right now."

The volcano inside her erupted and before realizing what she was doing, Juliet took a step towards Gabriel, and slapped him across the face, making her fingers sting from the impact. He lowered his gaze, making no attempt to follow when she walked away.

Chapter 29

Juliet drove around town, lost in thought, until she found herself in front of Secret's house. The spot where Secret used to park sat empty next to Kevin's vehicle. Another reminder of what she'd lost. She slowly climbed out of the truck and made her way to the door.

Kevin opened the door a few moments after she knocked. He looked shocked to see her. "Hey," he started then seemed lost for words.

"Hey," Juliet said, a wallowing pool of anxiety settling in her abdomen. Why had she come here?

"Um, is everything okay?" Kevin's startled face morphed into concern. "You look like you could use a friend."

"Yeah..." she stood awkwardly, unsure of what to say. Deciding she needed to trust something, Juliet picked her instincts. She had driven here for a reason, even if she wasn't sure what it was. "Can I come in?" she asked.

He opened the door, and Juliet shuffled in heading directly for the couch. Kevin sat in his old brown recliner, hands clasped together. The clock on the wall ticked the seconds away, marking their silence. Juliet looked at Kevin, and realized she had missed him; missed having him as a friend. Even though Juliet had always been skeptical of Secret's boyfriends, she liked Kevin almost instantly, and it became clear the three of them could spend time together without Juliet feeling like a third wheel. Of course she and Secret were best friends, but Kevin never felt like an intruder. Plus, it was nice to have someone to gang up on Secret with. A pang of guilt hit Juliet – the last thing she expected to feel right now: why had she pushed him away and kept him out of her life these past few weeks? If anything, she needed a real friend, someone she could trust. Kevin was still looking at the spot on the floor between his feet, his hands clasped together. Juliet could see his knuckles clenching and unclenching.

"So, what brings you here?" Kevin asked, breaking the silence.

The real reason for Juliet's visit came hurtling back at her, and she dropped her gaze to her lap. She could feel Kevin growing serious. "Jules, what's wrong?" Juliet didn't respond. What was she supposed to say? She couldn't tell him the truth – she was still trying to process it herself. But there were pieces she could talk about.

"Did someone try to hurt you?" The anger in Kevin's voice surprised Juliet, and she jerked her head up to meet his eyes.

"No," Juliet said, but then continued, "At least not physically."

Kevin was leaning forward in his chair, and the expression on his face made Juliet's hair stand on end. She couldn't remember ever seeing him this angry.

"Kevin, please, I'm okay." She saw him relax a little. "It's not even that big of a deal. I'm sorry to bother you, but I just didn't have any other place to go."

"It's okay," he said. "It must've been pretty big for you to drive out here."

"Well, it is and it isn't." Juliet thought carefully before she went on. "It's about Gabriel." Kevin's face remained blank, waiting for Juliet to explain. "I guess you and Secret were right: I do – or at least I did – have feelings for him."

Kevin's mouth twitched, but Juliet couldn't tell if he was holding back a mocking smile or resisting another surge of anger. There was a long pause before Kevin said, "Well, I can't say I'm surprised."

Juliet was trying to work out what else to say. Her feelings for Gabriel were complicated, but any romantic inclinations were not first on her mind right now. How could she talk about the real issue without sounding crazy?

"So, what's the problem?" Kevin asked.

Juliet sighed. She thought about all the truthful answers to Kevin's question. There were too many to count. As she listed off all her concerns in her mind, she could feel the rage from before returning. "I'm just so angry, and I don't know what to do. I feel like I can't see the forest through the trees." Juliet looked straight at Kevin, willing herself to stay calm.

Kevin wrinkled his forehead. "I don't understand."

"I've been adrift since Secret died; desperate to find something to hold onto. I thought I found it, and it turned out to be a hoax."

"Jules. I really am lost." Kevin scratched the back of his head.

"I got in a fight with Gabriel," she said delicately.

Kevin frowned. "About?"

Juliet shook her head. "It's not important. The important thing is he's not the person I thought he was."

Juliet thought she saw a flicker of recognition flash across Kevin's face, but when he stood up and moved to sit down on the couch next to her, all she could see was his look of deepening concern.

"He had been helping me deal with…stuff, and things were getting a little easier, you know? And then I find out he's been lying to me this whole time."

"Lying to you about what?" Kevin's brown eyes were so intense Juliet felt the need to drop her gaze.

"Just…everything. His past, who he is, what he wants from me." Juliet was teetering on the edge of just telling

Kevin the whole story. These half-truths were forcing her to dance around the real issue, and she wasn't getting anywhere.

In her silence, Kevin spoke up. "So, what do you need from me?"

Juliet looked up at him again. Though his words had been soft, she could see he was upset, and his eyes flashed with whatever he was holding back. No, she couldn't tell him the truth. Not now. But she suddenly saw a way to get the answers she wanted. "I need you to tell me what you would do to find Secret's killer," she said quickly.

A brief look of shock washed over Kevin's face and then disappeared, replaced with a new calm. "Anything that needed to be done," he said so coldly Juliet felt a shiver run down her spine. "Even if it meant making sacrifices to get to the end goal."

Juliet chewed on the end of her thumbnail, wrestling over his answer. The intense emotions he had been holding back were gone, and a fierce resolve now plastered his features. Her question had struck a nerve. Juliet could feel herself agreeing with his words. She knew what to do next. "Thanks, Kevin," she said, leaning over to hug him. Kevin looked surprised and then Juliet felt his arms around her back. She pulled away from him and stood up from the couch. "Sorry to be so cryptic, but I need to do something."

Kevin looked up at her. "I understand," he said, his tone still low.

Juliet managed a small smile. "I doubt it, but someday I hope to explain it to you."

Her light words seemed to bring Kevin out of the trance he had worked himself into, and he stood up to walk her to the door. As Juliet stepped out onto the front step, Kevin's usual ease and laughter had returned. "You do realize you haven't made any sense, right?" he called after her as she walked to her truck. She glanced over her shoulder and gave him a quick wave and a smile. She got into her truck and backed out of the driveway while Kevin stood at the door and watched her drive away.

Leaving Kevin's house, she picked up the phone and left a message on Dr. Silver's voicemail that she would not be into work the next day. With some hesitation, she headed back to her temporary home. As much as she had wanted to escape their family and their property, she was calm enough now to realize it didn't make sense for any of the Archons to hurt her. Even so, she was glad she didn't see anyone driving up the road to the guesthouse. Once inside, she locked the front door and pulled the curtains over all the windows. Then she went to work. Armed with her laptop, Shadow, and a bowl of macaroni and cheese, she Googled 'Shamar', 'Amoveo', and 'Venator'. What she got was a big ol' goose egg of nothing. If the Internet didn't have answers, where else was there? She decided to switch tactics and typed in the word 'werewolf'. She knew that was not what they called themselves, but it was the closest thing she had. She immediately had over 33 million results. Even if it wasn't what they wanted to be called, at least she was getting somewhere.

She clicked on the first link and started scrolling. As pages of pictures and written descriptions popped up about werewolves, her mind kept replaying the image she had seen the day before. How Gabriel's body had lengthened and twisted, his canine teeth growing long and sharp. In that moment, her ever-fragile hope of finding someone she could trust were dashed as he revealed himself to be just another man who had hurt her.

And what about the rest of the family? They were all in it together. Lorna and Sabra had just started filling some of the void she felt with Secret's death. Sterling and Cara had taken her in and had become like second parents. Was their friendship part of the lies and deception or had it been real? The children whom she had come to care about: what about them? Her inside ached.

What would she have done to protect her family? Would she lie? Would she keep secrets from her friends? If it meant protecting them from danger, then yes, she would, but at what cost? These questions kept creeping back into her thoughts as she continued to study the words on the screen.

By Monday evening, her eyes were sore from looking at her computer all day. She had only been able to get through a tiny fraction of the werewolf information she had found online. No one had stopped by or tried to contact her, though Juliet was sure they knew where she was. She was starting to feel a little stir crazy, and cautiously opened up some of the curtains. The woods around the house looked silent. Deciding she could risk going outside for some fresh air, Juliet headed out the front door. Immediately, the late summer breeze started to rejuvenate her mind and spirit. Juliet asked herself the question she had asked Kevin: what would she do to find Secret's killer? She filled her lungs with another cleansing breath, and the answer she had struggled with for days suddenly seemed so clear. It wasn't a question of what she would do, it was a matter of how far she was willing to go. With new determination, Juliet marched over to Sterling and Cara's house.

Cara opened the door when Juliet knocked. Her eyes widened and she straightened her back. "Come in," Cara invited.

Juliet walked in and followed Cara into the family room where Sterling and Gabriel were sitting. Their conversation halted, and Gabriel stood up. Juliet ignored him and focused her attention on the older of the two men. "I'll help you in any way I can to find Secret's killers." Sterling went to open his mouth, but Juliet cut him off before he could start talking. "But if I find out any of you have lied to me or kept me in the dark about anything else, I'm gone."

Sterling now stood up. His eyes filled with kindness and understanding. "Thank you. I know this must have been a difficult decision."

His words emboldened her. "I also want you to teach me how to fight. I'm sick of being defenseless." While keeping her face towards Sterling she pointed her finger at Gabriel. "And don't you even start trying to tell me you're going to protect me. You haven't exactly done a bang up job in that department."

"I'll have Sabra start working with you," Sterling said, his eyes brightening. "She's an excellent teacher, and it'll give her something to do while she's away from school." Sterling remained standing. His eyes darted to his son and then back to Juliet. "Is there anything else?"

Juliet turned her gaze to Gabriel. She wanted so badly to hurt him; not wanting him to think he'd won because she was agreeing to stay. "When it's over, I'm leaving. I want no part of your world."

Chapter 30

The cold piece of technology sat lifeless on the coffee table, the screen mocking its owner with a contorted reflection of a face. It hadn't rung for days. There was no one to call. Secret was dead. Her parents and brother wouldn't understand. The talks she'd had with Kevin had paved the way to renewing their friendship, but their conversations were still awkward. She wasn't sure how much he appreciated her cryptic phone calls that mostly involved her whining about Gabriel and the bruises covering her body from her new "self-defense class". Kevin had been supportive, telling her it was good she was doing something active. Of course, Juliet had left out the detail that this particular class was a one-on-one with Gabriel's sister.

"So, let me get this straight," Kevin's voice said over the speakerphone while Juliet was pulling every bag of frozen peas she could find out of the freezer. "You haven't seen him in two weeks, and you keep saying you don't want to, but he's pretty much all you think about?"

Juliet settled onto the couch, stretching her legs out in front of her and draping the bags of peas over her throbbing muscles. "He's not all I think about!" she retorted.

"Well, it's all I ever hear you talk about," Kevin said. Juliet glared at the phone on the coffee table beside her.

"It's just hard not to talk about him when I'm living in his parent's guesthouse," Juliet finally responded, though she knew the answer was weak.

"Right." Juliet could hear Kevin's eye roll through the phone.

Juliet sighed. "Sorry, I'll try to find other topics to discuss."

There was a pause and then Kevin said, "You know, my offer still stands, the one about you moving into the guest bedroom."

Juliet was glad that Kevin couldn't see her reaction, because she was certain he would mock her incessantly if he could see the red creeping into her cheeks. Even though Kevin had assured her many times the kiss was a mistake and his feelings for her were nothing more than platonic, Juliet couldn't help but notice how angry he became when she talked about Gabriel for too long.

"Thanks, Kevin. I really appreciate that." Juliet paused, suddenly considering what it would be like to escape the watchful eyes of the Archons. But, no, it wouldn't be fair to risk Kevin's safety in light of recent events. "I'm fine here, really. I just complain because I can." She tried to make it sarcastic, but it came out sadder than she had intended. "I've got to go. Thanks for talking."

"Of course. Any time."

That had been three days ago, and Juliet hadn't heard from him since. Since she had made her ultimatum to the Archons, Kevin had been the only person outside of the family Juliet had spoken to. She'd been wishing for an interesting case at work just to have an excuse to call him up. She knew all it would take was one good story about projectile vomit to bring her and Kevin back to laughing and joking. As it was now, she was alone with her thoughts which were filled with anger and heartbreak.

A knock on the door made Juliet jump and then wince. Her muscles, tired and sore from today's lesson with Sabra, screamed in protest with the sudden movement. "Come in," she called out not wanting to attempt to get off the couch.

Lorna's scarlet hair broached the doorway followed by her face. The green in her eyes looked like a soft spring meadow. "Hey, I came to bring you that book you wanted to read."

"Thanks. Sorry, I would get up and get it, but I think Sabra broke me."

Lorna crossed the room and sat down next to her, laying the book next to the cell phone. "I was a little worried when I heard about your request. Sabra's really good, but she's tough. It's hard being the youngest. I think Sabra feels like she needs to prove herself."

Juliet grunted. "Tell me about it. After fifteen minutes, I feel like I'm going to die. How about having your three-year-old train me? I might be better off."

Lorna laughed. "Unfortunately, Nora doesn't know her own strength. She might inflict more damage."

"Fantastic." Juliet accidentally moved, causing her neck to spasm. "Ow, ow, ow." Her hand went to the back of her neck, trying to stop the pain.

"Here, let me." Lorna massaged the knotted muscle. "Wow, you're really bad off."

Juliet grimaced as the pain continued but after a few minutes started to dissipate. "Thank you, that feels better."

Lorna got off the couch and disappeared into the bathroom. When she emerged, a small towel was in her hands. Crossing over to the kitchen she opened the freezer door and immediately placed several ice cubes into the cloth then returned to the couch placing it on the back of Juliet's neck. "There, that should help."

The cold felt good. "I feel like a broken record by saying this again, but thank you."

"It is the least I could do, considering..." Lorna's voice trailed off. "For months I've wanted to thank you for saving my son's life. If you hadn't found him before the V—" Her voice caught in her throat. She cleared it. "I don't know what I would've done."

Jacob. It was so hard to imagine the wolf caught in the trap so many months ago was just a young boy. Juliet had unknowingly operated on a child: Lorna's child. She could have accidently done more damage to him or worse. The thought made her shudder.

"I am forever in your debt." Lorna's green eyes met her blue ones. "I know you're still mad, but I would hope, in time, you could find it in your heart to forgive us."

Juliet had spent so much time being angry she failed to consider anything else. She and Secret had saved a life. Her friend had died a hero. Then there were these Venators, cowards, out there trying to kill innocent children like Jacob and Nora. They had killed her friend. Secret would've sacrificed herself to save a child. That was who she was.

"If I let go of the anger, then all I have left is the sadness," Juliet whispered.

"Yes, but it makes room for things like friendship and love," replied Lorna. "Things a person needs. The entire family cares about you, if only you let us in."

Juliet wiped a tear from her face. "How?"

"Baby steps. I bet with everything that has happened you probably really want to talk with someone. You've got a great selection of listeners to choose from; just pick one." Lorna made it sound so easy.

Juliet sat there stewing over Lorna's words. What did she want to say? What couldn't she say to Kevin that she could to someone who understood? What would she say to Secret if she were sitting there? "Your brother's a jerk," she blurted out then covered her mouth with the couch pillow. "Sorry."

Lorna smiled looking out the window. "That's alright. Gabriel can be difficult sometimes. His heart is always in the right place, but he goes about it the wrong way at times."

"He betrayed me."

"I know that's how you feel now, but think about it from his point of view. You were a stranger, if he had told you the truth would you have believed him?" When Juliet didn't answer, Lorna continued. "If you had, how did he know you wouldn't have done something to hurt us, his family?"

Lorna's arguments were logical: typical lawyer. "It's been a long time since anyone in this family has revealed what we are to a human. When you found Aiden sleeping on the front porch—" Juliet scrunched her face up in confusion. "Sorry, I think Gabriel told you his name was Ardent, it's hard to keep track. Mom and Dad allowed Gabriel to mislead you. In fact, from what I hear you came up with most of the story yourself. So, technically, my brother didn't lie, he just let you believe your assumptions. Not that I agree with his decision."

Juliet opened her mouth to protest, but realized Lorna was right. She had offered up her own theories, Gabriel had just gone along with them. "Why did you say your mom and dad allowed Gabriel to mislead me?"

"They're the alpha pair."

"I thought Adir, I mean Gabriel, is the alpha."

Lorna got up and went back into the kitchen. She poured two glasses of lemonade and brought them back, handing one to Juliet. "Gabriel is an alpha, but so are both my parents. Our family has two alpha males and someday will have two alpha females. Mom and Dad tend to handle the affairs outside of the family, while Gabriel handles internal conflicts, but ultimately my parents are in charge."

"So do all packs have two alpha males?"

"No, we're the only one."

"Why?"

Lorna took a long sip of her drink. "That's for my parents or Gabriel to explain."

"Are you keeping another secret from me?" The anger was beginning to rise inside her again.

"No, it's just not my place. I'm not an alpha, there are certain things only they can explain."

"Then I'll ask your parents." The last thing she wanted was to have a conversation with that infuriating man. Juliet timidly stretched her legs, testing the tenderness of the muscles.

Lorna took the empty glasses back to the kitchen and deposited them into the dishwasher. "Remember that forgiveness is not for the person who has sinned against you, it's for yourself. A person should not carry resentment. It will eat at you, destroying you slowly from the inside out."

Chapter 31

"Thank God your dress is long so I won't have to cover up the bruises on your leg," grumbled Sabra as she was applying makeup over one of the purple marks on Juliet's arm.

"I'm sorry I don't have supernatural healing," Juliet shot back.

Lorna came into Sabra's bedroom. "Lorna, I need to start on her hair; can you finish covering up this bruise?" Sabra handed the make-up sponge to her sister.

The soft strokes of the brush through her hair felt nice. The one place on her body that wasn't sore was her head. Training had left her resembling a grape.

"I think that should about do it." Lorna finished applying some powder on Juliet's arms. The once-visible bruise was now gone.

"Good, you can start on her face now," ordered Sabra. "By the time we are done with you, every single man in this town will be chasing after you."

Juliet tried to turn and face Sabra, but she had a firm hold on several strands of hair. "Did you ever think for a second I might not want that?"

Lorna started wiping a liquid on Juliet's face. "Why don't you tell us what you want?"

The desire that had been there the day they had kissed had all but vanished when she saw him change, but the tiny spark still present inside had grown slowly each day. Her mind kept thinking about that day he kissed her. How his wet skin felt against hers. The way she liked his strong arms around her body, and his lips, how very much she wanted those lips to kiss every part of her. Even now, when she thought about it, her body would get warm and tingly; however, she was leaving after this was over. Juliet knew she shouldn't get involved. But as much as her rational mind fought it, her feelings were winning the battle.

"You know, Gabriel will be there tonight." Lorna started dabbing something under Juliet's eyes.

"I know." She spoke softly.

Lorna stopped what she was doing. "He thinks a lot of you."

Juliet sighed. Sabra pulled on Juliet's hair a little too tightly causing her to wince. "Oh, for goodness sakes. I can't put up with this any longer."

Lorna cast her sister a weary look. "This is none of our business."

"Come on, you can't tell me you aren't sick of smelling the two of them." Sabra relaxed her grip on Juliet's hair. "Even now I can tell she's thinking about him."

"Sabra." There was a warning in Lorna's voice.

Juliet raised a hand like a student who wanted the teacher to call on her. "Could you please explain what you're talking about? I'm pretty sure you just said you can smell me thinking."

Unable to see Sabra's face behind her, Juliet looked to Lorna who was glancing at her sister. Her lips were pressed together. "Fine," Lorna stated. "But be very careful in how you explain this."

"I will," Sabra huffed and then resumed working on Juliet's hair as she spoke. "You know how wolves have a better sense of smell than humans?" There was a little more pep in Sabra's tone.

"Yes."

"Our sense of smell is just as acute as an animal's, and all of us have a certain personal smell. We just interpret that smell differently."

"So, are you trying to tell me that I should put on more deodorant?"

Sabra let out a short laugh. "No, you don't smell bad. Well, at least not to me." Sabra pulled another strand of hair back and pinned it in place.

"What my sister is trying to say is Gabriel finds your fragrance appealing." Lorna picked up a brush to apply eye shadow.

"What does me smelling good have to do with anything, and how would you guys know he likes it anyway?" Juliet moved her head so she could look at both sisters.

Sabra dropped the piece of hair in her hand. "When he's around you he releases a massive dose of mating pheromones, and it's getting annoying."

"Sabra!" Lorna smacked her sister in the arm.

"What!" Sabra bit back. "Every time you two are together, we can smell it. I know you can smell him too but only when he's really turned on."

Juliet's mouth fell wide open. The room had grown small and hot. Sabra walked around to the front of her and knelt down. "Think about it: at the picnic, in church, and definitely when he saw you in that bikini. Haven't you ever wondered why you can sometimes smell him and other times you can't? The first time he smelled your scent at the picnic, we were blown away by the pheromones he was pumping out. And don't deny you like it, because we can smell yours too."

Never before had Juliet really wished she could melt into the floor. If what Sabra said was true, not only could Gabriel tell she was attracted to him, but so could everybody else. "Then why didn't this happen the first time we met?"

"I don't follow." Sabra glanced at Juliet and then Lorna.

"I met Gabriel at the veterinary hospital. There was never any smell or release of anything except for him shouting at me. If I'm so appealing to him, how do you explain that?" Juliet felt quite smug in her response.

Lorna stepped in. "Were your wrists covered?"

Juliet thought back to that day months ago. "I still had latex gloves on over my surgical gown."

"That explains it." When she realized Juliet did not completely follow, Lorna continued, "Everyone's scent is excreted mainly around the inside of the wrist. Latex masks the scent."

Juliet put her hands to her face. "You're telling me, since the picnic, Gabriel has found me attractive?"

Both women nodded their heads in affirmation.

"And he knows I'm attracted to him?"

They continued nodding.

"And everybody knows because they can smell the hormones between the two of us?"

Lorna gave Juliet a sympathetic smile. Sabra just rolled her eyes. Juliet buried her face in her hands. "Why can't I have been mixed up with a normal family? I'm definitely not going tonight," she mumbled through her hands.

"Oh, yes you are," chided Sabra. "I haven't spent the last few weeks making this dress for you only to have you hide in the house."

"I'm sorry. You just informed me your brother has been in love with me from the moment I met him, and I'm supposed to sit here and act like everything's normal?" Juliet barked back.

Sabra put her hands on her hips. "He hasn't been in love with you since he met you. That's not how this works." The right side of her mouth angled upward. "He's just wanted to have sex with you since he met you, and, recently, from the smell of it, so have you."

"Enough!" scolded Lorna.

The heat of Juliet's face was practically unbearable. "Can I get a glass of water or something?"

"Go get her some water," directed Lorna.

Sabra sauntered out of the room. Lorna picked up a small book next to Sabra's bed and started fanning Juliet. "Just ignore Sabra. It's not as bad as she made it out to be."

"That's easy for you to say. Your hormones are not on display for everyone to smell," grumbled Juliet.

"That's where you're wrong." Lorna stopped fanning. "Almost all of the adults in this family have gone through this. We even know it will happen, and it's still embarrassing when it does. It's not a problem when we're kids, because we haven't hit sexual maturity so no pheromones. Having crushes is no big deal, but the minute the hormones kick in, it's all over. Everything is on display. I'd been in love with Ben for years when I was a child, but never told him. The minute I came of age, bam! There was no keeping it from him. I was so horrified; I hid in the house." She brushed a strand of hair off Juliet's shoulder. "Sabra's been off at school so there's no telling who she's been attracted to, but just wait until she meets a guy around you she thinks is hot. Then you can sit back and enjoy the show."

"Just because Gabriel's reaction to you was attraction doesn't mean you had to like the smell or even be attracted to him. You could've of thought he smelled like rotten eggs." Both women laughed at Lorna's comment. "But, you did find his scent attractive. It just means you two are physically compatible. The emotional part is up to both of you. There's always a choice. You don't have to be with anyone you don't want to."

"Thanks for explaining that to me."

"No problem." Lorna gently nudged Juliet. "I want to see both you and Gabriel happy. I like you, Juliet, and I think you're good for my brother."

The sting of embarrassment started to dissipate. That tiny seed of hope she had tried to keep buried for weeks fought its way to the surface. "Can I ask you a question about him?"

Lorna dabbed the eye shadow brush into the powder in her hand. "Sure."

"Can I trust him?"

Lorna's face was neutral. "Eyes closed, please." Juliet did as she was told. Lorna was quiet for a few moments, the only sound in the room was the soft sweep of the brush over Juliet's eyelid. Lorna pulled her hand away from Juliet's face, and she tentatively opened her eyes. Lorna was looking at her with a serious expression that softened ever so slightly as she started to speak. "Yes, you can trust him. He would die to protect any one of us."

Juliet peered at Lorna's face and could tell she was sincere. She closed her eyes again and felt the brush start across her left eyelid. Juliet heard footsteps coming into the room and felt something cold, hard, and cylindrical being placed in her hand.

"There's your water," stated Sabra.

She felt her hair once again being pulled and pinned to her head. The women worked on her hair and makeup while she sipped her water, mulling over the new information they had just presented to her. Juliet was a concoction of conflicting emotions: relieved to know she had not imagined the attraction between herself and Gabriel and yet scared of it. When they were both done, the sisters stood in front of their creation.

"I think we did pretty good, sis." A satisfactory smile spread over Sabra's face.

"I'm going to go get ready." Lorna turned to Sabra. "Behave."

"Let me finish my makeup and then we'll get our dresses," Sabra said in an overly chipper voice once Lorna had left the room.

About the time Sabra was applying her mascara, she pointed to a box on her dresser. "That's for you. Go into the bathroom and put them on."

"What is it?" Juliet picked up the box.

"Undergarments for your dress."

Juliet walked into the bathroom and closed the door. She opened the box and picked up the first item that she saw. What Juliet perceived as underwear was dangling from her fingers. She dropped it back into the box and then lifted up two silicone bra cups. "You've got to be kidding me."

"Sabra?" she said to the closed bathroom door.

"Yeah?" Sabra's voice answered.

"What is this?"

"What do you mean?"

"Is this supposed to be underwear and my bra?"

"Yup."

Juliet held up the underwear again. "Well, there's not much to it, and what little there is feels weird."

"It's a special, silver-infused material."

"Why?"

"Silver is toxic to us."

"You made me toxic underwear?"

"Did no one explain this to you yet?" Sabra called out.

"I think I would remember something about toxic silver," Juliet said.

"Fine. This is how Dad explains it: there are two metals that are extremely important in the New Testament in the Bible. The first is gold, which was brought by one of the wisemen as a gift for Jesus. Since it's associated with good, it's harmful to things that are evil like the Amoveo. Silver, on the other hand, was used as payment

for the betrayal of Jesus, which is why it's harmful to us."
Juliet had to admit Sabra did sound exactly like her father.

"Shouldn't you have made my underwear out of gold if you want to protect me?"

"Oh, I'm not protecting you from the Amoveo. I'm protecting you from yourself."

"Excuse me?" Juliet stuck her head out of the bathroom and looked at Sabra with raised eyebrows.

"Just think of it as a chastity belt," Sabra smirked.

"And what makes you think I need a chastity belt?" Juliet said, her voice losing its carefree and joking tone.

Not picking up on Juliet's sudden lack of humor, Sabra answered cheerfully, "Because, despite his flaws, my brother is a great guy."

At that, Juliet set the undergarments on the bathroom counter and walked into the room to Sabra. She folded her arms across her chest and tried to look as intimidating as possible. "And why would your brother be touching my underwear?"

Sabra shrugged innocently. "No reason. Now, go put it on so I can get you into your dress."

Juliet reentered the bathroom, shut the door, and began to get undressed. Her earlier giddiness over learning Gabriel had feelings for her had dissipated with Sabra's inferences he needed a physical barrier to prevent him from…whatever Sabra thought he might do to Juliet. It sent a wave of nausea through her. Thoughts of backing out of her agreement with Lorna and skipping the auction rushed through her brain. No, Lorna had just assured her Gabriel could be trusted, besides they hadn't spoken or seen each other since that day she'd slapped him. If he was even at the event, he wouldn't be bidding on her. She put on the bra cups, which stuck to each breast and were not as uncomfortable as she thought they'd be, and then put on the dental floss Sabra called underwear. Finished, she stepped out of the bathroom. Sabra was standing there holding the midnight blue material in her arms.

"Okay, you're going to have to step into your dress, and then we'll pull it up and fasten you in," instructed Sabra.

Juliet was unsure about all of this but didn't like standing almost naked in the middle of the room, so she hurried over to where the redhead was kneeling. She stepped into the dress and let Sabra bring it up. It felt silky against her skin. Sabra brought the material over Juliet's chest coming to a point at her right shoulder. Juliet noticed several silver-looking cords attached where the material ended forming an intricate design before separating into five individual strands. She could feel Sabra attaching them to different parts of the dress. Juliet also realized she didn't feel very much on her back. She went to look over her shoulder but Sabra gently brushed her face forward. "No looking until I'm done."

The redhead handed her some very 'Sabra-style' three-inch heals. Juliet fell directly over when she first put them on, then again when she took her first step. Next were teardrop sapphire earrings. Sabra then pulled out Secret's silver-cuffed bracelet. Juliet was shocked she was holding it in her bare hands.

Juliet pointed to the bracelet. "How are you doing that?"

Sabra smiled proudly. "This was something I came up with my freshman year of college when I was dating a chemistry TA. It's a liquid that coats the metal rendering it harmless to us. It does wear off, so you have to reapply it every so often, but it allows us to wear silver. The silver detailing in the back of your dress is dipped in it too. I'll give you a few bottles to use."

"That's amazing." Juliet took the bracelet from Sabra.

"Yeah, I wish I could come up with something we could put on our skin, but since the cells turn over so quickly it would wear off way too fast." Sabra handed her a bottle of the liquid.

Juliet looked at the substance in her hands. "It looks just like hand sanitizer."

"That's the plan. That way no one suspects anything if they find it."

"Are you sure you don't want to go into some kind of science field?"

"Yes." Sabra bent down and straightened out a kink in Juliet's dress. "This family needs my fashion sense."

At that moment, Lorna walked into the room. She looked absolutely gorgeous in her emerald, strapless dress, which made her eyes practically glow. She looked at Juliet and then circled around her. Her eyes grew wide, and she looked at Sabra. "Oh my."

Juliet shifted uncomfortably and looked down at the dress. The material was extremely thin, and it did seem to hug the few curves she had. She was about to ask to look in the mirror when Cara walked in. The smile on her face vanished into an open gape when she saw Juliet. How horrible did she look?

"Do I look that awful?" Juliet blurted out.

Cara walked over and put her arm around her shoulder. "Quite the contrary, my dear. You look absolutely angelic. Come look for yourself."

Cara guided her over to the three-sided, full-length mirror. Juliet gasped; she barely recognized herself. Even as an adult, she had always felt like her face had never fully matured, but the person looking back at her in the mirror was a regal woman. She turned and saw the back of the dress was practically nonexistent. The silver cords were the only thing covering her back with the center one making a straight line to the blue material barely covering her butt crack. Only a few millimeters of material prevented her from having plumber's butt.

Juliet continued to look at herself in the mirror. "Sabra, you and Lorna did a great job, but this isn't a dress I would wear. I'm showing too much skin and what is covered is very form fitting. I can't wear this out in public."

"Oh, yes you can, and you will," retorted Sabra.

"I know that you have worked very hard on this for Juliet, but we need to consider how she may feel about wearing this." Cara gave Juliet a reassuring smile.

"Oh, my God." Sabra threw her hands up in the air. "You need to come out of your shell. It's okay to be attractive." She pointed at Juliet.

"It's up to Juliet if she wants to wear this dress." Lorna placed her hands on her hips.

Juliet wrung her hands together. They were probably just being nice, nobody would be paying that much attention to her. "Oh hell, why not. What's the worst that could happen?"

Chapter 32

Two hours later, she was really wishing she hadn't said those words as she was standing on a stage feeling like a cow being led to slaughter. If she made it through tonight, she vowed to never let Sabra dress her again or allow Lorna to talk her into any kind of charity function involving auctions. From the minute they had walked into the ballroom, she and Sabra had been swarmed by men. While her younger counterpart had flirted and mingled, Juliet had done her best to become a wallflower. So when it was time for the auction to begin, Sabra was the bell of the ball and managed to drive the bidding up to $10,000 for a date with her. A few other single ladies had followed but didn't come anywhere close to Sabra's total. When it was Juliet's turn, it felt like she was betraying all the feminists of the world. She kept reminding herself this was for the sick children whose families couldn't afford treatment. As the bidding began, she plastered a smile on her face, but kept her mouth shut for fear she might throw up on stage.

The spotlight was so bright she couldn't see the men who were bidding. The bids kept getting higher and higher. Then Gabriel's wonderful smell slammed into her like a train causing her to step back. It was so overpowering she felt a little euphoric. Her ears heard the sound of his deep, husky voice say, "$50,000", snapping her back into reality. There was a generalized hush in the room and all eyes turned to look at the man who had just committed to such an unprecedented amount. The auctioneer pronounced "SOLD!", and Juliet was suddenly being escorted off stage.

Why had he done that? To bid so much money and make a spectacle of her after they hadn't spoken to each other in weeks. If the spotlight hadn't blinded her, she would have escaped through the nearest exit. With her eyes adjusting to the change in light, it took a few moments to focus on Gabriel's approaching form. He looked dashing in his black tuxedo. As he got closer, Juliet noticed his face was tense, his jaw was clenched, and his eyes were a brilliant blue, almost glowing. He positioned himself beside her and placed his hand gently on her bare back. Heat radiated from his hand and went throughout her body. He guided her through the room and spoke into her ear. "You look amazing."

They walked past the table where Sabra was sitting. The redhead winked at her and then pointed to her nose. Juliet wasn't sure if she wanted to laugh or throw something at her. Much to Juliet's surprise, Gabriel escorted her to a table filled with people she didn't know. She had assumed they would be sitting with his family. The only other person she recognized was Ben, the empty seat next to him most likely was for Lorna, who had been running around earlier dealing with some kind of party disaster.

Before pulling out her chair for her, Gabriel introduced her to the other people at the table who she discovered were all employees of the hospital and their spouses. She greeted each person politely and then took the seat next to her date. The muscles in his jawline had relaxed and the color in his eyes had softened. Juliet wondered what had happened to change his mood. Lorna returned, and Juliet leaned over to her. "I might kill your brother before the end of this evening for embarrassing me like that."

Lorna grimaced. "Sorry, he did go a bit overboard."

"What are you two ladies chit-chatting about over there?" asked a woman whom Gabriel had introduced as the head of surgery.

"I was just telling Lorna what a great job she's done with the charity event," responded Juliet.

"Oh, yes, and with the help of your fabulous date," the woman gestured to Gabriel, "We've raised more money than ever at one of these events."

"Thank you, Dr. Smith, but I think all the credit should go to Dr. Greene here. She was the one kind enough to be a part of this. If it wasn't for her, then I doubt we would have raised as much as we did." Gabriel gestured to her with his glass of champagne.

Dr. Smith looked back at Juliet with envious eyes. "You're so lucky, dear. He's such a charmer. If only I were twenty years younger."

"I'm right here, honey," murmured Mr. Smith.

"Actually, Dr. Smith, I'm the lucky one. Dr. Greene is everything a man would want. She is smart, kind, and gorgeous." Gabriel peered into Juliet's eyes.

Juliet felt her heart flutter. *Fickle thing*. She broke eye contact with Gabriel and turned so he could not see the color she knew was going into her face. Her brain was screaming at her emotions not to let a few compliments get her all mushy inside.

The salad being served distracted her from her internal battle. Juliet got a reprieve from most of the conversation during the meal since everyone was too busy eating. As much as she tried not to, she found herself looking over at Gabriel during the dinner.

The soft background music began to grow louder and change tempo after the dessert plates had been cleared. Several couples made their way to the dance floor and started dancing. Ben took his wife's hand and excused themselves from the table to join the other dancing couples. Gabriel stood and extended his hand towards Juliet. "Would you like to dance?"

Her cerebrum screamed no. "Yes."

She took his hand and let him lead her to the center of the room. His arm went around her waist, his hand resting gently on her back. Her breath increased with the touch of his fingers on her bare skin. He took her other hand in his and started guiding her along the dance floor. Regardless of everything else, she felt safe and relaxed when she was in his arms.

"I meant every word I said earlier." He leaned his head down close to her ear.

"But did you have to put on such a show in front of the entire town? I like not being noticed. It makes me feel safe." Her tongue didn't have the sharpness it normally had when she was chastising him.

"I'm sorry about embarrassing you, but you're wrong. When you are in a room, everyone notices you." Gabriel pulled Juliet closer to him and a new wave of his pheromones hit Juliet so hard she almost stumbled. "I am trying to be the man you deserve."

Sliding her hand out of his, she broke apart from his grasp. "I need something to drink."

Suddenly, the room seemed very stuffy. Why did he have to say things that confused her? She approached the bar and asked the bar tender for a glass of water. The cold water soothed the dryness in the back of her throat.

The small peace was interrupted when a man stumbled into her. "I'm sorry, sweetheart." He grabbed her arm to steady himself. "Hey, you're that girl that got all the money. You must be pretty special to be that expensive."

The stench of alcohol on his breath was overbearing. Juliet turned to leave but he stepped over to block her. "Hey, where are you going? I'm just trying to talk to you."

Repulsed by his presence, but knowing from previous experience a drunk like this could be dangerous and volatile Juliet chose her words cautiously. "I really need to get back to my date."

"Archon, that stiff." He maintained the grip on her arm. "Why would you bother with him when you can be with someone who knows how to have fun?"

"Let go of me." Juliet tried to pull her arm free.

His hand pressed harder in her skin, digging into one of the covered bruises sending waves of pain up into the arm. A large male hand reached across her and snatched the offending hand, pulling it off. Juliet looked up and saw Gabriel. His eyes were on fire and the anger on his face made her step back. "The lady told you to let go."

Gabriel bent the drunk man's hand back, and Juliet was convinced he might just pop it off. "You'll lose this hand the next time it touches her. Do you understand?"

Sweat was dripping down his face. "Yes."

People were starting to notice this altercation. To her surprise, Kevin approached the three of them. Somehow she had missed seeing him the entire evening. Gabriel let go, and the other man retreated back, clutching his released hand. "You and your family think you're entitled to everything around here. Well, someday that's going to change." He spit the words out.

Kevin grabbed Juliet's assailant by the back of the shirt. "Okay, pretty boy, let's take a walk and get you cooled off." He nodded his head at Gabriel and then Juliet.

She felt something light on her arm and saw Gabriel's fingers touching the red mark that had formed from being gripped so hard. "Are you okay?" he asked.

"I'm fine, thank you," she said, attempting a half-hearted smile.

"You're shaking." Gabriel took off his tuxedo jacket and placed it over her shoulders. It was still warm from the heat of his body. The side of the jacket started vibrating. Reaching into it, she pulled out his cell phone and handed it to him. "It's Marcus; he stayed at home tonight to guard things. I need to take this. Will you be okay?"

Juliet nodded yes and Gabriel walked away. After a few minutes, Gabriel returned to where he had left her. He bent down and placed his mouth closed to her ear. In a hushed tone, he said. "We need to go. Someone broke into your house."

Chapter 33

Marcus's car was already in Gabriel's driveway when they pulled in. The car ride from the charity event had been silent. From the death grip Gabriel had on the steering wheel, she could tell he was worried. This evening had already been filled with too much drama, and Juliet anticipated there would be more.

Gabriel opened the door to his house, and Marcus was standing in the middle of the living room. "Where are the others?" he asked.

"Dad thought it was best if only the two of us left while the others stayed and acted like nothing was wrong. We don't know whose watching." Gabriel undid his bowtie. "Now, tell me what happened."

Marcus glanced over to Juliet before he began, "We were doing our perimeter rounds when Kayla picked up six unfamiliar scents. We tracked them in both directions. One path led straight to where Juliet is staying. From the smell, they had been inside the house. Travis, Kayla, and Luke found the men trying to escape near the main road." Marcus paused, then cleared his throat and continued, "There was a fight."

"Was anyone hurt?" interrupted Juliet.

Marcus hesitated before answering. "No one in our family was seriously hurt." He looked at Gabriel. "They killed five of them, and the last one committed suicide before they could capture him."

Juliet pulled Gabriel's jacket tighter around her. It was happening all over again. By living with the Archons had she put them closer to harm's way? People were dying again.

"Another thing, they all had the tattoos on them." The lines on Marcus' face deepened.

Juliet was confused. "What does that mean?"

"It means that Venator are testing us and know exactly who we are." Gabriel turned to Juliet. "It's not safe for you to be alone anymore in that house. You can stay here tonight, and we'll figure something out tomorrow."

Juliet approached both men, her voice panicked. "Don't you think we should all leave? They know who you are, and as far as I know, we have no clue who they are, so isn't everyone in danger?"

"We're not running." Gabriel gritted his teeth. "We won't be chased away from our home."

Juliet knew the anger wasn't directed at her. She could feel the stress emanating from Gabriel. Her heart raced and her breathing increased. She wasn't as strong as she thought. "I need to excuse myself."

Gabriel walked over, reached out and rubbed her arms. "If you want to go up to my room, you can."

Juliet nodded and made her way up the stairs where she sat down on the edge of the bed. The first thing she did was take off the shoes that had been torturing her all night. Blisters had formed on both heals and on one of her toes. Rubbing her sore feet with her hands she wished Adir had been just a wolf so he could be there now. She wanted to run her hands through his fur and talk to him like before. To tell him her thoughts and feelings and have him not judge. This was too much. She wasn't brave. She wasn't a fighter. What had she been thinking agreeing to help this family when she had no business being in the middle of this mess?

Getting up off the bed, she went to the bathroom to wash her face, desperately hoping it might make her feel better. She scrubbed the make-up until her face was red.

Unfortunately, Lorna had used waterproof mascara. She needed make up remover. Her hair was pulled back too tightly and had started giving her a headache, so she tackled getting some of the bobby pins out. When she yanked out the last one, her golden locks cascaded down her back. All she needed was a pair of warm pajamas to attain the final level of comfort. Taking some liberties, she made her way to the walk-in closet in search of something to wear. Everything in the closet was as pristine and orderly as the rest of the house. She had to search several drawers before she found one containing worn tee-shirts. A few minutes later, she found a pair of ratty, old, cut-off sweatpants. She knew both would be huge on her, but they would work until she was brought her own clothes.

Juliet went back to the bedroom and tossed the clothes on the bed. She reached around to start unhooking the silver cords so she could take off the dress. With much frustration, she couldn't seem to figure out how to unlatch them. She went to the bathroom and turned her back towards the mirror. She looked over her shoulder at the reflection, trying to see how to undo the hooks. How had Sabra fastened these? Getting nowhere, Juliet decided to try and lift the dress over her head, but discovered she could not get it past her waist. She needed to get out of this dress, and she couldn't without help or a good pair of scissors. Panic began to set in. A knock on the doorframe caused her to almost jump out of her skin. She whirled around to see Gabriel stick his head past the opening of the door.

"Marcus left. Is it okay if I come in?" he asked.

"I was just about to come down." Juliet started walking towards the door. "I need you to call Sabra."

"What? Why?" The confusion was transparent on his face.

"I can't get out of this dress, and I need her to help me." Juliet was trying to keep her voice calm to disguise the rising alarm inside of her.

"Sabra's still at the event." Gabriel stepped towards her and reached out. "Here let me see if I can help."

Her nostrils filled with the smell of his pheromones. Juliet backed away from him. "I don't think you should help me."

Gabriel stopped and just stared at her. "Why?"

Juliet felt hot again. "Sabra told me about the phero-mones, and I don't want to have sex with you." Juliet cringed as she said it. That hadn't come out the way she wanted it to.

Gabriel's eyes widened while his skin blanched. "I – um." He shook his head. "I'm going to kill my sister when I see her."

"I think it's best if we go somewhere without a bed and have this conversation." Juliet padded past him.

She retreated to the safety of the kitchen. If Gabriel had not been standing feet away, she would have grabbed one of the knives out the butcher block and cut the damn dress off. As things were, she rested her hand inches away from the knife set and leaned against the countertop wait-ing for him to say something.

Gabriel cleared his throat. "How much has my baby sister told you?"

"Oh, you know, the basics: I smell incredible to you, every time you get turned on there's a massive surge of pheromones you emit that even I can smell, you can smell that I'm attracted to you, and to top it all off, everybody in your family knows and has found it entertaining." Her nails were clicking on top of the granite.

Gabriel reached up and rubbed the back of his neck. His cheeks became rosy. "You see… It's just that… If you let me explain…"

Juliet could not believe it. Gabriel was embarrassed. There was something endearing about this man being befuddled. Maybe it was the dress giving her the confidence, but before she realized it, Juliet was right in front of him. Standing on her toes, she pressed her mouth against his. Her pulse raced, and she withdrew her lips before anything could progress.

His arms encircled her, preventing her from putting too much distance between them. "What was that for?"

"You're cute when you stutter." Juliet gave him a sly smile. "I felt sorry for you."

"Are you telling me you gave me a pity kiss?" Gabriel's blue eyes darkened almost to the color of her dress.

Juliet shrugged and batted her eyes at him. Gabriel pressed his forehead against hers. "We do need to talk about what is happening between us, but I must admit, I really can't concentrate with you in that dress." His voice was deep and husky. "I'll give you scissors to cut it off or, if you let me, I'll help you remove it." Juliet tensed. "I swear on the life of my family I will not try anything," Gabriel promised.

She knew he would not make such a statement lightly. Hesitantly, she turned around, exposing her back to him. She glanced behind her to see Gabriel lower down on one knee. "I think I will only have to undo the three on your left side and then you can get out of it." He picked up the silver strand that led down to above her butt. "Let's see what Sabra has done."

His fingers lightly touched her skin giving her goose bumps. She heard him mutter something inaudible. "What is it?"

Gabriel stood up and walked to the opposite side of the kitchen. He opened up a drawer and rummaged through it. Finally, he grabbed something out of it Juliet couldn't see and came back over. "It looks like my darling sister locked you into the dress."

"What? Why would she do that?"

"Let's just say she has a funny sense of humor." Gabriel went behind her again. "I have to get the tension off the chain so I'm going to pull it up a little bit."

"Okay, I trust you." It was a simple phrase, but for Juliet it was a major step.

She felt movement right above her butt. "Shit!" Juliet jumped at Gabriel's outburst and turned her head to see what happened. Gabriel had pulled back his hand and the tip of his finger was smoldering.

Juliet's eyes grew wide. "Are you okay?" She reached out to look at his finger. It was red and blistered.

Gabriel gritted his teeth. "I'll be fine. There's silver somewhere on your dress."

Juliet remembered the underwear she was wearing and how Sabra said it was a silver-infused material. He must have accidently brushed it with his finger. It really wasn't funny, but a snicker escaped her. Gabriel's eyes narrowed. Juliet lifted her hand to her mouth trying to cover the smile she couldn't help. "You better apologize to Sabra, because you must have done something to her."

"What do you know?" Gabriel's finger had stopped blistering, and the skin was beginning to turn back to its normal color.

Shocked at how quickly he'd begun healing, she stared at the finger, not answering the question. Not until the skin had gone completely back to normal did she speak. "That's amazing." She grabbed his hand and examined it. "Oh, sorry, Sabra had me wear silver-infused underwear as a…precaution. I forgot about it until now."

"Humph" was the only response she got. He motioned for her to turn around again, and she did.

A few minutes later, three of the chains were free and the dress started to fall. Juliet held the left side of the bodice up for fear her breast would be exposed with the loosened material. She could feel air on the top part of her butt and was sure it was exposed. Without a word she turned, scampered out of the kitchen, and up to the bedroom to change. She felt relief wash over her when she finally had the dress off but opted to leave the underwear on just in case. Now in Gabriel's soft clothes, she made her way back downstairs.

A fire was burning in the massive stone fireplace. Gabriel got up from the couch where he was sitting and made his way towards her. He looked her up and down and the corners of his mouth turned upward. "My clothes never looked so good."

He reached for her, but she pulled away. "Nope; not until we talk. You should go change."

While Gabriel was upstairs, Juliet tried to make herself comfortable on the couch. Fidgeting every few seconds, trying to find a position she liked but failed. Her stomach was full of butterflies. Too busy squirming, Juliet failed to notice Gabriel until he was alongside of her. She jumped when she finally realized he was there. "Don't do that to me?"

He walked around and plopped down on the couch. "Sorry. It is my nature to be quiet: predator, remember?"

Juliet didn't pay attention to his response. She was too transfixed on his bare chest. He had chosen to wear a pair of black, cotton knit pants with no shirt. How was she supposed to concentrate now? "You don't believe in shirts?"

"It took me a while to find these." He pulled at the pants. "I'm normally naked" Gabriel flashed her a devilish smile and winked.

This was so not fair. Juliet's mind imagined what his naked body would look like and reflexively smiled. A chuckle from Gabriel pulled her back into reality. He moved closer. "I think we need to talk about us."

Suddenly shy, Juliet looked down and traced imaginary designs with her finger. "I don't think this is the time. You've got more important things to worry about like the Venator knowing who you are."

He placed a finger under her chin and guided her head upward so she was looking directly into his eyes. His pupils were dilated and intensely set on hers. "This is the perfect time." Gabriel's chest lifted. "My life is full of danger, and I've tried to protect everyone I care about from it. I have denied myself so much, and I don't want that anymore."

Heat radiated through her entire body. Juliet realized he could probably sense this, and her face reddened more. Gabriel continued, "My sister is right: my attraction to you in the beginning was primal. I couldn't get enough of your scent; it was addicting." His finger traced the outline of her jaw. "You have to understand I'm more in tune with my carnal instincts than people are in general. Growing up like this, we learn to control it early on, but you threw me for a loop. So yes, initially, it was purely lust I felt."

By this time both his hands were now holding hers. "The more I got to know you, the more I couldn't stay away, but I battled with myself. I didn't want you to know about my world. I knew becoming involved with you meant I was putting you in harm's way. Then the day we kissed: I never felt so normal."

Juliet drew her eyebrows together. Gabriel chuckled. "That's not a bad thing. I yearn for normal. To not have these responsibilities or abilities. To be able to date a woman and have a relationship with her free of the fear that any minute some mortal enemy might try and hurt her."

She remembered the story Cara told her of how Gabriel's fiancée had been killed. He had lost so much. How could she even try and fill that void? What about her safety? Would she end up like Natalia? "I don't know. If we start down this path, then it will only be harder when it has to end."

His hands tightened around hers. "It doesn't have to end."

Her chest contracted and her mind raced. Did he realize what he was saying? What he was asking of her?

"I'm just asking you give this a chance. To date me. Let me show you how much you mean to me." He reached out and brushed a strand of hair out of her face.

The barriers she had carefully constructed around her heart started to crack. Her chest swelled, and she felt alive inside. "We can try, but if you hurt me, I'll stab you with silver myself."

Gabriel released her hands. "Not exactly the answer I was looking for, but I'll take it."

"There are some ground rules though."

"I'm all ears."

"One, no secrets. Two, you aren't allowed to go super overboard on the whole protector thing. Finally, pheromones or not, I'm not ready to have sex with you. Do you understand?" Juliet straightened her spine.

The right corner of Gabriel's mouth turned upward. "I can live with that." He reached over, wrapped his hands around her waist, and pulled her into his lap. His chest was blazing against Juliet's bare arms. He leaned into to kiss her.

"Does it hurt?"

Gabriel's mouth stopped inches away from hers. He drew back cocking his left eyebrow upward. "Last time I checked kissing doesn't hurt."

Juliet's eyes met his. "No, not that. Does it hurt when you change into your wolf form?"

Gabriel scratched the side of his face. "Not unless you're fighting the change." He leaned in again.

Juliet put her hand on his chest. "What kind of special powers do you have?"

A rush of air escaped Gabriel's mouth. "Well, you know about the smell and saw my ability to heal quickly. We are extremely strong and all of our senses are heightened, which are amplified when we are wolves." Gabriel's eyes went slowly up and down her body. "For example, I can hear the increase in your heartbeat. Your eyes are dilated just a fraction more than they were a few minutes ago. The tips of your fingers are colder than the rest of your body."

Gabriel's free hand was lightly rubbing her lower back. "Why are you nervous?"

Juliet looked away from him. "It's nothing, just feeling a bit self-conscious at the moment."

Gabriel pressed his lips to the side of her neck. "About what?"

His breathe against her skin sent a shiver down her spine. "It's just that we're so different, and I know you've been in a relationship with someone of your own kind." Juliet hesitated. "I don't want you to be...disappointed."

"Close your eyes." The inflection in Gabriel's voice was not a command but a request. "Go on; close them."

Juliet did as he asked. Even though he wasn't touching her she could feel the heat of him against her face. When he finally spoke his voice had dropped an octave and his words poured out like warm molasses. "You are an incredible woman, which I think you know but sometimes forget. Anybody who is around you for more than a minute can see how beautiful you are." He kissed one of her closed eyelids and then the other. "Don't waste your time trying to compare yourself to people in my past." His mouth enveloped her right ear lobe and his tongue flicked over the end causing a soft moan to escape her mouth. His teeth skimmed the surface as he released the small area of flesh. "If I need to, I will remind you of this every day."

His mouth found hers. At first the pressure was soft but it quickly increased with need and desire. She opened her lips to him allowing his tongue to thrust inside. Her body ignited under his fingers caressing down her back. She gripped his taught arms with her hands. Gabriel's mouth left hers long enough to whisper in her ear. "You are my present and my future."

Chapter 34

"Earth to Juliet." Sabra snapped her fingers in front of Juliet's face.

Juliet blinked and focused on the bewitching green eyes of the woman in front of her. "I'm sorry, what?"

Sabra crossed her arms in front of her chest. "Were you listening at all to what I was saying about immobilizing your opponent?"

Juliet shook her head. There was no point in lying. "No."

Sabra threw up her arms. "You're useless tonight. Go home and daydream about my brother." She reached down and snatched the towel lying on top of her bag. "Next time I see you, I want your full attention."

Sabra's words did nothing to dampen Juliet's spirit. "We're going on our first real date tomorrow. Let me be excited! You have only yourself to blame: you locked me into a dress." Juliet rolled up the towel she had in her hand and flicked it at Sabra's legs. Her opponent used her lightning-fast reflexes to quickly move out of the way. Sabra retaliated, and her towel edge found its mark on the back of Juliet's left thigh.

"Ow!" squealed Juliet, rubbing her leg.

"Serves you right," Sabra smirked. "How is tomorrow your first date when the two of you have been nauseatingly inseparable since last weekend?"

Juliet picked up her bag and threw it over her shoulder. "Going to church and spending time at each other's houses after work doesn't count." She looked up at the wall of the gym. "Hey, when do I get to start playing with those?"

Sabra looked at the series of blades, knives, and swords that decorated the wall. "Not until you master the basics and even then I'm worried you'd cut your foot off."

"Not that it isn't cool, but isn't fighting with that stuff antiquated? Wouldn't it just be faster and easier to shoot those Amoveo things?" Juliet paused at the door to the gym.

"Bullets for the most part only wound, unless they are gold and, well, that metal doesn't really work." Sabra frowned. "However, cutting one's head off is another story. There is no coming back."

"Good point." Juliet opened the door and walked out.

Sabra walked out of the gym beside her and down the stone path. "So what grand plans do you two have tomorrow?"

"He's picking me up in the morning, and we're going to drive over to Cumberland Falls for a picnic. Then we're going to go back and watch the Auburn game. It's perfect. I don't have to dress up; I get to eat, watch football, and spend time with Gabriel."

Sabra opened her mouth and made a gagging noise. "You two have gotten worse."

Juliet wrinkled her nose. "I thought you wanted this."

Sabra rolled her eyes. "I wanted the sexual tension driving all of us nuts to go away. I didn't realize you two would turn into a Disney movie."

Trying to find neutral ground Juliet changed the subject. "What are you doing tomorrow?"

Sabra waved her hand lightly in the air. "Oh, the typical, chaperoning the kids while they're at soccer practice so they're not attacked by gun toting mercenaries trying to wipe out our entire family."

Her comments, though sarcastic in nature, illuminated a very real danger. Since the charity event, the entire family had been on lock down. No one was to go anywhere unaccompanied. Every day Juliet would car pool with Lorna and Gabriel. It was annoying not having her own vehicle, but she didn't object. She had saved her major protest for her sleeping arrangements. The morning after the ball, Gabriel, Sterling, and Juliet met to discuss the safest place for Juliet to stay. Not surprisingly, Gabriel wanted her to stay at his residence. Sterling, of course, offered his place with all its extra rooms. Juliet had calmly refused both offers. Citing her need for as much normalcy in her life as possible, she carefully and methodically explained how she wanted to remain in the guesthouse, which had pretty much become her home. Of course, this was met with objections from Gabriel, who paced back and forth in his father's study. She sat still as he said his piece, not interrupting him in the least. Finally, she got up from her seat, crossed over to him, kissed him on the check, and whispered the words, "Remember rule number two?" His face reddened, and she waved a finger at him and smiled.

That evening, Shadow started crying at something outside her living room window. When she glanced outside expecting to see a stray cat, she instead saw Gabriel's massive wolf-form on her front porch. Yanking the front door open so hard it bounced off the side wall, Juliet stomped out on the front porch.

"What do you think you're doing?" she asked, her tone accusatory.

Gabriel's eyes just stared at her as he proceeded to sit down on the wood in front of the swing. Juliet knew he couldn't speak, but the lack of communication enraged her nonetheless. "This is ridiculous, you know. Your whole family is guarding this place. If you want to sit out here all night then fine, but you better not complain to me you're tired in the morning." He had only responded to her with a howl.

Now, walking back towards the house with Sabra, Juliet wondered if Gabriel would be there again tonight. Lorna had picked her up this evening from work without him, saying he was caught up with an in-depth surgery that would take a while. Sabra had gone back to scolding Juliet for her lack of attention span. Juliet walked next to her in silence, electing to let Sabra carry on in her tirade. Her reprieve came when they got to the front yard and saw Gabriel leaning against the railing of the stairs.

Gabriel's tie was loosened and the top button of his shirt was undone. His shoulders were slightly slumped, and his eyes were bloodshot. He straightened when she came into his view and gave her a weary smile. Juliet let the bag on her shoulder drop to the ground as she pressed her body against his and squeezed her arms around his abdomen. She felt his lips press down on the top of her head as his hands rubbed up and down her back.

"Oh my God, you two are going to give me a cavity," Juliet heard Sabra say.

The cheek pressed up against his chest felt the vibrations of the low warning growl Gabriel emitted as a response to his sister. Juliet heard Sabra mutter something, but it was inaudible to her. When she turned her head to look at Sabra, she saw her stomping off in the direction of the main house. Her focus returned to Gabriel. "Tough day?"

"It's getting better by the moment."

"Let me make you dinner and then maybe a massage for dessert?" Juliet kneaded the muscles in his back with her fingers.

This time there was a deep rumble of pleasure. "I wish I could, but I have to patrol tonight. I just wanted to come by and see you."

Juliet drew her eyes together. "You cannot keep going like this. You're wearing yourself out. Promise me when you're done tonight you'll go home and sleep. If I catch you outside my house, I will cancel our date tomorrow."

Gabriel leaned down and kissed the tip of her nose. "You're adorable when you fuss over me. I'll be fine. Hanna and Aiden volunteered to watch your house tonight so I could get some sleep."

"Don't you think they're a bit young to be doing this?"

Gabriel tucked a stray piece of hair behind her ear. "They're fine. Remember, they're a lot tougher than you think."

Juliet pressed her lips against his and then broke apart. "Be careful, and I'll see you tomorrow."

"I wouldn't miss it." He kissed her again, delaying his departure for a few more minutes.

Chapter 35

Juliet enjoyed seeing Gabriel smile. His hand rested on top of her knee as they drove. Speeding along the road, Juliet took in the moments of peace just watching the man next to her. She was impressed he picked her up wearing almost the same thing as herself: jeans and an Auburn tee-shirt.

"When did you become an Auburn fan?" Juliet had eyed him suspiciously.

Gabriel picked up the edges of the shirt. "What? It's for later." But his doe-eyed innocent look didn't have her convinced.

He removed his hand from her leg to down shift the car. Juliet looked up and realized they were turning onto the road in the opposite direction of Cumberland Falls. "Where are we going?"

"You'll see," was all the response she got.

Juliet saw a green road sign with the word AIRPORT written on it. "Tell me we are not going to the airport." There was a bit of alarm in her voice.

Gabriel's eyes slid over to look at her then returned to the road. "You'll see."

In less than five minutes, Gabriel pulled his car in front of the private airport. Walking around the car, he pulled the door open and offered her his hand. She accepted it with growing curiosity. Walking around to the back of the car, he opened the trunk and pulled out a picnic basket. "Let's go."

"Just where are we going?"

He took her hand in his. "I'm taking you on a picnic. I just decided to change the venue."

Not able to think of something to say, she walked next to him staring at his face. They walked through a small building and out onto the tarmac. In front of her was some type of white jet. The door was open, and a lady dressed in a navy suite was waiting at the foot of the stairs. The woman smiled and gestured for both of them to board the aircraft.

Gabriel assisted her up into the plane. Juliet sat in one of the leather seats and Gabriel sat down beside her. "Are you going to tell me where we're going now?"

"Nope."

Juliet pursed her lips and decided to let herself be surprised. He reached across and threaded his fingers through hers. They'd been in the air for about thirty minutes, Juliet could no longer hold her thoughts back. "I know it's really rude to bring this up, but this must have cost a fortune." She chewed on the bottom of her lip, trying to figure out how to phase the next part. "It's just that I don't want you to be wasting your money on me."

His eyes locked with hers. "One of the fiscal rewards my family has, being what we are, is that we keep a percentage of what we find when we eliminate certain threats. The rest of it we donate to worthy causes."

Gabriel leaned over closer to her. "Being sensitive to gold, the Amoveo hoard it so it can't be used against them. They also collect silver to destroy us. Through time, as the packs raided groups of Amoveo, we've confiscated their wealth. After a while, the wealth accumulated and was divided amongst the seven original packs."

"You're talking in the past tense. Does that mean that you don't do this anymore?"

The flight attendant walked by and informed them they would be landing shortly. Juliet was a little surprised at how short the flight had been. Relieved they were at least in the United States, she relaxed ever so slightly, but was still a ball of nervous energy. She looked out the window to see if she could recognize any landmarks. On the ground below were trees and large open fields. Several barns dotted the landscape. She could see the interstate with cars racing along it. Nothing stood out to give her a clear idea of where she was. The ground grew closer and soon the plane had landed safely.

When they stepped out of the plane, Juliet saw a familiar logo with navy blue and orange and took a guess where they were. "We're in Auburn?"

Gabriel brushed his lips against hers. "I thought it would be so much better if we watch the game in person instead of on TV. I hope that's okay with you."

Juliet threw her arms around his neck and leaned into him. "You better be careful, because I might come to expect this for all our dates." She kissed him deeply.

"You know, we could just forget football and go find a nice quiet place for a while," he murmured between kisses as his hands lowered down her back to rest on her butt.

Her body responded to the suggestion by getting warm and tingly. Juliet's brain had different plans as she became very self-conscious. "I think we better go so we don't miss anything."

With a look of reluctant understanding, Gabriel placed his arm around her, and they walked to a convertible parked outside of the airport. Gabriel hopped in the driver's side and turned to her. "I have no idea where I'm going at this point, so I'm at your mercy."

Knowing by this time everyone would be tailgating near the stadium, she elected to head towards main campus. During vet school, she fell in love with football and had attended every game. She had even discovered a great place to park near main campus that somehow most people didn't know about. Gabriel carefully maneuvered the car down back streets, avoiding most of the traffic and people flocking to the game.

Once they'd parked, Juliet led him through the streets towards campus pointing out different buildings and giving him a brief narrative about the significance of each one. The lawn stretching out in front of Samford Hall, the historic brick building at the entrance of the campus, was littered with families tailgating. They found a space under one of the many trees, and Juliet helped Gabriel spread out the blanket. As they ate, Juliet watched the children in their blue and orange clothes passing footballs and waving their string shakers with the Auburn colors. Never before had she really imagined what it would be like to have a child of her own running around on game day playing ball and having fun together as a family. For a split second it was something she wanted, but then vanished before the thought could take hold in her mind.

Satiated by the food, Juliet leaned back and placed her head on Gabriel's lap. He ran his fingers through her hair, massaging her scalp. It hadn't gone without notice every time he touched her it was with precision and delicacy: the hands of a surgeon. Juliet could feel her eyelids getting heavy with every stroke of his fingers through her honey locks. Fighting the urge to sleep, she sat up, her muscles protesting the sudden movement.

"You want to walk around, and I can show you the campus?" she asked.

"If that's what you want to do. It's all about you today." His knuckles brushed her left cheek.

Juliet leaned in. "It's not about me. It's about us."

The corners of his mouth turned upward. He reached over and started putting away the remains of their lunch. Juliet helped and in no time everything was cleaned up. Picking up the basket once again, Gabriel turned to her. "I'm going to run this back to the car if you want to stay here. I'll be back in no time."

"Are you sure you don't want me to go with you?"

"Nope, I'm a little faster than you, and I'll be back in a few minutes." He winked at her.

"I'll stay right here and time you." Juliet grinned and pointed to her watch.

Juliet sat back down this time and resumed people watching. The blades of grass tickled her fingers. A group of children were running around playing tag, giggling as they chased each other. She was so engrossed in their playful antics; she didn't see three people approach.

"Juliet Greene, is that you?" shrilled a voice to her left side.

Juliet closed her eyes and prayed for a brief second she was wrong in identifying the voice. As she stood up, she plastered her best fake smile onto her face. "Hello, Hillary." She looked at the two other women. "Joyce. Michaela."

"Well, it sure is funny running into you like this." Hillary patted her on the arm. "What brings you back to Auburn?"

"I came for the game." She put her hands in the front pockets of her jeans.

"Well, isn't that sweet you came down by yourself." Her sarcasm was not masked by her thick Southern accent. Hillary glanced at her two cohorts. "The girls and I come down with our husbands every home game."

Like synchronized swimmers, all three ladies lifted up their left hands to show off their sparkling diamond rings. Juliet cringed. In her mind, southern society had many redeeming virtues. None were as repulsive as the way women justified their existence through their objectification of marriage to the correct well-bred man. She hated how some women thought their relationships were something to hold over each other as a prize. If they'd married the guys they'd been dating during vet school, she was not impressed. It was obvious their shallowness hadn't dissipated since graduating.

The sea blue eyes she adored came into view behind the strumpets. She could see him laughing quietly at her predicament, and she reminded herself to kick him later for it. For her own entertainment, Juliet allowed herself to sink to their level. "Bless your heart, Hillary, to be worried about me being by myself. No, I came here with my boyfriend. Here he is now."

She felt a hand slide around her waist pulling her into a hard masculine chest. She looked up into Gabriel's face as he bent down and passionately kissed her. Juliet felt the blood rushed to her cheeks as she realized they were definitely making a scene, but didn't bother to pull away. When his lips parted hers, they were swollen; his eyes sparkled. "Sorry I kept you, I helped an elderly couple across the street with their things."

He turned and extended his hand towards Hillary. "I'm Gabriel, Juliet's boyfriend."

Juliet saw the three women had their mouths hanging open with huge eyes. She stifled a laugh. "Gabriel, these are some of my old classmates from vet school."

He shook each one of their hands and by the third one had cast them all into a deep lustful trance. "If you ladies don't mind, I'm going to steal her away. She promised me the best lemonade in the South."

Gabriel didn't wait for their response before he turned both of them around to walk off in the opposite direction. Juliet hooked one of her fingers in Gabriel's belt loop. "You're bad."

He kept his eyes forward. "I have no idea what you're talking about."

Juliet bumped the side of her hip into his leg. "I didn't think you were going to kiss me like that, but it was an added bonus."

"It's nice to know I'm your boyfriend."

She really wished that she could keep herself from blushing every five minutes around this man. Without acknowledging his comment any further, they headed to Toomer's Drugs for their famous lemonade. Juliet told him how everyone comes to the corner and covers it with toilet paper whenever Auburn wins. Gabriel lifted one eyebrow. "You mean to tell me everyone comes out here to T.P. a street corner and this is what you do for fun?"

Juliet blinked. "Of course, it actually looks like snow sometimes by the time the fans are done. When I was in school, there were these beautiful old water oaks at the front gates of the school at the corner of Toomer and College St. Then some dumb-ass Alabama fanatic poisoned the trees. The doctors in the Ag department did everything they could to save them, but they died." A noticeable sadness was in her tone.

"I take it if Auburn wins tonight we'll be partaking in this activity." He finished his lemonade.

Juliet raised her eyebrows and nodded her head yes. Gabriel just shrugged in response. Four hours later, the two filed out of the stadium and participated in the rolling of Toomer's Corner. Auburn defeated the opposing team with a decisive victory. Juliet even spied a smile and heard a laugh from Gabriel as he chucked a roll of toilet paper up in the air. They walked back hand-in-hand to the car and made their way to the airport.

When Gabriel finally walked her up the steps to her house, she noticed how there was more of a spring to his step and an energy to his eyes. It must have been how relaxed the muscles in his face were that made him look younger. He cupped her face in his hands and kissed her softly. Maybe it was still the newness of everything, but her stomach fluttered every time his lips touched hers.

"Thank you for everything. This day was perfect," she said.

"I should be thanking you. It's been a long time since I've had a day this free. Today, I was just a man on a date with a beautiful woman." He paused. "You don't know how much that means to me."

Juliet's fingers softly touched the inside of Gabriel's wrists. "So you want to keep dating me then?"

He lifted her hand and pressed his lips to the inside of her palm. "Of course, you said I was your boyfriend."

Chapter 36

The tension in her head wrapped around her neck and traveled down her shoulders. It had been one of those days she would have rather been anything but a veterinarian. Juliet called Sabra and got a reprieve from tonight's training. She changed into jeans and a sweatshirt and walked down to the lake.

The days had grown shorter. Green leaves of the trees began to change into shades of red, yellow, and orange making the forest dance with color. The lake mirrored the beautiful colors with the enhancement of the setting sun.

She sat in one of the Adirondack chairs and pulled her knees close to her chest, thinking about the many changes that had taken place in her life. Her training with Sabra gave her new bruises and aches, but her arms had definition now and her legs were more toned. Her new physical strength hadn't caused as much chaos in her psyche as the newfound emotions Gabriel seemed to invoke in her.

The fall leaves showering down to the ground each day were like the stones from the wall around her heart toppling over. The imprisoned organ at first shrank away from its unexpected freedom but gradually began to have more confidence. Like the skeletal muscles she exercised, her heart grew stronger.

With every spoken word, stolen look, and playful caress, the warmth she felt inside her chest grew. Juliet found herself in unfamiliar territory: yearning. She craved to be near Gabriel. Content most times just to sit next to him at night watching TV or reading. They shared frustrations and challenges of cases, bouncing ideas off of each other and sometimes coming up with unique solutions. Regardless of all the time they shared together, it ended the same way every night: Gabriel kissing her goodnight at her doorstep not daring to press further.

Her thoughts were interrupted by the sound of crackling leaves behind her. She smelled Gabriel before he touched the back of her neck. He pressed his thumbs into her muscles in a downward motion and they responded to his touch by relaxing. "Sabra said you cancelled on her."

Juliet eyes were now closed. "I had four euthanasia's, told two owners their dogs had cancer, and my parvo puppy took a turn for the worse and died this afternoon. I really couldn't bring myself to be a punching bag tonight."

"I'm amazed how you vets do it."

"Do what?" Her headache was beginning to fade.

"You dealing with death on a daily basis. You're much stronger than most people." Gabriel's hands left her shoulders and she opened her eyes to watch him walk around.

She moved over, and in one fluid motion he slid in next to Juliet while placing her in his lap. She snuggled into the crook of his shoulder where her head seemed to fit perfectly. The two of them sat in silence, content just to be in each other's presence. "New plan: I give up the vet thing and you ditch the doctor/protector jobs and we go into something happy like…basket weaving."

Gabriel's chest rumbled with laughter. "God, I love you."

It took a second for Juliet to register the words that had just come out of Gabriel's mouth, causing her spine to straighten. She could feel her eyes widen as she pushed away from his embrace. His blue eyes looked like the tranquil lake: soft and still. He brushed her cheek with the back of his hand. "I love you."

Juliet opened her mouth then shut it again. She wiggled out of his arms and got to her feet. She felt like a deer in the headlights and needed to escape. With the words frozen inside her, she scurried away from him back to the house.

It was this action Juliet pondered the next day as she tapped the pen in her hand against her face. Juliet had just finished writing a script for her previous patient and was waiting for the next. What had she done or not done for that matter? She shook her head side to side replaying the scene over and over again in her head. What had stopped her from telling him how she felt?

Emily's face next to her interrupted her self-loathing. Juliet glanced up at the tech. "Whatcha got for me?"

"Mrs. Robinson is here with Angel." Emily handed her the tablet while Juliet's face paled slightly.

Her lip curled and then relaxed as she looked up to the ceiling. "Please tell me she's sedated?"

"Not even close." Emily pulled a chewed muzzle out of her scrub pocket.

Juliet took a deep breath in and blew it out. Pushing away from her desk, she ran down the mental checklist of things she would need to safely examine her canine patient. Walking into the hallway, she spied Hanna texting on her phone.

Hanna looked up. "Sorry, but Aiden needs me to pick him up from practice. Mom has some parent-teacher conference that's going long and can't drive him or Ava home."

"You can leave and go get them, but I need you to help me first."

She moved closer to Hanna so as not to be overheard. "I need you to go into this room with me and help persuade our next patient to not eat my face off. Do you think you can do that?"

Hanna nodded in agreement. Juliet turned to Emily. "I think I'm just going to take Hanna in with me on this one. Can you stand outside and keep an ear out in case I need you?"

Emily's eyes widened. "Are you sure?"

Juliet glanced over to Hanna. "I hope so."

Before turning the door handle to the exam room, Juliet could hear the snarling of the dog on the other side. She doubted Dr. Silver would approve of this approach, but since he and his family had all left the day before for vacation, Juliet was not concerned about getting his blessing. Hanna handed Juliet her phone. "Can you hold onto this for me? I broke my case in school today, and I would hate for it to get dropped in case I have to wrestle Fido."

Juliet pocketed the phone in her lab coat. Mrs. Robinson sat in the chair in the exam room trying to hold back the 100-pound dog at the end of the leash. Angel's teeth were bared and saliva dripped onto the floor. The chocolate lab attempted to lunge at Juliet but was pulled back by her owner.

"Good afternoon, Mrs. Robinson. I see we are here to check Angel's ears today." Juliet set the tablet on the exam table. "We are going to try something different today, if that's okay with you."

"Okay," agreed Mrs. Robinson.

Juliet pointed to the fixtures on the wall. "If you would please secure the end of her leash to the mounted wall cleat. I'm going to have you step out for a moment while we get the muzzle on her."

Mrs. Robinson looked at Juliet and then at Hanna. Her face had doubt written all over it, but the lady didn't protest and did as Juliet asked. When the door closed behind Mrs. Robinson, Juliet gestured to the dog. Hanna walked around to the exam table as the growling intensified. Juliet watched as Hanna's green eyes focused on Angel's brown ones. The angry sounds from Angel quieted into soft whimpers. The lab sat down and then rolled onto its back exposing her belly in an act of submission. Juliet handed Hanna the muzzle, which she fastened around the dog. With Hanna holding Angel, Juliet examined the lab's infected ears and was able to perform a thorough physical exam. After reading the ear cytology, Juliet cleaned the ears and applied the first dose of medication. Hanna opened the door and walked a calmer Angel out to her owner. Juliet came out to the waiting room to hand the medications Angel would need for the next week to Mrs. Robinson.

Hanna was standing by the owner with the lab lying at her feet. Mrs. Robison turned wide-eyed to the two of them. "I don't know what you did, but this is the calmest I've ever seen this dog at the vet. You two are wonderful."

Juliet patted Hanna on the shoulder. "I have a wonderful assistant. It was all her doing."

The two women turned and walked back down the hallway. "You were fantastic in there. I think you have a career in this. Especially with the aggressive dogs," complimented Juliet.

Hanna giggled. "Yeah, as long as you keep the cats that hate dogs away from me, I think I'll do okay." She looked down at her watch. "I gotta go get Aiden and Ava. I'll be back soon to give you a lift home."

"I'll be here," said Juliet.

Juliet had just walked out into the treatment area after completing another patient examination when she felt her lab jacket start vibrating. She put her hand in her pocket and lifted out Hanna's phone. Noticing that it was Lorna calling, Juliet excused herself to answer the phone. "Hello?"

"Hanna? Thank God you're alright?"

"Lorna, this is Juliet. Hanna left her phone here at the clinic."

"Juliet, where's Hanna?"

Juliet could hear the urgency in Lorna's voice. "She went to pick up Aiden and Ava from school." Juliet looked at the clock on the wall. "She should've been back by now."

"Oh my God, this is not happening." There was a panic in Lorna's normally calm tone.

The hair on Juliet's arm stood up. "Lorna, what's wrong?"

"None of the kids or mom, Kayla, or Leah came home today. Marcus went over to check the school and they're not there." Lorna started to cry. "They're gone."

Chapter 37

Juliet went back to her office. Her stomach was knotted and it felt like someone had pumped ice water through her veins. She took off her lab jacket, put on her coat, placing Hanna's phone inside the jacket pocket, and grabbed her purse. It was the end of the day and everyone was too busy trying to close the office to notice how sickly pale Juliet was. She made her way upfront to wait for someone to come pick her up. Juliet slumped over in one of the waiting room chairs with her head in her hands. She heard the front door of the clinic creak open and then felt a hand on her shoulder. Juliet looked up and saw Kevin's face looking down at her.

His mouth was pressed into a thin line. "Sheriff asked me to come get you and take you to some place safe."

Juliet stood up and made her way towards the door. She was surprised Gabriel hadn't come to get her, but he probably had more important things on his mind like trying to find his family. "Thanks for coming to get me," Juliet's tone was solemn.

"When I found out what was going on, I volunteered to come get you. I wanted to make sure you were safe," replied Kevin as he kept his head looking straight ahead.

The passenger side door of Kevin's police car opened and Joe stepped out. He opened the back door and gestured with his hand for Juliet to get in back. "Here, I'll hold your purse for you while you get in."

Juliet smiled at the young man and handed over her purse. Looking into the back seat she hesitated, the metal mesh separating the back from the officers in the front gave her a sense of being in a cage. She was aware this was standard in most police cars, but it still made her uneasy stepping into a car she would be locked into. With apprehension, she slid into the back seat. Joe closed the door behind her and climbed into the front. Juliet realized he had kept her purse. Her stomach contracted a little more.

As if he had read her thoughts Joe turned back to her. "Sorry, I know you're not a suspect, but its habit not to let women ride with purses. I'll give it back to you when we get to where we're going."

His words did little to calm the uneasiness building inside of her. Kevin climbed into the driver's side and started to drive. They turned not in the direction of the Archon residences, but towards the Sheriff's office. When they passed the building Juliet assumed they were going to, warning bells began screaming inside her head. "I thought we were going to the Sheriff's office," she said trying to keep her voice as even as possible.

Kevin glanced at her through the rearview mirror. "We're meeting everyone someplace else."

Juliet shoved her hands into her coat pocket and leaned back into the seat of the car. She felt a rectangular structure in her hand: Hanna's cell phone. It was then she realized by taking her purse, Joe had taken away any her phone. Looking back towards the front of the car, Juliet noticed something shiny reflecting light on Joe's right hand, which was propped against the window. She leaned forward and squinted, trying to see the design engraved on the glinting ring. Her grip tightened around the phone as her muscles started to tremble. Juliet blinked again to make sure that she was not imagining the Venator symbol decorating the silver ring on Joe's finger.

There was no way she could safely warn Kevin from the back seat of the car. She would need to tell him as quickly as possible whenever they arrived at her destination. Of course, he wouldn't believe her since the explanation would sound crazy.

Juliet desperately wanted to pull out the cell phone in her clenched hand and send a message to Gabriel, but she knew she couldn't do it without being caught. As luck would have it, her phone started ringing inside her purse. The ringtone was for Gabriel. Joe grabbed her purse and started rummaging through it to find the cell phone. Pulling Hanna's phone carefully out of the coat pocket she kept her eyes locked on both men to see if they would notice the movement. Placing it on her left side almost under her leg, Juliet used her thumb to text 9-1-1 to Gabriel, and hoped he would get the hint he should track Hanna's phone through GPS. By this time, Joe had found her phone and turned it off. "Sorry, Dr. Greene, we can't have phones on while in the car." He turned to look back at her.

Juliet plastered her best fake smile on her face. "Oh, I understand."

Pretending to smooth out her flowing skirt, Juliet moved her hand down her leg, slipped the phone into her left boot, and returned the fabric of the skirt back over it. By now, they were turning down a dirt road far away from the city, but still bordering the National Park. Juliet observed her surroundings as they drove. The road was covered mostly with thick forest but opened up to a wide, cleared piece of land. Juliet saw an old farmhouse to the right with a black barn set off from it. She also saw several dozen cars and trucks none of which she recognized. Where were the Archons?

"We're supposed to take you to the barn. That's where we're going to meet everyone," stated Joe.

Juliet was finding it hard to believe Kevin wouldn't find any of this highly suspicious. Before her death, Secret was always bragging about what an awesome cop he was, but obviously things were not registering with him right now. This screamed shady to her, and she was just a civilian.

Joe climbed out of the seat with her purse when they stopped and opened the door. Juliet extended her hands towards him. He handed her the purse. "Here you go."

"Thanks." Juliet was trying to keep up the masquerade but it was becoming increasingly difficult. She slowed her steps so she was walking next to Kevin. Keeping an eye on Joe's back in front of her, she leaned a little closer to the man next to her. "Kevin, I can't explain everything to you right now, but as your friend, you have to believe me when I say, we're in danger."

Kevin continued walking towards the barn. "Why do you say that?"

There was no way she could explain everything to him in the distance between the car and the barn let alone make him believe it. She decided to be as direct as possible. "I know Joe is working for some bad people, and you can't trust him. We're not safe."

By this point, Joe had disappeared into the opening of the barn door. They reached the open door. Kevin turned to her. "Juliet, it's fine. I know exactly who he works for." He pressed his hand on her back, pushing her inside the barn.

It took seconds for her eyes to adjust to the darkened space. When they did, what she saw caused her to retreat backwards, slamming into the person behind her. Like tentacles, Kevin's arms came down around her and squeezed her until she could barely breathe. He leaned down, his hot breath blew against her ear as he hissed, "He works for the same people I do. The ones that are going to kill those monsters you've been helping."

Chapter 38

Juliet struggled against Kevin as he lifted her by the waist and carried her further into the dark structure. A dozen armed men were standing in the room, all eyes locked on the two of them. Deciding it was pointless to even attempt to escape his hold, since she would probably be shot the minute she was free, Juliet didn't use anything from the months of training to free herself. Instead she resolved herself to look at the image that had instilled fear into her when she first walked into the barn.

Lining both sides of the building were large metal cells she assumed were made of silver. Entrapped inside were the missing family members. To her left, she could see Aiden, Hanna, and Ava were in one cell. Mathew was in a cell with some of Lorna's children. Several other cages contained at least a dozen teenagers and preteens of the family members that lived on the Archon property. It seemed none of the little ones Sabra was watching every day at the main house had been captured. To the right, she could see the crumpled bodies of several adult females lying very still on their cell floors.

Juliet tried to jerk forward in the direction of those cells. "What have you done to them?"

Kevin pulled her arms behind her back, making her shoulders scream in pain. "Those she-devils put up a fight at the school, so we sedated them. If I didn't need them, I would've ended their sorry existence."

Anger and confusion swirled in her mind. This could not be real. How could this have happened? He was her friend. How could Kevin be one of these people? "They killed Secret," she said quietly. "How could you work for the same monsters who killed your fiancée?" By this point, Juliet was screaming the question.

Kevin's haughty laugh made her quiver. "They didn't kill her." He let go of her arms.

Juliet swiveled around to look at him. "How can you say that?"

"Because I did." Kevin's eyes reflected the coldness inside of him.

Juliet felt the bottom being ripped out from underneath her. In seconds, confusion and numbness turned to rage. Forgetting her surroundings, Juliet saw red. Blinded by hate, she leapt towards Kevin, managing to dig her fingers down across his left eye and cheek before being pulled away by two of the men standing in the barn. "How could you?"

Kevin wiped the blood trickling from his wounds as he approached Juliet. Ignoring her question, Kevin lifted his hand to strike her, but then lowered it. "For now, let's not mess up that pretty face."

At one time, Juliet had thought he was handsome, but now the sight of him repulsed her. She cast her head to the side, refusing to look at him. With her peripheral vision she could tell he was circling her. "I originally hoped you wouldn't have to be a part of the end plan, but you choose the wrong path." Kevin reached out and grabbed the side of her mouth, jerking her face up and forcing her to look at him. "You should really look at people when they're talking to you. It's rude not to."

His fingers were digging into her cheeks. "Why?"

Kevin released his grip. "Why what?"

"Why did you kill my friend? She did nothing to you." Tears burned her face. "She was innocent. She loved you, and you killed her."

"Secret was a means to an end." His voice felt like icicles stabbing her with every word he spoke.

"I came here two years ago to investigate a report of a large family of werewolves living in town. Dating Secret was a way to get information about anything going on in the National Park, since we know the beasts like to run free sometimes. It was a good plan, but this group was careful. Unlike others of their kind." He stopped circling her for a second.

"We set up traps and motion cameras in the woods, but found nothing. Then you came along, and everything changed. Secret told me everything that transpired the day you found that wolf in one of our traps. I knew we were onto something then."

Kevin pulled out a knife and started picking the dirt from underneath his nails. "Raiding the clinic turned out to be a waste of time. Then those two idiots who worked for me got caught at your house. I had to eliminate them when a simple female was able beat up one and could identify the other. Lucky for us, they took you in after the fire. I knew something was going on with that family."

The blood was beginning to drain from her body. Juliet felt weak. "I ordered the attack in the woods hoping in your grief you'd turn to your only remaining friend. We were supposed to grow closer through our misery.

"I saw the stained glass wolves on the door and realized you had unknowingly been living with the creatures the entire time." Kevin chuckled. "They hid in the open right under our noses. Genius, really. Who would suspect a pastor and his wife as the leaders of a group of freaks?"

"I tried to be there for you. Spend time with you so I could help you grieve while gathering intel. I even knew the day you came over so upset you'd probably discovered the truth about them, and I hoped maybe you'd help us destroy them." He was waving the knife in his hand wildly.

"You're a psychopath!" Juliet kicked at him, barely grazing his shin.

He lunged forward and held the knife to her chest. The tip of the blade cut the fabric of her shirt. "I really don't want to hurt you until it's time, so don't try that again."

He removed the blade. "In your poor taste, you got involved with Archon's son. Do you know how annoying it was to listen to you whine about him day after day? Then, when I saw how protective he was of you the night of the ball, I knew he'd do anything to keep you safe. Unfortunately, our scouts were easily overtaken by the lesser family members that night."

Kevin pulled out his gun, looked at it, and then placed in back in the holster. "We realized they were a lot stronger than others we've dealt with in the past. In order to eliminate the threat, we would have to do it all at once, on our terms."

Juliet felt her knees starting to buckle. "So you kidnapped their children?"

Kevin made a clicking sound with his mouth. "Now, don't forget about you and the other women. The bitches will be worried about saving their screaming offspring when we set them on fire, and the strongest of the men will be too wrapped up in what we're doing to their females."

Bile rose in the back of her throat, and Juliet fought to swallow it back down. Kevin grabbed Juliet's arm and pressed the silver Venator ring he was now wearing on his finger down in the palm of her hand. He drew it back and examined her perfectly untouched skin. His eyes drew together, and he looked at her. "He hasn't turned you? Maybe you aren't as valuable to him as I thought."

"I never asked, Jules, how did you like all those flowers I sent you?" He leaned in and whispered in her ear, "Secret kept a diary. I read up on you when you got into town. I know everything that happened while you were in vet school. Looks like you have a way of picking the worst men."

He reached out and grabbed one of her breasts, squeezing it until she winced. "I always wanted to know what it would be like to be inside you. How much do you think your boyfriend will care when he watches me fuck you in front of him as he's chained against a wall?"

Juliet spit in Kevin's face, which became crimson. "Put her in a cell with the other human traitors."

The two men holding her started dragging her backwards. "Why did you tell me all this?" she gasped.

Kevin's face contorted into a devious smile. "I wanted you to know this was all because of you. The death of your precious friend. The torture and death of the others – even your lover – will all be on your shoulders. By the time I'm done with you, you'll be begging me to kill you."

Chapter 39

Juliet was thrown into one of the metal cells in the middle of the room. She pushed down the fear that was at the surface, willing herself to keep it together. Breathing in through her nose and out her mouth, she began to quiet her mind and focus. Juliet was grateful for Sabra's lessons on mental preparedness, knowing this would have been impossible for her to do a few weeks ago.

Still a little unsteady but feeling better, Juliet stood up, coming face to face with Nicole. Looking around she saw Gina and Brenda kneeling down next to a bloody figure. His eyes were swollen shut. Dried blood was caked on his lips and his nose was no longer straight but at a thirty-degree angle. If his family hadn't been next to him, Juliet wouldn't have recognized Dr. Silver.

"Why isn't he healing?" she asked Nicole.

Nicole looked perplexed by his question. "What are you talking about?"

Juliet pointed to Dr. Silver. "You guys heal so fast; I've seen it with Gabriel. Why is he not healing?"

Gina looked up from her father. "Because we're human."

"Oh." This definitely was not the time to ask about the family tree. Glancing down at her feet, she saw her purse on the floor. She picked it up and started to look through it to see if there was anything useful in it.

"Looking for this?" Juliet turned to see Joe holding up her phone. He dropped it on the ground, smashed it with the heel of his boot, and walked away.

The sight of the phone reminded her she still had Hanna's phone tucked away inside her boot. She peered between the cell bars to see several men walking up and down the aisles checking on their prisoners. Crouching down next to Dr. Silver, she pulled out the phone and concealed it in the palm of her hand. She whispered to his family, "I need someone to text Gabriel where we are and that this is a trap. Use my skirt to cover your hands. Stay around Dr. Silver to block things better."

Nicole took the phone from her hand and started furiously tapping on the screen. Gina kept an eye out for an approaching guard. Between messages, Hanna's phone received replies with Gabriel asking questions about logistics. The Silver family had been kidnapped the day before, and all three women were able to provide more information about how many men they had seen every time they were taken out to use the bathroom. The three of them guessed there were at least 100 men if not more, and every one they had seen was heavily armed. All of this information was sent through the phone, but it would all be useless unless they could escape. From the sounds of Kevin's psychotic rant, he would more than likely set the barn on fire at the first signs of attack from the outside.

Gina tapped Juliet on the arm and pointed to the guards. Almost all of them were leaving. The only remaining member was Joe who had changed from his sheriff's uniform into the black military gear the rest of the men wore. With a single guard watching, this would be their best chance of escape. Juliet looked in her purse again and found the bottle Sabra gave her that rendered silver useless against her family and one of her large bobby pins. She hoped her one-time lesson might help them spring free. If the guard was away, she could toss the bottle to Hanna or Aiden who were in the cell next to them, and hopefully they could coat the bars and bend them using their strength. It was not a well-laid plan, but it was the best she could come up with for the moment.

Juliet looked at the three women. "We need to get him out of the room for a few minutes."

"Leave that to me." Nicole stood up and strolled over to the cage door. "Oh, Joe." Her voice was smooth as silk. "Do you mind coming over here?"

Joe approached the cell. "What is it?"

"I need to go to the bathroom."

Joe scratched his head. "Can't take you while everyone's in the meeting. You'll have to wait."

"I really have to go, please." Nicole crossed her legs and rocked back and forth. "I'll make it worth your while," she added.

Joe took the bait. He opened the cell door and pulled Nicole out. Making sure he locked it behind him, he pointed the gun at Nicole's back and motioned for her to walk. As soon as the barn door was closed, Juliet was on her feet again.

"Aiden, catch." Juliet tossed the clear bottle of liquid to him. He caught it mid-air, careful not touch the bars. "Put it on the bars and see if you can bend them."

Aiden shook his head. "It doesn't work like that. These are pure silver. I couldn't bend them if I tried. I'm sorry."

Juliet's small amount of hope dropped a little. She still had her bobby pins and prayed they would work. She pressed her body against where the lock was and stuck her arms between the bars. By touch, she found the lock and inserted the bobby pin. Pressing the way Gabriel had shown her she attempted to open the door, but only managed to break the bobby pin inside the lock.

Juliet heard the barn door slide open and saw Nicole and Joe returning again. She backed away from the cell door. Nicole met her eyes, and Juliet shook her head no. Joe stopped in front of the door with Nicole positioned slightly off to the side in front of him. He pulled out the cell key and tried to insert it into the lock, only to find that it wouldn't fit. He allowed the gun to drop, supported by only the gun strap, placing his now free hand on the door in order to examine the lock. Before Juliet could register what was happening, Nicole had grabbed the knife strapped to Joe's side, whirled around, and sliced his throat open. Joe collapsed against the front of the cage while blood shot out from the wound, coating Juliet and the metal bars. Juliet heard a sickly gurgling sound and saw the blood bubbling around the center of his throat.

Nicole pulled Joe's body away from the door and opened it. Not wasting time, she stealthily ran to the other cells and opened them, releasing the children. Juliet helped Gina and Brenda get Dr. Silver to his feet, and they exited the cell, stepping over the body now pooled in blood. Several of the children had gathered around Cara, Kayla, and Leah who were still lying on the floors of their cages. Juliet checked pulses on all three; they were slow but strong and steady. Aiden with some of the other teenage boys picked up the unconscious women and brought them out to the center of the barn, resting them on some rectangular hay bales Hanna and Ava brought over.

Juliet walked over to Nicole and nodded her head towards the dead man. "Where did you learn how to do that?"

Nicole still had the bloody knife in one hand and the keys in the other. "I may be human, but everyone in the family is trained to fight. Just in case it's needed." She handed the cell key to Juliet. "Keep that in case we need to lock someone else up."

Juliet pocketed the key in her skirt. "Remind me never to piss you off," Juliet said and then turned her attention to the group. "We've got to get out of here. Does anybody have any ideas?"

"Right now there are two guards on the outside of each of the barn doors." Nicole started drawing lines on the dirt floor of the barn with the bloody knife. "When Joe took me to the bathroom, we went inside the house where most of the men are right now. They're eating and having some kind of meeting. I wasn't able to hear much, but I say we have about thirty minutes before people start coming back in here." She started drawing X's in the dirt. "I saw at least twenty men still patrolling the perimeter. From the house you can see the guards at the front barn door but not the back."

Juliet crouched down beside her. "How close are the woods from here?"

"The shortest route would be through that side." She pointed to the back end of the barn. "It's maybe fifteen yards to the tree line. But we'll have to go through the back door of the barn instead."

"Not necessarily." Juliet walked over to one of the sidewalls of the barn and examined it. She looked around and found a pile of five-foot-long sticks confirming her suspicion. Grabbing one of the sticks from the pile, she came back to the group. "My grandfather was a tobacco farmer. When you harvest the plants, you put them on these sticks and hang them in the barns to dry."

"How does that help us?" asked Aiden.

"The barns are built so that the side panels open to help vent the leaves. There are latches normally chest-height on the outside that keep the panels locked. We could open the side latch and go through," explained Juliet.

"Last night when they took us out to go to the bathroom it was pretty much pitch black out there except for flashlights," Nicole stated. "The sun was almost gone when I came back in here, but how are we going to get all of us unseen to the woods, probably carrying four people?" She pointed to the three unconscious women and her father.

Juliet clicked her tongue to the roof of her mouth and looked around for any ideas. Her eyes fell on Joe's lifeless body. She pointed to him. "We're going to change sides."

She looked up and saw every person staring at her. Most had looks of confusion, others were frowning. "We grab the guards outside the barn doors and the boys who are big enough to pass for them can change into their clothes. We'll need some kind of diversion, and while they're busy with that, we can sneak away." Juliet looked at the faces around her. Although they all looked grim, a few of the teenagers were nodding in agreement.

"Okay, let's do it," said Nicole.

"Good. Gina, text Gabriel and let him know what we're planning," Juliet instructed.

She stood up. "We're going to have to do this carefully and quietly. If somebody screams, we're all done for."

Aiden, the oldest of the group of children, and his cousin, James, stepped forward. "We've got the first two."

The two teenagers walked to the back of the barn door. "I need both of you to come in here for a second and help me with one of these scum," Aiden called out through the door.

The barn door opened, and as both men stepped through they were grabbed by the head. Juliet diverted hers eyes but heard the sickening sounds of bones popping. When she looked up, the two men were lying on the ground staring out with empty eyes their necks twisted to the side. Aiden and James stripped their clothes and put them on. They repeated the same action with the guards at the front of the barn. The disguised teenagers stepped outside to take the place of the men lying inside so no one from the house would see the post was empty. Marcus' teenage grandsons then dressed in the black military clothes. One went to watch the back of the door and the other changed places with Aiden.

Gina came up to Juliet and Nicole who were talking with the younger children about how they must move quickly when they were going to run. "I just got a text from Gabriel's phone. They've surrounded the clearing and are sweeping the area for traps."

Juliet looked at the phone screen. "They're not going to fight them, are they?"

"I think that's exactly what they're going to do," confirmed Gina. "Think about it. Just like they wanted to kill us all in one swoop, we have to stop them all at once. If any of them get away, they'll lead more here."

Juliet knew she was right, but feared for the lives of the family she'd grown to love. Battle may have been in their blood, but it wasn't in hers. She shifted her focus on Aiden. "Watcha got?"

"Some of the men have switched out with the guards patrolling the perimeter. The house looks quiet, but Nicole is right, I don't think that's going to last much longer. I did see two convoy-looking trucks parked near the house. I was going to take a quick look to see if we could use anything as a diversion. If not, I figure rigging it so one of them goes into the house would work just as well." The right corner of his mouth lifted.

"Do what you think is best, but be careful. If you see an opportunity, take it. We'll be ready." Juliet turned to Gina. "Let Gabriel know what we are planning. Tell him to wait for the diversion. Knowing Aiden, it won't be subtle."

Juliet waved to Hanna. "Go tell James to unlatch the sides of the barn where we need to escape but not to open them. We can do that from in here when we're ready. Also, let them know we're going to need them as soon as

Aiden sets off his diversion to carry Cara, Kayla, and Leah out of here."

While Hanna ran to do this, Brenda and Nicole got Dr. Silver to his feet. Gina informed them Gabriel and the others were ready. Sterling, Travis, and Luke would be in the woods near the barn to help carry and protect the children. Juliet kneeled on the floor to be eye level with some of the smaller kids. "Now, I don't want you to shift unless you absolutely have to."

"Ms. Juliet," interrupted Mathew. "We can't shift unless it is full moon or the day after. We aren't old enough yet."

"Oh." She was learning more and more tonight about this family. Things that would have been nice to know weeks ago. "Why?"

This time it was Jacob who spoke. "Momma says it's to keep us safe so it doesn't happen when we don't have control."

Juliet could imagine a temper tantrum with a child changing into a wolf would probably scare the crap out of most people. "That's okay. You guys can still run really fast, right?"

Several small heads nodded. "Good. So, when I tell you, you're going to run as fast as you can and follow Hanna and Ava, right?" This time all the children agreed. "No matter what happens, do not stop and do not look back."

"Ms. Juliet, I'm scared." Jacob's worried eyes found hers.

She put her hands on both his arms. "I'm scared too, but we've got to do this."

Juliet was unable to finish her pep talk, because there was a loud crash followed by an explosion that shook the ground and rattled the barn walls. Through the slits in the barn she could see a bright flash of light. The front of the barn doors opened and three teenagers rushed in and started picking up Leah, Cara, and Kayla. Brenda and Gina opened the slats on the side of the barn and started helping Dr. Silver out.

The air filled with screams of men and the popping of machine guns. Howls echoed in the air reassuring her help was here. Hanna peered outside the side of the barn. "Nobody's coming this way. Let's go."

The first group of children climbed out of the barn led by Hanna. When they reached the woods Ava lead the second group with Leah being carried by one of the older teenage boys. Aiden was next to Juliet cradling his mother. "What did you do?" Juliet asked.

"The truck had grenades in it. I took the keys from the guy who was guarding it, rigged the truck up so it would crash into the house, and then threw grenades inside as it went by." He leaned out to check for guards. "I think I did alright."

"Impressive, now go." Juliet pushed his back.

Even carrying his mother, Aiden climbed up and leaped out through the opening with the grace and agility that impressed her every time she saw it. James, who was holding Cara, went next, and Nicole and Juliet were the last ones. With his better vision, James checked to make sure everything was fine. Juliet could only see flashes of light from where guns were being fired outside. The noise was deafening. James motioned it was safe and started for the trees.

"You go next." Juliet was practically screaming in Nicole's ear to be heard.

Nicole was up and out, and Juliet stepped up to leap out into the open. A sudden pain around her scalp caught her by surprise as she was pulled backwards hitting the floor square on her back. Her lungs screamed in agony as Juliet struggled for breath, dazed by what happened. She had no time to recover before being dragged along the floor by her hair as the nerve endings of her roots sent waves of pain to her brain. She thought her scalp might be torn off. The assailant let go when they reached the center of the barn, and then Kevin was on top of her pressing his knee into her chest.

Blood was running down the side of his face from a wound at the top of his head. His hair was disheveled, and his eyes screamed of death. "What've you done, bitch?"

Juliet's lungs were still searching for air. She could not answer him. He climbed off her and yanked her up into a standing position using the front of her shirt, which tore under the strain. His hand came across her face, stinging the side of her cheek but not hard enough to draw blood. "Answer me!"

Juliet blinked trying to make the black dots in her vision go away. Her lungs had finally filled completely with air, each breath giving her the strength she needed to fight back. She didn't know if it was muscle memory or fear, but she thrust up the heel of her hand making contact with the underside of Kevin's nose. There was a crack, and blood gushed out of his nostrils. He dropped his hold on her, and Juliet backed away in time for his wild swing to miss contact with her face. She blocked the next assault of his fists like Sabra had shown her but his left hand contacted her abdomen. She doubled over and prevented herself from falling by grabbing onto Kevin's shirt. His hand came around her neck pulling her up and slamming her head against the metal bars of a cage. The collision jarred her body as his hand clamped harder around her throat. Juliet felt the life being squeezed out of her. Her vision began to fade at the edges.

"Let her go!"

There was a sudden release of pressure on her trachea, as she fell forward coughing, trying to get oxygen. Kevin's arm swiftly came around her body, pulling her back against his chest. The cold metal of the gun's muzzle pressed against her temple. Gabriel was at the other end of the barn. He looked like an avenging angel, with a sword gleaming red in one hand and blood splattered across his face and body. Juliet could see the calculating anger in his eyes as he stepped forward.

Kevin pressed the gun harder into her head. "Keep walking and I'll make sure her brains cover you too."

Gabriel paused. Juliet saw the sword twitch ever so slightly in his hands. "This is between you and me. Release her."

"Do you think I'm that much of an idiot?" Kevin's chest vibrated with laughter. "I've got all the control."

Gabriel's eyes narrowed. "Release her and I'll kill you quickly."

"I could just kill you first." Kevin removed the gun from Juliet's head and pointed it in Gabriel's direction. "Then, I can take my time with her."

The blue in Gabriel's eyes darkened. "I surrender." He buried the blade of his sword in the dirt floor, and then lifted up his hands. "Let her go, and you can have me to do what you wish."

Juliet wrestled against Kevin's grip. "Don't do this, Gabriel."

"Well, well, the mighty alpha gives up so easily over a female. I must say I'm a little disappointed." The gun remained positioned at Gabriel. "Get in the cage and I'll let her go. You have my word."

Juliet watched Gabriel walk into one of the open cells and step into the center. Dragging her with him, Kevin went over, shut the door, and locked it. Once this was done, he released her.

Juliet gripped the bars of the cell. "Don't do this. He's going to kill you."

"Trust me." His voice was calm as he moved closer to her. Careful as to not touch the bars, he reached out and caressed the side of Juliet's face. "I need to make sure you are okay." She reached up and clasped his hand in both of hers.

"That's enough." Kevin grabbed her around the waist.

Gabriel pulled his curled hand back inside his prison. "You agreed to let her go. Now do it."

"You're right, I did say I'd let her go." Kevin let go of her waist and pushed her to the ground. "But I never agreed not to have a little fun before she went."

Kevin's full weight was suddenly on her. She tried to strike him, but he grabbed both her wrists pinning them above her head. There was a blur of black and a sudden release of pressure from her entire body. Her ears were bombarded with screaming and a ferocious snarling. Juliet lifted her head towards the noise and saw her black wolf with his mouth clamped around Kevin's arm. He was shaking the man like a chew toy; Kevin's arm flapping as the bony attachments had been severed. Kevin screamed in agony making the hair on the back of Juliet's neck rise.

Juliet pushed herself up and stood several feet back watching the sight. Noticing her movement, Gabriel released his hold on Kevin but still bared his teeth with his hackles raised. She walked over to stand next to the wolf and pushed a remnant of his shredded shirt off his back.

Kevin was trying to prop himself up with his remaining good arm. "How did he get out?"

Juliet looked over to the cell door. The key she had given Gabriel remained in the lock. Kevin's eyes followed hers. Juliet's focused back onto Kevin who was moaning in pain. "Why doesn't he just kill me?"

Juliet looked down at Gabriel who was still in his attack stance. "I told him you were the leader. I think he wants you alive for questioning. However, after I tell him what you've done, he might just kill you instead."

Kevin's hand moved towards the gun holstered on his leg. Gabriel lunged forward, and Kevin's hand retreated.

Juliet walked over, putting the heal of her boot on Kevin's remaining good hand and pressed down while she bent over and relieved him of the weapons that were in her line of sight. She tossed most of the guns away, but kept the .45, pointing it at Kevin while placing his sheathed knife in her boot.

"Tell your men to stand down," demanded Juliet.

Kevin threw his head back and laughed. "It doesn't matter what I say. We'll keep coming." He jerked his head towards Gabriel. "Until they're wiped off the face of this planet, you won't be able to stop us."

Juliet felt her pointer finger twitch on the trigger. "How many more of you are there?"

Kevin had gotten his feet up underneath him and was attempting to stand. "I'll never tell you."

Gabriel let out a low growl and crouched lower. "I think you need to reconsider your answer." She nodded to his dangling arm. "That needs some medical attention unless you're ready to lose it."

"You don't get it, do you?" Kevin pressed his back against the bars of the cell and inched his way up until he was standing. "We're too well funded, and there are too many of us. Just tell Fido to kill me."

Gabriel lifted his lips higher, showing his gleaming canines that had traces of blood on them. She opened the door to the cell that Kevin was leaning on. "Get in."

Kevin slowly made his way towards the door. When he was a foot away from her, he threw a handful of dirt in her face then lunged for the gun. Unable to see, Juliet did not discharge her weapon, Kevin knocked her down, and was trying to rip it out of her grip with his remaining good hand. Juliet felt something wet on her face, and then Kevin's weight was removed. Using the back of her hand, she cleared the dirt from her eyes, but they were still stinging. Tears were rolling down her face, blurring her vision.

When she was finally able to focus, she saw Kevin's neck entrapped in Gabriel's jaws. Blood was welling on the floor beneath. Kevin stared at her with dull eyes as his head flopped around every time Gabriel jerked it back. Juliet stepped forward towards Gabriel when she heard a loud pop and saw her protector fall to the ground. The inhumane sound he made as he collapsed to the ground was like a dagger into her chest. Not thinking about anything else, she ran to his side and pressed her hands against the wound now spilling out precious blood.

Another Venator stepped into the dim light of the barn. The overhead fluorescents enhanced the evil in his contorted face. Movement behind the soldier caught her eye. She saw two red wolves with green eyes saunter through the door and down opposite directions in the barn. Juliet redirected her eyes towards him so as not to alert him to the encroaching wolves. "Why don't you shoot me first, and make it quick." Juliet lifted her head in defiance.

"I like your bravery. It won't save you, but I like it." He moved next to her.

The first of the wolves attacked, ripping off the arm with the weapon in one crunch. The muscular impulse caused the weapon to discharge, the bullet narrowly missing her head making Juliet's ears ring. She was not able to hear the screams as the second wolf grabbed the other arm. She watched as the two female wolves tore the body apart.

Juliet turned back to Gabriel. His breaths were shallow, and she could see the bullet had entered the left side of the chest. She reached down, tore a piece of her tattered skirt and placed in over the wound. The two wolves came up next to her. "I need to get him to the hospital now."

Sabra and Lorna phased back into their human form. Lorna crouched down next to her. "They're using silver bullets. Gabriel can't shift with that in him."

"Then help me get him to the vet clinic. We don't have much time."

Chapter 40

"Nicole, Emily, I need at least eighteen-gauge catheters in two of these legs." Juliet picked up an endotracheal tube. "Gina, tell me everything in surgery is ready to go."

Juliet gripped the plastic tube, trying to keep her hands from shaking. She took a deep breath and then carefully placed the tube down the trachea, tied it in place, and inflated the cuff, listening for leaks. "Maureen, I need you to ventilate pure oxygen until we are ready for surgery, do you understand? He's got a pneumothorax, and I don't know where that bullet is. Don't put him on the ventilator, got it?"

Maureen nodded in agreement. Juliet barked orders at other techs as they all buzzed about the clinic. Nicole had managed to get every technician that worked at the hospital to report back to work. No one questioned the state of Juliet's appearance. Lorna and Sabra were with her dressed in torn clothes they had taken off some of the dead men from the farm.

"I want hypertonic saline and hetastarch going at the same time once you get those catheters in, and I'll let you know the rates. Once we've got that, I need chest rads before he goes into surgery." Juliet listened to the weak but beating heart of Gabriel. "Gina, I need this chest clipped now. I'm going to go get ready. You call me if there's any change."

Juliet walked out of the treatment room and went to her office to grab a pair of scrubs and her surgical cap.

Lorna and Sabra followed. "Is there anything we can do?" asked Sabra.

Juliet whirled around. "Yeah, I need you to tell me anything medically important I might need to know about you guys before I go into this."

The two sisters exchanged looks. Lorna stepped forward and grabbed Juliet's hands. "Get the silver out of him and he should heal on his own. Anything the silver has touched will have been burned so it may take some time to heal."

Juliet pulled her hands away. "Oh, you make it sound so easy. Well, it's not. Gabriel's in there fighting for his life, Dr. Silver is unconscious, I can't call in the other doctors to back me up in this case or I risk exposing your family. It's all on me." Juliet felt like she was about to lose control. "The only thing getting me through this is by pretending he is not someone I lo— care about but some stray animal I'm treating."

Juliet pushed past the two women. "I need to get ready. Let the techs know if more of your family is coming to be treated."

Juliet didn't wait for an answer. She went to the bathroom and started stripping out of her blood-soaked clothes. Before putting on her scrubs, she washed as much of the blood off her face, hands, and arms as she could, letting herself cry while the water flowed over her hands. She allowed this small breakdown before she had to push all emotions aside and become the caretaker. Juliet twisted her blood-crusted hair into a bun and tied her surgery cap over it. Once dressed in her scrubs, she went back to the treatment room. Gabriel's chest rads were already displayed on the computer monitor. Juliet could see Nicole and Gina in the surgery suite finishing prepping Gabriel's body for surgery. She turned her attention to the images on the screen. "Shit." The word slipped past her lips.

The bullet was sitting at the apex of the heart. If it shifted at all it would cause damage to the precious beating muscle, and she didn't know if Gabriel would be able to recover from that before it killed him. The good news was it hadn't splintered into fragments.

She noted there were three broken ribs and scalloping of the left lung lobes, which indicated fluid around them, most likely blood. There were also signs of free air in the chest, which was not surprising since he had a gaping hole on the outside. Turning away from the screen, she headed to the sink to start her hand scrub.

While scrubbing, she mentally went over her approach while praying she would have the ability to do what needed to be done. Gowned and gloved, Juliet stepped into surgery. Gina and Nicole were the only two techs in the surgery room since Juliet didn't think she could hide anything else tonight from the others that weren't already privy to the family's secrets. Gina was ventilating Gabriel while Nicole was ready to assist.

"Gina, I'm going to tell you when I need you to stop breathing for him when I try to take this bullet out. The last thing I need is to hit an inflated lung and singe one of his lobes." Juliet picked up a scalpel and made a skin incision between two of his left ribs. The opening she made extended from near the wolf's back to his chest.

"Okay, Gina, stop for a second." She took a pair of curved Mayo scissors to cut the remaining tissue that separated the chest from the outside world. The pink left lung lobes came into view as dark blood and several blood clots spilled out of the incision. "Give him two more breaths, and then I'm going to have you stop while I put in the rib spreaders. Juliet grabbed the instrument and placed it between the ribs.

"Nicole, I need suction."

The plastic tubing started removing the blood giving better visualization into the field, but liquid was still welling up above the sternum. She suspected the bullet had severed one of the internal thoracic vessels. Juliet had to stop the bleeding so she could visualize the bullet, but blindly clamping could push the bullet in farther doing more damage. "Nicole, stop the suction for just a minute."

Nicole did as Juliet asked, and she stared down into the chest observing for any signs of where the damage might be. Then she saw a whirlpool forming in the center of a crater of blood. Juliet took a hemostat and clamped it in the center of the spinning liquid. "Suction, please."

To her relief, the cavity did not fill again. Gabriel's pink lungs expanded again in her field of view. Juliet looked at the monitors and reviewed Gabriel vitals, which for now looked stable. "Gina, give me thirty seconds before you give him another breath."

She gently pushed the lung lobes apart with her fingers to get a clear view of the massive beating heart and below it the object she was hunting for. It had migrated and was now a hair's distance from touching the heart. The tissue around the silver was black and singed. Juliet removed her hands from the chest, and Gina pushed air into the lungs.

Beads of sweat were forming on her forehead, and she felt droplets running down her back. One misstep and she would push the bullet into his heart and most likely send him into cardiac arrest. Unlike Hollywood's version of this medical emergency where most people survive, Juliet knew the reality was very different.

Juliet looked at the tray of surgical instruments and selected the hemostat she thought would be best to grab the piece of metal. "Alright, Gina, I'm going in again." She waited for the lungs to deflate and then proceeded.

Using her instruments, Juliet attempted to grab the bullet, but it moved away from the hemostat, slicing the tip of the pericardial sac like a hot knife through butter. "Dammit." Juliet's right hand froze in place.

"Doc, I need to give him a breath," stated Gina.

"Okay, but not so much positive pressure this time. I'm leaving my hands inside." Juliet could feel the lungs press against her gloves giving her seconds to think of a new plan, thankful she had long, slender fingers so both hands could easily fit inside the chest cavity.

Her mind calculated multiple scenarios trying to answer the problem before her and finally settled on one solution. "Okay, I'm ready to try again."

Her left hand slipped under the apex of the heart and she twisted it so she cupped the beating organ in her palm while feeling the hard metal against the back of her hand. She opened the hemostats and grabbed the bullet in the direction of her left hand so it pressed harder into the latex gloves. Now with solid resistance she was able to clamp the cursed object and backed the hemostats into her right hand curling her fingers around the metal to protect any tissue that may come into contact with it as she removed it from the cavity. Breathing a sigh of relief, she pulled the silver bullet out of the body. Juliet relaxed her fingers from around Gabriel's still-beating heart and slipped her hand out, making sure she had not displaced the organ. "I'm out. Start ventilating."

Juliet dropped the hemostat with the bullet into a surgical bowl. She stripped off her top layer of bloody gloves and replaced them with another sterile pair. "Alright, ladies, let's debride and lavage."

Her hands worked swiftly and with precision ligating the vessels she had clamped earlier. She removed black, necrotic tissue from the cavity. Taking one last look before she started closing the chest, she was satisfied by what she saw. Gabriel's heart rate and pressures were improving. Making a separate incision further down his ribcage to the primary one, Juliet placed a chest tube to help evacuate any air or fluid after surgery. She moved the suture in and out of the tissue, closing each layer completely before moving on to the next. When everything was finally closed, she placed sutures through the skin around the broken ribs and attached them to an external fixation device to stabilize them until Gabriel's body could heal. After pulling as much air out of the chest tube as possible to restore negative pressure inside the chest, Juliet wrapped the chest and tube.

A knock on the surgery widow redirected her attention. Emily was waving her hand at Juliet, beckoning her to come out. "Do you two have him?"

Nicole was wheeling the transport table over, lining it up next to the surgery table. "Go, we'll get you if we need you, and, Doc, you did great."

"Thanks." Juliet pushed through the doors. "What's wrong, Emily?"

Emily held the tablet in her hand. "They've brought in more wolves. Several with gun shots to various locations. A few with knives stuck in them. We went ahead and took radiographs of every patient and placed IV catheters. All of the animals are conscious right now, so I'll need to know who you want to sedate first and when." Emily hesitated. "Dr. Greene, do you want me to call in one of the other doctors?"

Juliet was already stripping off her gloves. "No, I can handle this. Emily, I know this is a very odd situation, but I need you to know this is extremely important."

"Dr. Silver and his family have been good to all of us techs." She started walking into the treatment room and then turned back. "We know you guys stopped a poaching ring tonight and you saved these animals." There was a knowing twinkle in her eye.

Juliet followed her tech into the treatment room and saw multiple wolves lying in every available free space: on the treatment tables and the floor. Techs and a human form of the Archon family were with each animal. Emily ran through the list of injuries, giving her the most critical to the least. None of the injuries were as extensive as Gabriel's.

Methodically, Juliet treated each wolf: removing bullets from legs and a few metal tips from broken knives. Sterling and a now-conscious Cara walked into the treatment room as Juliet was flushing out a superficial gunshot wound on Ben's left leg. Lorna was bent over him whispering in some language Juliet didn't recognize.

Juliet could see the patriarch's eyes scanning the room taking in all the activity that was occurring. He bent over and in a low tone asked, "Do you have a moment to talk in private?"

"Give me just a second to finish this, and I'll meet you in my office." She continued to flush the wound.

The couple walked off in the direction of her office. Juliet finished treating Ben and told Lorna to take him home. Her friend hugged her tightly with tears streaming down her face. "Thank you for saving my family."

Juliet returned the hug. "Thank you for saving my life."

Lorna released her, and Juliet turned to go meet Sterling and Cara. She closed the door to the office. Cara was sitting down in her chair while Sterling remained standing. The lines in his face seemed deeper and his eye lacked his normal gleam. He cleared his throat. "How is everyone here?"

"Stable. Everyone you saw in the treatment room will recover with no problems." Juliet leaned on the wall. Her muscles were beginning to ache.

"And my son?" Sterling's voice lacked his normal undertone of authority and confidence.

"Nicole is still with him. He's breathing on his own, but hasn't woken up enough for us to remove the endotracheal tube." Juliet looked down at the floor. "I did everything I could. I don't know if there is anything else I can do. I'm sorry."

Cara crossed the room and grabbed Juliet's hands. "Don't you apologize. We've asked so much of you tonight and will forever be in your debt. Because of you, we didn't lose our whole family."

Kevin's warning resonated in her mind. Juliet looked up at the two figures. "Kevin said there are more out there."

Sterling walked up behind his wife. "We managed to capture several men, and Marcus has them for questioning. Aiden's little distraction managed to destroy most of the farmhouse with the majority of the men that were inside. Travis is gathering any computers and information that wasn't damaged. We'll get this sorted out."

"People died tonight; surely that won't go unnoticed." Juliet involuntarily squeezed Cara's hands.

Sterling placed a hand on her shoulder. "You go worry about my family. I can assure you we're very good at covering our tracks."

Cara released Juliet's hands, and she walked out of the office to return to the chaos of the treatment room. She continued to work through the night. As she finished with her last patient, Nicole walked up to her holding the endotracheal tube in her hand. Despite the overwhelming desire to collapse on the floor and fall asleep, Juliet sprang out of her seat and rushed to the kennel area. Due to his size, one of the dog runs was set up for Gabriel's post-operative recovery. The fluid pumps and monitors were attached to the wall. Gabriel, still in his wolf form, was sleeping on several soft comforters. Juliet crawled into the cage next to him. She ran her hand down his fur looking for a response that did not come. His chest expanded and contracted with each breath. Juliet lay down next to him and weaved her hand in his fur. "Please wake up."

Chapter 41

"Have you lost your ever loving mind?" Juliet was so angry she could spit nails. "I mean seriously, what were you thinking?"

"I was thinking I needed to be in this form instead of the wolf who was being babied night and day for a week," grumbled Gabriel.

Juliet ripped another piece of medical tape and applied to the bandage over his chest. "I worked so hard making sure you didn't die and you thank me by changing back into a human, while no one is around, opening up your sutures, and probably damaging your ribs even more."

She wiped some of the blood she had missed earlier off his chest. "I just pulled your chest tube yesterday."

He held up some more gauze for Juliet to take. "I had it under control when you walked in the house. I do know how to apply my own bandages."

Juliet threw the tape roll in her hand on the counter. "Fine, then you do it!"

"Juliet, wait." Gabriel caught her hand. "I'm sorry." He looked down at the open incision that was only partially covered. "I'm not used to being taken care of."

Juliet pressed her lips together and forcefully pushed the air out her nose. She picked up the tape and began tearing strips again. "I'll get Sabra up here since she's been the one taking care of you during the day and have her do this."

"You mean Nurse Ratchet. No thanks."

"Come on, she watched over you, and called me when she had questions. I think she did a fantastic job."

Gabriel ran his right hand down the side of her arm. "I much prefer my night time caretaker. She has a much better bed side manner and is extremely beautiful, especially sleeping in my bed."

Juliet smacked his hand. "Flattery will get you nowhere. You're in the dog house." The anger from earlier was dissipating. "Well, now that you're back to this form, and I don't treat humans, you're on your own."

"Humph."

"I had Marcus look at those bullets since everybody who got shot is healing a lot slower than I expected."

"Did he find anything?" asked Gabriel.

"Yeah, Marcus and Travis discovered the bullets used were coated in a fine silver powder. I suspect some of it remained in the wounds despite all of the lavaging I did. I'm just thankful no one's developed any secondary infections." Juliet began to wrap bandage material around Gabriel's chest.

"That would make sense. The silver could have contaminated the blood stream affecting our ability to heal." Gabriel sucked in a sharp breath. "It's a little tight."

Juliet relaxed the tension. "Sorry, I'm not used to doing this on people." Her fingers began to tremble as the events of the last week and a half suddenly hit her. "I can't do this."

"You're doing fine. It was just a little tight. No big deal."

"No," her voice was wavering now. "I don't want to keep living like this where one minute you're telling me you love me and the next thing I know I'm pulling a bullet out of your chest praying you won't die."

The tears started to spill over her eyelids. "Do you know what it was like trying to keep it all together when you were bleeding out on the dirt floor in the barn? I thought my heart was going to stop right there if you'd died."

Gabriel pulled her hand urging her to come closer to him. "But I'm—"

"Let me finish," she cried. "I patched up a good portion of your family, and I never want to have to do that again."

Gabriel hopped down from the counter, crossed over to the family room, took a box about a square foot in area off the bookshelf, and then returned back to her. "I need to give you something, and I hope you'll let me explain once you open it."

Juliet took it from him and opened it. She stood there blinking at the neatly stacked piles inside. "Do you remember when I told you we divide a portion of what we find among the family? Well, this is your share."

Juliet looked up at him and then back down at the pile of one-hundred dollar bills. "Everything the Venator had was made of solid silver, which, obviously, we don't need. It will take a while to melt and sell, but I thought you deserved the money we found now. The majority of the rest will go to the animal charities I know you like. You were integral to our family's survival that night, so this is our gift to you."

"I can't take this." Juliet tried to hand the box back to Gabriel. "It's too much. I wouldn't even know what to do with this much money."

Gabriel pushed the container back into her arms. "It's yours to do with it whatever you like. You could pay off your student loans, give it all away, or, since you said you would leave when this was all over, you could use it to start somewhere new."

The last comment made her hands weak and the money spilled onto the floor. "Do you want me to leave?"

Gabriel's hand caressed the side of her face. "I don't want you to leave, but I don't want to stop you from living your life. I definitely want you safe, and I don't want you to be afraid. That's no way to live."

"I'm scared, but I've found something stronger than fear." She glanced from him to the money and then back to his face. A rush of warmth and happiness filled her chest. "I choose to stay. I've got my hands full here with the clinic while Dr. Silver gets back on his feet. You're mostly healed, but who knows when you'll do something stupid and undo all my hard work." Juliet pointed to his bandage.

"Is there anything else that would make you want to stay?"

"I like looking at you with your shirt off." Juliet's cheeks and ears were burning. She focused her eyes on the pile of money on the floor instead of his face. "You've been overbearing, frustrating, and downright reckless and yet you're kind and loving and you make me feel more alive than I've ever felt."

She poked her finger at him above the dressing. "You made me fall in love with you, and then you almost died. I held your beating heart in my hand while performing a surgery I've never done before. I'm frightened if something happens to you I won't be able to recover from it."

He moved closer to Juliet stopping inches from her. "Don't you think I feel the same way?" His fingers traced the healing bruises around her neck. "Kevin was trying to kill you, because of me."

He ran his hand through his hair, pulling at the ends causing it to stand up. "I don't want this for you; I want you to be safe, but I'm selfish." Gabriel slid his hand around her waist. "I want you more than I've ever wanted anything else in my life."

Juliet touched the bandages on Gabriel's chest. "When you were unconscious all I wanted was for you to wake up so I could tell you how I feel. I've never felt so vulnerable before, but no matter how much I fight it I can't control my emotions." Juliet took in a deep breath. "I love you."

Gabriel's hand enclosed the one she had on his chest. "You know I can't promise there won't be any danger being with me. In fact, I can guarantee something else will occur, but I swear on my life I'll do everything to keep you safe."

She leaned her head against him. "And I'll do everything in my power to keep you safe." Juliet sighed, "I can't promise I won't freak out the next time somebody tries to kill you or me."

Gabriel's other hand pressed against her lower back. "Sorry I'm not a normal guy."

Juliet lifted her face and pressed her lips against his. "I'm not."

Epilogue

The ringing of the phone stirred her awake. The tiny apartment was dark, which was exactly how she liked it, but the rude awakening did nothing for her already foul mood. "What?" she snapped.

"Did you receive the e-mail I sent you?" asked the male voice on the other end of the phone.

"Hold on." She reached for her laptop and flipped it on. She ran her fingers through her short, black hair. "What's so important you had to wake me up this early?"

"You'll see when you open your e-mail."

"Is this about the Venator screwing up?" Her computer was taking too long to load. "I told you I should've handled the situation. We handed it to them on a silver platter, it took two years for those idiots to attempt anything, and it still all ended up in failure."

"If you hadn't lost your temper years ago, we wouldn't have needed them. Subtlety is what we need to win," retorted the male on the other end of the receiver. "Besides, once you see what I've sent, you'll thank me."

The woman's red irises reflected off the screen as she brought up the e-mail that was so urgent for her to see. The image before her caused her eyes to narrow and her nostrils to flare. "She's obviously not from a Yesod pack, so it seems he's lowered himself to commoners now. You must allow me to handle this."

"There can be no mistakes this time," the voice warned. "What exactly do you have in mind?"

Her lips curled. "I'm sure that I can think of something special for Gabriel and his new wolf bitch."

"She's human."

Her red eyes glowed with hatred. "Then she'll be his downfall along with the rest of the family."

Meet our Author
Lydia Staggs

Dr Lydia Staggs' love for animals was acquired at a young age growing up on her grandfather's farm in Kentucky. An aquatic veterinarian for 10 years, she spends the majority of her time caring for her flippered and finned patients at Gulf World in Panama City Beach, Florida. As the largest marine rehabilitation center in the panhandle of Florida, much of her time is spent performing the necessary procedures to bring sick and injured sea turtles, dolphins, and small whales back to health. The unique career choice has provided many unusual and rewarding opportunities including the rescue of dolphins from hotel swimming pools after Hurricane Katrina and de-oiling hundreds of sea turtles during the BP oil spill.

A graduate of Auburn University's College of Veterinary Medicine and later becoming an affiliate professor for the veterinary school, Lydia is an avid Auburn college football fan and loves all SEC sports. An addiction to chocolate and great reads serve as simple rewards for stressful days. When she is not working, she is spending time with her husband, son, and pets in the Florida panhandle.